The Charm

Integra Press
Phoenix

The Charm

A Southwestern Supernatural Thriller

by

Adam Niswander

Integra Press

Phoenix, Arizona

The Charm
Publisher: INTEGRA PRESS
          1702 W. Camelback Road
          Suite 119
          Phoenix, Arizona 85015

This is a work of fiction. The events described here are imaginary; though many actual settings and institutions do exist, the portrayal of these settings and institutions is strictly fictional; the characters are fictitious and not intended to either characterize the places or represent living persons. In other words, it is made up stuff.

Cover Painting and Special Edition Frontispiece by Armand Cabrera
Printed in the United States of America
First Printing: 1993
1 2 3 4 5 6 7 8 9 0
Library of Congress Cataloging-in-Publication Data
Niswander, Adam, 1946-
    The Charm: a southwestern supernatural thriller
    by Adam Niswander
            p. cm.
    ISBN 0-9626148-1-5: $21.95
    1. Indians of North America--Southwestern States--Antiquities--Fiction. 2. Excavations (Archaeology)--Southwestern States--Fiction. 3. Archaeologists--Southwestern States--Fiction. 4. Southwestern States--Fiction. 5. Supernatural--Fiction.
    I. Title
PS3564.I86C43 1993   93-26241
813'.54--dc20   CIP

Dedication:

For Suzanne Stone (as promised),
and my mother, Olga.

And to all the dancers.

Acknowledgements

Thanks (it seems so inadequate a word) to all the following:

Arizona State Senator and superb weatherman Ed Phillips for aid and advice in creating Matt Sharp.

My friend and publisher Frank Wagner, who provided equipment and supported me through the publishing process.

My friend Larry Reiner—author of *Minute of Silence*—who helped with advice to assure that this book came out right.

The Adam's Bookstore Writer's Group who listened, advised, suggested, sometimes argued, and always helped improve the quality of my work. May we all soon be in print.

To Brian Lumley, Alan Dean Foster, Michael A. Stackpole, Thea Alexander and G. Harry Stine—all exceptional writers in their own rights—for their kind words and comments.

To Margaret Grady and Matthew Frederick, editors of Con-Notations, for aid above and beyond the call.

And to my other friends—too numerous to mention—who encouraged me and believed in me all these years.

What people are saying about The Charm

"An intriguing excursion into the mythology and wonders of both the old and new American Southwest."

Alan Dean Foster
Author of the *Flinx* adventures, *The Damned,* etc.

"I read the first few chapters, turned to my wife and said, 'He can write!'"

Brian Lumley
Author of the *Necroscope* series, *The Burrowers Beneath*, etc.

"Adam has written a yarn in the great tradition of (A.E.) van Vogt's *Voyage of the Space Beagle,* (Jack) Williamson's *Darker Than You Think,* and (Robert) Heinlein's *Glory Road* and *JOB*. It's true science fiction in which Adam has melded the science and technology of two cultures, the Native American and the Euro-American, to defeat a demon in the same league with Coeurl, Will Barbee, and the Soul Eater. And, if you don't believe it's about technology, you haven't read Arthur C. Clarke's *Second Law* recently. The book's an 'all-nighter;' you'll stay up all night reading it because you'll be afraid to go to sleep until you discover how it turns out."

G. Harry Stine
Author of the *Warbots* series, *Handbook of Model Rocketry,* etc.

Saturday, July 8th

Chapter One

Phoenix

"Shit!" Jack Foreman swore as he blistered his elbow on the chrome strip around the driver's window of the Rover. "Damn sun!" He squinted into the brightness and finally spotted the site.

The dozers, trucks, graders and other heavy equipment sat silent behind a heavy chain-link fence in the Saturday afternoon heat. Early July in Arizona meant temperatures hovering at just under 115 degrees. Heat exacerbated a second problem, for the barometer had risen steadily with the promise of evening thunder showers and dust storms. Aside from sounds of traffic simmering on the distant freeway, Jack saw no other living creature. Not even a dog would have been stupid enough to wander unprotected on that strip of desert. In a couple of years, the corridor would be the outer loop of the new beltway.

Although I-17 passed by only five miles away, the construction yard might have been in another world. Jack shook his head.

"Fool politicians!" he muttered.

The debate over freeways had raged for years. Everyone agreed to the necessity, but no one wanted all that traffic to pass through their neighborhood so moderate attempts to compromise brought further compromise until the freeway became a beltway by being pushed out of the city entirely and into the surrounding desert.

The battered landrover rumbled up to the fence and stopped by the sign that read "NO VEHICLES BEYOND THIS POINT." Only the hissing and creaking of the radiator disturbed the afternoon stillness. Jack looked at his watch, then scanned the dirt road behind him.

"Where the hell is that kid?" he asked himself belligerently. With a sigh, he reached over for the canteen and unscrewed the cap. The water remained ice cold. As he took a deep pull at it, he looked into the rearview mirror and saw a dusty red pickup pulling off the access road and onto the trail. Once again he looked at his watch. It read 11:30 a.m. They would have to buck the mid-day heat while on this fool scavenger hunt.

Grabbing his hat and walking stick, Jack opened the door, got out and waited for the pickup to arrive.

Even before the engine stopped dieseling, a younger man stepped lightly down from the other truck and crossed toward him. He smiled out from under a wide-brimmed cowboy hat. "Hi, Dr. Foreman. Sorry if I kept you waiting in this heat." The boy waved and his big turquoise ring flashed in the sun.

Don Hunnicutt, a promising third year archaeology student, represented one of the few bright lights in Jack Foreman's dreary professional life.

Resigned to teaching at Arizona State University and losing his chance to work in the field, Jack felt bitter disappointment when he found that students in his classes showed little promise. They evidenced an appalling lack of curiosity and, in his opinion, wanted nothing more from archaeology than an occasional dig and a passing grade. When he had finally realized he could not do a damned thing about it, Jack started drinking too heavily.

The boy, Hunnicutt, however, seemed an exception. He evidenced genuine interest and had a good eye.

"Hello, Don," Jack replied. "Hope this is going to be worth all the trouble. A beer back home by the pool is starting to sound awfully good right now."

"I know just what you mean," said the younger man with a grin. "I don't think I'm wasting your time, Professor. I found something out there." He pointed toward a cluster of rocks a little to the west.

"And you think it's some sort of Indian relic?"

Don shook his head. "I don't know enough to even guess. What I do know is that what I found isn't a natural formation."

The older man looked out toward the rocks which lay about a thousand yards away from the equipment site and shook his head. Ragged, overweight and hung over, his face already gleamed with perspiration. Only the gray eyes still held a glimmer of the competence which won him his position in the field of archaeology. Mopping his brow with a red bandanna taken from a hip pocket, he sighed.

"Well, let's go take a look, Don," he said. "It's too damned hot and disagreeable to stand here guessing. The sooner we check it out, the sooner we get back for that beer."

"Right this way, Professor," said the boy leading off.

Jack grunted to himself and followed slowly, his progress more a waddle than a walk.

Little else occurred to distract them. The desert had been cleared of scrub and debris by the dozers preparing the surface for the new roadway. The ground appeared level and featureless until just about fifty yards from the rocks which marked the end of the excavation. From there on, they saw simply desert with the usual cacti and weedy clutter. The professor stopped twice en route to mop his forehead and take a swig from his canteen. Young Hunnicutt waited with obvious impatience. Finally, huffing and puffing, Jack came up to join him at the base of the formation.

"Nothing very unusual about these rocks that I can see." He sounded gruff. "Where is it?"

Don looked apologetic. "We'll have to climb a little, Dr. Foreman."

The look Jack turned on the boy would have withered a desert flower, but the younger man, already making his way up the steep slope toward a jagged cut about eighteen feet above the ground, missed his expression entirely.

"It isn't far, Professor," he called over his shoulder. "I promise."

"Isn't far," muttered Jack, still winded from just walking across the level ground. "The little bastard is trying to kill me."

"Did you say something?" called Don from above.

"No."

"Are you coming?"

"Yes . . . but it may take a while."

Jack started up the side in silence, saving his breath for the climb. Much to his amazement, he reached the cut in only a couple of minutes. The path, as steep as it appeared from below, had steps chiseled in the rock face. At the top, he turned and surveyed the drop.

He shook his head. If you looked carefully, you could see the indentations. A casual glance would not have revealed them. He reminded himself to make a closer inspection on the way down.

When he turned around, Jack could not repress a grunt of surprise. Though Don watched his face with a certain amount of trepidation, he need not have been concerned. The professor became convinced his exertions had not been in vain.

They stood on an unnaturally level and nearly circular surface about twelve feet in diameter, its appearance rather like medieval battlements. The rocks facing outward were uneven and natural in appearance—the inner area quite obviously worked stone.

"Not a battlement, perhaps," Jack said under his breath, "but like the top of a tower."

In the center of the circular area lay a large flat-topped boulder. On all surfaces Jack could see, symbols had been incised. He moved up for a closer look.

"It is Native American, isn't it?" asked Don.

"Native American petroglyphs," replied Jack. He indicated one. "This is Yaqui." After a moment of silence, he continued. "And the Pai sigil," he added. "And Apache . . . and Hopi . . . and Pima . . . and others." He turned to Hunnicutt. "You've found something all right." He stepped back, his voice quieter. "Now all we have to do is figure out what."

Don cleared his throat and spoke. "I was here with a date, Dr. Foreman. Now that they've started working on the belt, it's becoming a popular place to park." He looked a little sheepish. "We had a clear night and I spotted these rocks. I thought there'd be a nice view of the city lights. As soon as I came over the edge, I knew." He kicked at the base of the wall. "It's too regular and smooth. It had to be worked. And the angle is a perfect 90 degrees—I checked."

Jack still looked at the markings on the stone. "Too many nations," he said in a low tone.

"Can you read any of that?" asked the boy.

"They're just symbols representing the different tribes, but I've never seen so many in one spot," Jack admitted. "Oh, it's not language as we know it. Most of these native tribes never had written language until recently. And," he added, "none of them are well known for cooperating with each other. To find something that obviously involved every tribe in the state is weird." He traced several characters with his finger. Hunnicutt came up to look.

"What's this one, professor?"

Jack followed the boy's finger as he pointed. Next to each petroglyph, another symbol had been cut into the rock . . . the same symbol carved by many different hands. "Whatever it means, it's common to all these tribes," he observed. "See? There next to the Hopi glyph, there by the Pima. I'm sure this one is Zuni."

"Isn't that unusual?" Don looked puzzled.

"Maybe . . . and maybe not. Remember, these people didn't write like you and I do. These symbols represent whole ideas and concepts."

"So certain symbols might be common for a number of different nations?"

"Why not? How many different symbols would people use for the sun, for instance? In every case, it's a disk with rays radiating outward. Some have faces, others don't, but the basic glyph is the same."

Hunnicutt scratched his head. "So what does it mean?"

"Damned if I know," replied the older man. "It could be anything. If you want me to hazard a guess, I'd say this is a well or cistern. This rock can probably be moved aside to uncover the hole. Want to help me try it?"

"Sure," answered Don, rubbing sweaty hands on his cut-offs. "Which way, or does it matter?"

Jack took a moment to examine the base of the stone, then answered. "From the grooving and wear on the surface here, I'd say it goes to our left." Jack indicated the desired direction and both men braced themselves. "On three," said Jack. "Ready?"

Don nodded.

"One. Two. Three!" And they put their shoulders to it.

The stone moved grudgingly about six inches to the side, then stopped. They pushed harder, but it would not budge.

Some kind of opening did lie below the stone. Both men could clearly see it. Perhaps it was just a breeze blowing over the hole, but a low whistling came up from beneath.

"Hold on a minute," said Jack. The effort took his breath away. He took his bandanna out of his pocket and wiped sweat from his eyes, then knelt and peered intently at the base of the rock.

"No wonder it won't go any further," he said. "It's been blocked." He pointed. "See? There are small shaped stone wedges all along that side."

Don reached into his pocket and pulled out a jack-knife. He offered it wordlessly and the professor took it.

After trying for a minute, Jack gave up in disgust. "It's no good," he said. "They've been in there a long time. All I'll do with your knife is break the blade."

Don leaned forward and looked. "You know, Professor, I have a hammer and screwdriver in the truck. I'll bet I can pound those suckers out or at least break them up some."

Jack looked at his watch. It was just 12:30. He glanced at the sky. There were clouds on the horizon, but only the barest hint of any weather nearby. "Okay," he agreed. "I'll wait here. You'll make a lot better time than I would. And, while you're down there," he added, "you may as well get the camera from under the driver's seat in the Rover and a roll of film from the cooler."

"Sure. No sweat, Professor," said Don. "I'll be back in a couple of minutes." With that, he moved to the cut and disappeared from sight. Jack turned and looked again at the writing while he waited. Around him, the wind began to pick up.

A few minutes went by as Jack tried to figure out the meaning of the unfamiliar symbol. It appeared to be a funnel on a level plain. He couldn't recall having seen it before.

Suddenly, Jack exclaimed, "Dammit!" He rubbed his eyes. The wind had started blowing dust. As he looked up, shielding his eyes as best he could, he found visibility limited to just a few feet in any direction. Funny, it had been so clear just a few minutes before. Now he stood in the middle of a huge dust devil. He looked over in the direction of the construction yard and the trucks but could see nothing.

"Great!" he muttered. "Just great!" He pulled the bandanna out again, poured water into it from his canteen, and held it over his nose. Crouching down behind the stone, he waited for the sudden storm to blow over. He hoped Don had sense enough to wait it out in the cab of his truck. The wind howled with enough strength to pick up small pebbles and hurl them with considerable force. One hit him on the forehead and hurt like hell.

Crouched down, with one arm over his head and the bandanna held over his face with the other, Jack could look down and squint into the hole under the stone. Only darkness could be seen below, but, suddenly, his eyes found something glimmering at the edge. He reached in and brought out a small metal object. It looked like a charm of some sort, but the dust kept getting in his eyes. He knew by touch that metal formed the object. He could feel the small rough places where it had been hammered.

"I'll be damned!" he swore when he finally got a momentary look.

The object reproduced the symbol on the rock he had been unable to identify. He slipped it into his shirt pocket. His watch read exactly 12:34 and 56 seconds.

Suddenly, as if released, the storm rushed off. The wind died quickly and the dust began to settle. Jack looked over toward the construction yard but a few minutes passed before the storm, moving coincidentally in that direction, swept over it.

As the cloud sped beyond the fence and into the desert, a surreal landscape met his eyes. What Jack saw sent him scrambling through the cut and down the steep face of the rocks.

The chain link fence stood no more. The pickup and rover squatted axle-deep in dust and sand, and both shone brightly in the returning sunlight for they had been denuded of all paint. Jack saw no sign of Don.

Chapter Two

Salt River Indian Reservation

That same morning, Danny Webb had awakened from a dreamless sleep filled with the excitement of anticipation. Today Tom Bear had promised to show him a secret place—a place at once sacred and terrible. Danny rose and went directly to the metal shower stall in the corner of his one-room house.

He hoped to find a day labor job with the road construction company that had contracted to widen Pima Road where it bordered reservation land.

After a quick shower, he dressed in clean but worn jeans and a loose-fitting shirt. Tying off his long fine black hair with a red bandanna, he walked the two miles to the site with an easy, loping, ground-devouring stride. The desert heat had only begun to build.

No one appeared to be in when he arrived at the mobile office the R.H. Sanden Company used as their on-site headquarters. He had been advised by his friend Mark Walker that the first few Indians to arrive could usually count on work for the day. No other members of his tribe waited at the trailer so confidence filled him as he knocked on the foreman's door.

Only after waiting for several minutes did he notice the "CLOSED" sign hanging to the left of the door. Well, perhaps he was early. Danny could wait. He had nothing better to do.

An empty nail barrel lay on its side to the right of the portable three-step platform that stood before the trailer door so he righted it and sat, content to wait, congratulating himself for being first today.

A hawk circled high in the air to the south over reservation land. It rose in the currents and dipped, swooping to the ground after some unseen prey. Danny's eyes followed the poetry of its flight.

For the Pima, life consisted of a mix of good and bad. The land that bordered Scottsdale constituted the best owned by the tribe. It held a number of leased parcels, among them one which housed Scottsdale Community College. They had signed a ninety-nine year lease with the city and, at the end of that time, the buildings would belong to them. The same applied to the government-operated farm to the south.

Though the white man, or miligan, misused the land, the people believed he would one day go away and leave them with the world they used to know. Until then, the Pima and other tribes played a complex game—a dangerous game—politics and economics and law all part of the package. Through it all, the tribe, nearly six thousand strong, maneuvered to survive, sometimes prospering, sometimes suffering.

No white man in the world can understand the Native American mind, thought Danny with a smile. *No magic. They have machines and we have the earth.* Not for the first time, he thought how he could never live away from his people.

Tonight, after a hard day of labor, he would go and visit his friend. Danny knew that Tom practiced witchcraft, but the wise had knowledge of the secret ways. The outside world's influence reached in irrevocably and wrought changes which might never be undone. Terms like witch, priest and medicine man were not really Native American, but even the Indians used them now. They had to do with the miligan's churches.

Tom Bear would take him to this place after sunset and then they would return to sit in the shaman's house and talk of sacred things. Danny's fondest dream would soon come true.

Many of the other men feared Tom Bear, but not Danny. The old man spoke with the spirits—something Danny wanted to do. Medicine ran in his family. His hands felt under the loose shirt for the small leather pouch that hung from a rawhide thong around his neck. He fingered it absently, imagining himself a powerful medicine man and commanding the respect of the rest of the tribe.

His thought was interrupted by the sound of a pickup pulling up along the gravel, a truck with the words "SANDEN CONSTRUC-TION—FOREMAN" on the door.

"Can I help you, son?" The man wore a blue hardhat tilted back over a very sunburned face and neck.

Danny stood with dignity and walked around to the driver's side.

"I was told there would be work for the day," he said.

"Not today, boy," said the foreman shaking his head. "Old man Sanden's wife died yesterday and we're closed down for the week."

The Indian stood there for a long moment. He appeared to be thinking. Finally, he looked up and spoke. "No work today?"

The foreman, a man named Jim Dobson, shook his head. "Sorry, probably not for a week or so."

Danny nodded and said gravely, "Thank you. I will go early to see Tom Bear." Without saying anything further, he turned and started to walk toward Ma Smith's Bar.

"If you'll come see me a week from Monday, I can probably find something for you," called Dobson out the window.

The Indian stopped and turned. "Thank you," he said. "I will be here." He began to walk away, then turned and spoke over his shoulder. "Tell Mr. Sanden I am sorry about his woman."

The foreman drove away smiling.

Danny could be philosophical about the lack of work. Next week would do just as well. He had many other important things to do. He turned and headed for Ma Smith's Bar. Perhaps he would be lucky and some of his friends could buy some beers.

Ma Smith's, a seedy dive farther down the street on the reservation side, enjoyed a measure of tolerance from the Reservation Police, largely because of the pay-offs they received and the regular fines the old lady paid to the tribe for violations real and fabricated. The bar attracted construction workers during the lunch hour and a few tourists who bought turquoise jewelry, baskets and weaving. The rest of the clientele were Indians.

Danny stepped into the relative darkness of Ma's out of the bright morning sun and breathed a sigh. He always felt good being there. The stale smell of beer, the humid half-light, the rows of baskets behind the bar and the familiar faces all combined to welcome him. He made his way to the bar and sat next to Jon Steele, a neighbor about his own age. "Ho, Jon! How are you today, my friend?"

The other man looked up from a full beer and smiled. "Ho, Danny. I am fine."

The game began. Sometimes Jon had money. He made baskets for Ma and sold others to one of the mall shops in Phoenix. Though his friends kidded him about women's work, he had a craftsman's eye and produced superior quality work. When he had been paid, he would stop at Ma's and drink until the money was gone.

Sometimes, Danny got money, though of late, it had only been when he received his tribal government check. When it arrived, he would meet Jon at Ma's and it would be his turn to pay.

"Would you like a beer, Danny?" Though only 8:30 a.m., it seemed obvious that Jon was already on his way to a short day. He beckoned to Ma and indicated she should serve his friend.

"I'll pay you back, Jon Steele," Danny replied as always. "I went to Sanden for work this morning, but they are closed. Old man Sanden's wife died."

Ma, who was almost as wide as she stood tall, put a cold beer in front of Danny.

Steele shook his head and gazed sadly into his beer. "I knew Sanden's woman," he said, more to himself than to anyone else.

"You foolin' around with white women, Jon Steele?" The raspy voice of Ma Smith was sharp and mocking. "Is that how you knew Sanden's woman?"

"Go on, get away old woman!" Steele raised a huge right hand and pretended to threaten Ma. She didn't flinch.

"Use that hand and I'll hang it on my wall, Jon Steele." But both of them were smiling.

Danny, used to the banter and the posturing, felt no alarm. The game-playing was part of being in Ma's place. He cleared his throat and spoke. "I must leave early today for a visit with Tom Bear. He has promised to show me something."

Ma Smith hissed like a cat and stepped back. "You should stay away from that old crazy man, Danny Webb. He's a witch. He's dangerous."

"Tom Bear is a great man, Ma Smith," said Danny. "He is not dangerous unless he is your enemy. I am proud to call him my friend."

"Friends like that can get you in a lot of trouble," retorted the old woman. "Your father knew that. He would be angry to see you wasting your time with the witch."

"My father walks with the spirits," answered Danny in a low voice, "and I have much time these days."

"Hey, lighten up, you two." Jon Steele smiled and tossed off the last of his beer. "We'll have two more, Ma," he said. "The witch has powerful medicine. He is respected by the Council. It is unwise to speak ill of so great a man."

Ma put the two beers in front of them and glared at Steele, but something in his words struck home. Uncharacteristically, she kept her mouth shut and moved away to wait on a lost-looking tourist who had just wandered in.

"What does Tom Bear have to show you?" Steele seemed casual as he asked, but his gaze was intense.

Danny shrugged. "I do not know. Once he made me drive to Flagstaff where he took me to a place with carvings on the rocks. He said it was very old." His face and voice indicated the experience had made an impression on him. "I could feel the weight of the years in that place, Jon."

"There are many places of power, my friend," said Steele. "Few know of them. You are fortunate that Tom Bear is your friend."

Danny nodded. "Yes."

They finished their beers in silence, each lost in thought.

Draining the last of his bottle, Steele glanced over and said, "Want another?"

Danny hesitated, but then shrugged again. "Why not? It is too early to visit my friend."

Jon ordered. Ma served.

After a few more minutes, Steele asked, "When are you supposed to be there?"

"When the sun sets," the other replied.

"Ahh, a good time to go calling on witches."

After two more beers, Steele's speech grew a little slurred and Danny felt a glow of well-being.

The morning passed.

They drank through the heat of the day, sometimes talking with great animation, sometimes sitting for an hour in silence. Those who made things, the weavers and jewelry makers, those who carved the dolls out of cottonwood root, came and went. Ma alternately cajoled or scolded depending on whether she wanted their wares or not. By two in the afternoon, Jon had put his head down on the bar and fallen into a drunken sleep.

Danny was little better. He looked over at his sleeping friend, realizing that free beer time had ended, then cast a bleary eye around the bar. Finally, his head in his arms, he too slept.

Danny awakened when he fell from the stool to the floor. He lay there a moment, stunned, before his outraged body began to complain. Several different areas of pain manifested themselves simultaneously. The first was in his right elbow and shoulder. These had taken the brunt of his impact with the unyielding concrete floor.

As the numbness of shock gave way to throbbing agony, his brain kicked in with the dull, remorseless pounding of his temples and the nauseous unease of his stomach. He kept his eyes closed against the pain. The worst combination imaginable is a hangover and physical injury at the same time. He rolled to the left, cradling his arm and resting his forehead on the cool slab.

Someone laughed.

Danny opened his eyes and looked for the source. He saw bad news leering down from a towering height, a familiar and hated face.

"Sorry, Danny boy," said Bill Watts without even a trace of sincerity, "I didn't see you there when I sat on the stool." He looked around the room, which had gotten fairly crowded for a weekday evening, and grinned, inviting the others to join him in his jest. "You should not drink so much, boy. It is bad for your health."

A few of the others present joined in the general laughter, but Ma Smith spoke up from behind the bar. "We want no trouble here, Bill Watts," she said in a quiet but menacing tone. "Danny was just leaving," she added looking directly down over the bar. "You okay, Danny?"

Rising and pretending he felt no pain proved difficult, but he carried it off. Grinning back, he spoke in a deceptively mild voice, "Yes, I am fine, Ma Smith. I need to be leaving now anyway." He had to concentrate hard to keep from brushing himself off and rubbing his arm. "You should be more careful, Bill. They say carelessness breeds carelessness. You would not want to invite trouble."

"There is no trouble I can't handle, boy, and don't ever forget that." Watts' voice rang harsh and threatening. He tensed up like a coiled spring, spoiling for a fight.

"You want a whisky, Bill Watts, or did you just come in for talk?" Ma Smith's sharp voice cut like a knife.

Watts looked around and then relaxed. "Yes, a whisky would be fine, Ma. And I will buy one for all my friends here." He added, "Too bad you are leaving, Danny boy."

The baiting might have continued, but Danny did not rise to it. He turned and walked without speaking out of the room and into the evening. Only after he had gone around the corner did he lean against the wall and allow a soft moan to escape his lips. His arm and shoulder ached and his temples felt like vibrating drums.

The sun set in an impressive orange blaze in the west, though Danny did not really have presence of mind enough to appreciate it. Nonetheless, the time had come for him to go and visit Tom Bear. Despite the pain of the shoulder and headache, he felt his pulse quicken at the thought of spending the evening with the wise man. He took a deep breath, focused his mind, and moved off toward Tom's house on the far edge of the reservation.

One day, he would have wealth and prestige. One day, he would own an automobile. For now, his feet would carry him where he needed to go. Bill Watts acted like a clown. The man did not know enough to recognize true importance. One day, Bill Watts would learn that Danny should not be ridiculed.

Danny moved silently and with inborn stealth across the desert sand. Tom Bear awaited him. It would be unwise to delay.

Tom lived in a house along the river, far up from the settled area of the reservation. Because all held him in awe, he had no close neighbors. As Danny moved across the desert, he remembered what his father had told him about the Pima lands before the white man took the water.

The green of the Pima fields once followed the river for many miles. On hot nights, the cattle stood on the banks up to their knees in mud to cool off. The Pima were great farmers when they had water. They would take shovels and lead the water to the crops, alfafa, corn and melons, by digging shallow ditches off the main flow. Black birds sang in the trees and seemed almost a musical blessing to the people. With plentiful water came abundance. The Pima worked their land, far from the stereotyped Indians who were supposed to be lazy drunks.

In the orange glow of the sunset, Danny looked around him. The river appeared as an empty bed of sand, and the trees that once flourished were dead, skeletal and dry, twisted and choked with tumbleweeds. Though some of the Pima still struggled to farm the land, the lack of water caused many to fail, the dying crops speaking eloquently of the crushed spirit of the people. The white man ruled the fields and crops and water. The people owned the land, but the miligan had the land's life blood.

Danny stumbled. He looked down in the fading light and saw that he had stepped into some fresh dug earth. The spot occupied only about a square foot. Curiously, he squatted down and put his fingers into the earth. Feeling something hard, he grabbed it and pulled. He withdrew a wooden wand, covered with feathers. *Pretty.* He tucked it in his belt and continued on his way.

As the sun faded from sight and the night sky began to glow with stars, Danny neared the house of Tom Bear. There would be no moon tonight—one of the reasons Tom had asked him to come. A coyote howled in the distance. Danny shivered but kept moving. He grinned in the dark as he recalled the comment of his friend, Jon Steele. *A good time to go visiting a witch.* Stepping lightly up out of the ravine, he saw the house.

Large and built of rock, it possessed a wide front porch where the old man could sit and watch the sun come up across the ravine. It had no city plumbing. A big rusty water tank sat on stilts beside it. Out back, a rag-tag collection of sheds harkened back to older days. They were made of arrow weeds held in place by mesquite posts, each built under a mesquite tree in the traditional Pima way.

Danny called out. "Ho! Tom Bear! Nam'i va dadrha? Are you there?"

When the voice replied out of the shadows just by his shoulder, Danny jumped.

"Ho, Danny," said the old man stepping from the darkness. "You have come as I asked. That is good. It is nearly time for us to go." Tom cocked his head as if listening. Then turned and spoke into the dark. "Do not hide there in the night, Jon Steele. You may as well come out of that ravine and join us."

Danny turned in consternation. "Jon? Here? Why?"

Tom Bear laughed. "Perhaps he will tell us when he gets his cojones up." Then he called again. "Do not keep me waiting, Jon, or I will grow angry."

The other man came up over the edge of the ravine. He stood there a moment, hesitant, then decided to brave it out. "Ho, Tom. Shapa'i chu'ig? How are you? Ho, Danny. I am here."

Danny said, "You followed me."

Tom put a hand on the younger man's shoulder and said, "Don't worry. He is here because I called him. We will need his help tonight."

Jon looked a little uncertain. All three of them knew he had not heard from Tom. He had probably followed Danny out of curiosity. Something important appeared to be going on and Jon must have acted on impulse. However, the old man had accepted him so it would be all right. He smiled and stepped forward.

"I am ready to do whatever you want."

"Good," said the old man. "There are some bags on the porch. Bring them here. Danny, you get the truck."

Both men did as they were told and, within minutes, the three were crowded onto the bench seat of Tom's old Ford pickup.

Danny got to drive. "Where are we going?" he asked.

"Into Phoenix," replied Tom. "Just get on Pima Road and head south to Thomas, then turn West."

They rode in silence. Danny concentrated on his driving. Tom Bear lit a cigarette. Jon lay back and tilted his cowboy hat over his eyes, content to await explanations when the old man chose to give them.

The roads held only light traffic. They passed a blue and white Scottsdale Police car, but it travelled north and probably failed to note the expired plates on Tom's truck. They had expired in 1955.

They drove through the heart of Phoenix, passing the businesses and walled developments, hospitals and topless joints, and on west past I-17. Three Indians in a dusty pickup drew little notice as the white men and women made their way home to swimming pools and fancy dinners.

"Go North," instructed Tom when they hit the construction. Danny complied and mused to himself that the miligan kept ripping up the old roads and building new. Yet the reservation roads were little better than pot-holes with crumbled edges.

"Slow, now," cautioned Tom. "It will be up on the left." The access road led off into the excavations for the beltway. Danny turned carefully and proceeded to the fallen chainlink fence, pulling up beside another truck that shined brightly in his headlights.

Tom Bear sat up suddenly and cursed. "Alu ge-ban!"

Danny laughed. Tom Bear had called someone a sneaky old coyote. Unfortunately, the old man appeared really upset.

"Stop here!" Tom ordered. "Get out, quick!" And then he led them at a fast pace beyond the fence, across the road construction and into the desert. Danny struggled to keep up.

"Fool miligan," said the old man under his breath, "they let it out!"

Jon had kept silent until now, but curiosity drove him to ask, "What is it, Tom Bear? What has the white man done?"

"I must see for myself," said the old man, hurrying toward a rock formation on the desert edge. "Maybe it is not too late."

To the astonishment of the two younger men, the older Indian moved up the rock face like a spider, disappearing over the edge while they still sought the path.

Climbing carefully, both joined Tom atop the rocks. Ghostly light transformed it into a strange place and neither Danny nor Jon felt comfortable there. As their eyes adjusted, they could see the old man bent down examining the base of a large boulder in the center. Close by, the lights of Phoenix lit the sky casting harsh shadows in the night.

"Gone," muttered Tom, then sat heavily with his back against the rock. He looked at the two others and they saw fright in his eyes.

Danny crouched down and put his hands on Tom's shoulders. He could feel them shaking.

"What is it?" he asked.

The old man hung his head. His voice was barely a whisper. "The white man has doomed us all, Danny. He has loosed the demon. We must prepare to die."

Chapter Three

Hopiland

Harold Laloma had earned his place among the priests of Coyote Clan in the village of Oraibi on Third Mesa. Bear Clan originally settled Oraibi but made room for Coyote when Sikyatki to the East of First Mesa failed. The Hopi—the oldest people on earth, the people of peace—lived in harmony with the world.

The meeting had been going on for two days and the afternoon sun slanted in through the open hatch above making dust motes in the air visible, like minute spiders suspended from invisible threads. The vagrant breeze from outside and above had kicked up all day creating unusual drafts and eddies. Harold prayed and fasted in the kiva with the other priests when the vision came. His consciousness had been uplifted after ingestion of datura root, so he could not be sure afterwards whether he had actually seen a physical manefestation or an inner vision.

Seated with his back to the wall in the largest circular chamber, Harold smoked his clay pipe, doing his part in the cycle of rituals that kept the sacred trust between Tiowa, the Creator, and his children. With eyes half closed, his surroundings seemed vague suggestions as in a dream. He could feel that place on the top of his head, the door, opening, enabling him to communicate directly with the spirits.

Then Taknokwunu, the spirit who controls the weather, spoke to him. "A storm is coming," it said quietly. "Look to the center of the kiva and see it."

Harold had not expected to hear the deep musical voice in his head—like a roll of thunder—and started. Immediately, he imposed discipline and, thereafter, remained motionless. Opening his eyes, he peered toward the middle of the chamber.

A breeze stirred where no breeze had a right to be, the dust began to swirl and a dust devil took form. It spun in one place, not at all the capricious, ephemeral funnel of dust so common in the desert. This cone of rapidly spinning wind current and debris sat firmly, revolving like a top.

The priest marvelled at the vision. He looked surreptitiously around at the others present, but they appeared unaware of what occurred in the center of the room. Each seemed asleep or entranced, and Harold realized that he alone had been given this sign.

The voice spoke again. "Once before, many years past, this storm swept the desert and preyed upon the people. Now, the pahana has set it loose to feed on the tribes. You are the one I have chosen to represent the people of peace when the wise attempt to imprison it again."

Harold sent his thoughts to Taknokwunu. "Oh Great Spirit of the Weather, I am honored that you have chosen this humble servant to do your bidding. I know this fourth world, Tuwaqachi, is struggling with the evil ways. Command me and I will do as you ask."

The whirling dust had still not moved from the point where he first saw it. His vision suddenly telescoped, every detail presenting itself clearly. As he watched, a lone fly buzzed frantically, struggling to avoid being sucked into the vortex. A strange feeling of dread flooded through Harold as he watched the insect imprisoned at the base of the dust devil. The ill-fated fly shrank in upon itself until it disappeared. Then the miniature storm stopped—one instant raging there, the next gone. A small, clean, round spot on the earthen floor showed where it had been.

"Fast, and cleanse your spirit," commanded the rumbling voice. "You will be contacted by others. Be strong and pure, and sing your praises from the hilltops as you have always done."

"I obey," said Harold under his breath.

"Until I summon you, hide from the wind," said the voice.

Harold felt the spirit withdraw and fell into exhausted slumber.

In the dream, he heard the voice of the beast. As if that did not impose enough awe, he sensed that the creature knew him—recognized his presence.

"Ahhhh . . . ," it sighed, "you are one of those who would return me to the dark."

Harold huddled into himself. The power of the beast felt overwhelming. Contempt and derision underlay the voice.

"You cannot trap me again, mortal. Not all the powers in the hands of men can chain me a second time. I will not idly await a gathering of the wise. I will come for you."

The words spoken rang, not with threat, but promise. Harold knew that certainty and confidence lay beneath.

"I know where you are, Peace Man. I will visit you soon. It will be as long ago when I first went forth to gather souls."

The Coyote Priest felt the presence of the beast. It hungered and rejoiced in freedom. Arrogance unbounded welled forth. The creature exuded absolute power and confidence and appeared determined to achieve its destiny. Harold felt despair flow through him. He knew the hopelessness of the merely mortal. He feared, as he had never feared before.

Chapter Four

Chaco Canyon, New Mexico

In Chaco Canyon, Northeast of Gallup, New Mexico, is a settlement of Navajos. Scattered through the area are the hogans and farms of nearly two thousand people. This one small group is but a part of the Navajo Nation, the largest single Native American tribe. Though the site in the canyon is off the reservation, the land is occupied and used by the Dineh—their word—which means simply "The People."

"Can I get you anything, grandfather?"

The speaker was Walks-In-A-Hurry, one of the three men, four women and six children who lived in the hogan. A mile away was another stone dwelling which housed more of the family. The old man sat with his eyes closed and did not reply.

After waiting a moment, his grandson went on toward the house of his sisters.

He-Who-Walks-In-Wisdom—Archibald Smythe when census takers stopped by—sat alone in the Hogan, singing and waiting. He did not know what he waited for, but he still lived and therefore must have something important yet to do.

Born to the Standing House Clan and for Bitter-Water Clan, the oldest of the Dineh at 108 years of age, he possessed the clarity of mind and physical health of a much younger man.

In his head, he had just finished singing the story of Changing Woman and the People. It had taken a long time. This project represented his choice of what to do with his last years. He knew he could not have much time left, so Archie had decided to sing all the songs he knew—and there were many songs.

"Grandfather. May I come in?"

Archie opened his eyes and looked at the younger man in the doorway. His great-great-grandson, educated off the reservation in the biligaana—white man's—schools, used the name Gordon Smythe. The family addressed him as Thoughts-Never-Stop, but Archie affectionately called him Fly. The nickname had first been used when the child reached six and pestered all the adults with questions. The constant and very un-Navajo interruption of his elders reminded them of the persistent buzzing of an insect.

"You are already in, Fly."

"I did not wish to disturb your singing." The young man moved closer to where the old man sat cross-legged on the west side of the hogan, opposite the door.

The old man gestured and the boy joined him. Archie watched and felt a surge of pride.

The elder man, acknowledged by all to be a great singer, still several times a year performed The Blessing Way, but his age caused considerable awe even in those closest to him. Others of the people, not of the immediate family group, approached him reluctantly, fearful they might incur his wrath. As it is with the Dineh, they respected the wiry old man.

Four years earlier, just before his college graduation, the boy had come to him and asked to be taught the songs.

At first, Archie discouraged him saying, "You don't want to be yataalii, a singer. You've been to biligaana schools and lived in the white man's world. The ways of the dineh are no longer your ways."

But the boy had answered well. "I am of the dineh, grandfather. Just because I can embrace some new ways does not mean I must abandon the old."

Fresh from his graduation from ASU in Tempe, Gordon had returned to the Canyon and to the hogans of his family where he spent the next year working twice as hard as anyone else, trying to put the experience of living away from his people into perspective. Many young Navajos faced the feelings of alienation that resulted from their excursions away from the homeland and into the wider world of the biligaana. Often when they returned, accustomed to speaking and reading English, use of their own native tongue seemed awkward and confusing. In time, the words came more easily but the change was never completely reversed.

It had been so for Gordie, but he set about the task of reintegrating himself into his family with obvious determination. He had set out to prove himself to the old man and the others, to show them by his deeds that Thoughts-Never-Stop still thought of himself as dineh.

Always, when the day's work was done, he came to his great-great-grandfather and asked, "Grandfather, will you teach me to sing?"

At first, the old man did not reply, curious whether the boy could be discouraged, an easy way to test the dedication of the young. Gordie came and made the same respectful request every night. Eventually, acknowledging the boy's sincerity, Archie began to sing for him.

No better teacher lived than He-Who-Walks-In-Wisdom. Archie remembered everything that had happened in his long life and had learned the songs from his father and his grandfather as well.

108 years of living represented a momentous accomplishment, and he had accumulated great power by virtue of it. The old man's father had been alive when Kit Carson led troops into Navajo country in June of 1863 and destroyed the crops and livestock. His father had made the infamous long walk to Fort Sumner, survived the bitter imprisonment there—lived through the diseases and famine—and made the return to their devastated homeland in 1868.

Born in 1882, Archie had grown up as white men encroached on the land which had always belonged to the people. He had sat on the councils by his father's side and seen the government trick, betray and cheat his people.

But he had learned that the white man had power too. He had seen the results of resistance and rebellion. If his people wished to survive, they must learn to accomodate and compromise.

Archie had served in the Navajo government when it was first established at Windowrock. After his service there, he moved his family to a nearby settlement and became the medicine man, his son becoming headman of the village. Here he had performed the sacred ceremonies, mediated disputes, and treated the sick. Archie's fame had once spread throughout the Navajo Nation, his name spoken respectfully even by the Apache, the Hopi, the Zuni and Pueblo.

Fame, however, in the Native American world is a two-edged sword which can cut deeply. To accumulate wealth and power is suspect. The very nature of personal gain is foreign to a people who habitually act for the good of all, who work with the spirits of the earth toward perfect harmony. Inevitably, when someone excels, there is talk of witchcraft.

Skinwalkers. Wolves. Witches.

Fear of witches is deeply ingrained in the Navajo.

The man had used the name Sam Pino. His family lived near Archie's about twenty miles from Windowrock, in fact had been related through marriage of the Pino's sister's daughter to one of Archie's grandsons. There had once been a nasty argument over ownership of some sheep, but they generally got along.

When illness struck down his wife, Pino had come to the medicine man seeking help. Unfortunately, Archie had been away at Windowrock and the neighbor had been unwilling to wait for his return. Instead, he went to a nearby village and enlisted the aid of their medicine man, Bent Man.

"Can you come look at my wife?" he had asked, quite properly.

"Where is the famous Archibald Smythe?" replied the medicine man.

"He is away at Windowrock," said Pino. "He will not return for several days."

Sam didn't know—none of them knew—that Bent Man harbored tremendous jealousy of Archie.

After examining the woman, he told Pino that his wife had been witched. He told Sam to go to a crystal gazer called Laughing Spring who could help him by finding the identity of the witch. Slyly, he asked if Pino had ever had bad words with someone in the family, someone perhaps powerful and dangerous.

Sam Pino was a man of peace, uneducated and uncomplicated. He had no enemies, did not quarrel or brawl, and could think of no one he had ever offended. Then he remembered the argument over the sheep.

"Archie and I had a disagreement over part of the herd last year," he said quietly. "I thought it settled, but he sure got mad at me for a while there."

Bent Man had nodded. "That is the way it sometimes is," he said. "The truly powerful can afford to wait to get even."

"Are you accusing Archie?" Pino didn't want to believe it, but Bent Man wielded power and Sam remained just a simple farmer.

"Even I would not have the courage to accuse the great Archie Smythe of witchcraft. He is a powerful man, a man who has accumulated a large herd and a big family, a man who has many friends." Bent Man shook his head. He added, "It could be someone else, Sam Pino."

But the seeds of doubt had been planted.

Bent Man treated the woman, finding, he said, a bump on the back of her head within which was lodged a small bit of ash.

"Corpse Poison!" he said. "Probably from a hogan where someone died. I can remove it," he looked up at Pino with a piercing gaze, "but you'll have to find out where it came from and who the witch is if you really want a cure."

"How do I do that?" Sam Pino had already decided Bent Man must be correct. It had to be Archie.

Bent Man sent Sam to Laughing Spring who identified Archie as the witch. Sam returned to the medicine man.

"We'll hold an Evil Way tomorrow night," said Bent Man, "and I'll prepare it for you. The easiest way is to load it into a blowgun or even a shotgun shell and shoot him." He shrugged. "You could arrange to get some of it into his food. A better way, a way that would take more courage, is to confront him and blow the loose ash right into his face . . . if you think you can do that."

The idea of confronting Archie gave Sam the shakes, but his wife was so sick and taken with fever he feared for her life. If Sam had to face the medicine man, he would.

Word quickly spread throughout the village. Archie was a witch. Archie had been named in the Evil Way. To be sure, most of the people thought it utter nonsense. Unfortunately, there are always some willing to believe the worst about the rich or powerful.

By the time Archie returned from his business at Windowrock three days later, even neighbors who had known him for years acted suspiciously and seemed nervous around him. He knew something was different, but no one told him what had happened.

That first night, Sam Pino had come calling, pulling up in his old green pickup and waiting, as custom demanded, for Archie to come to the door.

"Ya-deh-hay, Sam," called Archie in greeting and welcome.

"Ya-deh, Archibald Smythe," responded Sam. Pino felt scared half to death as he advanced toward the hogan, a small leather pouch in his hands. "I have brought you something."

Archie's face had lit with pleasure. He felt badly about the argument last summer over the sheep. The misunderstanding had been simple, but the bad feelings lingered too long. As the eldest in the family, he had gone out of his way to be nice to the Pinos. The gift must mean that Sam had finally put the incident behind him. He attributed Sam's awkwardness to embarrassment, but stood ready to be gracious in his acceptance of the gift. Unwary and off guard when

Sam opened the pouch, he knew genuine surprise when Pino poured something fine and grainy into his palm and blew it into his face.

The powder, mixed by Bent Man, contained many things, among them ground datura root and pepper. The unfortunate effects for Archie became immediately evident.

What Sam saw convinced him that Bent Man must be right, for Archie's face underwent a dramatic change. The welcoming smile faded quickly, replaced by a look of shocked surprise. The old man's eyes began to water. He sneezed and then clutched at his throat, stepping backward into the hogan and tripping over a rug just inside. He fell heavily, choking and gasping for breath.

Sam had fled, running back to his truck and racing off toward his home. When he got there, he found his wife awake and feeling better. Though he was frightened that Archie might come after him, Sam had been convinced that he had done the right thing and become a hero. Nothing would ever convince him that Archie had been innocent.

The effect on Archie's life had been devastating. Retelling of a tale always exaggerates what happened and the story of simple Sam Pino confronting the powerful witch spread throughout the reservation. The result had been a loss of prestige and the loss of many friends. Within two months, Archie took his family and moved away from the village all the way to Chaco Canyon where other relatives had settled. Archie never returned to the village again.

Now, looking with pride at his great-great-grandson, Archie knew why he still lived. He must teach this young man the songs of his people, train this yataalii who showed such promise. There were many songs he had learned from his own grandfather which he had never heard any one else sing. They would not be lost if Fly could commit them to memory. And the boy had a wonderful memory.

"One day, I must teach you the song of the Great Gathering," Archie said. "It is from long ago, starting before the biligaana came and ending when a great evil was shut away."

Fly looked at him with curiosity. "I have never heard of it before, grandfather. Is it part of a ceremony?"

The old man nodded. "It is very old, Fly, and was old when my father's father was yet a dream in the heart of his father. It tells of the demon loosed on the earth to punish those who had turned from the law."

"Teach it to me now, grandfather."

The old man looked into the boy's eager face. "It is a long tale, Fly, and it is late. Are you sure you wish to begin now?"

"Oh, yes, grandfather!"

Archie nodded, satisfied, and began to sing.

Chapter Five

Barrio Libre, Tucson

"It has happened," Juan told his wife.

Midday had arrived quietly in Tucson. Maria looked up from her weaving, automatically glancing at the wind-up alarm clock on the table next to her, noting the time. Juan always wanted to know the time when he was traveling. The timepiece read thirty-five minutes past noon.

"What has happened, husband?"

"The demon has been loosed."

Maria tilted her head and studied the gnarled old man through the open window. She had never understood him. He remained an enigma, a constant puzzle, always off to do strange things and meet with strange people.

Juan Mapoli, sabio, wise man of the Yaqui tribe, lived in Barrio Libre in South Tucson. He had grown up in Pascua, but urban renewal in Tucson had resulted in razing the village and resettlement of its inhabitants—some to the village just north of the San Xavier Reservation of the Tohono O'odham and most of the rest to Barrio Libre.

Juan lived quietly, an anachronism even though he resided in the center of an anacronistic society. He had never converted to the Church, but kept older traditions handed down from the days when the proud Yaquis lived along the Yaqui River in the rich land of southern Sonora, Mexico.

He claimed direct descent from the Surem, the Uto-Aztecan tribe that once flourished in that area. When the Surem lost their river, some died and the remainder scattered, one group moving north to the area which now borders the Yaqui River and becoming the Yaqui Tribe. Juan claimed to be able to trace his ancestry all the way back to a legendary wise man also named Mapoli, a key figure in the origin myths of his people.

"What do you mean, Juan?"

Maria had faith in her husband. He was one of the wisest men she had ever known and had been a good provider. Their children had been raised, loved and sent out into the world well-prepared for productive lives of their own. Juan and Maria had been married for forty years.

"The demon," he replied. "The beast without form that once roamed the desert. It is back."

He sat on an old collapsed sofa on the porch of their modest home, just outside the open window of the room where Maria kept her loom. Late that same morning, he had moved to the porch with a small jar and begun chewing dried mushrooms, *psilocybe mexicana*—magic mushrooms. Since noon, he had been sitting quietly with his eyes closed, traveling through some mysterious inner landscape.

Maria understood this behavior. She respected it. Her husband had a reputation as a great man, a man looked up to by all. Now she waited patiently to see if he would continue.

Juan opened his eyes. He appeared calm and his face showed no signs of discomfort or stress, but he seemed to be in a trance. "It rages in the north," he said. "It is very hungry."

She did not understand, but her husband often spoke strangely when he ate the mushrooms. He, at least, never showed any signs of being sick. She had tried one years before, but got terribly ill and threw up.

"What demon, Juan?" She said it in that patient tone all wives use when their husbands seem incomprehensible. When he did not answer, she shrugged and returned to her weaving. If she needed to know, he would explain it to her. If it was just one of the mushroom dreams, he would not. Either way, it would be as God intended.

Her husband had closed his eyes again and sat motionless. The woman could not see the crow perched on the railing. She did not see it suddenly rear its head in shock and freeze into immobility.

The crow closed its eyes, then opened them, and something else shone from within. Without uttering a sound, the large bird hopped down and looked at the still form of the man on the couch. It nodded to itself, turned, and launched itself into flight.

Juan Mapoli flew through the air. He had done this often, but it always filled him with wonder. Unencumbered by his larger physical body which now waited back in Barrio Libre, his consciousness followed the snake-like passage of I-10 north from Tucson to Phoenix and then beyond. The miles sped by and the old man felt like laughing.

The freedom of the air filled him. With merely a thought, Juan could dive down and flash along just above the ground or climb higher into the air. The feeling of speed and power was exhilarating. The keen eyes of the crow could see everything below, could watch the drama of life and death in the desert unfold.

He flew north, and time ceased to exist, there were no miles, only the thrill of the open skies. But, as he neared Phoenix, another feeling began to manifest itself. Following the highway, skirting the city, his uneasiness grew stronger. Juan felt the joy of his flight being wrestled from his grasp, felt the freedom of flight slip into the shadow of another emotion.

He slowed. The joy faded. The movement of his wings became a chore. The effort of his northward progress became a labor. His avian heart began to beat even more rapidly. He left Phoenix behind and continued northward.

Soon, as he looked ahead, he could discern a small grouping of buildings along the access road. There was a sun-faded, weathered old wooden sign. He landed on the ground before it and hopped around so he could read it. It said, "Agate Junction. Population 104." Suddenly, he became aware of something in the desert just to the west — not something seen, but a heightened anticipatory feeling. Taking wing again, he flew out over the highway and past the narrow cleared area separating the natural desert from the roadside. Beyond, stretching for miles, level sands were interrupted only by cacti and scrub. His keen black eyes searched for movement. Catching an upward current, he soared higher.

There! Just by that dilapidated farmhouse on the outskirts of the town—movement. Something large raced across the desert, the wind of its passage drawing the sand and dust into the air, whipping it into a funnel.

Juan turned in mid-flight, and sped away toward the south. He had seen enough. It was indeed free. Now he must return to his home and prepare. He would be summoned.

*   *   *   *   *

On the porch in Barrio Libre, the form on the couch shivered. A very soft and nearly inaudible sound came from the lips of the old man slumped there. Maria had gone into another room for thread and would not hear it. It was a mournful sound, an expression of fear and unease. The sound was "CAW."

Chapter Six

Havasupai

In the Colorado River Country of Northern Arizona, in Cataract Canyon, lived an old man named Rattle. In his youth, he had dreamed that a deer came to visit him in the night, speaking to him about the Pai, whispering to him about how they needed a medicine man. It had instructed him to make a rattle out of a gourd, to put within it pebbles from the very bottom of the gorge and attach a strong handle. Night after night it came to him in his wickiup and taught him songs, which he practiced diligently until they were memorized.

Now, at the age of 70, he constituted half the medicine men among the Havasupai. To "The People of the Blue Water," he served as both a respected elder and a great story-teller, one who kept the magic of their traditions alive.

On this day, Rattle felt unaccountably agitated and kept looking around the village for a cause. His wife, Naomi, whispered to her sister that the old man must be up to something, his restlessness hinting at the unusual.

"Don't whisper behind my back, wife," he snapped, venting his irritation on the unfortunate woman. "There is something in the air." He paused, looking northwest toward the spirit land, then shook his head in frustration.

"What is it?" His wife placed a skinny hand on his shoulder, her face contrite, her eyes bright with curiosity.

"I do not know, but I can feel that the gods have something to tell me," he replied, shrugging her hand away. "I will go walk in the gorge and perhaps I will understand."

"How long will you be gone, husband?"

Rattle looked disdainfully at the woman. "As long as it takes." Taking his rattle, pipe and walking stick, he strode off in the direction of Black Man, a red sandstone and black mineral figure carved by nature to resemble a sleeping giant.

Naomi watched as he disappeared from view, then turned to her sister. "This is not like him. His name among the wise is 'He-Who-Waits.'"

The sister, named Flower, merely grunted as she concentrated on her weaving. She had learned early in life not to comment on domestic tensions between her in-laws. Silence had proved wiser and safer when dealing with a medicine man.

*   *   *   *   *

Rattle passed by Black Man, wishing him continued rest, and came to the large boulder upon which the beautiful primitive art of his ancestors had been carved. Buckskin-clad warriors pursued mythical beasts in the hunt of life, the Great Serpent wove her way along the fissures of the rock, and handprints of those long gone decorated every side. Here he sat and rested under the four foot ledge.

The time would soon come for The Peach Dance, their fall festival, when they would give thanks to Those Above for the bounty of the harvest and ask the gods for continued blessings. Rattle nodded to himself. There would be visitors from the Hopi and the Piutes, even the Apaches. There would be songs and stories and dancing. A time of happiness approached.

Rattle would have duties at the festival. He would dance (a little) and he would smoke his pipe and tell a story around a large open campfire, much as he had done all his long life. He had been waiting for the deer spirit to show him which story to tell. Thus far, the spirit had been silent.

The shadows grew longer as the afternoon faded toward evening. Rattle felt a strange lassitude sweeping over him. He knew he should get up and move on, but the shade of the overhanging ledge was constantly cooled by breezes passing across the nearby water. It was so peaceful and so comfortable that his lethargy overcame his will. He did not sleep . . . exactly. He watched a tiny bright red spider weave its gossamer web on the edge of the overhang. It worked with patience as it crossed the anchor strands again and again, creating a mosiac of silver filaments.

With the web all but complete, the spider suddenly spasmed, thrusting its eight legs out from its body and falling on a single strand until it hung two feet away from the old man's face, exactly at eye level. It hung there motionless for a long moment and then began to climb laboriously back up the strand. As it moved upward, it began to revolve, as if some strange miniature whirlwind played with it.

It continued to climb upward, however, without missing a step. The eight tiny legs moved rhythmically, the little body spinning. When the spider reached the web again, it moved across in a similar manner. Starting at the far edge, it wove a new pattern in an ever widening spiral. The result looked like a tornado, a narrow conical base winding upward into a wide funnel.

Rattle could not move. He knew this must be a message for him from Those Above. He puzzled over it, but could not understand.

A tentative scrabbling sounded as the evening shadows spread over the gorge. Soon, a proud old buck deer stepped into view. Its antlers were high, a rack of horn seldom seen even in the wild. It sniffed the air, looked carefully but regally about, and moved toward the shadowed overhang.

The totem showed no fear. It moved sure-footedly over the rocky ground and came to a halt not more than three feet away from the edge of the rock overhang. It stood at least fifteen hands high at the shoulder and the medicine man could see only its body beyond the edge. Then, it lowered its head and peered under the ledge directly into Rattle's eyes.

The old man's heart beat swiftly, excitement and adrenalin coursing through him. He didn't move—didn't even blink.

Man and deer sat frozen in that tableau for a long and breathless time.

When Rattle returned to his wickiup later than night, his wife awakened and asked, "Did you find out what is wrong?"

Moving silently in the dark, Rattle lay beside her and placed a comforting hand over hers. He sighed as he lowered his head onto the mat.

"The Deer Spirit came to me, Naomi. He told me what lies in store and what I must do."

His wife waited for him to go on, but he was silent. "What is that, husband?"

The old man could see the glimmer of her eyes just inches from his face. He smiled. "I must go to my brothers," he said. "I must represent the People of the Blue Water at a great gathering." And then he closed his eyes, wrapped in the contentment of one whose waiting is over.

Chapter Seven

Apacheland

In Apacheland, George Buck, war-named Red Cloud, woke with a start. He was bathed in a cold sheen of perspiration and his heart raced. He had been dreaming the dream again.

Ever since his childhood, George had experienced a recurrent dream, wonderful yet frustrating. In the dream, he was Geronimo. In his heart, he knew that he was remembering another life—his own life. The white man called it reincarnation. His parents thought their boy a little crazy. George, however, felt certain he had been Goyathlay, meaning One-Who-Yawns, known in history as Geronimo.

Often when the elders told stories of the past, singing the story of the great leader, George recognized the events and could fill in details—details that were confirmed when the disgruntled singers went to check. It was unsettling, but not his fault.

Sometimes, as if entranced, George would do things without realizing it. He might make a sand painting, sing an old song, make a gesture he would normally not make. At such times he felt possessed.

Living on the Fort Apache Reservation, near Springerville, Arizona, was a good thing for George. Though his peculiarities set him a little apart from the others, his personable manner made him generally liked. He worked for the Sawmill in Cibecue, cutting and loading lumber, doing odd jobs in repair and maintenance for several stores, and as custodian for the supermarket and the clinic.

The good steady work made it possible for him to put a little money aside. He didn't drink or gamble so saving it proved easy. Work also gave him time alone, time to sort through the confusing thoughts and memories.

Those who knew George believed himself to be Geronimo reborn thought it strange he worked as a janitor, but it posed no problem for the youth. In his earlier life, he had been a great leader and warrior, despite an ignominious end. In these times, the leaders needed were accountants and business administrators, not fighters. Simple work done well and thoroughly could be quite satisfying.

After finishing the offices and locking up for the night, George would go out into the desert, southeast of town, and sit under the stars where he could look back on Cibeque and see how far his people had come.

Remembering brought no pain. The contrast of present to past demonstrated for George what could only be seen as miraculous. And this young Apache had a truly unique perspective.

There had been a lot of progress since the Western Apache made their peace with the white man. The Fort Apache Reservation alone contained over one and a half million acres of land. The people lived in permanent houses, maintained their clan ties, voted in elections and had developed a business acumen that brought them commendations from the white man's government. Cattle ranching took up 138,000 acres in the southeast corner of the reservation and the herd had grown to the point where there were eight livestock associations involved. The Fort Apache Timber Company developed, harvested and milled quality lumber, generating an impressive income for the tribe. Schools had improved and the opportunity for education had gradually reached out to embrace all the tribe. Whiteriver had a full service hospital run by the U.S. Public Health Service and there were clinics in each of the eleven districts of the reservation.

In short, life for the Apache was considerably different than the Geronimo-part of George remembered. In those days, the people had been raiders and nomads, fighting to retain the territories they roamed. Now they were residents of a greater nation without surrendering their own. Geronimo-in-George took pride in his people and felt happy to be at peace.

On this night, awakening from the dream, George found himself afraid. In all this present life, he could not remember fearing anything. Worse, he did not even know the source of the fear.

Sitting up in the dark, trying to get his heartbeat under control, George extended his senses in an effort to identify the threat. Nothing. His small room remained quiet and secure. The first glimmerings of impending dawn had barely touched the eastern sky. Everything around him reflected peace and quiet, as it should. Why then this rude awakening?

Turning to the self within himself, George asked the older and wiser warrior to help him ascertain the nature of the fear. In shock and dismay, he discovered that his usually steady and reliable other self *was* the source of it.

Closing his eyes, he tried to calm himself, imagining a blanket of warm comfort settling over his peculiar joint consciousness.

He regretted it instantly.

The Geronimo part of George felt the imagined blanket spreading around him and went into hysterical overdrive, flooding his body anew with adrenalin.

Like watching a movie in his imagination, George saw a great cloud of dust settling over him, heard the screaming of the wind mixed with other screams. In his mind, he and his other self fled in blind panic, legs churning, muscles pistoning.

When he ran full tilt into the bedroom wall, George sank to the floor in pain and exhaustion. He gently rubbed his forehead. It had been the leading edge of his assault on the wall.

As his mind cleared, he asked himself aloud, "What the hell is going on?"

Deep inside, at a level of consciousness he had not even known he possessed, an inner voice sang.

> The Demon wind cannot touch me
> Demon Wind with razor claws
> Peaceful spirits all surround me
> Death a stranger
> Harm illusion
> Warrior am I

The song repeated again and yet again, fading, even as his heartbeat slowed, to an inaudible chant that barely impinged on his awareness but continued somehow to provide comfort.

He rose from the floor and returned to bed. Lying back, forearm draped over his eyes, he tried to make sense out of what seemed nonsense.

Mentally, he cursed whatever gods had saddled him with memories of other times. In all his life, this dual nature of his personality had marked him as strange and different. He had no great ambitions. He had done that part of living before. He deserved a rest, a lifetime of contented solitude. Why had this weird emotional instability singled him out? What good did it do him to remember being one of the great men of his people when all he wanted was to be left alone?

As the dawn lightened the window curtains, George turned his face into his pillow and tried to return to sleep. Silently, he prayed. "No dreams . . . please."

Chapter Eight

Zuniland, New Mexico

Zuni is different, an anomaly, the language itself probably unrelated to the tongues of any other tribe. Autonomous and secretive, the workings of religion, politics and superstition intertwine.

The old shaman looked across at the child who stood before him, nervous and fidgity, perhaps reflecting the proper attitude for one who faced the chief priest of the Gray Wolf Clan.

"You have been chosen by the whirlwind god, little one. Of all the winds of heaven, only the whirlwind stands upright like a man, yet flies like an eagle on wings of flint. It is the most potent and midmost among all the six gods of wind."

The boy stood while the old man sat cross-legged so their faces appeared almost on a level. Pasqual could see that the boy wanted to meet his gaze, but knew he looked terribly formidable decked in his feathers and beads. Time and again the child raised his wide eyes to the seamed countenance of the elder only to drop them.

"The whirlwind god can twist about and vanquish the north wind or the south, the east wind or the west and even overcome gravity, the pulling breath of the earth. To be chosen by him is a great honor."

The child nodded solemnly but did not speak.

"Go now, little one, but remember this day—for you have been marked for him."

Still without speaking, the boy fled.

The old man chuckled. "Ah, my little Rodrigo," he said under his breath, "one day, if the gods are kind, you will sit in my place in the kiva."

Pasqual Quatero rose from his cross-legged position and stretched his sixty-five-year-old limbs, working out the stiffness that always resulted these days from sitting too long.

The instruction of the child had been his last official responsibility of the day, but it remained early. The sun hung high in the sky, just past zenith. Pasqual wanted very much to return to his house and nap, but it would be unseemly. He decided to take a walk through the pueblo. It would be a good thing that he be seen active and healthy among his people. Rumors about his health and questions about his leadership were all too common these days.

"Always happens in the summer," he said aloud to himself. "The young ones start to feel like they can conquer the world and then begin to question the wisdom of their elders."

Pasqual walked for three hours through the village, greeting friends and speaking to the women and children. He stood not far from his house when he suddenly felt as if he'd been kicked. The excruciating pain caused him to reel back against an adobe wall and clutch at his chest. It felt as if a vise squeezed his heart without mercy.

No one noticed him at first, and, though he tried to call out, he could not find his voice. He attempted to brace himself against the wall, but slipped down helplessly.

Is it time? He asked the question only in his mind, but had already begun preparing himself for this possibility. Slumped against the base of the building in the dirt, he remained conscious, though his vision swam in red waves of pain as the vise continued to close in his chest.

A small figure suddenly stood before him. He did not recognize Rodrigo, but the child looked at him for a long moment before rushing off again.

By the time he returned with help, the old man had lapsed into unconsciousness.

Later, in the hospital, the attending physician stood at the old man's bedside and shook her head.

"Lucky," she muttered. They had stablized Quatero quickly and, though the attack appeared severe, Pasqual had come through it with much less damage than the team of doctors first feared.

Dr. Rose Treadwell seemed as much an enigma as Zuni. She had been a high school pageant queen and once, for a year, a Playboy

Bunny. She had graduated at the top of her class from Johns Hopkins and gone on to a very prestigious career.

Now, at 52 years of age, she remained a handsome woman. Rose had come to Zuni for a one year stint, working with the Public Health Service. She had a reputation as one of the top cardiologists in the country. Pasqual could not know how fortune smiled on him by having her there. The old man remained unconscious, a matter of concern to the doctor. It seemed unusual for a patient who had sustained little damage to stay out for so long.

Rose had been looking directly at his face when he screamed. "Yaaaaaaaa . . . ." His whole body coiled, his arms and legs pistoning as if he were running. "No! No! I-shothl-ti-mon-a-ha-i!" Then he grew silent, though restless.

The attendant, who had rushed over when the scream began, backed off again and looked suddenly fearful.

"Carl, what did he say?" The doctor placed a hand on the orderly's shoulder.

"He called on the immortal beings. Ishothltimonahai."

"What beings are those?" Rose did not release her grip. The man looked as if he might run away.

"Priest business, Doc," he said, recovering his self possession. "The Ishothltimonahai are supernatural beings . . . not the gods exactly, but pretty powerful nonetheless. The Ahai are 'The Beings' or the ever-recurring ones."

Rose turned back, looking at the patient. "He must have been dreaming."

Carl looked at the old man and nodded. "Maybe," he agreed, "or maybe he's having a vision. It is said that the gods talk to these elders. This guy is the head man of his clan. You never know what they're up to."

"Get some restraints," instructed the doctor releasing her grip on the orderly's shoulder. "I'll stay with him to make sure he doesn't hurt himself."

"Yes, ma'am." The attendant hurried to the supply room and returned with the requested items.

When they had secured Pasqual to the bed rails so he couldn't hurl himself off the bed, Rose breathed a sigh of relief.

For the first time, the old man opened his eyes. "Where am I?" The question sounded more a demand than request. His hawk-like eyes swept the hospital room. "Who are you, woman?"

"I am Dr. Treadwell, Mr. Quatero," she answered reaching down and taking his pulse. "You are in the hospital on the reservation because you suffered a heart attack. You were brought in this afternoon and you've been sleeping for several hours."

Memory seemed to flood back into Pasqual's mind. "I 'member walkin' in the pueblo and a sudden pain in my chest." He closed his eyes. "It hurt bad." He shook his head, opening his eyes again and looking up at the doctor. "That's about all . . . except I seem to remember someone calling me." Suddenly, his eyes got wider. "Wait a minute! I remember the demon!"

The doctor looked surprised. "The demon?"

"Yeah, it spoke inside my head."

Rose rolled her eyes ceilingward but kept her voice calm. "What demon is that?"

Pasqual appeared about to answer when he stopped, looked around again and realized where he was. "I got to get out of here, doctor. How soon can I go?"

"I think you should stay tonight at least. We'll need to run a few more tests, just to make sure you're going to be all right."

The old man tried to sit up and discovered the restraints. "Hey! How come I'm tied up?"

"You thrashed around a lot before you regained consciousness, Mr. Quatero. I didn't want you to fall out of the bed."

"Would you untie me, please?" The old man seemed calm.

Rose paused before reaching down and slipping off the restraints. "Okay, Mr. Quatero, but you've got to promise to behave. You had a heart attack just a few hours ago and we have to talk about your diet, daily routine and treatment."

"We gonna do that now?" The old man rubbed his wrists once they were free. The look he gave her said very plainly he didn't want it to be now.

She smiled. "No, Mr. Quatero, it doesn't have to be tonight. After you've had some rest, we'll take you to another room for the tests and then you can come back and sleep through the night. We'll talk about these other matters in the morning. Okay?"

Pasqual looked relieved. "Don't wanta do it tonight," he said.

"Then we won't," she assured him. "If you'll just relax, I'll find the nurse and have her bring your medication. Then you can sleep for a while."

The old man closed his eyes when the doctor and attendant left.

Only five minutes passed before the nurse arrived with the pills but she found the room empty. Pasqual Quatero had disappeared.

Chapter Nine

Agate Junction, Arizona

"Onetwothreefourfivesixseveneightnineten!" Billy Mauldin pushed his face and arms away from the tree and scanned the immediate area, squinting against the bright afternoon sunshine.

He shouted, "You guys have had it!" Youthful bravado perhaps, but the other boys were bigger so he deemed it necessary.

Life in Agate Junction had never been stimulating for Billy and his friends. Everything in Agate could be classed as truly Mom & Pop. A total population of 104 provided limited opportunities for interaction.

Nearly a hundred years old, the town had survived from pioneer days. That it remained alive at all resulted from its location along I-17. The one gas station provided the only fuel for forty miles and even that pitiful influx of traffic gave the citizenry a meager excuse for hanging on.

Billy looked carefully all around his position. Benjamin Green, a boy two years older, would be somewhere close by, just waiting for him to step too far from base before racing in and catching him off guard. Ben always stayed close to home. Margie Croeller, on the other hand, could be characterized as a hide-and-find-me player. Billy could spend a half hour trying to locate her and never get a clue unless he got lucky.

Beth, his older sister, might be anywhere. Totally unpredictable, she could even have quit and gone home without telling the others.

Billy had spent hours looking for her in a game just last week, only to find she had gotten bored and left while he still counted with his eyes closed by the tree.

The twins, Joe and Jim Babson, were not really much fun in these games. They had a tendency to lie in wait and ambush the person who was "It." That always proved to be painful and embarrassing. Once, they had taken all his clothes and left him naked, hiding in the brush. Beth had found him and made his life miserable for a full week afterward. What a crummy situation! Joe and Jim were a year and five months older at 15 and bigger by a head and a half.

From Billy's point of view, playing hide-and-seek with this crowd involved peril.

They all shared the problem of having no other kids in Agate Junction to play with. The rest of the citizens were older, survivors from an earlier time. There were six farms, the gas station, a truck stop, the post office, general store and a scattering of houses. The children were bused to school over in Wickenburg. Thus they were forced to rely on each other when they got back home in the afternoon.

A rustling in the scrub by the old wooden shed caught Billy's attention just as he was about to risk moving away from base. He crouched low and followed the sound until he ran out of cover. At that moment Benjamin attempted to make his break. Too slow. Billy tagged him with a joyous whoop and Ben turned with an embarrassed grin, good natured despite his obvious failure at stealth. As first caught, he would be "It" next time.

"Thought I had you, Bill," he said moving over to sit at the base of the tree. "How'd you guess?"

"You always stay in close, Ben. It isn't hard to find you. I wish I could say the same about the others." He shook his head. "Margie and Beth are hardest to find, but the guys are liable to give me a difficult time. Do you want your parole?"

An innovation on the old game of hide-and-seek, added after they got older, was the practice of granting an early "catchee" the opportunity to help find the others—a parole. It kept them from getting bored with waiting around.

"Yeah, I guess so." Ben leaned back against the tree and closed his eyes. "Do you ever get tired of this, Billy?"

"I suppose I do, Ben," replied the other boy. "I just can't figure out what else we can do. It isn't like we have that many choices."

The task of finding the others remained. Billy felt a wave of frustration sweep up from somewhere deep inside, threatening to overwhelm him. Why bother with this stupid game? Maybe he'd be smarter to just quit right now and go home. That would teach Beth a lesson. Let her hide out in the bushes while he sat at home in front of the TV and ate candy. Then she'd know what it meant to waste an afternoon without friends.

It was early evening and supper would not be ready for an hour or two. The clear sky guaranteed miserably hot weather. The temperature—soaring to 116 degrees—kept the rhythm of all their activities slowed down and minimum exertion became the rule. Aside from bursts of energy when absolutely necessary, the children tended to proceed at a leisurely pace, even when playing hide-and-seek.

Billy and Ben split up and headed out past the shed, each planning to look in a previously successful hiding place used by Margie. They had not gone far, however, when the wind started to pick up, whipping sand into their faces. They instinctively closed the distance between them and met in the clearing just beyond the shed.

"Where'd this come from?" asked Ben, rubbing his eyes. "Everything looked clear a minute ago."

"Let's get under cover," said Billy. "Ow!" A pebble had just flown into his face. He wiped his hand over the spot and it came away bloody.

Both boys dove into the shed and burrowed into a stack of loose straw. They would not realize for some time how lucky they had been.

*   *   *   *   *

It had slept undisturbed for more than two centuries, imprisoned under the earth by the charm. It had no physical body as men understand bodies, but the energies that combined and gathered to form its consciousness were localized and compressed into a force which behaved as if it had physical proportions. Imagine the way particles are confined in a cyclotron—swiftly moving bullets of matter enclosed in a chamber which prevents their escape. The resultant collisions and combinings create new atoms with properties the original contributors had only in part. In a similar way, the physical world acted to force the elements of the beast into cohesion, kept it from diffusing and losing identity. A perfect organism, unencumbered by physical weakness, devastating in its ability to destroy utterly, nothing could stand against it—not nature, not man. Perhaps it is understandable, therefore, that it eventually grew arrogant and careless.

It remembered earlier days of freedom, dominating its environment. It had ranged across the great Southwest unchallenged by any predator except the two-legged biped called man. Even over that animal it continually demonstrated superiority. It fed on the tribes, settling like a cloud over their camps and villages, devouring them at leisure. Sometimes it flayed them, using the sands that surrounded and coursed within it to cut through the flesh and release the blood and fluids. Other times, it absorbed their energies directly by settling over an individual's head like a caul and sucking every bit of moisture from the body, down to the marrow in the bones.

In time, the beast became predictable—a near fatal error. Since it behaved as if it had form, it fell victim to the trap the ancients set and it remained confined in the dark under the rocks for five hundred years. It hungered. The scorpions and snakes that blundered into its lair provided only a fraction of the energy it craved. In the days before its imprisonment, it had known the luxury of satiation, the pleasure of gluttony.

The beast had devoured everything in its path back then. The wild things of the desert had no defense except flight. The beast could be invisible—except that matter surrounding it could be affected by its movements so sand and dust and other bits of material swirled around and through it in ever increasing volume when it was not at rest.

Anything living, large or small, provided energy that the beast could assimilate, could transmute, could use to sustain its growth— and it perceived growth to be its destiny.

Many times, through the centuries, men and animals had stood atop the rocks which formed its prison. At first, it had guarded the door, hoping one of the creatures above might open it, might remove the hated charm that bound it. It had always been disappointed. Sometime after the first century passed, it found such intrusions only a bitter reminder of its helplessness, of the freedom no longer possible. Instead of moving to the door, it fled into the deepest recesses and brooded.

It grew ravenous and only the blind worms of the earth and the insects of the deep came near. It had cried and raged and even given way to mad laughter—though such physical terminology did not really describe the processes of this non-physical creature. Even more than the hunger, more than the loneliness, more than the disappointment, it hated. It hated man for imprisoning it in the rock. It hated man for leaving it to languish in the dark. It hated man for being free.

When Jack Foreman and Don Hunnicutt climbed atop the rocks, the beast retreated once again to the depths, weak and despairing. The tantalizing nearness of men added a spur of insult. It tried to ignore them, tried to concentrate on the insects of the dark, sought escape from the cruelty of man.

But then the two acted as no others had before. They moved the stone.

The beast felt rather than heard the grating vibration as the stone moved a little to the side, allowing fresh air to enter the chamber. It passed from despair to frenzied glee in that moment. It raced to the door and waited.

Only six inches, but enough. Now, if they would move the charm, it could escape. It waited, wished, and willed them to take away that cursed metal fragment which bound it to the rocks.

One of the men began to leave. The beast panicked. It feared it might lose this chance. Without thinking, it moved part way out the door, into the air atop the rocks. It could not leave, but it reached out and spread as far as it could. The dust and sand began to swirl, shrouding the rocks in a blowing cloud. The remaining man crouched down to escape the whipping sand. Then he saw and picked up the charm.

It took a moment for the beast to realize what had happened. It felt the sudden wrench of release, looked down from above and knew it had cleared the doorway. The beast was free.

It could not touch Jack Foreman. He was protected. He held the charm. Whipping around in a circular motion, the beast drew more dust and sand into the gale, putting a curtain of darkness between it and the human atop the rocks. It hungered. It saw the other. It fell on him and devoured him entirely, almost tenderly. Young Don Hunnicutt never knew what happened. He had almost reached the trucks when his world ended forever. The beast never stopped. It fled north into the desert.

Now, outside the village, the beast felt ready. It had traveled swiftly over the forty miles, following the ribbon of dense material on which the metal howlers sped. It searched for a small settlement, a place without too many of the hated men. A long time had passed since it last fed freely, and then it had been trapped. It would be conservative this time in case these men had learned new tricks.

The beast moved into Agate Junction in a furious blast of wind, sand and dust. Using the edge of the access road as the beginning point, it anchored itself and began expanding eastward over the town on toward the farms.

This choice of an anchor point spared the lives of the children. They dove into a shed just across the road.

Will Jensen owned the general store. The old clapboard building lasted approximately six seconds before the pressure put on it by the beast caused it to explode as if it had been bombed. Will perched on a ladder restocking a high shelf when the blast struck, lifting him into the air and into the center of the beast's leading edge. He became raw hamburger in seconds. The beast's hunger sucked him dry upon initial contact, so dry that the marrowless bones crumbled to dust while still in the air.

Audrey Green, Benjamin's mother, worked as a waitress in the truck stop adjacent to the store. The building itself had been constructed of concrete block much more recently than the store. It lasted only a few seconds longer.

Feeling its power grow, the beast churned like a fury over the flat tar roof of the building, ripping with fingers of concentrated force and razor sharp rock at the seals along the edges. The beams and joists that formed the roof structure were forced outward and upward as if they had been yanked free by a giant hand.

Audrey and her four customers were lifted up as Jensen had been, as if some huge vacuum cleaner was suddenly placed over a shoebox.

One moment they flew upward, mouths opened to scream their terror, and, the next, they exploded into red mist—a mist quickly replaced by a rain of white chunky dust.

Ed Bronson, the cook, grabbed at the handles to the huge walk-in freezer when he first heard the roof start to go. For a timeless instant, he managed to cling to the old half-ton unit. Unfortunately for Ed, the backs of the handles were not smooth and, in another moment, his fingers ripped from his hands as the rest of him flew upward to feed the hunger of the beast.

Grandon Mauldin, Billy's dad, the only mechanic for forty miles around, lay under the front end of an eighteen wheeler when the beast hit the gas station. Though everyone else in and around the station perished, including the driver who sat above him in the cab of the truck, Grandon survived. It would be a while before anyone knew it. The sharp whipping rocks flying within the sands surrounding the beast shredded the tires and the truck dropped down to the rims. He was pinned but not crushed.

The town of Agate Junction ceased to exist. Nothing of any consequence remained standing. The force of the beast's attack overwhelmed it. When the first driver pulled off the highway onto the access road looking for gas, he figured he must have misread the map and signs because Agate Junction could not be other than a ghost town.

The beast, somewhat satisfied with it's first significant meal in five hundred years, decided not to wait for the council to form. It would set out now to eliminate the threat posed by the men. Start with the peace man? No. The eldest first! The young pups could be no threat. It moved to the east, picking up speed as it crossed uninhabited stretches of desert.

Chapter Ten

Phoenix

The Phoenix weather forecast for Sunday, July 9th, called for partly cloudy skies with a 10% chance of thunderstorms and blowing dust through the day increasing to 40% chance in the evening hours, a typical monsoon season.

Matt Sharp, meteorologist with KTVC, doubled as the weatherman for KUAM, a talk-radio station. Early that morning, he entered his office and hooked up through his information net, Zephyr, with the National Weather Service. On the screen, he could now study satellite photos and weather forecast maps. In addition, his network of local spotters called in a steady stream of surface reports. The radar showed the usual blue and green patches of storm activity starting in the mountains to the north, crossing through the upper part of the state, then sweeping in a southeasterly direction just at the border between Arizona and New Mexico.

Monsoon weather always fascinated Matt. The swirling patterns of the storms built and dissipated quickly, sometimes surprising even the weatherwise. Three inches of rain in an hour had been recorded more than once and such storms wreaked havoc with Phoenix Metro traffic.

As a result, when activity stayed as high as today, he kept an extra sharp eye on the radar, even on a day off, trying to pick out the emerging patterns and forecast the areas in danger of flooding.

You could get a real feel for the weather when you saw the radar superimposed on the satellite shots. The flow of activity ran in a logical and inexorable curve as the mountains forced the wind currents into strange and almost beautiful swirls and arcs.

As he watched, the line of the predominant front moved across the state for all the world like a rainbow, beginning up in Kingman and arcing over the Grand Canyon before starting south along the border with New Mexico. The flow remained even and uninterrupted.

When the phone rang and one of his Mobile Weather Spotters reported a major storm about 40 miles north of Phoenix, Matt checked his radar and found no signal at all from that area.

"What the hell?" he asked himself aloud.

"What have you got?" Diedre Carroll, the new weather girl on KTAX-FM came up by his side and leaned over the console. Matt smiled as he felt her left breast come to rest on his right shoulder.

"Roger Milton reports a major weather center about 40 miles north but there's nothing on the radar."

"Could it be some sort of malfunction?" Diedre pushed back a little, then swooped in and nipped at his ear.

"No, everything else is right on," he replied. Picking up the phone, he called Roger's mobile line. When it connected, he could hear the wind howling and lots of interference.

"Weatherwatch. This is Milton."

"This is Matt. What exactly have you got, Roger?"

The weather chaser had to shout to make himself understood. "A hell of a blow. Everything not anchored down is in the air."

"We show nothing on radar," complained Matt.

"Because there's no rain," shouted Roger. "It's like a miniature hurricane out here but dry as a bone."

"Which way is it heading?" Matt was trying to find a way of plotting it.

"It's right alongside I-17, not far from Agate Junction, heading right toward me. It's moving along at a pretty good clip."

"Keep an eye on it and call me every ten minutes," said Matt. Hanging up, he dialed the number for the Wickenberg remote. "Hi, Pat," he said into the phone. Pat Harris owned the Wickenberg Mercantile where KTVC had installed a remote sensor. Matt called her whenever he needed on-site confirmation. "This is Matt, the weather guy. You got anything unusual out there?"

He listened for a few moments, then said goodbye and hung up. "Nothing to report, she said. Must be some freak." He dialed Roger's number again, but got a busy signal.

"I guess we wait," he said, turning his face to the delicious neck that leaned over him. He kissed and nuzzled her.

"Stop that," she commanded, but didn't move away. Instead, she sighed and reached over for his hand. "You have to stop doing that," she whispered. Her eyes—beautiful eyes—held a pleading look.

"You don't really mind, do you?" He grinned up at her and squeezed her hand gently.

"You're supposed to be working and I'm supposed to be learning, Matt," she said seriously. "When I got this job you said you'd help."

The two were new lovers. Neither worked on weekends. They had gotten together for the first time over the Fourth of July and engineered considerable fireworks of their own.

Matt turned his swivel chair, capturing her other hand, and she perched lightly on the edge of the desk. She smiled.

"I do mind, honey. I've wanted this job for a long time. Now that I've got it, I don't want to do anything to threaten it—no stupid errors because of my inexperience. That's why I need your help. I want to learn from the master, my hero. Then, when I choose to move on, I will."

"Today Phoenix, next year LA?" Matt only half-joked.

"Maybe," she said and winked.

"Okay with me," he said turning back and studying the screen. And it was okay . . . well, more than okay. Diedre did not act like other professional women he knew. Some were positive tiger sharks about their careers, but this girl impressed him.

She reached over and ruffled his hair, then rubbed his shoulders. "It hasn't been too bad for you so far, has it Matt?"

He leaned back into her, feeling his head nestle between those truly spectacular breasts. She massaged his temples.

"Hell no," he admitted. "I feel like a teenager in love, and you won't hear me complain. I hope you feel the same way."

She studied him from her vantage point behind and above. She too felt lucky. Matt fit—both a nice guy and a good lover. His full, thick hair had been cut in a shaggy mop covering the tops of his ears and hung just perfectly at collar length.

She moved her hands back to his shoulders, feeling the broad muscular expanse as she kneaded it with strong fingers. *Almost perfect—and single,* she thought to herself. Why, then, did she still have such reservations about even a little commitment? For the past two days, he had been urging her to move in with him. He said he understood her reluctance to get into anything complicated, but it would be so much easier for them if they shared the house.

He was right, of course, in that it would enable her to save a fair amount of money. Rent and food would be equally split and, he insisted, cooking for two was more fun than cooking for himself alone.

The cooking thing mattered. She hated to cook while Matt loved it. More than that, he was really good. Whether grilling steaks or creating a delicate souffle, he had the magic touch in the kitchen. She sighed. Maybe she just stayed ornery and independent for no reason.

Leaning forward, she whispered into his ear. "Everything so far has been just perfect."

"Are we on for dinner tonight?"

"You bet," she said and kissed him lightly on the cheek. "Meanwhile, explain what's happening with this storm."

He looked again at the screen, indecision written on his face. "I don't know." He dialed Roger's number again. This time an operator told him the line was out of order. He looked at his watch. "He's late. That isn't like Roger. It must be the storm."

Diedre smiled. "It's almost 4:30. If we leave soon, we can get in a quick swim before the sun goes down."

Matt's eyes strayed from the screen to look at her. She was so damned pretty. He could see her now, her sleek body cleaving the water like some magnificent creature of the sea. Swimming without suits provided the best excuse for having a block privacy fence around the yard. She looked like a living advertisement for naturism. "Just a few more minutes, honey," he said at last. "I keep thinking that . . ." he stopped. "Shit! There it is!"

"What?" She stepped up to look at the screen and they both saw the same thing.

A blue spot of activity blossomed on the radar, expanded as the color intensified. It blanketed an area a few miles wide and settled there for a few long minutes before it began to fade. They watched in awe.

"If that isn't a rain squall or a tornado, it must be kicking up a hell of a lot of debris or it wouldn't show at all."

"It can't do that, can it?" Diedre looked at the plot.

"I don't know," said Matt. "Damn!" He reached for the phone and dialed the National Weather Service. "If that was a wind storm, Roger was right. Somebody just had a hell of a blow."

Chapter Eleven

I-17 Near Agate Junction

Officer Daniel Lopez had just pulled over a little red Fiero that had been weaving erratically along I-17. The driver, returning to Phoenix, had been excited and panicky.

"I was heading south, Officer," he reported, "and I saw the gas sign for Agate Junction. When I checked my gauge, I figured I'd better stop. I was still about a quarter mile from the exit when I saw the storm. Jesus, it was a bitch! I slowed down and finally pulled over. It was moving from the west or northbound side of the road or I don't know if I'd still be here to talk about it. It didn't move fast, but it sure chewed up that town. When the buildings started to explode, I made a U-turn and hit the gas. The first emergency call box was out of order so I'm damned glad to find you."

"This storm," said Lopez, "what did it look like?"

"Like a tornado . . . sort of. It looked like something out of the Wizard of Oz, you know? Except the funnel didn't taper down like that. It just kind of whipped up the desert and sucked all kinds of debris into it." He shook his head. "I never saw anything like that in my life, man. It was a killer."

Lopez called in and reported right away. "I'm about six miles from Agate," he told the dispatcher, "so I'll get over there and call in again after I look around." Thanking the driver and cautioning him to slow down, the officer turned around and sped down the highway toward Agate Junction. Despite the monsoon season, most of the clouds he could see lay north. To the west, he saw nothing that looked like a killer storm. The Agate turnoff came up quickly and Dan pulled into a scene he could hardly believe. "Holy Shit," he exclaimed. Taking the microphone, he spoke urgently. "This is Officer Daniel Lopez. I just pulled in off I-17 at what used to be Agate Junction. You aren't gonna believe this, but it's gone. I mean the whole town is gone, levelled, wiped clean. It looks like some kind of bomb went off or something."

"Take it easy, Daniel," said the voice of the dispatcher. "I'll call the sheriff and get you some back-up. Do you see any people? There are 104 residents. Some have to be left. Do you need medical and emergency equipment?"

"Send everybody, Doris," he said wiping a suddenly sweaty hand over his brow. "Something happened here . . . something big. But I don't have any idea how to start looking for survivors in this mess. There doesn't appear to be anything large enough to hide people under."

Where the general store had stood only a cleanly swept concrete slab remained. Little pieces of splintered wood crunched underfoot. He saw roof shingles, badly scarred, and broken glass. Big pieces of lumber that would have framed the building had vanished. They were just gone.

The gas station and truck stop, a roofless block shell, now held only the big freezer and the bases of some counter stools that had been bolted to the floor. The counter, stove, tables and chairs that had been there when Daniel stopped for lunch a little before noon were absent.

In front of the station stood what must have been a semi-rig but Daniel couldn't have sworn to it. The tires had been shredded and blown, the box gone entirely and the truck itself denuded of all trim and paint. He climbed up and looked in, but saw no driver. The windows had been blown out, the seats were shredded rags, and even the glass on the gauges had been scored to opacity.

Over all of it lay silence—an eerie absence of sound, like the hush after a loud Fourth of July ear-banger. It shrouded the place like a lid on a jug.

Then Daniel heard the soft bubbling sound. When he looked under the truck, he saw what he took to be a corpse—had to be because the body appeared to be all chewed up. But then it moved and cried and Officer Lopez turned and vomited up his lunch. He ran back to the car and called in again.

Ten minutes later the area was a circus of emergency vehicles and various kinds of cops. The first reports had also attracted the news media. It took a tow truck brought up from Phoenix to lift the rest of the semi off what remained of Grandon Mauldin. When the truck fell on the blown wheels, it had covered him from head to crotch, pinning him but leaving his arms and legs free. These were mostly gone now, just shredded stumps of bone. That the man hadn't bled to death seemed a mystery until he babbled about the fire. A ruptured gas pump had ignited, resulting in a flash fire that neatly cauterized the stumps before the wind blew it out. The raw flesh had still been razored by sand and rock, but the main arteries stayed mostly closed.

Daniel closed his eyes and tried to shut out the memory of Mauldin's screams when they lifted the truck off.

They found the two kids in the shed across the access road. Despite being scared half to death, they were able to report what they had seen—howling wind, rocks and sand blown with enough force to cut flesh, horrible screams and ultimately silence.

A check of the sites where houses and farms had stood just a few hours earlier that day showed nothing but devastation. No bodies were found, not even animals. It was as if the hand of God had reached down and swept Agate Junction from the map.

No one could explain it. No one understood it. The media went a little crazy and Arizona made the national news. The Killer Storm became a subject of controversy almost immediately. Expert after expert tried to explain how it could not have happened, but the mute barrenness that had once been home to over a hundred souls remained. Grandon Mauldin died before the ambulance got to a hospital. The only two survivors were Billy Mauldin and Benjamin Green.

Daniel Lopez went home that night and got quietly drunk.

Sunday, July 9th

Chapter Twelve

Phoenix

Jack Foreman awakened with a terrible hangover. He had been up all Saturday night and into Sunday morning. After the freak storm ended, he had searched for young Hunnicutt without success. Finally, growing alarmed, he got the truck started, drove to a phone and called the Tempe police. It had taken some heated argument but they finally agreed to meet him at the site. They were as perplexed as he about the storm. It had apparently been so localized that nowhere else in the Phoenix Metro area had been affected. If not for the evidence of the sandblasted pickups, even he would not have believed it possible. The officers found no trace of Don anywhere near the yard. When he got home, Jack drank a fifth of bourbon before passing out.

Even this morning, a little before noon, Jack still could not figure out what happened. He worried about Don, but also felt concern that this might be some sort of joke, a chance to blow the professor's mind. *If that proves to be the case, by God, I'll fry the boy's tail for sure!*

His head throbbed and his mouth tasted like week-old garbage. He groaned as he sat up in bed. He still wore his clothes from yesterday. Rising, he started shucking them as he moved toward the john, leaving a trail of discards behind. Down to jockey shorts by the time he entered the bathroom, he paused in front of the mirror.

The face glaring blearily back at him looked like a rotten melon in a cactus patch. His eyes were so bloodshot, they resembled wounds.

"Jesus Christ!" he exclaimed. "What a night!"

Dropping his shorts, he stepped into the shower and turned it on. The warm summer weather meant he left the handle on cold all the time. Even then, what came out of the showerhead was tepid.

Nothing disturbed the silence of his house but his own breathing and the running of the water. After scrubbing furiously and washing his hair and beard, he pushed the handle in and towelled off.

Usually at this time of the day, after his morning ablution, being alone affected him the most. Evelyn had been dead now for eleven years and he still couldn't get used to her absence. An important part of his mind expected her to be just around the corner or down the hall whenever he moved through the house. Late at night, when he had been hitting the bottle too much, he would sometimes forget and wander from room to room calling her name.

He shook his head. "I'm pathetic!" he said aloud. "When am I going to straighten up?" But the question was rhetorical. He knew the answer, or at least thought he did. *Never.*

"Meow."

The plaintive cry came from Useless, his tomcat. Huge and lanky, striped like a zebra, the feline carried scars earned in a hundred back alley brawls. He was a big cat, not an ounce of fat on him, though Jack fed him well and conscientiously. Useless remained the only link to his life as it had been with Evie. Everything else including furniture, pictures, clothing, dishes, had been replaced or at least purchased since her death. He wanted nothing to remind him.

"Hi Furball," he said pleasantly, bending to scratch the cat under his chin and stroke the full length of his body from head to tail tip. He was rewarded with a loud purring and continued stropping of his ankles as the cat wound back and forth between his feet. "Hungry?"

Useless sat on his haunches and yawned.

Just like him, thought Jack. *He wouldn't admit it to me if he hadn't eaten for a week.* To the cat he said, "Okay. Gimme a minute."

He picked up the shorts from the bathroom floor and crossed, naked, back into the bedroom. As he went, he kicked the pile of discarded clothing into a heap at the bedside. With that kick, however, something metallic shot out of the pile and hit the wall.

"What the hell . . .?" Jack bent and fumbled behind the bedside table until he had retrieved the object. The Charm. He had forgotten about it in the excitement and confusion of the night. He sat on the bed and tried to look at it carefully. Cursing, he reached over and picked up his bifocals.

He studied the object for a full minute, humming unconsciously to himself. Made mostly of silver, the exquisite workmanship could not be denied. Though small, it boasted of intricate detail. Whoever sculpted the relief of a whirlwind had been a consummate artist, even by today's standards. The cloudy funnel seemed to turn and move over the desert, the illusion of motion enhanced by tiny spots of turquoise and gold.

"Meow."

Jack looked over his bifocals directly into the cat's eyes. The animal seemed both curious about the object and impatient about his breakfast. "What do you make of it?" he asked, holding the charm out where it could by sniffed and examined.

Useless nosed the metal, sneaked a lick with a pink tongue and then backed away from it, suddenly growling. The cat turned and jumped down off the bed and ran from the room.

"Not a fan," mused Jack aloud to himself. He rose from the bed and dressed in clean clothing. Checking himself in the mirror, he grunted in satisfaction. "Better," he said.

Moving to the living room, he went directly to the phone and called the campus directory, getting the number for the dormitory where Don Hunnicutt lived. He dialed and waited for an answer.

"Hello, this is Harper Hall, third floor. Who do you want?" said a female voice.

"This is Professor Foreman and I'd like to speak with Don Hunnicutt."

"Hang on, I'll get him," came the reply.

Little son of a bitch is there! he thought with satisfaction. *Wait until I get my hands on him.*

Minutes passed while Jack seethed. Finally, the voice returned.

"I checked his room. His roommate is there but he says Don didn't come back last night. The bed hasn't been slept in."

"Can you take a message?"

"I'm gonna be late for class, Professor. Can't you just call again later?"

"Yeah," he answered. "I guess I can." Hanging up, he sat back in the chair, closed and rubbed his eyes. The anger faded quickly to be replaced by worry. The damned kid hadn't gotten back after all. What the hell could have happened?

He dialed the police, getting the number from the card given to him by one of the officers the previous night. It rang several times before being answered.

"Tempe Police. Sgt. Bowers. How can we help you?"

"This is Professor Jack Foreman of A.S.U. I reported an incident last night by the beltway construction and met Officers . . . uh . . . ," he referred to the card . . . "Bilks and Carruthers there. I reported the possible disappearance of one of my students, Don Hunnicutt. I'm calling to tell you that I just checked his dorm and he didn't return there last night. His bed hasn't been slept in."

"I'll get one of 'em for you. Hang on, sir."

Hold music replaced the silence for a few moments, only to be interrupted by a familiar voice, that of Officer Bilks.

"Hi, Professor Foreman. This is Gene Bilks. What can I do for you?"

"I just called Hunnicutt's dorm and he never returned there last night."

Bilks cleared his throat and sounded apologetic. "Uh, Professor, are you suggesting there is something unusual about a young college boy staying out all night on a Saturday?"

"Dammit, Bilks, I know better than that. Hunnicutt could have just gone off by himself as a joke. I know it. I also understand college boys better than most people. This is different."

"Look, Professor," replied the officer patiently, "I appreciate your concern. I can't explain the trucks either. You can be sure that got our attention. Given your position, we took a missing persons report yesterday evening and a detective has been assigned to the case. I appreciate your calling with the additional information. If you come up with anything else, call . . ." he paused, obviously referring to some document . . . "Detective Greg Johnson. He's the detective assigned to the case—a real up-and-comer, a hot-shot. I'll make a note to see that you're informed if Hunnicutt returns or we come up with anything significant. Okay?"

"Thank you, Officer. I appreciate your help." Jack shook his head. "I guess I am getting worked up over something that may turn out to be nothing."

"Think nothing of it," said Bilks. "It happens all the time. Anything else I can do?"

"No, thank you. Goodbye." Jack hung up the phone.

"Meooowwww." The cry from the kitchen doorway sounded more insistent.

"Okay," he said to the cat, who had just slunk into the room, "no help from the police right now." He got up and went to the cupboard for a can of catfood. Opening it, he dumped the contents into a plate and set it on the floor. Useless ate rather noisily, the smacking sounds accompanied by a continuous purr.

Jack leaned against the kitchen counter. Deep down, he had a sick feeling that Don Hunnicutt was dead. It manifested as a cold emptiness, a near certainty, but he had no idea how it could have happened. Freak storm or not, bodies do not totally disappear. Don was not the jokester type. He had been a fine student. This had gone beyond the stage where it could turn out funny.

He came to a decision. He would have to go back out to the site, look around for traces or . . . something . . . and he would have to climb up those damn rocks again and open up that hole. The boy's disappearance and the place had to be linked, but he was damned if he could figure out how.

Looking down, he realized he still carried the metal charm in his left hand. Putting it in his pocket, he went to get his gear together. Ten minutes later, he drove his obscenely shiny truck off in the direction of the site.

Arriving once again at the construction, Jack went immediately to Don's truck. It remained parked where they had left it, gleaming in the afternoon sun. Taking his equipment from the bed, he began a thorough and systematic search of the area around the vehicle. No one else appeared to be about, except a large crow that stayed well away, perching on a rock.

Only another archaeologist would understand the care Jack took in his search. Using a fine brush, he worked down through the loose sand until he had established the level of the ground before the storm. Painstakingly, he worked on a foot wide channel all around the truck. Finding nothing, he began to work outward with the patience and care only one of his profession could exhibit.

He occasionally stopped to take swigs from his canteen, but his mind stayed in what he called "dig gear." Working on a site meant examining everything. Nothing could be too small for consideration, no deadline or timetable would be allowed to cause hurried or careless work. While that part of his mind took control of his actions, the rest wandered into the past and relived the years with Evelyn.

After two and a half hours, Jack had cleared a ten foot wide area all around the vehicle. Taking a break, he returned to his truck and turned on the engine, hitting the air conditioner control. He sweated profusely but a part of him knew that he was eliminating the toxins and the alcohol from his body. It felt good.

He looked up at the sky. It was a cloudless July Sunday. With a little luck, the monsoon would leave him alone long enough to cover the ground. Another wind storm or rain would make it damnably difficult.

He decided to take a break from the brushing and walk over the ground between the truck and the rocks at least once in case something easy to spot lay out there. He pinned no real hope on that, of course, but it could save him hours of time and he wanted very badly to have something that would kick the police in the ass and get them moving.

He mapped out a route in his mind using various cacti or scrub as markers and began a long leisurely weaving walk toward the rocks. He did not hurry, or dawdle either. Desert landscape might be great for a front yard but it could not perk up anyone's interest except, perhaps, a scorpion's.

He had covered about half the distance when he saw something shiny in the sand. Staying back, he crouched down and used his brush to expose it. He had uncovered a ring, the turquoise and silver ring Don had worn.

Carefully, Jack lifted it. Sand filled it in a strange way, completely clogging the center. Brushing patiently, he gently cleared it. The clog seemed stubborn, clinging to the metal. As he persistently jiggled and brushed at it, he began to see something darker, as if the sand itself had been stained. Then, finally, the blockage fell out. Palming the ring, he reached for the chunk of material that had fallen to the sand. Midway, however, he had a horrible thought that caused him to lean forward and examine it more closely where it lay.

Suspicion became certainty. He finally recognized the pallid softness of flesh. It looked peculiarly pale and bloodless, but he knew it for human tissue. Poking at it with the handle of his brush, he exposed more . The last doubt faded. He had found the knuckle of a human finger. It had to be Don's.

"Jesus Christ!" he exclaimed.

A lighter patch of sand caught his eye, a foot away from where he had found the ring. Carefully, he brushed at it and found it almost an inch deep and running in a fairly straight line. He followed it and came upon another line of the same whitish substance running at an angle to the first. This was quickly crossed by another line.

He took his time, patiently exposing more and more of the substance until the realization of what he had uncovered struck him with enough force to send him pitching backward onto his ass in the hot sand.

No doubt about it. Once he was far enough back to discern the pattern, he couldn't deny the evidence. The shape marked by the white chunky powder was a human skeleton. He had already uncovered the legs and pelvis, blurred, but undeniable.

What to do? He could bag the piece of finger and cover the powder with a light coat of sand. Would that be right? Or should he leave it exactly as he had found it so far and go for the police?

He looked again at the sky. It stayed clear. He decided to take the chance.

If Jack had been dissatisfied with the reaction of the police to his first call, those feelings were dispelled by the response to this one.

The Phoenix and Tempe PDs, the DPS and the sheriff all arrived within minutes.

Chapter Thirteen

Salt River Reservation

After their return to the reservation, Danny and Jon stayed at Tom Bear's house, sleeping on couches in the main room. The old man had spent the night rooting around his place, digging through boxes, rummaging through drawers and gathering things in a small pile on the kitchen table.

Now, as the sun rose, they sat together while Tom made coffee on the stove. They all agreed that coffee had been one of the white man's great contributions to the world. Before them lay the items Tom had gathered—an old rattle made of gourd, a bunch of feathers, a clay pipe, a war club and a small feathered wand. All these rested in the center of an old war shield.

Danny reached over and lifted up the feathered wand. "This looks like the one I found on my way over here last night," he said, pulling it out from where he had tucked inside his shirt.

"Let me see that," demanded Tom.

Danny handed it over wordlessly and the old man examined it.

"Where did you find it, Danny?" asked Jon, curious as usual.

"He found it buried in the ground, Jon Steele," said Tom. "He found it there and took it because it was pretty, right Danny?" He rose and walked over to a drawer by the sink and brought out another wand, similar in appearance. "That's how I got mine." He held them up side by side. One looked older; the other newer, but they appeared identical. "This is a good sign, Danny."

"How?" Young Webb's eyes widened.

"It is a step toward power," replied the witch.

"Hey, can I have one too?" Jon felt left out.

"No," replied Tom. "If you ever get a wand like this, you've got to find it yourself." He indicated the items on the table. "Those belonged to my grandfather. I have my own stuff. Those have been handed down in my family from grandfather to grandson for generations. They have more power. This demon is bad medicine."

"What's all this about a demon, Tom?" asked Danny.

The previous night, the old man had refused to speak of the demon. He pointedly ignored all their questions. Now, he returned to the table and sat, looking straight at Danny. "A long time ago," he began, "way before the miligan came west in large numbers, the people lived closer to the earth. The Pima have never been warlike unless they had to be. We have been in the Gila Valley and along the Salt River for many generations, tending our crops, hunting game, trading with those who came to us peacefully."

Both younger men settled back to listen. It appeared Tom had a long story to tell.

"We've been here for hundreds of years," he continued. "We aren't a large tribe and never have been. There were enough people for the land to support and no more. In the old days, the Yumas and Apaches used to raid our villages. That was when we got painted up and fought—and the Pima were good fighters, true warriors. Don't ever let anyone tell you different than that! A Pima warrior with a shield like this one could dance around arrows, deflecting them and closing with his enemy. He used a war club like this and killed the man who would have killed him, taken his supplies and burned his village."

"How come nobody talks about the old days any more?" asked Danny in fascination.

"Those days are gone," said Tom with a shrug. "The miligan changed things." He paused, lit a cigarette, then continued. "Still, that raiding by the Yuma and Apache was about the worst we had to cope with. The only other problem was the weather. There were times of little rain and that stopped the river flowing. Without water, we had poor crops or none. Sometimes, there was too much rain and the river roared down from the north, overflowing the banks, to sweep people or cattle away."

"We still get floods," commented Jon.

"Yeah, but only fools build anything where it'll get washed away," said Danny.

"You two still interested in hearing about the demon?" asked Tom.

"Oh, yeah." said Steele, smiling in embarrassment. "Sorry. Please go on."

"The weather and the raiders were the dangers we had to face for all the years we've lived here, but way back in the beginning . . . oh, maybe six or seven hundred years ago . . . there was something worse. It was the demon." He let out a deep sigh. "No one knows where it came from except it seems like it may have been drawn down from the north. It must have been around for a while with no one knowing because there were no survivors left when it attacked." Tom stood up and walked to the window. "It's invisible," he said quietly, peering through the curtains. "It sneaks up on people and then sweeps over them like the worst flood you can imagine, only this flood is wind and sand.

"Whole villages just got swallowed up. The demon would come and settle over one and it was said you could hear the screams even over the howling of the storm. When it passed on, there was nothing left, just empty ruin—not even bodies. It had no mercy, that demon. It took everyone . . . women, children, babies, even great warriors with the strength of ten men. Nothing could stand against it."

Danny sat spellbound.

"When the people finally figured out what was happening, they set a watch on a high hill. I guess it was a hard job, holding the watch. Whoever did it had to have good eyes and a lot of patience. The demon was impossible to see unless it was moving. What it would do, you see, is travel at night and get close to the village or camp that it selected. Then it would rest. When the sun came up, everything looked peaceful and normal. It would wait all through the day until everyone was gathered for the evening meal and then descend on them without warning.

"Sometimes, the ones on watch would see it moving, getting into position, and ride into the village yelling the alarm. The people would, by prearranged plan, scatter in all different directions, like the ripples when you throw a stone into a pool. The beast would have to choose a direction and, even though it still got a lot of them, some would escape."

Danny let out a low whistle. "Sounds like it couldn't be beaten."

"It wasn't just the Pima, Apache or the Hopi," Tom continued. "The demon attacked everyone." He chuckled. "The Pima did better than some. Why do you think we had our villages scattered so many miles apart? Didn't you ever wonder what happened to the Hohokam of Casa Grande? Anyway, the wise men got together and tried magic to keep it away, but it didn't work. No one had enough power by himself, no village had enough medicine men or shamans to stop it."

"What did they do, Tom?" Danny asked the question.

"When they realized they needed to get all the wise men together, the Pima sent runners to all the different tribes—to the Yaqui down south, the Apache and Navajo, the Pai, the Utes, the Hopi on their Mesas, even to the Zuni Pueblos in New Mexico. In those days, the Pima were great runners. They would carry a supply of vi-hog cakes, made from mesquite beans, and run all day and night when they had a message to deliver."

"The Pima were the first to figure it out?" Jon sounded incredulous.

"Yeah," said the old man, nodding in satisfaction. "The Pima were the first. We were a little tribe, but we did a lot that no one knows about, a lot of good things. Deciding to gather the wise of all the tribes and sending the messengers may have been the biggest, though."

"Did the other tribes come?" asked Danny.

"All but the Utes," said Tom. "They had been pretty badly cut up by the demon when it passed through their settlements on the way south. They didn't have any medicine men left."

"Damn," said Danny, his eyes wide as he pictured the scene in his mind, "that must have been a council like no one's ever seen before!"

"Or since," said Tom. "The Hopi feud over land with the Navajo, the Yaqui keep to themselves—all the people are struggling with the times and trying to find out how they can change and still hang on to the important stuff that makes them what they are. It was the only time in the known history of the tribes that they all cooperated on anything. They had no choice, of course. They had to work together or die. So they had their Great Council and they chained the demon under the earth in the very spot we visited last night. It has been imprisoned there all these years, alive and hungry, and now some damn fool miligan must have let it out."

Jon looked from Tom to Danny. Seeing the look on their faces, he began to laugh. "You've got him, Tom," he said trying to stifle his mirth. "You sucked him in good." He spoke to Danny. "Do you really believe all this?"

"You mean you don't?" Danny felt surprise.

Jon looked at his friends and smiled. "I think Tom Bear tells the best stories I've ever heard, but I live in the twentieth century. If you really think I'm buying the idea of a malevolent dust devil, you are sadly mistaken."

Tom and Danny exchanged glances.

Jon continued. "It makes a fine story, but who is gullible enough to believe it? I don't, but I can appreciate the skill you told it with, Tom."

The old man looked across at Jon Steele. Pointedly, he said, "Yeah, it's all bullshit, Jon. I just wanted to see if I could string you along as long as I did." Looking to the clock on the wall, Tom rose and crossed to the door. "You're too sharp for me Jon Steele," he said with a half smile. "And the pun is intended." He opened the door. "Meanwhile, it's been fun but I want to talk to Danny alone for a while. See you around, huh?"

Jon felt the tension in the air and decided to get out while he could. Tom must not be provoked. He laughed as he made his exit.

"You sure had us going for a while there, Tom. That's a hell of a story! Thanks for telling it and for the fun." He turned and waved at Danny, who still sat at the table looking more than a little confused. "See you at Ma's, Danny," he said with a wink, and began the walk back across the reservation.

Tom stood silently at the window and watched him depart, peering through the curtains to make sure he really did. When Danny tried to ask a question, the old man shushed him and waved him to silence without leaving the window. Finally, he sighed loudly and came back to the table. "A young fool, that one. I should have realized we couldn't use him in this. He doesn't have the power like we do."

"The power?" Danny still felt bewildered by the shift in the conversation. "You mean . . . ?"

"Everything I told you this morning is true, Danny Webb. We have very little time before the demon starts taking his revenge on the people. We must get word to the wise of all the tribes and somehow arrange another Great Gathering. If we fail, everyone is going to die."

Chapter Fourteen

Hopiland

Harold Laloma stayed in the kiva. The ceremonies had concluded and the rest of the priests were leaving, but he had to remain. Only in this way could he obey the spirit and remain away from the wind.

"It is time to go," said John Lakona, another priest. "Why do you linger here in the sacred place?"

"I had a vision," replied Harold. "Taknokwunu spoke to me. There is something important happening in the world."

"What?" asked John. Other priests stopped and turned to listen in on the discussion.

"There is a demon loosed upon the world," said Harold quietly. "I saw it . . . here . . . in the kiva during the ceremony."

"What," said John, " even here?"

"I have said so," affirmed Harold. "It spoke to me."

"Why did I not see it?" John did not indicate doubt, merely curiosity.

"I looked around at all of you," said Harold, "but the spirit who controls the weather spoke only to me." He shook his head. "You appeared to be entranced. I saw the demon. It takes the shape of a great whirlwind. Also, I fear, it hungers for lives."

"This vision is a wondrous thing," said Joseph Lansa, one of the others present. "What did the spirit say to you?"

"He told me to fast and cleanse myself in preparation," said Harold. "He said I would represent the people of peace in an attempt to imprison the demon once again."

"Why do you suppose Taknokwunu spoke to you instead of Yaponcha, the wind god?" asked Joseph.

"Yaponcha remains in his crack in the black rock," said John with a smile. "Do we not go every March and deliver pahos and reseal the crack with cornmeal?"

Harold only smiled. "I do not know, my friend. I only know that it was he and that I am bound to obey."

The other priests exchanged glances.

"Then you must remain here, my friend," John said to Harold. "I will see that water is brought to you. How long will you stay?"

Harold shrugged. "I think things in the outside world are happening quickly. I will wait for the spirit to speak again."

"This is as it should be," said Joseph. "Come. We must return above." He placed a hand on Harold's shoulder. "Be careful, my friend. When the spirits talk aloud, great dangers usually follow."

The others exited, leaving Harold alone.

He sat in his accustomed place and closed his eyes. Why had he been chosen? He could no longer be considered a young man. He was not the most powerful priest, even of Coyote Clan, let alone the Hopi Nation. Why him?

Harold opened his eyes and looked around the empty chamber. It looked larger now that the other priests were gone. Many priests had come here over the years. The atmosphere seemed heavy with spirits.

He closed his eyes again, fingered the pahos, held the cornmeal in his right hand and prayed.

"Taknokwunu, great spirit, instruct me. I await and obey as you told me. When shall I act and what then shall I do?"

The kiva remained silent as Harold waited. The spirit did not speak.

Hours passed and Harold continued to wait and pray. The juniper branches kept out the light from above. He offered more feathered prayer sticks, pahos, scattered more cornmeal and tried to clear his mind—to cleanse his spirit.

Eventually, the priest fell asleep, but not into the kind of sleep he expected. Instead of the languid drifting into dream which he normally experienced, he moved from one state of consciousness to another. Instead of sitting in the kiva, he found himself standing in the desert on a high hill from which he could see the mesas rising before him. He recognized something strange about this view, however, for he could clearly see people moving about. It seemed as if he looked through a telescope.

The voice spoke almost at his ear and he jumped. "Ah, Peace Man," it said. "I thought you would like to see your past. This is what your world offered when I was free before."

Harold became aware of a stirring off to the west. Something large moved across the desert toward the mesa. A vast cloud of sand and debris swirled and billowed into the air, stretching almost a mile high.

"That was my aspect then," said the voice with pride. "I waxed strong and fed well." Anger flared in the voice as it continued. "I am not so strong now, nor half so large, but I will remedy that soon. Within days I will have doubled in both."

"Why are you showing this to me?" Harold felt no fear as he had the first time. He stood alone and remote, as if watching a newsreel.

"I want you to see the futility of this struggle against me, Peace Man. If you can prevent the others from acting, I might decide to spare your people."

"What?"

The voice mocked and dripped with sarcasm. "Wouldn't you prefer it if I spent my time feeding on the ones called Navajo? If you serve me, I might leave your peace people alone."

The roiling storm approached the mesa and it had been spotted by the people closest to the path of attack. They began to run in panic, almost swarming like ants. Like a spreading tide, the panic moved eastward as more and more of the tribe became aware of the approaching storm. By the time it topped the western edge of the mesa, people fled down the east.

As it moved to a position above the first village, the great cloud settled over it, the swirling sand hiding what happened below. Then the screams began.

Harold wanted to cover his ears, but it did no good. This was, after all, a dream, and he could not escape reliving the horror the demon wanted him to see.

"Ah," said the beast, "it is like music, is it not, Peace Man? The voices of your people were raised in chorus, like a great ceremony."

"Why are you doing this?"

"I told you, Peace Man. I might consider showing mercy if you'll agree to serve me."

"You must give me time to think." Harold had managed to shut out the screams and concentrate on what he had seen. The demon seemed unstoppable.

"There is time," agreed the voice. "I have errands to run."

The decimation of the village on the storm enshrouded mesa faded from view and Harold woke with a start back in the kiva. The voice had gone and he could no longer feel the presence of the beast.

The demon had expressed a willingness to bargain. If Harold would cooperate, he could save his people. An interesting thought. He pictured the beast ridding the Hopi of the troublesome Navajo. There were some who would counsel him to do it.

On the other hand, the very fact that the demon had been willing to offer its "mercy" meant that it must have weaknesses. It had already admitted to not being as strong or as large as it had once been, yet it had been imprisoned even then. Willingness to bargain could only mean it feared this gathering of the wise.

Harold smiled to himself, content for the first time since the initial vision to wait for the spirit to tell him what to do.

Chapter Fifteen

Chaco Canyon

He-Who-Walks-In-Wisdom felt tired but triumphant. His great-great-grandson, Gordon, had just completed the entire song of the Great Gathering without error. Pride filled him as he watched the boy walking toward his family's hogan just a mile away. Fly had surpassed even the old man's expectations of him, singing the story in a clear and pleasant voice.

Now the tale of the chaining of the demon would not be lost to his people. Archie had learned the song from his grandfather and he had never heard it sung by anyone else in all his long life. Fly would keep it in that remarkable memory of his and pass it on when his time came.

Tonight, despite their mutual weariness, Archie would teach Fly the ceremony itself. It was long and complicated, with many parts, some only known to medicine men from other tribes.

The boy would have to learn the order of calling and understand the shifting focus of the rite. Each tribe had a part to play. Archie looked over at the drum sitting on the far side of the hogan. It had been far too long since the heirloom had been used.

Archie yawned and stretched. For a long moment, he held his hands out in front of himself and studied the changes age had brought. Two fingers on his left hand had been broken and improperly set during his childhood so they led off at an odd angle from the others. They worked well enough as long as the weather remained dry, but damp monsoon evenings usually set them to aching. Veins stood out on the backs of his hands—hands that had short stubby fingers, working hands.

Now, as he made fists, he could see how fragile they had become, seeming almost transparent. His wrists looked too thin and bony—his forearms were wasted stalks with little flesh covering them. Still, he marvelled at his durability. Other than a few aches and pains, his health remained excellent. Perhaps he needed more sleep. Frequent naps seemed to work, but that was to be expected.

He yawned again and realized that his eyes were about to close on their own. He lay down and hummed an old song to himself, a song from childhood that just popped into his head.

> Little Flower
> Sunny Face
> Standing proud in fields of green
> Brightening the village
> Like a child's smiling face
> Or a mother's tender touch
> Little Flower
> Bring to mind the years gone by
> Keep my little one in smiles

Archie got through it only one time before he had fallen into a deep slumber.

Three hours later, Gordon came to the hogan. Finding the old man asleep, he entered, walked carefully around the peaceful form, sat quietly and waited.

The song of the Great Gathering had been a bitch to master, but it filled him with excitement. Nowhere else had he heard the tale of the dust demon and the wise men. It had all taken place so long ago that he had difficulty accepting that it might really have happened.

The old days came down in legend, changed and embroidered by the singers to suit some particular purpose at that time. If the listeners needed to be encouraged to act for the good of the tribe, the tale would be inspiring and geared to demonstrate the importance of working for the common good. The same story, however, might be told in such a way that its effect would be to inspire the young to strive toward heroism, or, again, reconstructed so differently that all it did was discourage marriage with someone too closely related.

Yataalii had great power to change the minds of the people. Though many ceremonies were as fixed and stylized as a ballet, some songs might be used to motivate the hearers to some specific course of action. Stories, of course, were also entertainments. As far back as he could remember, Gordon had loved the stories told by his great-great-grandfather.

Though young, Fly had a fine quick mind with a penchant for philosophical speculation. In deciding to be a singer, he had turned his back on much of what the outside had to offer. Choosing to return to the reservation and follow in the old man's footsteps had required that he ask himself and answer some basic questions. *What is the value of singing? Are the traditions of the tribe really worth preserving, especially at the cost of my newly acquired understanding of the white man's world?*

Largely because of Archie, his answers had been easier to find than he expected. Singing remained the oldest expression of art. Holding those gathered around your fire with the breathless excitement of a tale had been the first of entertainments. The traditions of the dineh were not only worth preserving, but might ultimately prove to be the salvation of the world—even the white man's world.

The questions that came after his decision had been easier to live with, but just as challenging. *Which of the old tales is most in danger of being forgotten? Just how much capacity do I have for remembering? How does one separate the truth of the old tales from the trappings of legend?*

Some of these answers were obvious, others had yet to be learned.

Preoccupied with these thoughts, the boy did not, at first, hear the old man speak in his sleep. Soon, however, Archie's voice rose in volume and could not be ignored.

"Get away from me, demon!" The old man's voice was filled with anger, not fear. Archie had opened his eyes, but they were focused on something beyond the room, perhaps beyond the world itself. "Whisper to me no longer," said the old man, disdain written on his features. "Your very existence was a mistake, your release at this time an aberration. The spirits will not suffer you to remain free."

Between the utterances, the old man had the aspect of listening, as if to a voice only he could hear. Now, he sat bolt upright, fear written on his countenance for the first time.

"Here? You would dare come here?" Archie's eyes darted from right to left, whites showing, pupils contracted. " If you remove me, another will come forth. If you remove him, yet another!"

Suddenly, the old man fell back, eyes closed. There was a hitch in his breathing and, for a moment, it stopped.

Gordon, kneeling at his side, saw and understood. He placed his hands on his great-great-grandfather's chest and pressed firmly down. The air whooshed out, followed only a second later by a deep intake of breath, then another. Archie breathed on his own.

The old man opened his eyes, this time conscious of his surroundings. Gordon leaned over him, concerned and intent.

He-Who-Walks-In-Wisdom smiled. "Do not worry, Fly. There will be time to teach you the ceremony." Despite his ashen pallor, the old man looked happy. "And now there is a need worthy of you, Thoughts-Never-Stop."

"What are you saying, grandfather?"

"Let me up, Fly. We have much to do and we must hurry. After I have taught you the ceremony, and you have shown me that you know it, you must go to Shiprock on an errand for me. You must leave before morning so there is no time to waste."

"To Shiprock? And learn the ceremony today?" Gordon was filled with doubt. "How can this be done, grandfather?"

"It must be done, Fly. We have no choice." The old man pointed to the drum over by the wall. "Bring the drum here and I will show you how it is used. Hurry, my boy. We must begin now."

Gordon brought the drum and the old man began to play upon it, a steady rhythm that seemed to urge the boy's heart to keep time with it.

"This is what you must do, Fly . . . ."

Chapter Sixteen

Barrio Libre

Juan Mapoli had made his preparations. He carried a military duffle bag, a blue-jean jacket over his shoulder and a small velcro belt pouch that contained peyote buttons, mushrooms *(psylosibe mexicana)*, datura root and *rivea corymbosa* or morning glory powder. These were the tools of his profession, his passport, if you will, to the world beyond the world.

Very early in the morning, a little before 7 a.m., he stood on the porch with Maria. Despite being a big woman, she looked extremely fragile and forlorn. Her fleshy frame seemed dwarfed by Juan's tall guant aspect. He embraced her and gave her a long, lingering kiss.

"I must leave you, wife," he said formally. "I go to join others who must face the demon. It is quite possible that I will not return to you."

Maria choked back a cry. She looked into his brown, lined face and spoke quietly. "I do not understand, husband, what it is that draws you from me and into the unknown." Her penetrating gaze never wavered from his. "I have never really understood you, you know."

"There is nothing to understand, Maria," he replied. "We have lived under the same roof, slept in the same bed and brought our children into the world together. In a way, we enter into this new thing together as well. Perhaps you do not understand, but you will be with me. You are so much a part of me that it is not possible for me to go anywhere or do anything alone. Your quiet strength will support me even in this time of trouble. If fortune is kind, I will return to you. If things go badly, you will have the memory of all our years together. There are many who have no such good fortune."

She continued to gaze for a long moment at his face, her own brown eyes expressing what was unexpressible in words.

He embraced her once again, then pushed her away gently. "It is time," he said.

The old man kept himself tall and proud as he walked down from the porch to the street. He gave her a studied, careless wave, as he had once seen an actor do in a movie, and then moved off with dignity, quietly pacing down the street. Only after he turned the corner, where she could no longer see him, did he allow the weight of his own fears to change his posture from a strut to a tired ambling gait.

Juan felt plagued by doubts. He alone of the Yaqui knew of the danger and could act for them as a true representative. Despite being the most powerful of the sabio, he carried no consensus of will from those he was to represent.

Reaching a more travelled street, he turned and put out his thumb. Since he knew most everyone within the Barrio, only minutes passed before someone came by and offered the ride he needed.

The Romulos, a Yaqui family with relatives of their own in Phoenix, were glad to help the old man reach the home of his son, Carlo. They stopped once, enroute, at Picacho Peak, but Juan stayed in the car, uncomfortable with the restaurant and traffic.

They took him to his son's door and dropped him off, wishing him health and happiness. He did not, however, trouble them with talk of his purpose. That undeniable inner voice had spoken to him and told him to go to Phoenix where, when the time was right, he would know what to do next.

Carlo Mapoli expressed joy at seeing his father that morning, though his home was small and his family large. They made room for the old man by moving the three younger boys into the same quarters. Carlo's wife, Juanita, was unhappy with the prospect of the sabio living under their roof for an undetermined period of time, but her husband told her it would be all right. She could make no argument under the circumstances. Nonetheless, she would have a headache when she retired for the night and planned to have the same headache until the old man left. Carlo would have to learn to consult her about such things in the future.

Juan, for his part, felt content to go to his room, asking his daughter-in-law not to disturb him till supper. Closing the door, he unpacked, made himself comfortable on the bed and began chewing his mushrooms.

He stayed patient and relaxed, despite the initial misgivings that had plagued him. He had faith his inner voice would know what to do when the time came. Meanwhile, he waited until he heard the fluttering of a large bird outside the open window. He looked over at the crow and smiled. He glanced at the clock on the bedside table. It was already afternoon.

Juan flew again, only a little way this time, until he came to the place his inner voice told him had been the prison of the demon. He circled over it, but experienced no feeling of fear or nervousness and concluded the beast was, indeed, gone. He landed on the boulder and cocked his crow's head so the eyes could see the carvings on the surface. The sigils of the different tribes were interspersed with depictions of the demon, the whirling spiral of a dust devil or tornado.

He hopped down and approached the edge of the hole underneath. A soft breeze whistled over the opening, the sound it made hollow and strange like a deep flute.

With a flutter of wings, he flew to the edge of the formation, strutting along the rough stone and looking at both sides of the wall —the inner worked, the outer rough.

Looking east, he saw two shiny trucks parked on a leveled lot by a chain-link fence. One of the trucks was axle deep in sand. Both vehicles caught and reflected the afternoon sunlight. He launched himself off the wall and glided nearer.

A man sat on the ground using a brush. He worked at clearing an area around one of the trucks. *Sifting the sand? Why?*

Juan sailed down and landed on a small outcrop of rock where he could sit in the shadows and watch.

After two hours of brushing sand, the man moved back to the other truck and sat inside, running the engine, but soon got out again. After standing and looking over the ground for a few minutes, he began a winding, leisurely walk that seemed to cover a big area. *Searching for something?*

Almost midway between the parking area and the tower of rock that had been the demon's prison, the man stopped and squatted down. Juan's keen crow eyes watched with curiosity. *Something found.*

As he watched the activity, Juan heard his inner voice telling him all this had to be connected. The site had become the crux point in the drama and the man must have some part to play in what needed to be done.

After a few more minutes, during which the man used his brush again, he suddenly stood. Indecision written in every movement. He started toward the trucks, turned back and looked at the ground, then up at the sky. Finally, he ran back to the vehicles, started one and roared away.

When the truck had gone, Juan flew over to the spot. He found a piece of human flesh and what had apparently been human bones, now crumbled almost to powder. He knew even without confirmation from his inner voice that this must be the work of the demon. Interesting. He would watch for a while longer and see if the man returned.

Chapter Seventeen

Havasupai

Rattle awakened Sunday morning and began to pack. It was not a complicated task. He took a change of clothing, his magical paraphernalia and his walking stick. The deer spirit had told him to travel light.

His wife accepted his journeying. At 70, the old man had no real duties any more except telling stories, and the Peach Dance, his next obligation, remained more than two months away. Naomi worried about him, but knew better than to try stopping him once he had made up his mind to go. In this case, his mission had become a holy quest at the direction of his guiding spirit. She knew it would be futile to try and hinder his departure.

"Where are you going, husband?"

"Phoenix," came the one word reply. He offered no explanation.

"How long will you be gone?"

"As long as it takes." This time, however, the reply sounded not sarcastic, but gentle. He went on. "I must meet with my brothers and do a great thing, Naomi. I do not know how long I will be gone."

"How will you get to Phoenix?" She knew the old man distrusted motorized vehicles of any kind.

"I will ride the mule," he replied.

"All the way to Phoenix? That's two hundred miles!"

"I know that, woman." He had that stubborn look on his face that she could spot a mile off. Intractable was an understated description at such times.

"I guess it's okay if there is no hurry," said Naomi.

The old man sat, tightlipped. "I had not thought of that," he said at last.

Naomi knew better than to give directions. If it wasn't his idea, he would resist it till his dying breath, the loveable old fool.

The old man looked up at his wife. "I don't want to ride in a car," he said simply, "but I guess I will have to."

"You can take the mule up to the rim and let someone else bring it back. Then you can probably get a ride with one of the tourists." She spoke for the practical course, the down to earth plan.

"I hate cars," he muttered sadly to himself.

Still, there seemed no way to avoid it.

During the mule ride up from the canyon floor, he kept hoping the deer spirit would tell him he didn't have to go, but it made no appearance. When he reached the rim, he went to the Ranger's Station. His friend, Joe Cochran, of the National Park Service, arranged a ride for him with a couple of young tourists.

Riding in the back of their pickup truck, Rattle closed his eyes and tried to quiet his stomach. The roads were none too good for the first few miles and he bounced in the back every time they crossed a rut or pothole. One of the problems with being 70 was that he had a lot less padding on his butt than he used to—another reason he disliked automobiles.

The tourists drank beer from a cooler on the seat between them—too many beers—one after the other. The guy on the passenger side, named William Lampley, gestured through the rear window and offered one to Rattle, but the old man shook his head. No liquor was allowed on the reservation, so Rattle had never developed a taste for it. He had seen the effect of alcoholism too often among the tribes. Let the white men have the fire-water.

The driver, Tod Harris, turned to his companion and said, "Hey Bill, I hear these Havasupai guys are good hunters. I'll bet this one could show us where the deer are hiding."

"He's an old man, Tod. I don't know if that'd be a good idea. The way our luck's been runnin', he'd have a heart attack and croak or somethin'."

The driver spoke in a low voice. "No one knows he's with us except that park ranger and he never even saw us get in the truck. He doesn't know who we are or where we're from. This Indian may be an old fart but I'll bet he can show us where to find the deer."

"Hell, don't we need a license or something?"

"No one'll know. We can ditch the Indian after we bag the deer and it'll be a day or two before he can find anyone and tell 'em. We'll be clean out of Arizona by then."

Lampley shook his head wistfully. "I sure would like to try out that thirty-aught-six you've got under the seat." He opened another can of beer. "Why don't we ask the old guy? He might just be willing to do it for five or ten bucks."

"All right, we will." Tod applied the breaks and pulled over onto the side of the road.

The two got out of the truck and spoke to the old man.

"What's your name, old dude?" asked Harris.

Rattle looked at the two of them, then said, "Some have called me Deer Man." It seemed unwise to give out one's real name to strangers.

The two exchanged delighted glances and Lampley spoke up. "That's great, Deer Man. In fact, it's really funny. That's why we stopped. We were hoping you might help us find a deer before we get back to civilization."

Find a deer? The old man was puzzled. *Were there not many deer all around in the woods? Why did they need his help?*

"Oh, not just any deer," protested Harris. "We need a really large one with a big rack. We want to find the most special deer in the area, right Bill?"

The other man nodded.

"You seek the Great Deer Spirit?" Rattle felt shock. He had not known the white man also was adopted by spirits. That these two smiling men might also seek guidance from the deer spirit seemed strange but wonderful. Perhaps the distrust he automatically felt when near such strangers had been unfair. He never knew what occupied their minds.

"Yeah, that's it," said Harris slapping the old man on the back. "We want to find the great deer, the biggest deer of them all."

Rattle had a chilling thought. He spoke carefully. "You wouldn't hurt the great deer spirit, would you?" He looked around for hunting gear, but he saw none in the bed of the truck.

The others exchanged glances again and shook their heads. "No way, Jose," said Harris. We just want to see him and maybe speak to him, you know?"

"Yeah, we want to give him something . . . a sort of gift like."

This was beyond Rattle's wildest imaginings. These two white men wanted to meet the deer spirit and talk with it and give it a gift!

"So, uh, deer man, would you be willing to help us find this deer?" asked Harris.

"We'd sure be grateful," said Lampley.

The old man thought about it. The deer spirit had been silent since their meeting in the gorge. If he took these two white guys to meet it, perhaps it would be pleased and release him from this damned journey. Sure it would. Maybe it would even send them instead.

Mistaking the old man's hesitation for a bargaining ploy, Lampley reached into his pocket and took out a ten dollar bill. "We'll give you ten bucks as well, okay?"

Rattle didn't understand. He did not lack common sense. He had grown up smart and savvy. He had not, however, had many dealings with white men. Other than his friend Joe, he had avoided them all his life. The school teacher and agent were not particularly close to him since he was a medicine man and they believed in white man's doctoring. In his own environment, Rattle possessed wisdom. In this circumstance, he was an innocent.

It all made a strange kind of sense. These two were the ones selected by the spirit to take him to Phoenix. They spoke to him about the Great Deer Spirit and assured him of their good will toward it. All this seemed too much a planned thing—it banished any doubt or suspicion that they were not as they purported to be. Rattle agreed.

That night, they camped near good water. Harris and Lampley pitched a tent but Rattle only put down a blanket. He had promised them that in the morning, before sunup, he would call the great deer.

A full hour before dawn, Rattle awoke and started chanting softly, calling to the deer spirit and asking it to come to him. The others awakened and came out to watch. He waved them to silence.

They spoke together in whispers and Lampley went to the truck, though Rattle did not know why.

Before long he heard the rustling of hooves on the forest floor. The deer spirit approached. Rattle stood in the clearing, facing away from the white men to greet it.

He remained aware of the two behind him, but his concentration stayed fixed on the calling. He could see the great form moving now in the dense brush and made ready to present his new friends to the spirit. Then he heard the click of a round entering the chamber of the gun.

He turned, incredulous. "What are you doing?" he asked. The two men stood side by side, Harris sighting the rifle on the approaching deer. "Stop!"

"Out of the way," said Lampley, moving forward and grabbing the old man roughly by the arm. He yanked to his right and Rattle went tumbling to the ground.

The shot sounded loud in the still wood. The old man lifted himself painfully off the ground and turned in time to see the two men rushing into the brush after their quarry. Horrified, he struggled to his feet and stumbled after them. He saw no sign of the deer spirit, no spore, no blood trail. That, at least, was good, but Rattle had become enraged. The white men had lied to him, threatened the spirit which had adopted him in childhood and guided his every action. He drew his knife.

Lampley leaned into the bushes, calling to Harris and asking whether they had made a good shot.

The knife moved quickly and efficiently, stopping his voice in mid shout as it severed the vocal chords and cut both carotid arteries. The man spun around, clutching at his throat, and Rattle saw the light of life fade from his eyes even as he fell.

Harris called from a position just ahead, asking if Lampley had seen which way the deer went. "I'm sure I got it with that shot," he shouted in excitement. "Listen," he instructed, "and see if you can hear it moving around."

Still without thinking, Rattle had closed the distance between himself and the remaining hunter. Harris had a loaded rifle and the old man had only his knife. It would be a close thing.

The white man was just turning to look when Rattle's knife took him in the chest and penetrated his heart. It took a moment longer for him to die. Rattle stood and watched passively.

When it was over, he called out to the deer spirit. "Forgive me, my friend. I was a fool. Do not turn from me at this time of need. Come back and tell me what I must do."

Then he sat, right where he had been standing, and began to chant again, prepared to wait in that spot until the deer returned or death arrived instead.

Chapter Eighteen

Apacheland

George Buck's quarters in Cibecue were small—just a livingroom, kitchen, bath and one bedroom. The windows looked out on Canyon Creek. Children playing nearby were often a challenge for George since he worked at night and slept during the morning hours. Weekdays weren't too bad, but weekends and summertime invariably meant more noise and shouting.

The figure on the bed stirred and the eyes opened. A moment of confusion followed as they roved around the room, then opened wider in shock.

"Whaaaaa?" Geronimo-in-George did not know where he was. He stood up and the mirror on the door showed him the face and form of George Buck. "Anah-zont-tee! Begone!" Geronimo shouted at the stranger, but then saw the reflected shape echo his facial and physical movements and figured it out. He moved closer, looking at the face which, apparently, now belonged to him. Young, definitely Apache, but the jaw line did not look square enough somehow and the corners of the mouth turned slightly up instead of down. Turning part way around in front of the mirror, he looked critically at the body. Lanky and muscular, taller than seemed right to his rapidly adjusting mind, obviously well-fed and healthy.

He sat heavily on the side of the bed, dizzy and nauseous. He bowed his head and put his face in his hands.

Geronimo's memories came flooding back. At first, they were hazy and unclear. Moment by moment, as he remembered bits and pieces, more came. Anger erupted within. The hated Mexicans had massacred his family. He had sworn to take revenge and raided northern Mexico . . . for fifteen years? How could that be? It seemed so long ago. He could still see clearly in his mind the day he led his Bedonkohe Chiricahua to the stronghold in the Sierra Madres. The white eyes had sent that general with an army . . . General Crook? Yes, and that other one, Miles. There were victories at first, then later defeats followed by imprisonment in Florida, Alabama and finally Fort Sill, Oklahoma. Bitterness filled him anew as he remembered the years in Fort Sill. And then he remembered . . . death?

He raised his head and looked again at the visage in the mirror. What had happened? This could not be right. He didn't belong in this body.

He heard sounds, turned and noticed the window. Pulling the heavy curtain aside, he consciously looked out on the modern world for the first time.

By modern standards, Cibecue is a hick town. To the eyes of Geronimo, it represented a marvel of magic and sorcery. Vehicles moved without horses to pull them. The dwellings were larger and much better made than he remembered even from Fort Sill. It seemed like a miracle to the old soul.

At the same time, a dual set of memories reconciled all the strangeness. George Buck remained locked into the hidden recesses of his own mind, but his memories and his modern socialization were accessible to Geronimo. The old medicine man understood, at least in part, that he had become a displaced personality. He could not have explained it in words, but his mind—utilizing the memories of George Buck—had already begun the complex process of reconciling the present with his own past. Still, it remained difficult to assimilate, especially for a man who had died in 1909.

Looking around the rental house, Geronimo could not accept the existence of modern amenities—the TV, the microwave oven, the stove, the couch. It all looked too foreign. He let himself out the front door and moved, nervous and unsure, away from what appeared a strange and foreign world to him.

He could see open land just to the southwest, so he headed into the canyon. When he had left the last of the settlement behind him, he breathed a sigh of relief and went eagerly into the desert. The familiar surroundings of cacti and scrub soothed his spirit. The wind, even in July, caressed him like a familiar lover. The world returned to what it had been before.

Geronimo was not only a warrior and chief, but a medicine man. He searched the desert and found the plants of his own era growing in abundance. In very little time, he had found both morning glory and datura. He elected datura, morning glory requiring more time to dry in order to create the powder.

Something nagged at the edge of his mind—had been restlessly impinging on his thoughts since his first awakening—but the disorientation of his encounter with the modern world had kept him from recognizing it. Now, in the desert, he was able to isolate and examine his hidden thoughts.

There must be a reason he had awakened in this strange place, in this strange time. He had some task to do—probably a task his alter-ego, George, would not be able to accomplish. He knew George, suddenly, and with a total understanding that at once touched and inspired him. The man he would become was the logical extension of the personality that had been both war chief and medicine man. George was himself matured.

Tentatively, Geronimo called upon George. At first, he felt as if his attempt had been smothered by a blanket of misunderstanding, but he sensed George hovering just beyond the realm of his consciousness and redoubled his efforts at contact.

In a supreme effort of will, he established contact—not just with the memories, but with the conscious mind of George Buck.

"Why am I here?"

"I do not know or understand."

"Who are we?"

"I was—am—an Apache named George Buck, but I remember being you."

"I was—am—an Apache named Goyathlay, whom the Mexicans named Geronimo. I remember many strange things, including my death."

George, more in control than before, spoke in his mind to this other self. "Something has happened. I felt it in the night. Something has come back into the world which should not be."

Geronimo used George's head and nodded. "I knew this. It is the demon of legend, come to life."

"What is this demon?"

"It takes the form of a great whirlwind. It kills. My grandfather told me of it."

"What shall I do?" George knew confusion and uncertainty. His other self did not.

"We must join with others in an attempt to chain it once again."

"Others?"

"We must represent not only Apache or Hopis or Pai, the Yaqui or Ute or Navajo or Zuni, not only Tohono O'odham or Maricopa or Yuma or Pueblo. We must serve all the Native American tribes. We must assemble a great council of the wise to act for all the people. In this way, we shall save the world . . . or we will all die."

George spoke again in his mind. "So hard to believe, my brother."

"I know how we shall do this thing." Geronimo was quicker to reach the core of the matter. "The Phoenix," he said. "From the ashes of ruin shall our hopes arise."

"Can you let me out?" George worried that he might be trapped within Geronimo.

"Right now," said his wiser self, "we are in the desert. I think it may be better that I stay in control. It may be I have an important part to play. Can you await your own moment of truth?"

Looking out on the waste through his own eyes—but his vision being colored by that of his warrior persona—the modern man acknowledged the superiority of his wiser self.

"Good," said Geronimo. "I will try to lead us."

Chapter Nineteen

Albuquerque

Pasqual felt himself pressed back into the seat as the airliner raced down the runway and took off. His eyes were screwed shut, his hands talons that gripped the armrests with all his strength, his mind occupied with a chant of protection. He did not move as the plane climbed up to cruising altitude, banked and turned away from the morning sun, heading west. The Southwest flight was crowded with passengers, all seats filled. The old man had spent the night at the airport and purchased the first ticket of the morning to Phoenix so his boarding pass had been number one. He had taken a window seat and now found himself trapped there by a woman and child who occupied the other two seats in his row.

When the captain spoke over the intercom and turned off the seatbelt sign, the priest sneaked a quick look out the window on his left and then closed his eyes again, concentrating on breathing regularly. His grip on the armrests relaxed only a little. In his mind, he reviewed the events of the night before.

He had not wasted a moment. As soon as the doctor left the room, he had risen from his bed and followed her out the door. He quickly replaced the open-backed hospital gown with jeans and a loose shirt that he found in a closet just three doors down from his room.

He had felt no ill-effects from the attack earlier that day. In fact, he had been filled with energy and strength since awakening. His heart pounded steadily in his chest. He felt his blood coursing through his sparse frame. Dressed, he had simply walked out of the hospital and into the evening.

The old man hitched a ride back to the pueblo, taking almost an hour to get home. Since he lived alone, no one required explanations from him. He had packed a small duffle, called a cab, and gone directly to the airport.

Upon arrival at the airport, that energy had deserted him. He had spent the night outside behind a baggage cart in a deep healing slumber, untroubled by dreams.

Now, he flew above the surface of the earth in a white man's machine, something he had only done once before. It made him nervous. He kept his eyes shut and ignored the attendant when she offered a beverage. Pretending to be asleep might have resulted in actually sleeping, but for the child in the seat next to his. Several times, the woman had addressed her as Beth.

"Mommy," said the little girl, "the man looks so different from us. How come?"

Judith said "Shush, Beth, you'll wake him." But she answered in a low voice, "He's an Indian, Beth. He's a Native American." Pasqual sighed, opened his eyes and turned to look down at the little girl.

She felt no fear, but remained curious. "Is that right, mister? Are you a . . . ," she hesitated over the words, ". . . Native American?"

"Yes," replied the old man. "I am Zuni. My people was here in the Southwest long before the white man come west."

"Were," corrected the girl, "your people 'were' here and white men 'came' west."

He smiled, his craggy face lined with wrinkles born of both sorrow and laughter. "I don't talk English so good," he said simply. "We gotta language of our own."

Beth studied the old man's face, frankly staring.

After a full minute of this, Pasqual laughed. "Am I so different?" The girl delighted him.

She looked thoughtful for a moment, then spoke, the innocence of childhood granting her immunity from the reluctant embarrassment that sometimes afflicts adults. "You're darker," she said, "and your face is all scrunched up."

"There is lotsa Americans darker than me," he said, "and don't white old people get . . . ," he stumbled over her word, ". . . scrunched up too?"

Beth thought about this for a moment and smiled. "Yeah," she agreed. "My grandma has more wrinkles than you do." She hesitated. "Yours are prettier than hers, though."

Her mother, scandalized by the trend the conversation had taken, tried to apologize. "Please forgive us," she said. "Beth has never met a real Native American before. She's just naturally curious."

"No worry," Pasqual assured her, "your child is okay. I like little ones. They talk truth."

"Are you going to California?" asked Beth.

"Phoenix," he answered. "Gotta do somethin' there."

"What's that?"

The old man thought about it for a moment. Struggling with the language presented difficulty enough, but trying to explain his reason for going to Arizona seemed nearly impossible. He hadn't even answered that satisfactorily for himself.

"Did you hear me, mister? I asked what you're going to do there?"

Pasqual smiled. "I was thinkin. Sometimes you gotta look in your head before you say things," he explained.

"Oh." Beth waited a couple seconds before she spoke again. "Don't you know already?"

"Sorta," he said at last. "I gotta find some guys there and we gotta go huntin."

The little girl looked troubled. "Are you going to shoot Bambi?"

Pasqual had never heard of Bambi, but guessed the girl meant some animal or another. "No," he answered carefully. "There is a bad thing. It used to be locked up but it got out. These friends and me, we gotta find it and lock it up again."

"Oh." She sat silent as she thought it over, hands in her lap, eyes downcast. "Is the bad thing going to hurt people?"

The old man nodded. "It did a long time ago, but the people made it stop. Now the bad thing got loose, it wants to hurt people again."

"Then I hope you and your friends can stop it," said Beth. "It isn't nice to hurt people."

"Thank you," said Pasqual reaching over and patting her hand. "We gonna do the best we can."

"Will I hear about it on the news?"

The old man considered this for a long moment. Actually, he didn't think so. If the work he and his peers were setting out to do went well, the white world might never know. "I think you will hear when it starts hurting people," answered Pasqual at last, "but I dunno if the newspeople will understand what it really is."

The two spoke together through the remainder of the flight. The little girl's mother had fallen asleep earlier so the old man did his best to entertain her.

When the captain announced their arrival at Phoenix Sky Harbor Airport, Pasqual knew genuine surprise at finding he had forgotten his nervousnous about flying. He said a solemn goodbye to Beth and deplaned.

Chapter Twenty

Phoenix

Jack led Detective Greg Johnson to the base of the rocks, still laboring over the level ground because of his poor physical condition, explaining as they went. "Hunnicutt told me he'd found this place," he said, trying to control his breathing, "and that it contained some kind of Native American artifact or monument. I agreed to come out and look at it."

Though it was only about ten a.m., the sun already rode high in the sky and the temperature had reached 115 degrees. Jack had crossed the ground at an unhurried pace, but still perspired like a racehorse.

Johnson looked fairly young to hold a shield, but he had a good reputation and a quick mind.

"So you met him over there," he indicated the parking area, "and the two of you crossed in a straight line from there to . . ." he paused and reached out to touch the base of the formation . . . , "here. Is that correct?"

"That's correct, Detective. He climbed up there first," Jack indicated the top, "and I followed considerably more slowly."

Johnson looked up and then nodded with resolution. "Show me," he said.

"What? Again?" The professor felt less than enthusiastic. "Why can't I stay down here?"

"Because I need to watch you walk through everything that happened here on Saturday," he explained patiently, "and because it might just help your student."

Jack looked up again, then nodded. He moved into the cut, his feet finding the hidden indentations in the rock face. Surprisingly, he reached the top in moments. Stepping over the rough outer wall and onto the level stone, he turned and looked down. The detective had not even begun the climb yet.

"Are you coming, Detective Johnson?" He enjoyed seeing the younger man below hesitate. He felt gratified to find he was not the only one who dreaded working too hard at things better done by others.

However, Johnson came up over the edge in seconds and looked around without confusion. "This is it, huh?" He walked over to the boulder. His finger traced the symbols and he turned to look back over his shoulder at the professor.

"What does it mean?"

Jack shook his head. "I'm not sure. When Don asked me that question, I told him I thought this rock might cover a cistern or maybe a cave with a spring. I figured that might be why everyone—all the tribes—knew about it." He sat on the edge and leaned forward, shaking his head. "Now I don't know. I keep thinking I missed something." He looked up, his face haunted. "People don't just crumble into dust, do they detective?"

Johnson put a hand atop the boulder and leaned close to study the carvings in the side. "I never used to think so," he admitted quietly, "but your boy Don isn't the only one to come up missing like that. We've got a whole town full of them."

"What?" Jack turned and stared at the other man face.

"Yep," said the detective with an uncomfortable look, "we found a whole town where everybody died or disappeared. It looked as if a line had been drawn at random along the road—on one side, everything stayed okay, on the other, everyone disappeared."

"Where?"

"About forty miles north of here along I-17, a little place called Agate Junction. Just a gas station and truckstop, but it had been there for about a hundred years. Anyway, it got levelled yesterday . . . reportedly by a freak storm . . . there were several witnesses—and we found the same sort of powdered bone as you did."

"Jesus!" The professor swore. "I knew it couldn't be my imagination. What kind of goddamn storm does that?"

The detective placed a hand on the older man's shoulder. "Don't make any assumptions, Dr. Foreman. It didn't show up on radar. The experts say it just couldn't have happened. Even our own weather guy is in hot water with them. He says it could be a storm, but that it would have had to be moving contrary to every other pattern of weather in the state to start here and end up there."

"Who's your weather guy?"

"We use that forecaster from TV and radio named Sharp, you know the one?"

"Yeah," Jack replied. "I like him. He's good." Then he turned and looked off toward the parking site where the shiny truck waited for Don Hunnicutt.

The other man followed his gaze, saw the truck and spoke, persistently. "Sharp's the only one who says it might be a storm."

"How else can you explain it?" Jack really wanted to know.

"I can't, Professor," admitted the detective. "I just investigate what they tell me to. I haven't had this shield long and I don't want to lose it."

Jack turned and knelt at the base of the boulder. Suddenly, he looked thoughtful, stood and began patting his pockets.

"Looking for something?" asked Johnson.

"No," Jack shrugged, "not really." He pointed down at the base. "You can see where we slid it aside, but it had been wedged and we couldn't get it any farther. When Don went back to the trucks for a hammer and chisel . . . uh . . . it happened."

Johnson came over and got on his hands and knees, peering at the bottom of the stone. "Okay," he said. "I see it. Let's get some help and find out what's under it." The detective stood and leaned over the edge, whistling for the officers who waited down below. "YOU MEN! COME HERE AND ROLL UP YOUR SLEEVES. I WANT TO MOVE A ROCK!"

The two patrolmen hustled up the side from below and were soon braced against the boulder with both Foreman and Johnson helping.

The wedges didn't hold this time. The rock slid to the side under their combined effort in one smooth motion revealing a clean round hole.

Jack pulled his flashlight from his belt and looked down inside.

"What do you see, Professor?" Johnson was crowded up close, but there was room for only one at a time in the entrance.

Jack leaned back out of the hole and turned. "The opening is worked stone. Looks like it used to be a kiva. Once, a ladder probably led from here to the floor below, but—if this place is half as old as I think it is—I guess it would have fallen by now."

"How old?" asked the detective.

"I'd say five hundred years or more," replied Jack. "Could be three times older than that, but some of those symbols are newer."

"Are you going down there?" Johnson looked like he wanted Jack to say no.

Always contrary, Jack replied, "Yes." He watched the other man's face as he said it. "Okay, Detective Johnson," he said with a grin, "just why don't you want me going down there? I'm certainly qualified to do it and, in fact, may have a professional obligation."

Johnson lowered his eyes and spoke quietly. "I hadn't realized I was so transparent," he said. "I worked on a murder case over in New Mexico last year. Questions arose about the border so I had to liaison with a New Mexico cop as well. We were doing great till the guys who protect antiquities stepped in." He shook his head and chuckled. "You never saw so much red tape in your life! We had to have permission in writing in triplicate for sneezing . . . and samples of the snot for analysis."

"I hadn't really thought about it before," said Jack, "but this really is an archaeological site and ought to be protected until someone does a thorough study of who built it, who used it and why." He scratched his head. "I should have reported this through the university when we first found it. I guess Hunnicutt's disappearance kept me from realizing it until now."

Johnson cleared his throat. "Uh . . . Professor, could we talk about that for a minute?"

The professor looked at the younger man, a twinkle of amusement in his eyes. "What did you have in mind, Detective Johnson?"

"Suppose you were to hold off on that report for a couple more days while we sort through this mess."

Jack thought it over. "Are we talking about a day or two, or are you suggesting a lengthy delay? I might be willing to hold off, but I won't just ignore the matter."

"If this isn't figured out before the end of a week, you can report everything you want to anyone you want with my full cooperation, Dr. Foreman. I don't want to hide anything. I just think we'll get further in this investigation if we leave the other agencies out of it as long as we can."

The professor nodded. "Agreed."

Johnson let out a sigh of relief. He sat on the side wall, opposite the other man, and smiled for the first time. "In that case, can we talk turkey?"

Jack smiled back. "Suits me."

"Call me Greg when we're not around the others, okay? This isn't a case where any of the usual rules are being followed. To tell you the truth, I don't think anyone has the faintest idea what's going on. Do you?"

"Difficult question," answered the older man. "I agree that no one we're aware of knows what has happened so far, but I'm beginning to think someone must know. Seems like it may be our job to find out who."

"You think this site is involved with that storm up north?" Johnson sounded really interested.

"It has to be, Greg," replied Jack. "I know it seems crazy at first glance, but I think there was something here—something under the stone—and Hunnicutt and I let it out."

The detective smiled and shook his head. "I can't swallow that, Dr. Foreman, even though it would answer a lot of questions." He rose and looked out over the edge into the desert. "There are still a lot of mysteries in the world. I don't say it couldn't be, but you'd have to show me evidence I can't refute."

"Look at logic first, Greg. What kind of storm passes across an area of land and leaves powdered bones behind?"

The detective shook his head. "I don't know."

"I was here when the storm hit. I looked out from the top of these rocks just like we're doing now and there wasn't so much as a small cloud within miles. Not until we moved the stone did the wind begin to rise. It isn't just a storm!"

"What is it then, Dr. Foreman? Come on, give me a break! I want to find answers as badly as you do, but you'll have to give me something I can believe if you want me to work with you."

Jack shrugged. "As to what it is, I don't know. But, returning to logic again, whose story is harder to believe, Greg? What you guys seem to be saying is that a freak storm killed my student, leaving him a pile of powdered bone. That same storm apparently wiped out an entire town just forty miles from here. It would all be neat and tidy except you found more powdered bones there as well. Come on, Detective Johnson, you aren't any more credible than I am."

Johnson looked sour. "I know. The problem is that no stretch of the imagination can account for what happened—neither here nor there—and the guys I work for want very badly to buy the killer storm theory. That eliminates a lot of troublesome questions."

"I think we're missing something," said Jack. "I think we ought to consider what we have here before desperately settling for the best guess."

"What exactly is it we have?" Johnson's frustration was beginning to show in his voice.

"A Native American sacred site," answered Jack, "and it just might be time for us to go and talk to some Native Americans about what it means."

The detective sat silent for a long moment as the suggestion sank in. Then a look of satisfaction came to his face. "Makes sense to me. Let's go find us some Indians." He rose, preparatory to climbing down.

Jack held up his hand, halting the younger man. "Don't rush off, Greg. We may not have to go very far, after all."

Johnson stopped with one leg already extended over the wall and turned back toward the archaeologist. "What do you mean?"

The older man pointed down.

Arms folded and looking back at them stood a dark-skinned man.

Jack said, "Yaqui, unless I miss my guess." And then he waved and called out, "Hola!"

Chapter Twenty-One

Salt River Reservation

Tom Bear wasted no time. "Go to the Tohono O'odham—those who used to be called Papago—Danny, and see their Medicine man. Tell him there is a thing needing done that only he can do. He lives on the Gila Bend Reservation, about sixty miles from here. You can use my truck. Bring him back with you."

"Okay, Tom," said Danny, taking the keys off the table. "I'll be back as quick as I can."

Once the younger man had gone, Tom locked up the house and set off toward the Maricopa section of the reservation. He had determined to gather as many of the wise as he could and achieve some sort of consensus of will, but the action had been born out of desperation.

Tom knew the truth. He had never been as frightened as he felt now. The legend of the demon had been told to him by his grandfather and passed down from others long before. All spoke of a thing so horrible that only the direct intervention of the spirits had enabled the people to win. A great gathering of all the wise men had been the course followed before. It had to be the answer now.

As Tom hurried along the road, he tried to remember what he had been told. The demon could not be seen, but it was real—and it could kill. It was smart and cruel, but could be fooled by a clever man. It could only be defeated when attacked on all levels at once—the reason for the gathering of the wise. The demon must be fought in the underworld, the middle world, the upperworld, in the mind and in spirit. Five battles with five victories required. Nothing less would do.

Tom thought despairingly about how little he really knew. The last of the Pima medicine men, Danny's grandfather, had died a couple years before. No others remained now, except a few who dabbled in magic like Tom—and he was the best of those.

He thought about Danny. The boy was descended from a wise man. He could become what Tom could not. The old man had intended all along to lead Danny into the path, but this turn of events made it critically important the boy move more quickly toward his destiny. *What if I am not up to it?* Tom tried to be brutally honest with himself. *What if we fail—not because of the boy or his ability—because I am too old or too arrogant to do it right?*

These thoughts plagued him as he crossed the reservation, but he eventually concluded only the gods would be able to decide the right or wrong of this thing. Tom could only do his best. With this acceptance warm in his heart, he arrived at the home of Kade Wonto, the only Maricopa medicine man on the Salt River Reservation.

Wonto lived in a nice house constructed of brick. It had many rooms, for Kade and Estelle had seven children. The Maricopa enjoyed great popularity among both tribes who shared the land, his own and the Pima. They had lived together in peace for many generations.

When the door opened and Estelle saw who had come calling, she let out a joyous squeal and threw her arms around the old Pima, calling out, "Oh! Kade, come quickly! It is the Bear dropping by to see us!"

Wonto must have been just out of sight within the front room for he came around the corner with his hand outstretched in greeting and a wide smile on his face. "Ho, Tom Bear!" he exclaimed. "I did not think I would see you so soon again. Come in and eat with us."

"Ho, Kade Wanto!" replied Tom with a matching smile. "I had to come, my friend. There is work for us to do. Something once imprisoned has been loosed."

Kade stopped smiling suddenly. His face froze momentarily in a strange and foreign look before a voice spoke through his mouth. Unfortunately, it was not Wanto's voice.

"Why waste your time, Pima man? There is nothing you can do."

Tom, who had reached out and clasped the hand offered in friendship, felt the whole of Wonto's body vibrate as the voice spoke—almost like a speaker grill resonates with sound. In another moment, however, Kade's face cleared and his cheerful expression returned, to be replaced a moment later by a look of slight confusion. He had missed something. "What happened?"

Estelle had stepped back and looked on in fear, her knuckle in her mouth, her hands white with the tension.

"That which has been loosed just spoke," said Tom gravely, "but do not be afraid, Estelle. Kade and I can do what must be done."

Wonto turned to his wife. "It will be all right," he said. "I will go with Tom Bear to his house and return when I am done." He turned to look at Tom. "Is this right, my friend?"

"This is so," agreed Tom. "Come, get your stuff and we will go. There is no time to waste."

The two friends made their way uneventfully across the reservation to Tom's house, arriving just after noon.

They found Danny waiting for them.

Tom could not help but notice the boy fidgeted and appeared agitated. "What is it?" inquired the old man. "Did you do what I asked?"

The younger Pima looked uncomfortable. "Yes, Tom. I did it, but . . . ." He trailed off.

"What is it, boy?" The witch had grown impatient.

"Well . . ." Danny stammered," . . . uh . . . I went to the Tohono O'odham and asked for their medicine man. They sent me to a house on the far side of the reservation. There I found the . . . uh . . . person who . . . ." He faltered.

"Who did you find, boy," demanded Tom Bear, finally at the end of his patience.

Danny looked miserable and was about to speak when a new voice spoke from the end of the porch.

"He found me, witch," said the smooth alto voice, "and persuaded me to come here against my better judgment."

"Tom," said Danny in explanation, "that's what I was trying to tell you. May I present Lotus Farley, Medicine Woman of the Tohono O'odham."

The old Pima witch turned and could not repress a gasp when he saw the woman called Lotus. She stood about five-foot-seven in moccasins, dressed in a tight skirt and flower print blouse, and absolutely, stunningly, heart-breakingly beautiful. Her jet black hair glowed, as fine as silk and brushed to perfection. Her dark eyes flashed a challenge that at once intimidated even the outspoken old man yet made him wish he were forty years younger.

For a long moment, the silence of shock reigned. Tom could not speak, Danny had made his introduction and Kade Wonto remained intentionally—wisely—quiet.

Lotus Farley threw back her head and laughed, a full, feminine but robust laughter, filled with warmth and sympathy and friendly good humor.

In that moment, all three men felt inexplicably that the situation had suddenly gotten better.

Chapter Twenty-Two

Hopiland

"Awaken," commanded the voice of Taknokwunu. "It is time to begin your journey."

The Hopi priest opened sleep heavy eyes, slightly disoriented. "What?" He ran his hand through his hair and then momentarily covered his eyes, ending by massaging the bridge of his nose. He looked around the kiva.

An unnatural hush lay over everything. Harold sensed the spirit even before he finally heard it.

"I said it is time to begin your journey, my priest. You must go quickly and quietly. You must be cautious. The storm seeks to destroy you and the others. If it can prevent your gathering, it can defeat us all."

"Where shall I go, oh spirit?"

"The city to the south. In Phoenix shall the hope of the past rise again."

"What do I need to do?"

The spirit did not immediately reply. Harold looked around the chamber but saw nothing. Still, the presence remained.

"Speak to me of what I must do," Harold said again. "What shall I take with me? What words shall I speak? How shall I do your bidding?"

"When the time is right, I shall reveal these things to you," said Taknokwunu. "For now, you must simply obey. Is this not what you want to do?"

The Coyote Clan priest was quick to respond. "Oh, Weather Spirit, I will gladly do whatever you ask."

"Then listen. The demon has touched your mind and spoken to you twice now. It can sense what you think almost as well as it senses what you feel. Part of what it feeds on is the feeling, the emotional energy generated by fear and uncertainty. If you know too much too early, you might, unintentionally, betray us."

"I understand, Spirit-of-the-Weather, and I will wait to learn what next must be done until you deem it time." Since Taknokwunu was apparently aware of the dream communication between the demon and himself, Harold decided to tell all. "Taknokwunu, I am troubled."

"What is it, my priest?"

"The demon has spoken of sparing the people of peace. He has spoken of passing us by and concentrating on those called Navajo. He offered this if I would stop the gathering."

The spirit remained silent for a long moment before replying. "And what will you do, Priest?"

This time, Harold was the one slow to answer. Finally, he said, "I do not know. I would save my people if I can, but would Taiowa accept the sacrifice of another tribe to save this one?"

"What do you think?"

The Coyote Priest spoke quietly. "We are the People of Peace. It would be wrong to deal with the demon. It would be wrong to betray the Navajo." He shrugged. "I cannot do it."

"That is why you were chosen, Priest, even though you are not the wisest, nor the oldest, nor the most powerful. I chose you because you are one who sees the connection between all life, all tribes, all peoples. You are not one who hates and schemes for advantage over others. It is this which will enable you to join with others and create a thing of beauty and power."

Harold stood speechless. The god *had* heard everything all along. He knew now that his heart held no secrets from Those Above.

"You must go quickly," said Taknokwunu. "Take only what you need for two days, plus your finest ceremonial clothing. Since you will represent all of our people, you must look every inch the priest."

Harold stood and bowed his head. "I will do as you ask," he affirmed.

"Be brave, my priest," said the spirit. "I will never be far. For now, because the storm is coming, I must stay in the shadows. Farewell."

Taknokwunu withdrew and Harold felt a sudden easing of pressure, a light-headedness that seemed a palpable thing. For the first time since the spirit addressed him, he knew where he needed to go and what he would do. How to do it remained the only unanswered question in his mind. He placed a stack of pahos on the altar he had made for the spirit that controls the weather and finished his prayers. Then he moved to the ladder and began his ascent.

"Peace Man! Stop!!" The voice of the demon sounded loud and shocking after the gentler spirit.

Harold missed his step, lost his grip and fell heavily to the floor. He heard the snap of bone as he hit and braced himself for the pain. He looked down at splintered ends of the bone poking through the skin midway between the right knee and ankle. The initial shock passed in an instant, replaced by screaming pain as the tortured flesh sent frantic signals to his brain. He closed his eyes, trying to retain some semblance of sanity.

"Ahhhh . . . Peace Man. Look what you've gone and done. How can we talk when your mind is occupied with pain." The beast's voice sounded smug and confident. "Would you like for me to ease that pain, Priest? I can do it, you know. There are many things I can do that you cannot imagine. Let me show you."

"No!" Harold protested feebly, but then he felt the presence of the beast settling around him. His visions of the storm settling over the village caused him considerable agitation at first, but then he almost felt the sensation of the beast grabbing and shutting down the nerves that brought pain from the injury to his mind. One moment, the reaction of his body threatened unconsciousness and the next, there was the soothing absence of pain.

"Isn't that better, Peace Man?"

Harold marvelled at the transformation. He felt a warm sense of contentment, a euphoric surge of good will. Yet he could look down and still see the bone protruding from his flesh, could sense that, under this illusion of comfort, lay the damaged agony of reality.

"Avert your eyes. It will be easier if you do not see that which contradicts the feeling."

"How can you do this?" A part of Harold's mind was wondering if this trick could be learned. *What a healer he would be if he could take away even the most severe pain!*

The beast knew his thoughts even as the priest had them. "This teaching could be part of it, Priest," said the voice. "I could show you how it is done and empower you to reach in and control the nerves involved."

Harold could sense the beast's amusement.

"There are so many things about you men that I am only now beginning to understand. You are soft and foolish, like grubs, and there is nothing you can do to stop me when I wish to feed on you. And—more than any other food—you make me grow stronger and give me your power. Yet you are the only creatures ever to defeat me. You are strong within and have powers of thought far more subtle than mine."

"What is it you want of me?" Harold hoped to draw the beast out, to encourage it to reveal more of itself. Perhaps in this way, he could discover its weaknesses.

"Have you thought about my offer, Peace Man? Have you thought of how I might spare your people? What do you think?"

"I admit the idea is tempting. What man would not wish to save his people?" Harold prayed fervently that the beast could not read much beyond surface thoughts.

"All you need do is agree, priest," said the beast, "and I will set about ridding you of your enemies."

"I am not ready yet to decide, Demon. I must have more time." Harold suddenly realized that only the beast stood between him and the pain of his injury. Worse, he was by himself in the kiva—left alone at his own request. It might be hours or even days before anyone came down to find him and his broken leg.

"Ahhhh, very well." The voice again contained amusement.

Suddenly, Harold sensed feeling returning, coursing up the nerves from the injury and speeding toward his brain. He braced himself but found no way to withstand the assault. His body trembled with the pain, his hands knotted into fists and slammed into the floor, his throat tried to close down over vocal chords that sought release in a wail of sound.

"Not too much time, though," said the voice. Again the pain receded, leaving an aftershock of outraged nerves and tissues. "You won't be long, will you?"

"No. No, I won't be long," moaned Harold. "Give me a few hours. Hold back the pain, block it off just for a few hours so that my mind is clear and let me think."

"As you wish," said the voice. "A few hours of respite I can grant you. Have your injury tended to while I take your pain. This time I will help."

The priest sighed with relief.

"But do not take overlong, Peace Man, or I will see that you and your people enter into the substance of my body as food and energy and growth."

"I understand, Demon," said Harold. "I do not promise I will agree, but I will consider your offer carefully and tell you what I decide."

"You really have little choice, man. Do you really think you can stand against me? What happened in the past was a fluke, a bizarre incident that cannot be repeated. Work with me and save your people. It is the sensible thing to do."

And then Harold felt the presence of the beast withdraw. He lay alone upon the floor of the kiva, his ruined leg bleeding onto the rock and hard-packed earth. He knew no one would be coming for him so he steeled himself for the ordeal and crawled to the base of the ladder. He could feel the nerve block keeping the pain at bay. The beast was as good as its word so far.

Laboriously, careful to keep his injured leg out and away from all other surfaces, Harold Laloma began to drag himself upward, one rung at a time. It would take until dawn.

As he climbed, he prayed aloud.

Chapter Twenty-Three

Chaco Canyon

Archie sat cross-legged on the rug on the west side of the room and waited. He knew he waited for death.

The night had been long and arduous. He felt exhausted and, in a way, ready to welcome the end of his journey. He only regretted being unable to witness the defeat of the demon.

As he waited, He-Who-Walks-In-Wisdom glowed with pride. Fly had surpassed himself. The full ritual had been learned. Now it lay hidden in the boy's memory. The ceremony itself took almost a full day, composed of many smaller ceremonies. Most of these were already part of what Fly knew, what he had previously learned. Some parts were known only to the other tribes. This had made the task of committing it all to memory in a single night possible, though not easier. The order of the calling was complex, and the boy had struggled to learn the proper placing of blanks representing the contributions of others. Archie knew that, when the time came, Fly would learn all of it even though he would hear it only once.

The night faded quickly, the eastern sky lightening perceptibly. The demon had to be nearby. Archie could feel it, hovering in the desert. He could not repress a wave of pleasure as he anticipated its disappointment. It thought to end the battle today. It would discover too late that the struggle had not yet begun.

Gordon, after learning the ceremony, had left for Shiprock—and then on to police headquarters. Almost as soon as the boy departed, Archie went to the post and used the phone to call the police switchboard and leave a message. This further message instructed Gordon to go to Windowrock and then on to Phoenix. There he would be contacted by others. In this way, the old man could insure the boy would not be caught by the demon. Fly's survival took precedence over everything. He had become the key.

Archie regretted he could not save the others. The large settlement at Chaco Canyon had a population of more than two thousand. It would be a long and bloody killing time for the demon, but the slaughter itself would actually contribute to the greater good for it would allow the boy time to escape and ultimately guide the final battle.

Archie felt surprised at himself for being so cold-blooded about the whole thing, but he knew neither fear of death nor of what might come after. Though he would have spared his children and their families, he could think of no way to whisk them all to safety with the beast en route. Since the demon wanted him specifically, there seemed nothing the old man could do other than sacrifice himself and the others to save the boy.

Now, as he sat waiting, he continued to sing to himself. He had nearly finished. The last of the songs he knew would soon be sung. Then he would die gladly.

*   *   *   *   *

The beast had moved cautiously after levelling Agate Junction. It knew now that men were different in this time than they had been before. The things they built, the solid things they lived in, were made to last—not at all like the flimsy hide structures used so commonly before. The effective destruction of these things in order to get at the man fluids within them depended on how much energy the beast chose to expend. It understood suddenly the point of diminishing returns.

It could tap into the minds of many. The greatest shock had been realizing how far these creatures had come in so little time. They understood more about their universe, about life, about the way things worked, than they ever had before. They still had the magic, if these wise men were any sampling, but they also had technology.

Crossing over Arizona, the beast avoided contact with the men. It had—through tapping into the minds around it—a rudimentary sense of how quickly the bipeds could communicate with each other.

It would not be wise to call attention to its progress. All of its past successes had been the result of stealth and surprise.

It had no sense of geography. The beast homed in on the thoughts of those it sought. Sensitive to other minds that it encountered while moving, it had been able to adjust course and avoid concentrations of men when it wished to do so.

Right now, the beast wanted Archie. The Navajo was the eldest of all the wise and knew the most. To eliminate the old one would be to destroy the potential for a gathering of any kind. Combined with deal-making through the Hopi, the two acts would ensure that no significant power could be assembled against it.

It lay silent and unmoving at the mouth of the canyon just before the settlement. It had arrived under cover of darkness and waited now for first light to swoop down on the unsuspecting hogans that lay spread out before it. It could sense all the sleeping minds as well as the alert mind of the old Navajo.

Now that there was no escape, the time had come for the beast to speak. Taunting always had rewards. "Ahhhhh . . . " it sighed in satisfaction, "He-Who-Walks-In-Wisdom. You did not try to flee. How proper."

Archie heard the voice in his mind and sat up straighter, his face a stubborn mask. He would give no satisfaction to the beast.

"Such a disciplined mind, old man. I am indeed impressed. I want you to listen as I destroy your home. I want you to wait there while I visit the rest of your family. I want you to pay attention as I crush your neighbors. Then, when you are the only one remaining, we will get together, you and I."

Archie ground his teeth and chewed the insides of his cheeks. He fought to keep his mind a blank page, to keep knowledge of . . . *no, no. Blank pages. Keep them blank.*

As the sun rose, the sound of the wind began to rise as well. Archie could hear it through the walls of the hogan, could hear the wailing and whipping of the increasing gusts as dust and debris were sucked up into the cone that was the body of the beast.

Above the wind, he suddenly heard the first human cries, the sounds made by those who had at last realized there would be no escape from this storm, the despairing cry of the hopeless.

The hogans in Chaco Canyon were constructed of stone due to the shortage of wood in the desert. They might on this morning have been made of straw for all the good it did. The beast descended on the settlement and established a running boundary that swept counter-clock-wise until all the buildings lay within the enclosure. Once the great hurricane-like winds encircled the settlement, they began to accelerate and grow in intensity.

The feeding at Agate Junction had been good, had provided much in the way of sustenance for the hungry demon. The 101 souls that died there had provided enough energy and mass for the beast to double its size and strength. This feeding would allow it to double again. Soon it would be prepared to attack the larger concentrations of energy represented by what the men called cities.

The dwellings on the perimeter were the first to go. Rock itself lifted into the air by the wind and the beast began to alter it, to use it like a blasting machine. The larger stones collided, breaking into smaller and more usable sizes and shapes. Every new piece or particle became part of the mass that pounded and cut away at the rest. When enough mass had been brought to bear, the walls of even the strongest hogans crumbled under the assault and those who sheltered within were sucked forth like soda through a straw.

Cries sounded above the din. Screams of agony and fear rose up in the early morning against a backdrop of blinding, blasting storm. One, ten, a hundred, five hundred! The chorus of voices cried out above the roaring wind and the beast fed gluttonously on the fear and the fluids.

Once the outer part of the ring had fallen, the beast concentrated its force on the next inner circle with an even more devastating effect. The small stone dwellings burst asunder like cork struck by a chain-saw.

The beast began to sing, a strange sound starting somewhere in the indefinable center and radiating outward. Thus, it came first to Archie as he sat in his home, waiting for the beast to get around to him. The eerie keening rose and fell in alien ululations, howls and tumultuous noise, inarticulate utterances from mumbles to sonic screams. It banished thought. It shattered sanity. And the beast sang joyously.

There was no separating the cacophony of sounds into individual voices after that. The din tortured Archie's ears and it became a monumental accomplishment just to remain seated through it all. Long before the beast actually reached him, his hearing had been destroyed, the auditory nerve coming apart under the assault. Still, the beast did not need Archie's ears to communicate.

"Are you there, Old One?" The voice in Archie's mind came tinged with barely suppressed laughter, a satisfied conceit that wanted now to take pleasure in tormenting the soul of the Navajo.

His voice barely a croak in the blackness of his home in the thick of the storm, Archie sat up straight and proud. "I am here, Demon," he said.

"Are you afraid, wise man?" It reached him not as a question, but a taunt.

He-Who-Walks-In-Wisdom did not dignify the taunt with a reply. He did not fear. He realized it even as he marvelled over it. The demon would take him now, but it only sealed its own doom.

"I see you," said the beast. "I see you and I can read your mind. You are . . . ." But the voice trailed off. After a brief moment of confusion, disorientation, the voice spoke again—this time, touched with incredulity.

"You are not afraid! Why not? I am going to destroy you, to crush you utterly, to flay the flesh from your bones. I will release the moisture within your cells and devour it, use it to grow stronger and more powerful until there is nothing on your world that can resist me. Why are you not afraid?"

"Because you cannot defeat the dineh," said Archie, his face wrapped in a smile of peaceful contentment. "I am only one. There is now another. You may defeat me, but the other will do what must be done. You are already too late."

"WHAT?" The beast grew so agitated it forgot restraint, disdained control, desired only to reach in and rend the old man to tatters.

The inarticulate rantings of its rage swelled in volume until the very rock began to explode and burst from the intense vibrations.

So, also, did Archie. Like an exploding pressure cooker, the hogan split and crumbled, leaving nothing between the fury of the beast and the fragile flesh of the man. The old man died instantly, the smile still on his lips even as his body tore itself to pieces under the lash of the demon.

At the last moment, Archie sang the last note of the last song. He died content and fulfilled.

Chapter Twenty-Four

Phoenix

Juan had followed the white man to the site. This time he did not wear the body of the crow, but his own form. He found it harder to travel in his own body than to fly. The Phoenix heat could not be called insignificant.

He had no difficulty sitting unobserved in the shadow of the rocks, watching the two white men move across the desert toward the site. They were intent on their journey.

Juan felt curious as he observed. He kept himself in harmony with the day, unmoving and invisible to all eyes.

He saw the two policemen called to aid in moving the stone and kept his place as they climbed back down, returning to the parking area and the shiny pickup, leaving the other two alone atop the rocks. He waited, knowing the proper moment would come in time. His inner voice, that voice of truth which always guided him, told him that he would soon recognize that key moment, that crux point, when action would be required.

The two white men, one obviously a policeman, spoke together. Juan did not know what they said, but he knew they were speaking of the demon. He reached into his pouch and withdrew a mushroom. Putting it into his mouth, he chewed slowly, savoring the flavor of the earth, tasting that indefinable essence—the embodiment of truth.

The time had come time. He knew it. As inexorable as a sunrise, the light of understanding blossomed in his mind. For this he had traveled to Phoenix, the next step for him on a path destined since his birth.

Juan Mapoli stood and walked toward the rocks. He moved in harmony with nature, still invisible to the real world around him. He reached a point in the cleared area about twenty yards from the rocks and stood, arms crossed on his chest, waiting for the white men to summon him. He would wait as long as necessary.

Within minutes he had been spotted by the older man. He knew it the moment it occurred. A few seconds later, the man called to him.

"Hola!"

"Hola!" Juan felt a deep satisfaction as his inner truth was born out. He waited with the patience of a sabio.

"Should we come down, or will you come up?" The two men stood on the edge of the summit and looked down.

Juan made the transition in his mind from Spanish to English.

"I will come up," he said, and moved swiftly to the base of the rocks. His keen eyes saw the path. As clear as it seemed to him, it might have been highlighted in glittering gold.

When he stood atop the rocks, he looked toward the stone which now lay off center to the side. "You have done a thing," he said quietly.

The older white man looked at him with an expression of regret and confusion. "I suspected as much," he said. "But what is it that I have done?"

"You have loosed the demon," said Juan.

"Demon?" said the other man, the policeman. "What do you mean?"

The old Yaqui looked at the stone and pointed to the hole in the rock. "There was a demon long ago. The people imprisoned it beneath these rocks. You have set it loose."

The two white men exchanged a meaningful look.

"What kind of demon?" The older man was troubled and obviously wanted to understand.

"It is a wind demon, a storm that sweeps over the unwary and takes their souls."

The policeman shook his head. "Oh Christ," he muttered, "not another one!"

"Hold on, Detective," said Jack Foreman. "I told you there was something to be learned from the Native Americans. Give this man the courtesy of suspending your disbelief long enough to get an explanation." Jack turned to the Yaqui. "Tell me of this thing."

The old Indian looked from one to the other and shrugged. "I have already done so," he said. "What more can I say?"

"Where did it come from, this demon?" Jack wracked his brain trying to figure out how best to approach the subject.

"No one knows," replied the Yaqui. "It came down from the cold north long ago and moved freely across the desert, feeding on the people. It was a great task to lure it here and imprison it beneath the earth in the underworld."

Jack sat on the ledge and looked up at the Indian. "What can be done to capture this demon?"

"It will take another great gathering of the wise," said Juan as he squatted on his heels in the center of the rocks. "But it may not be something that can be done at all."

The policeman turned and spat in disgust. "Come on, you two, give me a break. I can't deal in demons and magic. The facts are that a man was killed here in a freak storm. There is nothing to show that it has anything to do with ancient evils or the supernatural."

The old Indian kept silent. Jack looked at the detective with ill-disguised disappointment. "Won't you at least listen with an open mind, Greg?" He wanted the police on his side, but he sensed the importance of this meeting.

"I haven't time for this kind of nonsense, Professor," said the detective. "If you want to waste your time with ethnic superstitions, I can't stop you, but the police have to deal in facts." He shrugged. "I'm sorry, Dr. Foreman, but I have better things to do. There is an active investigation of Hunnicutt's disappearance to pursue and I can't honestly say I'm willing to spend even a minute on this demon crap."

The Yaqui remained silent, merely watching the two white men disagree.

"I think we have to look at everything, Detective." Jack stayed resolute. "I think this man may have something relevant to tell us."

"Sorry," said Johnson, moving to the cut. "I can't take the time." He crossed to the edge, pausing only long enough to speak over his shoulder as he started down. "I'll be downtown if you come up with anything tangible. Keep me informed." With that, he turned and started down.

Jack watched him reach the bottom and head off toward the other officers. He sighed.

"The policeman is not capable of accepting what he cannot see," observed Juan.

Jack sat wearily. "I'm not certain I can either," he muttered more to himself than to the Indian. "All I know is something big has happened here and I don't understand what it is."

Juan sat opposite the archaeologist, calmly and with dignity. "I will tell you what you need to know," he said simply. "There is something important to be done and you have a part to play in it. I am not certain what that part will be, but I will teach you when the time is right. Then you will have to decide."

Jack looked at the old man, trying to take his measure. "Do you drink beer?" he asked.

"Bet your ass," said Juan with a grin. "You buyin'?"

The two men, each from different worlds, climbed down from the summit and walked in silence back to the archaeologist's truck. They got in and Jack drove to a bar not far from the site where he bought two cold beers and took them to a quiet table in the back.

"What the hell is going on . . . uh . . . ," he suddenly realized he didn't know the Indian's name.

"Juan Mapoli," said the other. "And you?"

"Jack Foreman. I'm a professor at ASU. Archaeology. Call me Jack, please."

"Okay, Jack," said the Indian. "Why don't you start by telling me what happened to you?"

"A student of mine came to me . . . Christ! Was it only three days ago?" He shook his head in disbelief. "Anyway, he said he'd found this place in the desert, marked by a boulder with a lot of carvings on it. He said he thought it was a Native American relic. I agreed to come out and have a look. That was Saturday. We got here a little before noon and he took me up to the top. After looking at the stone, I knew it was something important, but couldn't for the life of me figure out what it meant. I figured, since the sigils of all the tribes were there, it must be a place common to all the tribes—a well or cistern maybe. The student, a boy named Hunnicutt, and I tried to move the stone aside. We only got it a little way before it jammed. Don went back to the truck to get a hammer and chisel. That was when the storm came up. It was really sudden. After it passed, I went looking for the boy. I found no sign of him. He might as well have dropped off the edge of the world."

Juan remained quiet for a long moment, then asked, "How come it left you alone, Jack?"

"I don't know," replied the professor.

"Is that everything?" The question implied that there must be more, but Jack just shook his head. "We got to go and find some people, Jack," said Juan. "I don't have wheels so I'll need your help."

"Who are we looking for?" Jack was willing, but he couldn't have explained why if asked.

"We got to find some Indians, Professor."

"Where are we going?"

"Where else? You can't find Indians in Phoenix. We got to go to the reservation in Scottsdale."

"When?"

"You can pick me up at sunrise tomorrow morning. I got to tell my son not to worry and pick up some things."

Jack nodded his agreement. "Okay. Can I give you a lift somewhere now?"

"I was hoping you'd offer, Jack." Juan smiled. "At my age, I fly a lot better than I walk."

The white man didn't understand and his face said so.

Juan's smile rapidly developed into a deep, rich laugh. "That's a Yaqui joke, Professor," he said, trying to control himself.

"I don't get it," admitted the archaeologist.

"You aren't supposed to," said the old man rising from his seat. "C'mon, let's get out of here."

They left with Jack still trying to figure it out.

Chapter Twenty-Five

In the National Forest

Rattle sat in the wood and waited. Reaction had set in and he began to shake. What had he done? How could he, a man of peace, have taken two lives in the space of moments? What else could he have done?

The two men had lied. They threatened the deer spirit when the old Pai called it. He had reacted without thought. Now he had to find a way to make peace with the spirit. If he could do that, he still had his mission to Phoenix—a mission he didn't understand. He only knew he had a thing to do, a task no one else could perform.

He continued to chant, calling on the spirit to return. He struggled within himself to achieve the kind of harmony with nature that would open his heart and summon the spirit. The onerous act he had committed made it difficult for him to find peace.

A long time passed before he heard the tentative sound of hooves in the wood.

Rattle felt the presence of the spirit even before he heard it. He felt suffused with a warm glow of peace, his conflict banished with the arrival of his totem. The great deer had answered his summons. It had forgiven him.

The huge animal came regally out the wood and stood shyly before the old man, head low, great horns a forest of polished bone.

The Havasupai medicine man lowered his head and wept with gratitude.

The voice of the spirit spoke softly in his mind. "Why do you weep, old man?"

A thousand thoughts raced through Rattle's head—protestations of innocence, expressions of relief, feelings of regret, questions—yet none of these reached his lips. Instead, he said only, "I love you."

The large brown eyes of the deer grew soft and gentle. It approached slowly, raising its head and standing close. The voice spoke again. "I know, my friend. You have always been mine and I yours. You did right in bringing the two men to me as they asked. It is a sad thing that they did not understand what you did for them."

"BUT I KILLED THEM!" Rattle shouted and his voice echoed through the woods.

"You had no choice," said the spirit in a low, comforting voice. "They would have taken away the thing that links us. They would have prevented me from telling you what you must do in the great task that remains before us."

The old man continued to weep without shame. The deer stood over him protectively, waiting patiently.

When he could again speak, Rattle wiped the wetness from his face and said, "Tell me what I must do."

"Move the machine to the edge of the slope and let it roll down into the dense growth," instructed the spirit. "Then continue your journey to the south. You are needed and there is little time."

"But what of the . . . " the old man gestured to the bodies of the two hunters.

"I will see to them," the spirit assured him.

"How can this be?" The old Pai knew amazement.

"Have you so little faith in nature and in me?" The voice reproached him.

"Oh no!" protested the old man, "I only wondered how this can be done?"

The deer looked all around, its gentle gaze growing steely and hard. When it spoke again, the tone in Rattle's mind was as cold and final as death. "I will summon others who will dispose of what remains," said the spirit. "I will call the bear and wolf and coyote. There will be nothing left to show that your knife drank of these lives."

Relief flooded over the medicine man. Despite his feelings of guilt, he knew now he had done the right thing, knew the spirit still protected him.

"It is time for you to go, my friend," said the spirit. "Move the machine as I told you and then go back to the highway."

"I am yours," said Rattle.

The large deer sniffed the air once, then moved slowly out of the clearing and into the wood.

Rattle took down the tent and packed it carefully into the back of the pickup. He carefully went through the area and gathered every trace of the white men's presence, putting empty beer cans and utensils in the cab. It took him a few minutes to start the truck and drive slowly to the edge of the slope. When the front wheels were over the edge, he cut the engine and got out of the truck, making sure the brake was released. Though seventy, the old man possessed a wiry strength and was able to push the truck the few feet necessary for the forward momentum to carry it on over the edge. It rolled downward smoothly with ever increasing momentum and buried itself with a crash in the heavy growth, disappearing entirely from view.

He turned then, gathered his meager possessions, and returned to the road. With a prayer of thanks, he began to walk briskly back toward the highway. Behind him, in the wood, he heard the roar of a bear.

An hour later, he was picked up by a delivery truck coming from the reservation—its destination Phoenix. Rattle decided he didn't mind motor vehicles so much after all.

Chapter Twenty-Six

Apacheland

Moving further into the desert, Geronimo/George found a cluster of rock that provided shade from the late morning sun. Seating himself, he took the datura root and scraped away the sand that still clung to it.

George watched through the medicine man's eyes—his own eyes—and understood. Still, he had never in this life taken any of the drugs that grew wild in the desert. He wanted to know what to expect. In the back of his mind was concern that his other self might do injury to the body they shared. "What will you do, my brother," he asked.

"It is nothing," replied Geronimo quietly. "The root will upset the stomach but soon reach the mind and open it."

"Why do this?"

"Because part of what we must do lies beyond the sight of the real world and in the spirit realm. We must open the door between the two and see what may be seen."

"Is there danger for us?"

"From datura?" The medicine man laughed. "Not as we shall use it. No danger, my brother. The root is highly toxic if taken in too great a dose, but it is given to us by the gods."

"I will wait and watch," said George.

Geronimo used their knife to cut into the root and took a small portion. Biting into it, he chewed and swallowed the juice. It was not a pleasant taste. He took another bite, chewed furiously and swallowed what he could of the pulp. Within moments his stomach rebelled. Leaning to the side, he spat into the sand. When he inhaled again, he felt the rush as the drug spread through his body.

George recognized it as a cleansing thing, necessary somehow to speed the drug into his system. When the rush came, he felt the barriers fall. It was a new experience to the George consciousness. In his long term memory, he knew his warrior persona had taken datura and other drugs in the past, but this awakening signalled the beginning of a journey.

They closed their eyes and could at last see with inner sight. Their minds now permitted them separate forms—a wondrous thing.

Geronimo saw himself seated across from George, both cross-legged, both relaxed and at peace. Between them lay a sand painting of great beauty, depicting all levels of the world. The underworld loomed dark, and a maze of lighter lines twisted through it, like veins or arteries within the earth. The middle world glowed sand colored with spots of green and yellow, and animals with large eyes peered stylistically out from the background.

Warriors from all the tribes were also present. The upper world shone pale blue and birds sang, notes of gold stretching from their beaks. The spirit world crowned the circle. The gods looked down from the upper edge—gods of all the tribes.

George could not disguise his feeling of awe. "What is this that we see, my brother?"

"It is the world," said Geronimo. "The under, middle, upper and spirit worlds are here presented to our sight."

"It is very beautiful," said George.

"The world is beautiful," agreed Geronimo, "but I think there is more for us to see."

Even as he spoke, the sand painting began to change. Starting in the portion of the circle that represented the under world, a dark spiraling blackness began to appear. It rose from the earth under the painting, a dark stain like black oil or tar. The spiral rose slowly from the base of the circle, gradually opaquing the web of lines. "It came from the underworld," said the medicine man, pointing at the spreading blackness. "See how it rose from the depths."

George could see the darkness consuming everything around it. He felt a chill starting at the base of his spine and climbing slowly even as the spiral rose through the painting. "What is it? Is it the whirlwind?"

Geronimo nodded. "It nearly destroyed all the people long ago. Some say it was sent by the great spirit to end the world because the tribes had fallen away from what is good."

"Could this be so?" George believed the world perfect, that all things exist as they are meant to be. He found it difficult to conceive of a god that would destroy the world.

"No one knows, my brother," replied Geronimo. "Perhaps we will find the answer by the time this journey is through." He pointed again at the painting. "Look, it continues to grow."

Indeed, the dark stain continued to rise and obliterate the rest of the painting. Now it had moved into the middle world, staining the light sand, erasing and engulfing the animal shapes.

As they watched, George noticed other movement within the painting. "Look," he said, "the tribes are moving together."

Geronimo studied the changing sands. "Here!" He pointed at one of the figures. "This is the Apache. See!" He indicated another. "The Navajo is coming to us."

As they watched, the whirling darkness that represented the demon began to move erratically into the middle world. First, it moved a tendril in a straight line upward, stopping and then appearing to grow, expanding into a thicker cone. Then it moved to the right on a zig-zag course and stopped again, once again growing larger. Suddenly it doubled back and began moving toward the figures that represented the tribes. It seemed to move most directly toward the Navajo, adjusting its direction as that figure moved toward the Apache.

The vision faded. Geronimo/George opened his eyes and found himself still in the desert. The sun sat high in the sky and shone unmercifully, the sand around him radiating an oven-like heat. He rose. "We must move on, George Buck," he said aloud. "We have an appointment to keep."

Within their mind, George agreed.

Chapter Twenty-Seven

Phoenix

Pasqual Quatero carried his bag out of Sky Harbor Airport in Phoenix. The facility remained under construction so there were numerous traffic barriers, reroutings and twists of the road. He caught a cab and told the driver to take him to the Salt River Indian Reservation. He knew the Maricopa medicine man there, the one called Wonto. He needed to talk with that one. Filled with curiosity about how the demon had gotten loose and thinking so hard about it, he did not realize that the cab driver took him by a scenic route.

He chuckled to himself as he recalled his conversation with Beth. The little girl had done more in the short flight to ease his mind about the white man than all his previous years experience of them put together. In essence, she had shown him that children are the same no matter where they come from. It had been a heart-warming experience for the old man, one he had needed.

Weariness dragged at him. Though he still felt physically strong, he realized his time might by almost done. This task might well mark the end of his life on earth. Strangely, this filled him not with fear, but with peace.

This city called Phoenix seemed a strange and wonderful place to the old Zuni priest. He had not done much traveling despite his years. His one previous trip by airplane had been to Washington, D.C. where his people had signed the papers that finally granted them autonomy. He remembered visiting the white man's capitol city with awe, but, of the sights they had seen, the Lincoln Memorial had impressed him most of all.

He remembered standing inside and looking up at the huge statue of the great American leader and being moved by the beauty of the place. The words inscribed on the marble walls had been translated for him and he remembered, in particular, the single phrase, "Here in the hearts of the American people for whom he saved the union the memory of Abraham Lincoln is enshrined forever." Those words, the almost rose glow of the night lights and the kindly visage of the martyred president had combined to show Pasqual white men were also capable of glory and honor.

Now, the tall buildings along Phoenix's Central Avenue stood high above the streets, towering over the wide modern thoroughfare. There were many automobiles. The air smelled of their exhaust fumes and the day shattered with the noise of their passing. Radios blared as some went by, causing the old man to stare in wonder as strange base rhythms and harsh shrilling music assaulted his senses. What a mass of contradictions these people were—so dynamic and energetic yet so unaware of the truly important things in the world.

While the gathering was necessary in order to save his own people, it would also preserve this brash and incomprehensible society around him. Today he felt better about that than he ever had before.

Upon arrival at the reservation, he asked for directions to Wonto's home. Ten minutes later he knocked on the door and a subdued Estelle greeted him. She explained that Wonto had left two hours earlier with Tom Bear, the Pima.

"They acted very strange, Pasqual," she said. "Kade spoke in a voice not his own. It frightened me."

"Don't be afraid," said the Zuni in a comforting tone. "That is why I come here also. We gonna take care of it."

"What is this thing that has been loosed?" Estelle remembered the conversation between the Pima and her husband.

"Somethin' old," replied Pasqual. "I gotta go find them guys. Can you tell me how?"

Estelle knew better than to persist in questioning the priest, but she worried about Kade and didn't know what to do. "Why don't you wait a minute while I close up the house and I'll drive you over there."

The old man began to nod, then suddenly grimaced and clutched his left arm with his right.

Estelle saw his face go ashen and barely had time to keep him from toppling over. Fortunately, a lawn chair stood only a few feet away and she helped him into it. "What is it, Pasqual? What's the matter?" she cried.

The old man breathed deeply and felt the tension lessen. He looked up at the woman and composed himself. He found it difficult to speak. "I gotta little heart trouble," he said. "I'll be okay in a minute. You go get your keys and I'll wait out here."

"Are you sure you're okay?" The woman felt relief at his apparent recovery but still worried about his health.

"I'm all right, Estelle, but I gotta hurry. I need to get with Kade and the other fella quick."

"I'll only be a minute." She rushed into the house. Pasqual could hear her yelling to the older children, telling them to watch over the younger ones, and she soon came out the door with a ring of keys in her hand.

"Okay," she said. "I'm ready. Are you up to walking to the car?"

"Yeah," said the old man, pushing himself up out of the chair. "I think I can make it." He had to lean on her for a moment as a wave of dizziness passed over him, but then he straightened and smiled down into her face. "I'm really okay. Let's go."

Estelle led him to the car and helped him into it. She drove a late model sedan and the Zuni sank into the seat, leaning back with his head against the rest. She kept an eye on the old man through the windshield and slipped behind the wheel. "It isn't real far," she said as she started the car and got it in gear. "It shouldn't take but about fifteen minutes or so. We'll have to go around to the road that leads to the Bear's place."

Pasqual smiled reassuringly. "I think I gotta rest a little, Estelle," he said. "If I sleep, it isn't cause I wanta ignore you."

"Oh no," she protested. "I know that. You just rest if you need to."

The old man closed his eyes with a sigh and became silent.

All the way over, Estelle kept one eye on the twisting road and the other on her passenger, watching to see that he continued to breathe. She struggled with worry, but knew that Kade would take charge once she got the Zuni to Tom Bear's.

At last she pulled up in front of the Pima's home and reached over to awaken Pasqual. He did not stir. She watched carefully and experienced relief when she saw his chest expand and contract. He lived, but something must be wrong. She shook him and he would not come to. Estelle leaned over and opened his left eye. The pupil had fully dilated and did not contract. She thought for a moment and decided to go to the house and get Kade.

Suddenly, with no warning at all, the old man's left hand snapped out and grabbed her. His body fairly leapt into an upright position and his eyes opened wide. Staring not at her but somewhere into the distance, he spoke in the same voice as had Kade Wonto only hours earlier.

"Tell your husband to get out of this, woman, or he will surely die." Then the old man collapsed again, his grip loosened and he fell once again unconscious.

Estelle threw open the door and ran from the car to the house screaming.

Chapter Twenty-Eight

Chaco Canyon

Gordon Smythe followed Archie's instructions to the letter, unaware of the old man's true motive for sending him away. After learning the ceremony, he took the drum and his gear and packed them on his horse. He said goodbye, promising to return in a day or two, and left for his Uncle George's hogan northwest of Chaco.

The trip took two hours and he got there only to learn from his aunt that the old man had gone off on a hunting trip. He left Archie's message with Martha Smythe, and, in the dark, continued on toward Shiprock.

The journey by horse to Shiprock took hours but it was easy riding since he followed the road. When he arrived there, still early in the morning, he stopped first at Archie's suggestion at the tribal police substation, introduced himself and asked if there were any messages. The one from Archie had been short but clear.

Fly,
You have made me proud. I am sorry I fooled you
but there was no time for explanations. The demon
will have been here by the time you read this. Go to
Phoenix. The others are gathering.
Goodbye, Thoughts-Never-Stop.
        Archie
P.S. Just about finished singing.

Gordon kept his reaction under control until he stood back outside, the crumpled message in hand. Then he leaned against the wall and choked back the anger and sorrow that flooded his every thought—anger at the subterfuge employed by the old man to get him to safety, and sorrow at the realization his great-great-grandfather had probably died.

He went immediately across the street to Twoleaf's Bar and—though it was not yet open—awakened the owner, his cousin Bertram Twoleaf. With hardly a word of explanation, Gordon raced behind the bar and turned on the big TV that sat on a shelf where the patrons could watch the sports contests. He changed the channels till he had one of the morning news shows. He saw nothing about Chaco Canyon, but Gordon decided to make a call home. Though Archie did not have a phone, their neighbor did. The call did not go through. What he had heard was, "I'm sorry, but your call cannot be completed at this time. Please hang up and try again. Thank you."

"What's going on, Gordie?" Bert saw the worried look on the boy's face, but didn't understand.

"Archie sent a message. I think he's dead."

"What?"

Gordon fumbled in his pockets and came up with the paper, then thrust it at Bert.

His cousin read through it carefully, twice. "We can check on this," he said moving to the phone. Pulling a small notebook out of his back pocket, he flipped through a few pages and came to a list of phone numbers. "These are all the families that have phone service in Chaco," he said. "I'll get someone." But, though he dialed every number on the list, he did not get through. Finally, he called the operator. "I'm trying to call some relatives in Chaco Canyon," he said into the phone, "but all I get is a recording."

"That's right, sir," the operator replied. "I'm afraid the main lines must be down. We haven't been able to get through to the canyon since early this morning."

After hanging up, Bert turned to Gordon. "What the hell does he mean by a demon, Gordie?"

Gordon shook his head. "I haven't time to explain, Bert. I have to get over to Arizona as quick as I can."

"You remember my brother, Charlie?" Bert shifted thinking gears quickly—all the Twoleafs did.

"Yeah," said Gordon, "the Vietnam vet who wants to be a doctor. What about him?"

"He's working on a medical chopper based right here in Shiprock. I'll bet we could get him to dump you off at Windowrock."

Gordon considered it and then nodded. "That'd be great, Bert. It would save me some time. Can I leave Rosie with you?"

"Your horse? Sure. She's no bother. The kids love her."

"Great. Can we call Charlie now?"

They did and Charlie answered. When he heard the explanation, he said to hurry out to the pad since he was scheduled to make a run over to Windowrock within the hour to deliver medical supplies.

Only ninety minutes later, Gordon walked away from the chopper and stood in Arizona. He didn't stay in Windowrock but caught an immediate ride south to Springerville. There, despite his haste, he knew he had to stop and rest. He checked into a motel and slept for several hours.

Chapter Twenty-Nine

Phoenix

Matt Sharp logged into Zephyr at 5:00 a.m. and turned on the news channel in the background.

Everyone still talked and speculated about the destruction of Agate Junction just the afternoon before. Matt had been the only one to spot the pac-man sized blue spot on the radar. When he first reported it, the guys over at National had laughed him off the air. Later, when the DPS reports came through, they had sung a different tune. Matt got interviewed on the evening news nationally and even got to talk on the air with Willard Scott. Suddenly, he was the hottest thing in weather.

Coordinating satellite photos, surface reports and weather forecast maps took considerable time. Nothing on any of them had shown a trace of activity in the Agate Junction area.

Weather radar is designed to reflect off rain droplets, not dust. The result is that a dry storm would have to be huge and thick in order to register at all—it would have to literally block out the sky.

The two brief instances where Matt's equipment had shown activity might have been just a glitch in the system—and even he and Diedre had thought so—until the town had been, in fact, destroyed.

The weather spotter's car had been found wrecked inside Agate Junction, but no trace of Roger Milton turned up. No one knew for certain what had happened except for the eye witness accounts of the two children who survived—and, for many, their claims stretched beyond plausibility.

No one else had spoken to Milton after he reported the storm to Matt. Only Diedre had been present when the spotter called and she had missed the first report. Fortunately, she did hear the storm howling in the background when Matt called back, but it wasn't much as far as proof goes.

Worse, Matt usually recorded everything for later review, but Sunday had been a day off and he had not turned on the machine. He had been distracted by his lovely colleague—not that he had any regrets on that score.

Matt had already taped a second interview with Willard Scott for the morning show and his weathercast, done as a remote while standing amidst the ruins of Agate, had been carried nationally the night before.

No one would be able to say Matt Sharp failed to take advantage of his breaks. Though it was truly a case of being in the right place at the right time, he knew enough to seize an opportunity and run with it. All his professional life had been leading up to a situation like this. He was ready.

The station had been bombarded by calls from all over the nation. Not only was Matt a good-looking professional, but his arguments in favor of the freak storm theory were persuasive. The fact that almost every other weather professional in the country said he had to be wrong only added spice to the situation. His broadcast at noon and six today would be carried through the network to nearly all its affiliates. Matt had started on his way to becoming a national personality.

Diedre thought it wonderful and enjoyed hanging in the background. He knew she wanted the exposure as well, but he didn't mind sharing the spotlight. As long as he stayed generous there was no reason to think she would not be generous in kind. That idea brought a smile to his face. When Diedre expressed her generosity, the experience became memorable.

At this point in his ruminations, the first story about Chaco Canyon was broadcast on the news channel. Coming one day after Agate Junction, it got a huge amount of coverage. Matt stopped everything to watch the initial reports. Speculation held to the theory there must have been an earthquake, but when the photographs began to appear on the screen, he leapt out of his seat like a shot and rushed to the phone.

Pictures of rectangular concrete slabs swept clean and small mounds of rubble that had been stone hogans were identical in nature to what he had seen in Agate Junction on the remote. It couldn't be coincidence.

He returned to the partially completed plot Diedre had begun. Whatever it was had been heading north until it stopped over the little town. Where had it gone then?

He pulled out an area map and traced a direct line to Chaco from Agate with his finger. The line passed through several major urban centers. It seemed highly unlikely that a storm—especially a storm even he called a freak, a once-in-a-lifetime oddity—could get from one state to another without touching down and leaving a trail between. But, Jesus, the pictures!

Meanwhile, he dialed National for an update. They stoically reported no storm activity in or around Chaco Canyon. Matt slammed the phone in someone's ear.

Then Diedre arrived on her way to the radio station. She had spent the evening at home last night, but still needed to use Matt's equipment.

"Hi handsome," she said in greeting. "How's it hangin'?"

"Low and to the right," he replied without humor, "but I swear I'm going to break someone's bones if they don't quit trying to tie it in knots."

"What's the matter?" She crossed to him and embraced him, careful to pat his ass when she got her hands behind his back. It was a kind of payback after all the times and all the jobs where the men she worked for patted hers. She had sworn such familiarities would be initiated by her or not happen at all. The fact that Matt seemed to like it took away none of her pleasure at having the choice. Besides, she felt sexy today.

"Damned National Weather Service refuses to acknowledge we have a killer storm out here. Did you hear about Chaco Canyon?"

Diedre looked at the screen and answered absently, "Just heard it on the news on the way over. Sounds awful. They think it might have been an earthquake or something."

"Guess again, darlin'."

Diedre suddenly caught on, turning quickly and putting her hand to her mouth. "Oh my God! Are you saying it was like Agate Junction?"

"Turn on the tube and look at the pictures. It's exactly the same. I tell you there is something strange going on."

"Has anyone else realized it yet?"

"No, but I'm networked tonight and I'm going to break it wide open." Matt looked excited and determined.

Diedre could not contain her excitement. "Can I come to the studio tonight and watch the show? Please?"

Matt held out his arms and she rushed into them. "You bet, honey." He smiled happily as she nestled within his embrace. "Old Matt is going to kick'em all in the teeth tonight."

She returned his hug, making sure he felt every curve, breathing hotly in his ear. "And afterwards, I'll see we have a night you won't forget."

"Ummmmm . . . " he sighed into her ear. "It's early yet. I don't have to be at the studio for the morning show until ten. How about you?"

"Mmmmmmm . . . " she responded moving her hips forward seductively, "the same for me."

"Maybe we could take a few minutes now . . . ?"

She laughed with pleasure. "I was thinking the same thing. We can take almost an hour if you promise not to mess up my hair."

He felt himself responding and she did too.

Her hand dropped down between them. "My, my," she said in a husky whisper, "what have we here?"

He chuckled, happy and eager. "Why don't we head upstairs and find out."

She put her tongue in his ear and and breathed, "What's wrong with the floor in here?"

Matt pulled away enough to look into her eyes. She met his gaze levelly and without shyness, a challenging, promising stare.

Without further words, they started hastily removing their clothing.

Chapter Thirty

Phoenix

Detective Greg Johnson admitted to being an unhappy man. Nothing in the Hunnicutt case made any sense. Jack Foreman, the reputable ASU professor, had started acting like some sort of mystic, talking of demons and Indian magic. The physical evidence was impossible. Those two pickup trucks had been neatly sandblasted out of their paint and the tires on both were scored as if they'd been sandpapered with a particularly coarse abrasive. The police lab had confirmed that the ring belonged to the missing student and the tissue samples matched medical records. The white powder had been confirmed as definitely bone, but bone so dehydrated that it might have been in the desert for a hundred years. All this had happened on a day that had been otherwise clear and nearly cloudless only a few miles from the main artery that was I-17.

Add to that the utter destruction of the town of Agate Junction, the testimony of two minor witnesses—who happened to be the only survivors out of a hundred and four inhabitants—who swore that a killer storm had swept through the town. Then throw in the mutilated body of Grandon Mauldin that could not be satisfactorily explained by a flash fire, the same powdered bone found all over Agate, and now—beyond belief—the Navajo settlement at Chaco Canyon had been destroyed, levelled in such a similar way that it banished any possibility of calling it coincidence.

To top it all, the normally dependable weatherman who regularly consulted with the police had just called to tell Johnson he believed the same freak killer storm had been responsible for all three events, two on Saturday and one on Monday—the most recent all the way on the northwest side of New Mexico. "Is everybody going nuts?" he asked aloud.

The Tempe Police would not usually have been involved in the Phoenix case, but, since it concerned an ASU student, Johnson had been assigned to the Phoenix PD. When the Agate Junction incident occurred, that assignment had been extended to include DPS. In the wake of the Chaco Canyon incident, he had now been ordered to work with a Navajo policeman named Twohats—Twohats for God's Sake! —Redfield, and he found himself on his way to the airport to catch a flight to New Mexico to meet with the Indian cop.

He pulled into the elevated Parking area in Terminal Three at Sky Harbor and had to drive all the way up to the roof before he could find a parking space.

He carried a single garment bag. Unless something even more disastrous happened, he would only stay a day or two. His shaving kit, changes of underwear and socks were in the bottom pocket and his clean suit hung inside.

By the time he made his seat selection and cleared the weapons checkpoint, the plane had begun its final boarding stage and he had to run all the way to Gate 41—the farthest Southwest Airlines gate from the entrance. When he got there, sweaty and out of breath, he found they had just buttoned up the craft and he had to argue with the boarding supervisor before they would reopen the door and let him get on.

When he finally got to his seat—after walking past over a hundred passengers who glared at him for his delay of their flight—he told the attendant to bring him three double bourbons as soon as the seat belt light went out.

For a seatmate, he had an eighty-two year old Italian woman, who apparently spoke little English, with an aged chihuahua dog in a travel case strapped into the seat in the middle. As they taxied down the approach preparatory to take-off, the dog let loose with a loud liquid fart that stank like an open sewer. Adding insult to injury, it stuck its rat-like snout through the barred end of the cage and locked its teeth on his sleeve, growling.

The old lady leaned toward the detective and said very carefully, "Pleesa meester, don'ta teasa my doag. She'sa very olt and she gotta bad keednies."

Pulling his sleeve free, Greg heard the material rip and watched the cuff button pop off and disappear under the seats. He turned his head to the window and tried not to weep. Behind him, the dog waited until acceleration for take-off had them pressed back in their seats, then squatted and filled the bottom of the cage with dark yellow urine.

Greg closed his eyes and remembered the fantasy writer, J. R. R. Tolkien. The author of *The Hobbit* had coined a word—who knows whether original or not—the word "scroaned." The writer defined it as "a cross between a scream and a groan, delivered with great feeling."

Turning away, trying to banish the smell from his senses, the detective lay his head against the cool window and tried to sleep. He had nearly made it when the flight attendant tapped him on the shoulder and informed him that they were out of bourbon. By this time, he didn't really care. He slept.

His next recollection was of the same flight attendant leaning across, asking him to please raise his seat to the upright position in preparation for landing in Albuquerque.

When he deplaned, he discovered that Sergeant Ed Twohats Redfield had come to meet him.

The Navajo policeman stood tall—nearly six-foot-three—and had a wide toothy smile. "You must be Johnson," he said extending his hand.

"That would make you Redfield?" He took the offered hand and tried not to show he had an attitude, but the Indian laughed aloud and pumped his hand.

"My friends call me Twohats. Hell of a handle, isn't it? My first name is Ed. As a kid, I went to white schools and got a teacher who worshipped Sherlock Holmes. I went out and bought one of those two-brimmed hats and the name sort of came with it."

"Sherlock Holmes?" Greg kept his voice neutral.

"Why do you think I became a detective?" The Navajo's eyes twinkled and a smile played on his lips.

It would have been hard not to like Redfield. The Sergeant loomed over him like a bear, but had a ready wit and catching sense of humor. In Greg's short career he had encountered few Indians under pleasant circumstances. Unfortunately, those he had occasion to deal with in Tempe were mostly drunk and disorderlies who brawled and ended up in the tank.

"Been up here before?"

"Not really," said Johnson. "I'm not even sure why they sent me."

The Navajo looked apologetic. "My fault, I'm afraid. I saw the coverage on Agate Junction—it did, after all, go national. What you had down there is exactly what we had up here except you only lost a hundred and some. We lost over two thousand."

Greg shook his head. "I heard the reports and saw the pictures, but I just can't believe they could be related."

"Do us both a favor," said Twohats seriously, "try to suspend that disbelief for the next few hours. This one has more kinks than a carnival drag show."

They retrieved Twohats' jeep from the lot outside and headed northwest toward Chaco. The Navajo drove and Greg sat back in his seat breathing a sigh of relief, glad that the ordeal of flying was over.

The trip to Chaco took two and a half hours, and the temperature stayed cooler than in Phoenix for most of it. The open jeep and the rush of air kept the heat away, though the Phoenician wished he had brought a hat.

The country became rocky and, as they drew nearer their destination, they began to pass small holdings and homesteads, clusters of hogans, a few roadside stands and commercial enterprises. However, they saw no one. There were not even any cattle.

"Where is everybody?" Greg asked.

"Those that haven't already left are hiding," said Twohats quietly. "They're afraid it may come again."

"What? The earthquake?"

The Indian cop looked surprised. "Didn't have any earthquake here," he said. "We got tons of equipment in this state for sensing that sort of thing because of all the federal installations, military and scientific. They didn't see so much as a flicker of a needle. The guys with the seismic stuff say it couldn't have been a shake."

"Then what was it?"

The Navajo didn't answer. His eyes had gone hooded and he stared straight ahead.

"Hey, Ed, did you hear me?"

Twohats looked uncomfortable. "Message at Shiprock from the old medicine man who lived up here mentioned a demon."

"Oh Christ!" Johnson leaned back and put both hands over his eyes. "Not you guys too!"

He would have said more, but the jeep turned off the paving and up a slightly inclined dirt road and came to a halt on a promontory where Greg could look down on Chaco Canyon. When he saw what lay below, he shut up.

From where they stopped across to the surrounding mountains stretched a tortured field of rubble. Nothing that looked like a human habitation or even resembled any intentional work of man remained.

Johnson could find no words. He tried to reconcile the sight with pictures he had seen of Chaco Canyon—pictures recently taken that showed a well-organized Native American settlement. He couldn't do it. The destruction overwhelmed imagination.

Twohats turned to face him. "The message we got from Archie Smythe, the medicine man I told you about, was for his great-great-grandson, Gordon, whom he had sent to Shiprock on an errand. It instructed the boy to go to Phoenix where others would contact him. It said the demon had come to Chaco."

"Where can we find this Gordon?"

The Navajo shook his head. "We don't know. The boy picked up the message early this morning, and, apparently, left before we got any reports about this . . . ," he gestured at the scene before them, completely lost for words.

"Did you check the airport in Albuquerque?" Johnson had begun to get his mind working.

"Yeah, the Lieutenant called this morning and I checked it personally before I met your plane. No Gordon Smythe flew out of Albuquerque today."

"Do you have people checking the busses and trains?"

Twohats nodded. "We have it covered like a blanket, but we aren't gonna find him here. I'd bet anything on that."

"What makes you so sure?"

"Found his horse hitched up nice as you please at a relative's home about four hours ago. Remember that there are a lot of ways to be related in our tribe. The relative wouldn't tell me anything, but the boy wasn't there. The problem is that we don't have any idea what he looks like yet."

"Highway Patrol?"

"We called 'em," said the Navajo, "but without a description of either the boy or a vehicle, they won't be a lot of help."

"What now?"

"After you've looked around here and satisfied yourself that this isn't the work of a freak storm or an earthquake, you and me are going to Shiprock. Maybe we can trace the kid from there."

For the next three hours, Twohats and Greg made their way on foot into Chaco Canyon. Rescue workers and investigators worked in small clumps as they sifted through the debris. No one spoke. A frustrating sense of futility reigned. No one had found anything to get excited about.

Earlier that morning, when the digging first began, the workers had unearthed several pockets of powdered bone. Since that particular aspect of the Agate Junction incident had not been publicized, it took a while for them to figure out what they had found—and even longer for their superiors to make the connection between both events. There had been considerable excitement then, but now, after finding over a thousand of the pulverized skeletons, the only response from the teams was a deep oppressive silence.

Standing alone together, away from the busy workers, the two law officers spoke in quiet tones.

"Were you in Agate Junction after it happened there?" The Navajo looked washed out.

"Yeah," said Greg with a shrug, "but not until yesterday when the first teams had already been through it."

"Well?" Ed Twohats waited.

The Tempe detective didn't answer at once. Instead, he squatted down on the rubble and shifted a flat rock. In the lee of a boulder which partially protected the space behind it, lay a tiny human skeleton—a child-sized chalky outline in the sand. He sucked air through his teeth. At last Johnson replied, though he did not rise or turn. "Yeah. Exactly like this."

Ed sighed with relief. "I thought for a minute you were going to deny it. I put my job on the line getting you sent up here. I need for you to say that again later in front of the Lieutenant."

Greg nodded. "I will."

The little form in the sand could not have been older than two or three. Both cops sat silent for a long time before Greg rose and turned, stalking back toward where they left the jeep.

They had begun the drive to Shiprock when Twohats checked in with his dispatcher by radio. He was told to stand by and then a gruff, very business-like voice came through the static.

"You there Twohats?"

Ed darted a look at his companion and rolled his eyes. "My boss," he whispered. Then he spoke into the mike. "I'm here, Lieutenant. What's up?"

The voice sounded impatient. "We found out what happened to your Smythe kid."

"What?"

"He hitched a ride in one of the medical choppers from here to Windowrock." After a moment of silence, the voice continued. "It seems the medic on the flight is a cousin of his."

Ed released the transmit button and turned to Johnson, raising his eyebrows. "What do you want to do?"

Greg didn't even pause. "To Phoenix—quickly as possible."

The Navajo nodded. Then he pushed the com button again. "Okay, Lieutenant. I'm going to accompany Detective Johnson back to Phoenix and see if we can't find the kid before he disappears completely."

"No more than three days, Twohats," warned the voice, "or I'll come down there after you."

"Yes sir," replied Ed. "I won't be longer, sir."

"See that you aren't." They could hear the button click off at the other end, then click back on again right away. "Uh . . . good luck, Ed."

"Thanks Dad," said the Navajo and signed off.

"The Lieutenant is your father?" Greg smiled in surprise.

"Yep," said Ed. "Ain't it a bitch? It's Navajo nepotism at its best."

Tuesday, July 11th

Chapter Thirty-One

Phoenix

Jack Foreman picked Juan Mapoli up at Carlo's home and drove to the Salt River Indian Reservation in Scottsdale. Juan did not know exactly where they were supposed to go, but they stopped first at the Information Center.

Juan asked the clerk, a young woman named Mary, if they could get directions to the home of a Pima medicine man and was disappointed to learn that there weren't any still practicing. "Last one died a few years back," said the clerk. "We're modern people now. None of the younger men went into it."

"How about the Maricopa?"

"They've got one. I think his name is Wonto or something like that."

Jack asked, "How do we find him?"

"He lives on the Maricopa part of the reservation. Go east about eleven miles. I suppose you can ask someone then."

"Thank you, Mary," said Jack. "You've been very helpful. We appreciate it."

"Nada," said the girl.

The two men got back in the rover and drove to the east. Jack wanted badly to ask questions, but the old Yaqui stayed uncommunicative and preoccupied.

This part of the reservation was flat, stretching miles to the east and dotted by small square looking houses. The roads seemed made of potholes studying to be canyons. As they bounced along, the archaeologist contrasted busy Scottsdale, just a mile or two behind them, with this open desert solitude. Despite the obvious poverty of the people who lived here, the comparison did not flatter the more successful white men. The crowded shops, restaurants and streets of the city spoke of a hurried, perhaps desperate, civilization. The reservation remained an island of sanity.

The block and wood-frame houses were well-spaced and their squat one-level simplicity detracted little from the expanse of sand and bristling cactus. In the distance, water towers stood like giant mushrooms, disturbing the harmony of nature but giving to the people the wherewithal to plant gardens. It seemed like a fair trade.

Like dinosaur skeletons, the carcasses of old cars and trucks sat baking in the sun. Nearly every house had one or two. The hulks seemed out of place, intruders in a world never meant to see them. Even here, the white man's influence had reached in and left imperfection.

They asked directions of a man seated on an old wooden chair in front of his house. He sent them south and further east. Soon the homes began to show more affluence.

Another stop for directions from a young boy brought an offer of help in exchange for a ride. They gave it gladly. Finally, the two men found themselves in front of a very clean and modern looking house made of brick. The name on the mailbox read Wonto.

Juan got out and knocked at the door. Jack didn't see who answered it. The Yaqui returned shaking his head.

"What's up?" asked the archaeologist.

"We must go North. Kade Wonto is at the house of a Pima named Tom Bear."

"Who is he?" Jack already wondered about the wisdom of this mission, but he started the rover and headed back.

"A witch," replied the old man. "He will be one of those that represents the Pima at the gathering."

The professor shook his head. "I still don't understand what this is all about, Juan. I don't want to be impolite, but I have a lot of questions."

"Be patient a little longer, my friend," said the sabio. "You will learn what you need to know this day."

Forty minutes later, they pulled up in front of Tom Bear's home. Together, they walked to the door and knocked. A young Indian answered the door, saying Tom was not at home. He and Wonto had both gone to the hospital with a Zuni priest. When Juan explained he was a Yaqui sabio, the younger man apologized, introduced himself as Danny Webb, a Pima, and invited them inside. They exchanged introductions.

"Are you involved in this, young man?" asked Jack.

Danny nodded. "Tom Bear has been teaching me," he said. "My grandfather was medicine man here for many years."

The old Yaqui smiled. "But why did you not learn from him?"

"He tried but my father did not hold with superstition and would not let me learn."

"I understand," murmured Juan.

The archaeologist and the Yaqui were seated on folding chairs around the dinette table. Danny served them cold water and looked in vain for some kind of food. It was impolite not to offer it, but Tom did not keep a well-stocked refrigerator or storeroom. Both Jack and Juan assured the young man they were not hungry and urged him to sit with them. He finally did.

"Tell us of this Zuni," said the sabio. "Who is he and how did he learn of this?"

"I never got to meet him," said Danny. "He got sick on his way here and Kade Wonto's wife brought him. They never took him out of the car. It looked pretty bad to me. The old man was gray."

"How long ago did they leave?" Jack felt growing concern. He had taken the day off only to spend it chauffeuring the Yaqui around. Now he was sitting in an uncomfortable house on the Pima reservation waiting for still more strange Indians and seemed no closer to knowing what was going on. In the light of day, the notion of a demon that threatened the lives of thousands seemed ludicrous.

"A couple of hours," replied Danny politely. He, too, felt discomfort. Who was this white man and why had Mapoli brought him along?

The sabio spoke to both of them. "Relax. Be patient. When the others arrive, all questions will be answered."

The three men sat in awkward silence for another forty-five minutes before they heard a car pull up out front. Danny leapt out of his seat and crossed to the window in a moment.

"It's Tom and the others," he said. "And the old man is still with them."

Juan looked relieved at that. "Good," he said to himself. "We need the Zuni."

In a few minutes, all of them were gathered in the front room. In deference to their ailing colleague, they perched on metal folding chairs, old bar stools, and Danny sat on the floor. Pasqual lay on the sofa with Tom Bear seated beside him.

Jack looked around from face to face. A strong resemblence shone in all of them. Oh, they didn't look physically alike. The Zuni appeared almost regal as he sat propped up on pillows to Jack's right. Tom looked intense, but had already taken charge. Kade Wonto, the Maricopa medicine man waited with dignified grace. The woman, Lotus Farley, of the Tohono O'odham, was both beautiful and distracting. Juan Mapoli looked scruffy and disreputable, but his eyes danced with pleasure as he sat among his peers. Danny personified the eagerness of youth. Yet each of them possessed the same look of confidence and serenity. There appeared to be no confusion, no worry, no fear. Each seemed poised, prepared to do whatever became necessary.

Juan spoke first. "I am Juan Mapoli of the Yaqui. I have been to the north and seen the demon. I have come to represent my people in a great gathering."

Tom was next. "I am Tom Bear of the Pima. I am not a medicine man, but a witch. The boy, Danny Webb, is the grandson of a great medicine man and he will represent the Pima."

The Maricopa spoke. "I am Kade Wonto of the Maricopa. I have come because my friend Tom Bear asked it. I am ready to represent my people."

Pasqual looked out at the others, smiling despite his exhaustion. "I am Pasqual Quatero of the Zuni. I have answered the summons."

Lotus looked at the others from under perfectly formed dark brows, her hair a lustrous tent of softness. "I am Lotus Farley of the Tohono O'odham. I have come for my people."

All eyes turned to Jack. He felt a moment of panic, but quickly brought it under control. When he spoke, he shrugged helplessly. "I am Jack Foreman, an archaeologist and professor at ASU. I fear I am partly responsible for our being here. A student of mine came to me with a story of an artifact in the desert. I accompanied him to a place not far west of here and found a rock covered with carvings. We thought it might be the marker for a well or cistern and tried to move it aside. We managed only inches before it jammed but . . . ," he hesitated, "I guess it was enough."

"Did you see the demon?" Danny asked the question.

"If the demon is a sandstorm or huge whirlwind, then I guess we did," said Jack, "but we didn't know it at the time."

"What of the other?" asked Wonto.

"He disappeared," replied the professor, "but I have recently concluded that he was killed."

Tom looked at the others. "We have begun," he said, "but there are several still missing. I have looked at the stone. We await the Navajo, the Hopi, the Pai and the Apache. The Ute were the only tribe not involved when the demon was first chained."

"Would someone please tell me I'm not crazy," pleaded the archaeologist. "Are we really all sitting here because I set something loose in the desert—some sort of creature?"

"You did not know, digger," said Juan, placing a comforting hand on the professor's shoulder.

Danny spoke. "This is the time when I return to my heritage. The Pima have been without a medicine man for too long."

Tom said, "And it's about time."

Lotus grew impatient with the others. "Would you all shut up and stop mouthing off about how dedicated you are? This thing in the desert has apparently been loose now for only a few days and it has already killed over a hundred people in the north. We'd better start deciding who's going to do what!"

"But we don't know yet, sister," said Wonto. He looked over to Tom and the Pima nodded. "The Navajo is the only one who knows the singing. Though we all have parts to play, only he can lead. We must wait until he reaches us."

"What if he doesn't make it?" Pasqual asked the question.

Tom's voice was iron when he spoke, harsh and uncompromising. "If the Navajo does not come, we will have a little time for farewells before the demon does."

"Who is this Navajo?" asked Lotus.

"The oldest and the greatest singer," said Tom. "He is called Archie Smythe."

"Archie Smythe?" Jack was shocked. "The Navajo medicine man who lived in Chaco Canyon?"

Tom and the others turned to the white man and nodded. "Yes," said Tom."That is he."

The archaeologist shook his head. "After I left Juan last night, I watched the news. Didn't you hear? All the networks featured it. Chaco Canyon suffered a disaster yesterday morning. The medicine man, Archie Smythe, was prominent among those who died."

Chapter Thirty-Two

Salt River Reservation

That night, Jack left Juan at Tom Bear's house and returned home because he had classes to teach the next day. All the shamans stayed together from then on. Lotus slept out on the porch, the others inside.

About an hour after the rest had gone to sleep, Danny wandered outside for some fresh air. There had been too much excitement. He couldn't sleep. His mind struggled with the anticipation of finally becoming the medicine man he had always dreamed he would be.

As he sat at the foot of the steps, the image of his father formed in his mind. The face looked stern, hawk-like and the eyes flashed in angry impatience. He could almost hear the voice—the harsh, grating sound of a voice nearly destroyed by too much alcohol and smoking.

"You're wasting your time," it seemed to say. "Didn't I tell you all that superstitious crap was nonsense? I am ashamed of you—ashamed! Wasn't it enough that your grandfather wasted his whole life, pursuing a career for which he received little gratitude and no money?"

Danny looked up at the moon. Superimposed over it he saw the face. He whispered aloud into the night. "Do not speak to me of shame, Father. I watched you stagger back in the early mornings from drinking in the white man's bars, beaten bloody by those who robbed you or by bouncers who found another drunk good exercise or at least acceptable entertainment." His eyes glittered as they filled with tears. "I listened to the taunts of my schoolmates who called you the D.I. —only they didn't mean Drill Instructor like in the marines, but Drunken Indian. I stood up to you when you tried to bully me. I let you hit me and never struck back. But I learned of shame, father. I understood all about shame. There is nothing now that you can teach me about it."

The face faded in the moonlight. The accusing voice fell silent. The spirit fled, perhaps, from truth, but Danny found his face wet. He blinked, passing his sleeve over his eyes to dry them. He had believed himself beyond tears for the past. He wondered how many more lay inside, threatening escape.

Then he became aware that he no longer stood alone on the porch. In the shadows to the left, he felt a presence. For a long moment, he feared turning around. What if it were the spirit of his father? Or the demon? Both Quatero the Zuni and Mapoli the Yaqui had already seen it.

"I had a childhood like yours, Danny," said the cool, rich voice of the medicine woman. "Come here."

Danny still did not turn. He felt embarrassed but not ashamed. He spoke in a low tone. "Forgive me, Lotus Farley. I forgot that you slept there. I did not mean to speak so loudly to the moon."

"Moon, my butt!" said the woman quietly but intensely. "You spoke to your father much as I used to speak to mine. I understand your pain, Danny. Come here and put your head on my shoulder. Speak to me of it. Perhaps I can help."

Danny stood up reluctantly and turned. He could not see her there in the darkness except for light reflected by those beautiful mahogany eyes. She remained silent, watching, and after a while, he moved up the steps toward her.

He stood before her looking down into that incredible face.

She reached out and took his hand, pulling him gently to the couch at her side, then reached with her other hand to turn his head by the chin until he looked into her face.

"I'm a healer, Danny. I can soothe that hurt, cure your restlessness, heal your heart. You have to ask for it, though. I never insist."

He tried not to answer. He held his eyes steady and tried to harden his heart, tried to put his sorrow aside. The next moment, his face was buried in her shoulder and he wept silently but bitterly. In the night, as if it were happening to someone else, he heard her voice soothing, saying "Shuuuuu . . . shuuuuu. Easy. There. There. Shuuuushhh."

How long they sat like that he did not know. Time stopped for a while. The moon shone, the cool night caressed them and he heard the soothing comfort of her voice.

He became aware at last of her body pressed against him. It was a warm, soft, wonderful body. He felt embarrassed all over again when he felt himself responding to her. He started to pull away, but she would not let him go.

She whispered, "It's all right. That can be part of healing."

Danny tried to tell her of his feelings. The only sound he could evoke came out a harsh sob.

Again she comforted him. "Don't try to talk, Danny Webb. Let your body speak. Tell me of pleasure and joy. Take what you need. Give what you can."

She pulled only far enough away to put her hands between them and began unbuttoning his shirt. He looked at her face. He could do that with her eyes downcast, watching the buttons. When she looked up again, her eyes met his and he flinched away. She looked so beautiful.

"Look at me," she said, her voice husky and low. "Don't be afraid."

So Danny watched as she unbuttoned her own blouse and slipped it off her shoulders.

He had never seen such a perfect figure. He wanted to act cool and controlled, but a soft moan escaped his lips and he found his hands moving of their own accord to fondle, caress and cup her breasts.

She responded, her nipples coming rapidly erect. "Love is healing, Danny," she said as her hands moved without timidity to his lap. Her lips curved into a bright smile and she darted a quick, almost shy glance up under dark lashes when she found what she sought.

Again Danny moaned softly under her touch.

"Lotus," he whispered, "what of the others?"

"We'll be quiet about it," she said simply. "Besides, who would object? I am my own woman and free to choose my own path."

She had unsnapped his jeans and urged them down over his hips. He half stood so she could slip them over his buttocks, meanwhile trying to find the catch that kept her denim slacks tight at the waist. As soon as his trousers fell around his ankles, she stood and quickly shucked her remaining clothing, moving into his embrace without hesitation.

Danny kicked his pants aside and turned into her at the same moment. Both of them ran eager exploring hands over each other—hands soon urgently followed by lips and tongues.

It lasted forever, the ecstasy lighting them up from within, and the night gentle around them. Through it all, they kept silent . . . well, near silent—in deference to those who slept within the house—but, for a while at least, they lost track of time and place and dwelt only in the land of touch and feeling.

Afterward, they lay snuggled warmly on the couch, kissing and caressing, and watching what they could see of the night sky. They still did not need to speak.

Eventually, they slept.

Chapter Thirty-Three

Hopiland

Harold Laloma emerged from the Kiva slowly and with great care. The climb had been arduous, negotiating the ladder a task requiring all his concentration. It had taken him all night to get out. He saw that both John Lakona and Joseph Lansa sat nearby, watching. He called to them. "Come here my brothers and help me up. I must have this leg set immediately."

The two other priests came closer and finally saw the injury, the bone still protruding through the skin. They looked at Harold but his face showed no pain. They exchanged glances.

"How can this be?" asked John of Joseph in a whisper.

"What happened?" asked Lansa as the two lifted their friend carefully between them. "I fell," said Harold, "but it is nothing. What matters is that Taknokwunu has spoken again and told me what I must do."

"The spirit talked to you again?" asked Joseph Lansa, obviously impressed.

"Harold, my brother," said John Lakona, "is that leg not painful? How is it that you can be here and talk of the spirits? This is a magic I cannot understand."

"Another has taken the pain."

The two other priests spoke simultaneously. "Who?"

"The demon," said Harold.

"The demon!" Lakona grew wide-eyed. "Tell us of this demon."

"It came to me and spoke of the past," said Harold. "It told me how it ranged across the mesas many years ago. It showed me," he hesitated, struggling for the words, "in a vision. I saw it descend on First Mesa and destroy a village. It told me nothing could stop it. It showed me its power."

"Then why has it taken the pain?" asked Lansa.

"It offered a bargain," said Harold. "It offered to spare the People of Peace and attack the Navajo if I would prevent a gathering of the wise."

"You should do it," said Lakona immediately. "After all, it is your duty to protect our people."

"No," protested Lansa. "That would be wrong. The gods could not smile on such a bargain."

Harold smiled. He looked at Joseph with real affection. "So I have already decided, my brother. But now you must carry me to my house and help repair my leg. I must leave immediately for Phoenix and the confrontation this demon seeks to avoid."

"You should think again about a bargain," said Lakona, his face troubled. "If this demon is all you say, there is nothing to prevent it from sweeping over us and leaving nothing behind."

"The spirit has already spoken of this, John," said Harold, "and my decision has been made. Now, please, my friends, take me where we can set this leg for I have little time and many miles to travel."

The two other priests carried their injured friend to his house and settled him on the bed. Though they would have conferred and even brought in others, Harold prevailed upon them to act at once while the pain remained blocked away.

Lakona and Lansa straightened the leg between them and the bone withdrew from sight. Though it continued to bleed, the ends went together smoothly and they splinted and bound it tightly into place.

Harold watched it all with a peaceful look on his face. The pain remained far away even when he felt the ends grind slightly as they met. He thought with regret that it was too bad he would not be able to learn this trick from the demon. What a healer he would be!

John fed his friend a tea made from powdered morning glory and, in very little time, Harold felt very well indeed. One of the villagers agreed to drive him to Phoenix and, helped by others, they put him in the back seat of an 1960 Ford sedan within a nest of pillows and rolled blankets.

The last thing Joseph put in with him was an old suitcase holding Harold's ceremonial garb and paraphernalia.

"Go with our blessings," said Lansa. "I shall pray to Taknokwunu for your success."

The villager, called William Concha, felt nervous with the priest in his car, but Harold spoke quietly to him and soon the man grew more comfortable in his role as chauffeur.

"Why do you go to Phoenix?" asked Concha.

"I must attend a meeting of priests and medicine men from all the Southwest," he said. "We have a difficult thing to do. There is a danger and we must lock it away before it creates more harm."

"Has it anything to do with the weather?" asked the driver.

"Why do you ask that?" Harold was surprised.

"Because of the storm they say is killing people here and in New Mexico."

"What storm?" But Harold already knew.

"It struck a place on the highway near Phoenix," explained Concha, "a town called Agate Junction. It was completely destroyed two days ago. Only two survivors—children."

"What happened in New Mexico?"

William gained confidence, warming to his subject. "It wiped out Chaco Canyon—killed off over two thousand Navajo."

"Two thousand?" Harold involuntarily recalled the vision. No doubt remained in his mind that the demon could live up to its threat.

"It's been in the news all day," said Concha. "Want to listen?"

"Perhaps that would be a good idea," agreed Harold, partly out of curiosity and partly because it would cut down on the talk with the gregarious William Concha. In very little time, the demon would return in his mind and know his decision.

As the car sped south toward Phoenix, the radio spoke to them of the disaster at Chaco Canyon. No one knew what caused it. It had not been an earthquake. It had not been a storm—or at least it had not shown up on radar. It caused considerable debate. No one, however, knew for certain except perhaps, thought Harold, those who had been called to the gathering.

He hoped most fervently that someone involved knew more than he did.

The priest had almost drifted off to sleep with the radio continuing to chatter in the background, when the demon, discerning his intent, removed the nerve block. Harold could not prevent a cry as the swollen leg began to throb with excruciating pain.

Concha turned around in his seat, shocked at the outburst. He saw the priest writhe in pain, watched the color drain from his face, and then slump over.

Chapter Thirty-Four

Apacheland

Geronimo/George moved across the Fort Apache Reservation, passing from desert to mountain foothills, gradually heading northeast. He skirted Whiteriver by hitching a ride on 77 to Carrizo and then along 60 to the edge of the reservation. Connecting then with 191, he got a final ride all the way to Springerville.

In reconciling the vision of the sand painting with George's memory of modern day road maps, they had decided that Springerville seemed the logical place to meet the Navajo. Once the Apache had arrived, however, he felt uncertain about the next step. Neither consciousness had any idea what the Navajo would look like—in age or appearance. The Sitgreaves and Apache National Forests which bordered the reservation on the north and east left a lot of alternative routes if someone travelled south from Windowrock. Still, Springerville offered a stopping place on the road if the Navajo took the most direct route to Phoenix.

The vision had certainly implied they were destined to meet. Geronimo/George moved as that inner voice seemed to indicate and simply had faith it would work out as intended. He did not feel surprised, therefore, when walking along the street in town, he saw coming toward him a young Navajo with a bag over his shoulder. He raised his hand in greeting. "Ya-deh-hay."

The younger man looked startled for a moment, his eyes darting from side to side as if he would flee. Seeing no obvious danger, however, he gave a tentative nod.

"Ya-deh," he responded. "You're Apache, aren't you?"

"Yes," said Geronimo quietly, "and I seek a Navajo medicine man. He is waited for in Phoenix."

"There was one who understood it all, but he is gone now." The boy looked sad.

"Then it must be you I seek," said the Geronimo part of the dual personality. "I know I am to meet with one who can sing the ceremony of the great gathering."

"I am that one," said Gordon, "though I wish it were not so. My friends call me Fly."

"I have been called . . . uh, Gerry." Geronimo and George had agreed upon this name for the time being. It seemed strange on the old medicine man's tongue, but George had assured him it was common enough.

"I am a yataalii," said the Navajo, "a singer of my people. If you seek the secrets that will banish the demon, I have the songs."

"That is what we seek, Fly," said the Apache. "Forgive me, but I cannot help but observe that you have not many years. How is it that you know the song?"

"I was taught by the greatest singer, my great-great-grandfather."

"And who was this great man?"

Gordon looked uncomfortable. "We do not mention the names of the dead, Gerry."

The Apache looked immediately contrite. He knew the Navajo fear of ghosts. They never mentioned the name of the dead because they believed that, in doing so, they might attract the spirit of the departed, a ghost which often brought danger. "I am sorry, Fly. I should have realized. How far have you come?"

"I left Chaco Canyon yesterday before the sun rose. The one I have not named sent me to Shiprock. I did not know why until it was too late."

"What has happened at Chaco Canyon?" Geronimo/George had heard no news since leaving Cibeque.

"The demon visited yesterday," said the boy in an angry voice. "It took all of them."

"All? How many?"

"The news said over two thousand died. No survivors. I would have been one of them if not for my . . . for the one of which we speak."

"Has this demon struck elsewhere?" asked Geronimo/George.

"It is said that it destroyed a town near Phoenix." Gordon shook his head. "I hope those I am to meet are strong enough to defeat it. I wish to watch it die."

Geronimo/George looked into the distance. What the boy had said could mean only one thing—the demon had pursued Gordon's great-great-grandfather all the way into New Mexico. If that was so, then it must be aware of them and hoped to eliminate them one by one before they could gather. Suddenly, he found himself searching the horizon for signs of wind or dust. "The others have gathered in the city and it is there we must go," he said to Fly. "I would guess the demon is trying to stop us. We must move swiftly, my friend."

"Have you a car?" Gordon looked around for a vehicle.

The Apache shook his head. "No," he said.

"Wait!" The voice went unheard by the Navajo but was clear in the mind of Geronimo. George spoke. *"There are credit cards in my wallet and I know how to drive. We can rent a car and drive directly to the city."*

"I know nothing of this," Geronimo answered furiously. "I could not drive such a machine."

"Then perhaps it is time to let me take control, my brother," said his modern-day self. *"You brought us through the desert and across the reservation. Let me take us to the city."*

"Hey, are you okay?" Gordon had been watching the Apache's face and seen some sort of struggle going on.

Geronimo could see no alternative that would take less time. Simultaneous with his inner agreement, he released his hold on control of their body and George's mind came to the fore.

The transition left both parts of Geronimo/George disoriented and the Navajo saw him stagger and sway like a drunk before he suddenly steadied and . . . changed. The features were the same, but the intelligence behind the eyes was . . . different somehow.

The Apache sighed and stretched. Then he looked at the Navajo and smiled. "Don't worry, Fly. I am all right. It is just that there is more to me than you can see at first. I have a credit card here," he fished his wallet out of his back pocket, "and we can rent a car. We should be in Phoenix tonight."

"What do you mean by more than you can see?" Gordon had backed away, unsure about this stranger.

"I am called Gerry though it is not a name I have used before," said the Apache. "I awakened on July 9th with a guest." He tapped his head. "In here."

Gordon returned a quizzical look.

Geronimo/George felt at a loss to explain. He asked, "What happens when we die?"

"Nothing." The Navajo's answer sounded guarded. "We return to the Holy People . . . unless we become ghosts."

"There are some who believe we live more than once. There are some who remember the past before they were born. I am one of those."

"You're talking about reincarnation?" Gordon shook his head. "I didn't just get off the bus, Gerry. I'm an ASU graduate."

"The truth remains that I remember being someone else, Fly. It has always been so, but, when I got up on Sunday, the other guy started to walk around."

"Who?"

It proved difficult for George. He wanted very badly to make friends with this young Navajo. How much could he expect the boy to accept? Still, he answered.

"I was Geronimo."

But Gordon didn't laugh. He nodded once and then said, "Might be a useful person to have around."

"He tells me that's why he's here," said the Apache. "Geronimo knows something about this demon and was once the most powerful medicine man of our people."

"I will look forward to knowing him better," said the Navajo, "but I think we would do well to get started toward the city. Where can we rent the car?"

"Let's check the dealership over there," said George, pointing just up the street. "In smaller towns they sometimes handle rentals. If they can't help, we'll get to a phone."

Twenty minutes later, their gear stowed in the back, they were driving a Ford Tempo out of Springerville on 60.

Chapter Thirty-Five

Phoenix

The delivery truck let Rattle out at Central Avenue and Van Buren in the center of downtown Phoenix. The old man stood on the street corner and waved as it pulled away, but he inwardly cringed at what surrounded him.

The streets were packed with traffic and all of it appeared stacked bumper to bumper. The cross street, Van Buren, had been barricaded into one lane each way and three lanes of cars tried to merge. Though Central had not been torn up, a US West truck sat parked in the center lane in front of an open manhole. Orange traffic cones forced the lanes on each side to merge for approximately two hundred feet. There were shouted curses, occasional horns and steaming radiators.

Towering over the street like huge monoliths rose tall buildings, old and new, buttoned up against the summer heat which radiated from the pavement beneath Rattle's feet. People dodged through the traffic on foot, crossing wherever they could because the construction crew building a highrise had severed the lines that worked the traffic lights. One lone, harried and sweaty patrolman tried to bring order out of chaos.

Rattle stood on the corner and thought about the deer spirit. What could he do in a place like this? He had been told to join with others and save the world. Why save this place? It would be kinder to let the demon take it.

"Hey, oldtimer," said a youthful voice at his elbow. "Can you spare a buck? I ain't et in two days."

Rattle turned. The speaker, a young white girl, probably weighed two hundred pounds. Her hair looked dirty and her complexion blotched. She appeared to be about fifteen.

"Did'ja hear me, old dude?" She watched his face, but her expression seemed neither eager or hopeful. She looked mean and bored.

"No bucks," he replied quietly. "I got no money."

"No money! Hey, don't bullshit me." Her eyes strayed to the roll of clothing that hung at the old man's back. "What's in the bundle, oldtimer?"

Rattle placed a protective hand over the blanket roll that contained his clothing and magical gear. The other hand took a firmer grip on his walking stick.

"Just clothes," he replied. "Nothing you would want."

"How'd I know that 'fore I look?" said the girl edging closer. "Whyn't ya let me take a peek." Her stubby fingers reached for the strap.

The old man lashed out with his stick and cracked her one in the shins.

"Ow! Son of a bitch!" She danced backward, bending and hopping, grabbing the spot. "Jesus Christ! The bastard hit me." She sat on the pavement and rubbed her leg.

Rattle moved closer, his stick at the ready. "You are a child," he said in a steady voice. "Go and play but do not come around me and act like a thief."

"I'm gonna get the law on you, you crazy old dude," shrilled the girl. "You got no right to hit somebody for no reason."

The ruckus began to draw a crowd. They made comments and shouted questions.

"What happened?"

"The she-pig tried to snatch the old man's bundle and he hit her with his walking stick."

"Good for him."

"Hey, ain't he an Indian? Yeah, he's a stinkin' Indian beatin' up on the little girl."

"Little? Look at her down there. She looks like a beached whale."

"Is there any blood?"

The noisy crowd finally attracted the police officer. "Hey," he shouted, "what's going on here? Move along, folks."

The girl looked slyly around and then turned on the tears. "That old man hit me with his stick." She pointed an accusing finger to where Rattle had been standing, but he had gone into the crowd.

No one pursued, but the old man didn't realize it for a few minutes. He frantically turned corners and changed directions in order to elude the policeman. If the girl accused him, he felt sure the white man's law would take her side.

He finally came to an alley between two of the hotels. He went a few feet down it and then saw a hidden area behind a huge trash dumpster. He moved quickly into it.

The air stank, but the dumpster banished the sun. Rattle perspired from his exertion. He sat wearily against the base of the wall in the shade and tried to calm himself.

"You wouldn't have a smoke, would you?"

The voice came from the deeper shadow to his right and the old man jumped up, ready to flee.

"Whaaaa!"

"Whoa, pardner!" The voice sounded contrite. "I didn't mean to startle you. I was just hoping for a cigarette."

Rattle peered into the shadow and made out the form of another man, seated with his back against the wall much as he had been. "I use a pipe," he replied, taking his seat once again. "I am sorry."

"No problem," said the man.

Rattle could see him now, a white man wearing old levis, a faded denim shirt and old shoes.

"Jumpy as you are, you must be hiding from someone." The comment was off-hand.

"Just getting out of the sun," said Rattle in reply. "I've never been here before and it is strange."

"Never been behind this dumpster? In this alley? In this town? On this planet?" The other chuckled. "Help me out. Give me a frame of reference or two."

"Never been to Phoenix before. I live up north. Havasupai. It isn't like here."

"Ahh. I thought you were probably an Injun." He shrugged. "Don't matter to me none. My name is Bob Murphy." He gestured around them. "Welcome to my home."

Rattle stared at him, astounded. "You live here?"

Bob nodded. "All this week, anyway. The cops find me, I'll have to move on again. The shelters are all full. They usually are in summertime. Too hot outside." Bob smiled at the old man. "You got a place to stay?"

The Indian shook his head.

"Then stay here with me," said the white man. "Hell, there's worse places."

"I must meet some others," said Rattle. "Only I don't know how to get there. It's on the Salt River Reservation. I must get there or they will not be able to do what must be done."

"Who are they?"

"The powerful men from all the tribes. The medicine will be very strong when we do this thing."

"More Injuns?" Bob sounded delighted. "I'd like to see that."

Rattle, however, worried. He had a little money tucked in his shoe so he knew he would not have to sleep in the alley. He knew he must make haste to this gathering, but did not know where to begin.

Bob studied the old man. "You must be pretty important," he said, "if the others can't do without you."

Rattle understood neither modesty nor bragging, but spoke the truth. "The others cannot do what they must without me. I am the Upper World Warrior."

"Interesting," Bob replied. "Well, just where are you supposed to go?"

"To the house of the Pima, Tom Bear, but I don't know how far it is."

"If it's on the Salt River Reservation, it's not too far," said the other man. "It's about seventy blocks in that direction." He pointed west.

"Blocks? How far are blocks?"

Bob smiled. "About a quarter of a mile each." Actually, he had no idea whether if he told the truth or not, but Bob Murphy liked being a helpful guy. He had always been that way. It accounted for his being on the street. Too many snappy answers to snappy questions—only the answers were usually wrong.

"That's over seventeen miles! I guess I need to start walking." Rattle stood and hitched up his bundle.

Bob stood also.

"I've got a friend with a car. Say, what's your name anyway?"

"Some have called me Deer Man," replied the Indian.

"Well, Deer Man," said Murphy, "we can go see my friend and he might be willing to give us a ride over there."

"I used to hate cars," said Rattle, "but I've been getting over it."

"I'll talk to my friend if you'll let me come along," said Bob.

The old man looked hesitant. "I cannot promise that," he said at last. "You can come with me for now, but I may have to tell you to leave when the time is right. Will you go when I ask you to?"

"Yeah," said Murphy, "but you gotta introduce me to all the other Injuns before I do." He smiled happily. "I haven't met no medicine men before."

As always when dealing with white men, Rattle agonized about whether he had made the right decision. He thought longingly of his gorge and the forests and the Great Deer Spirit. Secretly, he hoped this would all be over soon so he could return to the blue-green water of his home.

Bob Murphy did know a man with a car, a Volkswagen Beetle. Speed Perkins worked at the Hyatt as a bartender. Coincidentally, he had just finished his shift.

After a hasty conference that Rattle couldn't hear, the bartender agreed to transport them to the reservation if they would cough up six dollars for gas. Bob contributed a dollar and Rattle grudgingly gave up a five dollar bill from his shoe. The deal was done.

They waited in the lobby of the Hyatt and the old Indian kept gazing up at the ceiling high above, watching the glass-fronted elevators climb and descend.

When Perkins came to collect them, it dismayed Rattle to learn that the man seemed in a terrific hurry. Speed believed a VW has only two functional states—one is sitting at rest when not in use, the other is skittering along the road with the pedal to the metal.

They ran more than one red light.

Riding in the back seat of a Volkswagen Bug in Phoenix rush-hour traffic with a maniac behind the wheel reminded Rattle once again that he hated cars.

Chapter Thirty-Six

Fort McDowell Indian Reservation

Michael Coyoma, medicine man of the Mohave, awakened early that same morning in his cinderblock house on the Fort McDowell Reservation. He had spent a busy night in dream time talking to his Uncle. This Uncle had been dead for fifteen years but came in dream time to advise his nephew. The Uncle had told him of the demon and the gathering. Michael had been told to go.

He sat on the edge of his bed, head in hands, sleep still fogging the edges of thought. Michael had been up with one of his clients, a Mohave businessman who still clung to the old world ideas. Benjamin Reyes had developed blinding headaches and had been so incapacitated by them that his business suffered. Ben's construction company had been awarded many of the contracts for housing on the reservation.

Much of the construction got done under a self-help program administered by the BIA. Materials were furnished at cost and Ben's foremen served as advisors and supervisors while the soon-to-be residents provided the unskilled labor. Ben began as a plumber, but he knew every facet of the construction field.

He had come to Michael in the strict belief that the white man's medicine worked fine for broken bones and stitching up wounds, but the old ways were more important in dealing with those intangible ailments that had no apparent cause.

In recent years, Michael had obtained and studied many of the white man's books on medicine. He had a basic understanding of anatomy and an uncanny ability as a diagnostician. He possessed no arcane secret. He simply remembered what he read.

In Michael's opinion, Ben's problem resulted from stress. Although there were only about two thousand people to provide for on the whole reservation, meeting BIA standards and deadlines meant Ben had to spend a large percentage of his time pushing the outside of the envelope. This produced an ulcer—not yet serious—and tension headaches.

Treatment called for relaxation, creative visualization and affirmations, and frequent massage. These things Michael couched in traditional forms, thus attracting the conservative Benjamin Reyes to his approach.

This morning, however, Michael had awakened with a sense of urgency. His Uncle had shown him the demon, a completely evil creature with no form but the outline of storm and violence. He had understood that it was not a new thing, that it had been here in the distant past and plagued his people.

How he understood this he could not have explained—would not even have tried. For the Mohave, dream life was important as waking life, often more so. He sat now, on the edge of his bed with head in hands, planning his journey.

Michael understood what he needed to do. There would be a council, the like of which had not been seen in five hundred years. He would be part of it. He rose from the bed and began assembling the things he would require—his pipe, his ceremonial garb and his flute.

He went out and stood on the shore of the Verde. The summer sun blazed. It would be be 106 degrees today, but the cool morning air had been further conditioned by the running water. His toe informed him the water remained cold enough to raise goosebumps on his arms and legs. He smiled and broke into a light chuckle. He would not remain slow and sleep-laden for long.

Good. He must depart for Phoenix later today. By tomorrow he would have contacted the Pima Witch, Tom Bear. The dream required this of him.

He would have to get a message to Ben telling him to continue the visualizations and affirmations. Young Rain, the girl he was training in his craft, would be able to do the massage until he returned.

He smiled again as he realized this would be no hardship on Ben. Young Rain, a truly beautiful woman in the making, had gentle and strong hands and a distracting shape. No, Ben would not suffer for the change.

He waded out into the running water, iron discipline keeping his breath even and deep despite the cold. When he reached depth to his waist, he stopped and immersed the rest of his body in the clear swift water. All traces of sleep fled.

Since no one else could be seen, he bathed naked in the sunrise. The beauty of this spot had always touched him, ever since childhood. The land had not been allocated and the families could live where they pleased. It happened that his father, as a medicine man, had been given the choice of locations and his privacy respected. This, then, had been Michael's family home.

He climbed out of the river and ran along the bank in a ground-devouring stride to dry himself. His back stayed turned to the house no more than three or four minutes.

When he returned, however, he became dismayed to discover it had been ravaged by something. The corral was down and his cattle scattered. His sweat lodge lay completely destroyed, only the rocks still lying undisturbed. The house had suffered a broken window and the porch rail hung askew.

What could have happened? He looked around on all sides of the house. Nothing. Then, as he watched with wide eyes, a dust devil formed on the ground not twenty yards away, and swept the rest of the porch rail with it into oblivion.

It wasn't uncommon for dust devils to be destructive, but this might be more than a freak of the weather. Maybe it had been sent as a goad to help him understand the urgency of the calling.

Michael moved back inside and completed his packing. He would stop at Ben's and deliver his message in person, then leave final instructions with Young Rain. Repairing the damage would have to wait.

He would be delayed only in that he wanted to stop by the home of his friend Cord Hames on the Chemehuevi part of the reservation. When he explained it to the other medicine man, he felt certain he would not have to make the trip across the reservation alone.

Dust devils still played havoc outside. Watching them, he found it impossible to shake off the cold chill of the river despite the rising temperature of the day.

Chapter Thirty-Seven

Somerton, Arizona

In Somerton, just outside of Yuma, Cocopah medicine man James Bluesky had also been dream-directed. When he awoke, he showered and dressed and went to the ranch house to see the owner. "I've got to take off for a while, Mr. Crawford. I have some personal business to take care of down in Phoenix."

"Okay," said the white man. "I guess I can spare you. Any idea how long you'll be gone? We have a drive next month."

James nodded. "I'm pretty sure I'll be back for that."

"Is this medicine business, James?"

The Cocopah nodded. "Yeah."

Crawford looked unhappy. "Dammit, Jim, you're one of the best ranch hands I've ever had. Why can't you give up this witch doctor medicine man stuff and settle in. I've already told you I'd give you an interest in the spread."

James shook his head. "You know better, Mr. Crawford. You know how I feel about it. I'm the only one down here now. I'm needed."

The rancher sighed. "Yep, I do, but I'm not going to stop trying to change your mind."

They looked at each other for a long moment.

James thought of all the kindnesses extended by the older man. He had taken James on as a hand when the reservation suffered through an economic crisis so severe the tribe had been in danger of extinction. Housing had been substandard—many families living in cardboard shelters. In 1970, the only income most of the people received came in the form of a welfare check of around $65 per month.

Now, twenty years later, things had improved but were still far from secure. They had electricity and running water, housing had been upgraded and there were even a few families making a go at farming the 609 acres of land that constituted the reservation. However, most of the eight-hundred-plus members of the tribe worked either for other ranchers, like James, or as wage earners in and around Yuma.

James owed a lot to Kent Crawford and both men knew it. Still, James had proven himself a good hand and worked unstintingly to improve the ranch. Both men felt it was an even exchange.

Crawford, who had no children, cared for Bluesky as he would have for a child of his own. James knew the old man wanted to leave the property to him, but he felt uncomfortable with tying himself so completely to the white community. In his position as medicine man, he had a responsibility to his people that prevented him from taking individual opportunities like this one.

It was already difficult enough. Few of the people sought traditional medicine anyway. Surrounded as they were by the white community, employed by the outside world and able to enjoy the benefits it could provide, they went instead to the hospitals and clinics in Yuma for their ills.

It was James' turn to sigh. "I guess I'll see you in a week or so," he said at last.

Crawford nodded in answer but did not speak.

James turned and walked back to the bunkhouse. He could feel the old man's eyes on his back all the way across.

An hour later, he stood in downtown Yuma at the Greyhound Bus Station waiting to board the bus to Phoenix.

Chapter Thirty-Eight

Phoenix

Matt Sharp stood before the screen under the hot lights waiting to be cued up. He had prepared a special segment of the weather spot expanded to fifteen minutes. He had satellite photos from the appropriate times and an electronic pointer that would allow him to trace the hypothetical path of his killer storm north from Phoenix to Agate Junction, then across the state into New Mexico, finally to Chaco Canyon.

In addition to his best recollection of Roger Milton's phone call, he had tracked the Fiero owner from Daniel Lopez's report and interviewed him about what he saw. That tape already sat in the machine, ready to roll. There were three spot reports besides; the first from a family in Northeastern Arizona reporting the devastation of one of their outlying barns, the second and third relayed by the New Mexico Highway Patrol from tourists who had witnessed a swiftly moving dry storm apparently moving east over some less frequented roads. His one frustration remained that he had been unable to track down the ASU professor who reported the first incident in Phoenix itself. Still, his plot started on the west side of Phoenix and ran directly up I-17. Finally, waiting to be slammed into the machine after the sixty-second break, he had footage of the Chaco Canyon aftermath as well as more on Agate Junction. Matt had done his homework. He felt tired and a little sweaty, but triumphant. *This was IT*. This represented the big break he had struggled for all his young life. This would make him. He could already hear the phone ringing with offers from New York.

"Ready on set." The director had just come in from the adjoining studio where the regular news was about to break for weather. "Ready on camera one." Bill Thorp, the experienced camera jock on the team gave a thumbs up.

"Ready on camera two." Young Randall King, still a little shaky behind the lens, gave a second thumbs up.

"Ready Matt?" Jane Carter, the best director working with the local channel, looked as eager as Matt felt.

He nodded, not trusting himself to speak.

"Ready for count down to lead-in." Jane made a circle of thumb and forefinger. "Five—four—three—two—one—roll lead!"

Over the speakers came the voice of Carnaby Ford, well-known voice of KTVC as the logo appeared on screen and the music started. "Welcome to the KTVC weather show, the best and brightest of Phoenix, Arizona with meteorologist Matt Sharp. Tonight we bring you expanded coverage in the wake of the Agate Junction, Arizona, and Chaco Canyon, New Mexico, disasters." He paused dramatically, then continued, "And now, KTVC meteorologist Matt Sharp!"

"Good evening ladies and gentlemen, and welcome to KTVC weather. Because of the extraordinary events of the past two days, our coverage tonight has been expanded and, I am proud to say, is being carried nationwide on NBT."

The file film on Agate Junction began to run. People in all fifty states saw the devastation left behind when Agate was destroyed.

Matt spoke over the pictures. "Yesterday, I reported the total destruction of an Arizona town, Agate Junction." The stills showed the concrete pads on which houses and buildings had stood. "One hundred and four people are known to have lost their lives, one hundred and two residents, and two people who happened to have the misfortune of being in Agate at the critical time." The film changed to the cab of the semi, a fine white powder on the seat and floor. "One appears to have been the driver of a long haul truck, his identity as yet unknown, and the other, sadly, was a weather spotter who worked with me named Roger Milton." The scene changed once again to the two boys, shivering and pale, surrounded by police and rescue workers. "There were only two survivors. Both of whom, in a happy serendipity, were playing a game and had hidden themselves outside of the area of danger."

The cut back to live delivery went smoothly and Matt spoke directly to the camera. "As I told you all yesterday, this is the result of a freak, killer storm that hit twice in the Phoenix area. It began just west of Phoenix, resulting in apparently only one casualty. The name of the victim is being withheld pending notification of next of kin. The storm then moved parallel to I-17 northward," he used a pointer to trace the area map on the screen behind him, "until it reached Agate Junction, forty miles from the first report. Here, in a burst of activity, it created the destruction you have just witnessed. We all know the tragic results."

Matt turned back to the camera. "Thermal updrafts often result from heating of the earth's surface by the sun. Common over dry surfaces where very high temperatures arise, a layer of warm and unstable air begins to form near the surface. Being lighter than the cooler air above it, this layer has a tendency to rise. However, it cannot rise all at once in a sheet so small pockets of it begin to rise upward in the form of thermals."

"When the rate of ascent passes a certain velocity, the air takes on a rotary motion. Any additional flow of low level warm air fuels the developing spiral, increasing its rate of rotation. In the desert, such phenomena are called dust devils or whirlwinds. The tornado is a larger example, except that tornadoes are most often associated with thunderstorms."

Matt looked intently into the camera and allowed himself a grim smile, showing white teeth. "After we come back from this message, we'll trace the course of this storm after it left Agate Junction."

"Cut!" Jane gave him a high sign as the commercial began. The technician loaded the footage from Chaco into the primary machine. Matt looked around the studio.

It was more crowded than usual. Several executives were present as well as every tech and clerk unessential to the broadcast. Even the news team had come quietly up to the door and stood watching in fascination. Diedre stood in the back and smiled widely, nodding her approval.

"Coming out of commercial," Jane called out. "Ready Cameras One and Two." Again both camera men gave the thumbs-up acknowledgement and the director counted down from ten to one.

On cue, Matt continued. "Reports from several sources, including tourists on the road and the New Mexico Highway Patrol, indicate the storm took a dramatic eastward turn after leaving Agate Junction." He used the pointer to follow the projected path. "We have accounts from Baker Butte and then Corn Creek in Arizona," he traced the route across the Mogollon Plateau, then an arc over Winslow to the Grand Canyon Plateau, "and the Chuska Mountains north of Gallup in New Mexico."

Matt turned back to the camera. "And then, yesterday morning at exactly five-oh-three, the same storm laid waste to the Navajo settlement at Chaco Canyon."

The Chaco film began to run and the weatherman spoke over it. "You can see the similarities between this and the Agate Junction aftermath," he said quietly. A picture of a concrete slab swept clean centered on the screen. "This used to contain a trailer, a home to a family." The picture expanded and swept back until the total area of devastation could be seen. "This rubble strewn plain contained stone hogans, sheds, trailers, a few houses and businesses—all the structures that make up a human settlement. You can see the results." He looked directly into the camera, a hard penetrating stare. "This storm is a killer, a freak, and it doesn't seem to be dissipating as such scattered weather events usually do, but appears instead to be growing stronger."

Matt shrugged. "Where is it now? We don't know. In a minute, I'll show you where I think it may have gone."

As the show cut to the second commercial, Matt felt limp. The evidence seemed overwhelming to him, but he had received no backup from the National Weather Service or any other recognized authority. He would either make his career or destroy it.

"Thirty seconds, Matt." Jane glowed. She, too, sensed that her future rode on the strength of this broadcast.

Matt shuffled his notes, wishing it were over so the response could be assessed.

"Okay, this is the last segment," said the director. "Kick'em in the teeth, Matt."

He looked into the camera as the light came on. Inanely, he remembered what they had told him in broadcasting school about seducing the camera, acting as if it was a beautiful woman he wanted to bed. Involuntarily, his eyes flicked to Diedre as she watched from the rear of the room. *No comparison*, he thought.

"From the sequence of events in Chaco Canyon, as we have been able to reconstruct them, the storm came from the southwest and hovered over the settlement for nearly two full hours. Phone lines were blown out at five-oh-three according to telephone company sources but the power was cut a few minutes later. Location of the substations thus indicates entry from the southwest."

Again, Matt used the pointer. "As the event developed, there were additional recordable failures of utilities and even such little things as the times watches and clocks stopped. Based on this data, which we hasten to admit is purely speculative, it would appear that the storm headed off in a northwesterly direction when it left the canyon."

Matt used the pointer to trace the arc from Chaco, then turned and looked into the camera again. "It has reversed course," he said. "It has recrossed the border here at the Chuska Mountains and come back into Arizona even stronger than before—and where it goes from there is still an unknown." His face grew grim. "As a public service, we have established a toll free line for calls outside of the greater Phoenix-Metro area. The number is 1-800-555-KTVC. If you observe any trace of this storm, call us! If you have suffered any damage as a result of a freak storm in the past two days, call us! In the meantime, stay tuned to KTVC for bulletins and further updates. This is Meteorologist Matt Sharp saying be careful and stay safe."

The camera light went out and a long silence trembled on the air before the room erupted into spontaneous applause. Diedre rushed up and threw her arms around him, the crew came up to pound him on the back, offering loud and enthusiastic congratulations.

Jane Carter stood in the back of the room and smiled a wide, happy smile. "Son of a bitch," she said quietly. "He did it. He scooped the networks and the NWS and everybody. And you saw it here first, folks." She chuckled. "Son of a bitch!"

Chapter Thirty-Nine

The Desert Near Chaco Canyon

The beast had been sated. It still seethed knowing the Navajo had trained his replacement. The youth had escaped. The satisfaction of gorging itself on Chaco Canyon tasted less sweet as it realized all the frantic cross country stealth it employed had gone for naught. The gathering could still occur.

The Hopi had asked it to wait, to have time to choose a course of action. When it finished with Chaco, it had touched the mind of the priest only to find him already en route to Phoenix. Withdrawing the nerve block became only the first of the agonies it planned for the Peace Man.

As it lay hidden to the northwest, separated from human dwellings, the beast suffered angry consternation. Men refused to learn. No matter how it tried to teach them, they failed to benefit from the lessons. What kind of creature failed to preserve itself? What perverted instincts drove the Hopi to join its opponents and leave its people vulnerable to attack?

It had waited for darkness, lying still and dormant in sight of Chaco, all through the day. It had watched with curiosity as the rescue teams descended on the ruin. Though it did not possess sight as man knows it, the beast was able to "see" as long as there were living things nearby, for it tapped into their minds and experienced what they felt and saw. Still, it had seen displays of emotion that filled it with satisfaction, deep sorrows and lamentations of loss.

It did, however, luxuriate in the sensations, wallow in the wealth of feeling. It could sift through the thoughts of those below in search of even more pleasure. As it examined the minds of the workers in the torchlight, it suddenly learned something wonderful, something unexpected. Amazement colored its discovery that, of all the men below, none so much as suspected its existence.

Many blamed an earth tremor, others thought the cause to be a storm, but none knew of the demon—no man of those hundreds sifting through the wreckage below knew of the beast.

Joy flooded through it. No matter that the Navajo had won the contest, no matter that the Hopi was a fool. It was free and it had grown strong. Now it would move back to where it had been imprisoned and destroy the fools who thought they could stop it. Once they were gone, it could range freely throughout the land, feeding and collecting lives, for the rest of time.

Under cover of darkness, it moved off to the northwest, retracing its course over the Grand Canyon Plateau. This time, however, it would not avoid the smaller groupings of men. Larger and stronger by virtue of the feeding at Chaco, it would need to continue supporting its growth with frequent consumption. The isolated farms and ranches in its path would serve.

It huddled into itself, compressing its now massive body into the smallest possible size, in order to pass unseen and leave the narrowest trail. Its senses stretched ahead, picking a path that skirted settlements and towns but no longer avoided the single dwellings.

The beast moved quickly, turning south after crossing the Chuska Mountains, carrying its bulk above the ground as much as possible so as not to create a cloud of dust. It felt the power surging within, the strength and confidence of a creature that, even compressed, measured almost a half-mile across from edge to edge.

*   *   *   *   *

Larry and Sandra Baltus drove along Highway 40 from Gallup, New Mexico, to Winslow, Arizona. They had decided to travel at night so they could arrive early and see the sunrise at Meteor Crater.

They had been married for three years but remained childless by choice.

Larry worked as a security guard at K-Mart and Sandra as a convenience store clerk. Since they both worked nights, the traveling plans were simply a continuation of their normal daily schedule.

As usual, Larry drove and Sandy navigated—not exactly a difficult task since they never had to leave Highway 40. Unfortunately, their path and the course of the beast intersected.

The night shone clear, the sliver of moon bright and the sky ablaze with stars. They drove with the windows down, taking advantage of the cool desert night air.

When the beast slammed into their Chevrolet station wagon it ripped off the roof with a wind force in excess of three hundred sixty miles per hour. Sandra was lifted out of the vehicle like a sardine out of an opened can and burst into red rain before Larry's wild eyes. He tried to cling to the car, but his feet rose until he was stretched between the hungry wind and the wheel like a clothesline.

The car itself left the road and rose into the vortex that was the beast in what seemed to Larry to be slow motion. It rotated once on its axis and then his feet hit the leading edge of the blasting sand and rock. For a moment, he felt only the impact of the wall of force, but then his brain received the signals of outrage that had been sent by now non-existent legs. He screamed and let go of the wheel but the scream quickly cut off as the rest of his body flew apart.

*   *   *   *   *

The beast barely noticed except for a momentary feeling of gratification. It reminded itself that moving cross country used incredible amounts of energy that needed to be replaced. The two humans in the car had been nothing. It needed more of the precious fluids living things contained if it was going to travel and maintain size and bulk.

Hungrily, its senses reached ahead seeking other life.

*   *   *   *   *

Bucky Reese was a Vietnam vet and a societal dropout. He and a group of friends were living in Canyon Diablo illegally. Their van, painted garishly with portraits of their heroes, Charles Manson and Adolf Hitler, served as their base. Around it lay a scattering of tents and shelters.

He had called one of the pretty girls to him and invoked his right as leader to the pleasure of her company for the night. Just seventeen, she had been traveling with the group for two weeks.

Bucky lacked physical appeal, being slight and wiry, afflicted by poor eyesight that required the wearing of thick glasses. He seemed an unlikely leader, but had saved his money during the war and taken advantage of his position in supply to stockpile a huge cache of contraband. After the war, he had turned this stockpile of goods into a sizable nest-egg.

Born too late to be considered one of the beat generation, too straight to consider himself a hippie, he had used his money to attract a group of freeloaders who traded their loyalty for his financial support. The group numbered seven men and thirteen women.

They had stolen a calf from a farm before they came into the canyon and sacrificed it to Satan in a gory ceremony a few nights past. They had been eating the beef ever since, though it had gotten a little gamy. Tomorrow they would have to pack up and move on.

The girl, named Shoshona, with raven hair and a lovely body had run away from home in Albuquerque. Bucky had lusted after her since she joined the group, but tonight would be his first chance to sample the product.

"Strip!" he ordered.

Obediently, she pulled off her tee-shirt and shorts. She wore no undergarments and Bucky licked his lips as he watched the disrobing. The dark triangle of hair between her thighs was a lush growth, her breasts were bullets, high and proud.

As he undid his belt and dropped his shorts, a strange sound came out of the north, the whine of wind and sand driven by terrific force.

Some instinct drove him forward, tackling the girl and hurling her to the sleeping bag. With no foreplay, no consideration whatsoever, he buried his erection in the softness of her, driving himself up and into her with brute force. She cried out with the pain, but then the storm had come upon them.

The moment of ecstasy was brief.

*   *   *   *   *

The beast swept over the encampment like a buzz saw. The humans delivered what they had to give without a whimper, falling apart under its onslaught with no warning and total surprise. The demon never even slowed its progress.

Wednesday, July 12th

Chapter Forty

Salt River Reservation

Tom Bear arose first on Wednesday morning. He wanted to take those who could travel out to the site of the demon's long imprisonment. Juan had already told him it now lay open and the police and the archaeologist had looked inside.

Tom felt curious about the old kiva. Legend said it had once been a very holy place, used by the Hohokam, his ancestors.

A change had come over Tom in the last few days. He stood taller, spoke with more authority and felt the heavy burden of responsibility weighing on him. He knew, after all, he could not claim to be a medicine man, merely a dabbler. He had never meant to become involved in such a thing as the gathering, only to lead young Danny into the tradition and duty that should be the boy's legacy.

Danny's grandfather had been Tom's close friend. They had spoken of the boy many times, Donald Webb complaining that his son, Jed, prevented Danny from spending time with him. It had been sad to see the old man left alone by his family as he declined and finally died. Though Tom loved Danny as he would have loved his own son, the boy's father had been a drunken bastard.

Tom went outside and showered using the stall he had built under the watertank. He found it convenient, private, and it had simplified his plumbing problems when building the house. In the winter, he used the bathtub inside.

He stood and watched the sunrise. The sky glowed red in the east. A reader of classic literature in his youth, Tom had much more familiarity with the miligan's world than he usually let on. As he looked at the sky, his mind repeated the old maritime rhyme, "Red sky in the morning, sailor take warning—Red sky at night, sailor's delight."

There was, indeed, a storm coming—a storm absent from the world for five hundred years. The people of Agate Junction and the Navajo of Chaco Canyon had seen it. They died.

Tom wondered if they would have enough time. The demon had already been loose four days. It would have grown in size and strength in that interval. If the Navajo they awaited must really be counted as one of the dead of Chaco, what would they do?

"It is beautiful here, Tom," said a voice by his ear.

The Pima jumped in spite of himself.

"I'm sorry, my friend," said Juan Mapoli, grinning. "I did not mean to startle you. I came out to watch the sun and saw you down here."

"It is all right," said Tom. He turned back to look at the sky. "You speak truly. It is beautiful."

A moment of silence ensued before the sabio broke it. "Lotus Farley and Danny Webb seem to have struck up a friendship." It was offered tentatively, apologetically.

"They are both adult and able to make their own decisions. I have faith in the boy's judgment." Tom turned back to the Yaqui and saw the other man's eyes twinkle with amusement. He smiled in return. "She makes me wish I were a youth again," he admitted quietly.

Juan nodded. "She reminds me of my Maria when we were first married," he said.

Both men seemed content to maintain silence. They stood at ease and watched the sky, lighting up a couple of Tom's cigarettes.

Finally, the Yaqui spoke again. "I dreamed last night. It was a dream filled with answers."

The Pima said, "What questions had you asked?"

"I asked about the Navajo. I asked if Archie Smythe had really died."

Tom's voice was hushed. "And?"

"He is gone, but the dream spoke of another. We have not much longer to wait. The Navajo will arrive today."

"Another?"

"I have not seen his likeness yet," admitted Juan, "but I am sure he will arrive. There was something about the Pai as well, but I did not understand."

"What of the Pai?" Tom's interest quickened. He had met the Havasupai named Rattle once many years before. If that one planned to attend, their chances improved. The Deer Man had powerful medicine with his totem.

Juan looked confused. "I am not certain, but I think there are those who would prevent him from joining us. It is as if a cloud hovered in the middle of my sight. I see the old man and yet I see some great horned animal as well, almost as if he were two things at once."

Tom nodded and smiled. "I know that one. He will be important to us."

"If he gets here," said Juan.

Tom checked his own inner voice. He pictured Rattle as he had last seen him, dressed in buckskin with antlers on his head, dancing and singing at a festival. The thought picture was clear for a moment, then clouded and he saw that the Pai's face was red with anger.

"It may be that we will have to seek him," said the Pima. "I can do a finding call. The Pai is in tune with his totem. I can probably call him."

"If he does not arrive today, perhaps that would be a task for both of us tonight." The Yaqui put a hand on Tom's shoulder. "Maybe the boy can help."

The witch smiled at the sabio. "Yes, that would be good."

They were interrupted by the sound of a car pulling up in front of the house. The Pima went around the side, beckoning Juan to join him. It was a cab containing James Bluesky, the Cocopah.

"Are you the one called Bear?" he asked of Tom.

"I am that one," replied the witch.

"Then you are the one I seek," said Bluesky, paying the cab and sending it away. He turned. "I am Bluesky of the Cocopah. I was sent here for a gathering."

Tom indicated the sabio by his side. "This is Juan Mapoli of the Yaqui. I am Tom Bear of the Pima. Others are inside sleeping."

"Tell me of the demon," said James. "I know nothing of it except that we must stop it."

"It is a powerful wind, this demon," said Juan.

"It kills," added Tom.

"It is coming here," said Lotus from the porch behind them. All three men spun in surprise and faced her.

"Lotus Farley of the Tohono O'odham." The Pima completed the introduction. "James Bluesky of the Cocopah. What do you mean, Lotus?"

The woman shrugged. "I felt it this morning as I awakened. The demon is on the move and coming here." She added, "With some urgency."

Juan closed his eyes. "She is right," he said after a moment. "It comes quickly toward us, though we still have some time."

Tom led them toward the house. "There is much to do," he said, worry evident in his voice. "We are not yet all here." He looked at Juan. "We need that Navajo!"

The Yaqui was confident. "He will arrive today."

The witch shook his head. "Let us hope so. I doubt the demon will wait."

Chapter Forty-One

Phoenix

Detectives Johnson and Redfield had arrived at Sky Harbor late on Monday night. After a fruitless day of inquiries concerning the Navajo, Gordon Smythe, they met this morning, and sat, drinking coffee, at a fast foodery in Tempe.

"Where do you want to start?" asked Greg. He and Twohats had become friends over the past two days. The Phoenix detective found he liked the easy going manner and professional expertise exhibited by the tribal cop. Everything was done thoroughly and by the book, but there never seemed to be any hurry or pressure.

Greg knew, of course, that Twohats was under pressure. The Lieutenant wanted him back in Shiprock and there were cases he should be working on, but the gravity of the Chaco Canyon disaster made finding and interviewing young Smythe very important.

"Time to look up some Indians, Greg," said Twohats lightly. "If the boy came here, he would seek out his own. I think the Salt River Reservation is the place we start today."

They drove up to Scottsdale and onto the reservation, stopping at the Information Center. This time the tribal clerk, Mary, sent them directly to the home of Tom Bear. As they left the Information Center, she shook her head and wondered aloud where the old witch was putting all the people.

It took a while on the back roads before they found the house. When they pulled up out front, a group of people came from inside and stood on the big front porch watching them.

"You'd better handle this crowd," said Greg in an aside to his associate. "I'd probably do something wrong and they'd all clam up."

Looking at the assemblage on the porch, Twohats shook his head. "I don't know if I'll be any better than you, buddy. This looks like a pretty powerful bunch."

Indeed, the group had grown from three, when they first drove up, to seven.

Twohats spoke sotto voce to Greg. All from different tribes," he said, his tone indicating disbelief.

"What do you mean?" Greg felt off balance with this one. He hoped the Navajo could carry it off.

One of the old men stepped forward. "He means that it is unusual to find so many different tribes gathered together." He then turned his attention to Ed. "Are you the one we have waited for?"

After a moment's pause, Twohats understood. He smiled and shook his head.

"No, my brothers. I am not. This one is a policeman from Tempe and he accompanies me in a search for one of the Dineh named Smythe."

"Why do you seek this one?" Lotus spoke.

Greg took a long look at the woman and sighed.

"He was the last to leave Chaco Canyon alive," said Redfield. "We hope there are things he can tell us of what happened there."

"No mystery," said Danny. "It was the demon."

The others turned and looked at Danny passively, but that was enough to remind him they had secrets to keep.

Twohats tensed up as soon as he heard the boy's words. His dark eyes grew hooded. "I have heard talk of this demon," he said quietly, "but I know little of it. What kind of demon wipes out two thousand people in New Mexico and over a hundred in Arizona?"

Danny would have answered, but Tom glanced at him and the look said "Be silent."

Juan spoke. "It is an ancient evil that roamed here in our past, free and unchecked. Back then, the wise of all our people made a great medicine that forced it into the earth where it could do no further harm."

The look on Greg's face as he heard this was one of cold, superior disbelief. He could not help himself. This had to be superstitious nonsense. There were no such things as demons.

Tom saw his expression and spoke. "You asked, policeman, what kind of demon. You have been answered."

Twohats laid a restraining hand on Greg's shoulder. The Navajo's expression had undergone a change. He appeared almost awestruck. Still looking at the group before him, he asked with respect, "May I know what all of you are called?"

"Tom Bear of the Pima."

"Danny Webb of the Pima."

"Pasqual Quatero of the Zuni."

"Lotus Farley of the Tohono O'odham."

"Kade Wonto of the Maricopa."

"James Bluesky of the Cocopah."

"Juan Mapoli of the Yaqui."

"Ed Twohats Redfield of the Navajo and Detective Greg Johnson of the Tempe Police. We apologize for intruding."

The others did not speak but gazed at the two with calm, peaceful faces.

"What the hell?" Greg suddenly realized that Twohats had backed off. He did not understand.

"Quiet!" It was not a request. Twohats turned angry eyes on his companion, his expression a challenge and more.

This warning Greg decided not to test.

The Navajo turned once again to the group before him. "Would you call me when my brother arrives? It is important we speak with him. We will come to you here that we interrupt your important task as little as possible."

Tom and Juan exchanged glances, the Pima nodding slightly.

"We will call," said the Yaqui.

"Thank you, fathers," said Twohats sincerely. He turned, then, and left Greg no choice. Steering him back to their car with an iron grip on his shoulder, he ignored the policeman's attempts to speak until they were in the car with the engine running.

"What the hell was that, Twohats? Have you gone nuts? That collection of misfits knew a lot more than they were telling. We've got to go back and shake it out of them."

"That collection of misfits," said Twohats in a measured voice that indicated suppressed rage, "is the most powerful group of medicine men in the state . . . and they aren't even all there yet." He pulled over to the side of the road and shut off the engine. He lifted shaking hands and showed them to Johnson "You still don't get it, do you?"

"Get what?" The Tempe detective felt disgusted with him.

Redfield rolled his eyes and sighed. "This is big medicine, here, Greg. Something very important is going down in that house. If that many of the wise have gathered together, forgetting their own differences, then this may be one of the most important events in history."

"Oh, c'mon, Twohats! Don't give me that bullshit! You're an educated man. You can't seriously believe all this demon crap!"

The Navajo turned and looked levelly at his companion, his eyes as hard and black as obsidian. "You're starting to piss me off, white man," he said in a quiet but strained voice. "I haven't told you how the government should run your police force. I haven't called the President and his cabinet a collection of misfits. I haven't even asked what you believe as far as your religion is concerned—and I wouldn't ridicule it or call it superstitious nonsense. Nonetheless, that seems to be what you're telling me about my tribe, my leaders, my beliefs." He faced forward again, took a deep breath and let it out slowly.

An awkward silence prevailed.

Greg cleared his throat and spoke quietly. "I apologize, Twohats. I keep forgetting you're a Navajo Tribal Policeman and not a Tempe cop. I didn't mean to offend."

Redfield didn't say anything, but reached forward and started the car.

They had driven in silence for about five minutes when the Navajo turned and gave Johnson a sad smile. "I'll forgive you if you'll buy the beer," he said.

Greg burst out laughing, his words stumbling over themselves. "You bet, Twohats! It'll be my pleasure." He looked down, embarrassed. "I am sorry," he said again.

"No problem," said the Navajo, "but you ought to go spend a day at the Heard Museum sometime soon. You don't know shit about Native Americans and you, of all people, should." He shook his head, bemused. "Whatever it is those people are gathering for, I wouldn't want to be on the other side."

Chapter Forty-Two

Salt River Reservation

A car arrived at Tom's house an hour later containing Harold Laloma and William Concha of the Hopi. Tom went to greet them but found Concha upset and Harold unconscious. One look at the priest's swollen and bleeding leg frightened Tom enough that he sent Danny off with them to the hospital while he followed in his truck.

Harold was admitted immediately. His color looked ashen gray and his breathing stayed shallow. He occasionally regained consciousness, but those moments were obviously times of severe pain. X-rays showed that Joseph and John had done a good job setting the leg, but infection had set in because of the ragged break and wounds. The doctors put the Hopi on antibiotics to prevent it from spreading. They removed the splints, put on a cast, and, once he had been medicated, the tortured look left the Priest's features. In two hours, his color had vastly improved.

They waited through the afternoon for Harold's condition to stabilize, Tom fretful and impatient because all those they waited for were not yet assembled. When the Hopi regained consciousness, he demanded to be released from the hospital and taken back to the house.

Unable to do more, the doctors agreed to allow the priest to leave after Harold signed a release and Tom assured them he would take responsibility. The same thing had happened only the day before with Pasqual so the hospital staff had gotten used to it.

After the Pimas had left for the hospital with Concha and Harold, Lotus reminded the others that they had planned to visit the site of the demon's imprisonment. All expressed an interest in going, though Pasqual demurred because of his fragile health. Juan agreed to guide them.

So Lotus, Kade, James and Juan went by car to the West Phoenix beltway construction site, parked and walked across the desert to the rocks. Having brought torches and a rope, they were able to descend into the ancient kiva.

The experience proved eerie. The musty smell of ages hung in the air despite the opening above. The large chamber appeared much bigger than any of them expected, with smooth and glassy walls and a strange, rough floor.

Lotus looked around at the slick walls and spoke to the Yaqui. "This isn't constructed, Juan. It looks like a volcanic tube." She ran her hand along the glassy dark rock. "This is as smooth as obsidian." She knelt and touched the dark floor with her fingers. "And this is lava."

"What are you saying, Lotus?" he asked. James and Kade came over and joined their colleagues.

"This is a volcanic vent. See? At some time in the distant past, an active volcano stood nearby. This is one of the outlets where lava escaped. The heat has melted the rock on the sides. This floor is lava. It's probably only a plug. Our ancestors found this tube and dug out the lava floor, creating this chamber." She put a hand to her forehead, brushing away a strand of hair that kept hanging prettily before her face. "I wonder how far down it goes? There could be another chamber below this."

Juan smiled. "How is it, sister, that you know so much about this volcano business?"

Lotus smiled selfconsciously. "I have a graduate degree in geology." She shrugged. "I had planned to pursue it further but my people needed me."

"What does this . . . ," the Yaqui hesitated, ". . . vent mean to us? Will it serve as a trap for the demon?"

"Remind me to talk with Jack about this," said the woman. "Something about it sounds promising."

The chamber had both concave and convex walls so part of it curved away and created a separate room, rather like a comma. When they turned round that corner, they saw what remained of the paintings.

On an almost flat black wall were pictures that must once have been beautiful. Now they were scoured and scraped to the point of being unrecognizable.

In the torchlight the group could see figures within the renderings but they found it impossible to determine what the subjects had been depicted as doing.

"Look!" James pointed up toward the top of the wall.

As Lotus moved along the passage, she recognized the figures as representations of all the different tribes. In some cases, they had been all but obliterated, but the paintings obviously had been of the original Great Gathering.

"The others should see this," said Kade. "Perhaps it will help us when we are called."

"You're right," said Lotus. "I wonder what Pasqual would make of this?"

Though they searched every foot of the chamber, nothing else of significance caught the eye. The beast had, after all, ranged within these walls for hundreds of years. They were surprised anything remained.

Late that afternoon, they decided to return. All the way back in the car, Lotus sat quietly opposite the driver, apparently lost in thought. When Kade reached over the seat and tapped her shoulder, she started, then apologized.

"I'm sorry, Kade. It's just that there's something about the floor of that chamber that's important. I wish I could figure out what it is."

*   *   *   *   *

Pasqual had been glad to see the others go. Weariness lay heavily upon him and he needed rest. He felt better, but had begun to worry about his part in the task ahead. He sensed an urgency about this thing that could not be denied. *If anything happened to me, what would the rest do?*

He admitted to himself there were certainly other Zuni Priests who could represent his people, but it would take precious time to locate and then persuade one to leave Zuniland. He doubted much more than hours remained before the demon would come. In such a case, the council would be forced to scatter.

He had returned inside and lay upon the couch. He closed his eyes and tried to rest. This took more courage than in the past. He, among others, had directly touched the mind of the demon. Dread came with the thought of surrendering to sleep.

A knock on the door ended his attempt. He rose with a feeling half relief and half regret, and crossed the room to peer out the window. Outside stood two more men, obviously Native American. Pasqual opened the door.

"Is this the home of Tom Bear?" asked the taller of the two.

"This is his home," answered the Zuni. "He is not here now. He hadda go to the hospital with a Hopi."

The other nodded and spoke to his companion. "They have begun to gather. We are still in time." He turned back to the older man and introduced himself. "I am Michael Coyoma of the Mohave. This is Cord Hames of the Chemehuevi. We have been summoned."

Pasqual nodded. He stepped back and gestured for them to enter. "Welcome," he said. "I am Pasqual Quatero of the Zuni."

Michael looked around. "Where are the others?"

"The Pimas and the Hopi are at the hospital. The others are visitin' the place the demon come from."

"Is everyone here now?" asked Cord.

"No, not yet." Pasqual sat back on the couch. "We await the Navajo." He thought a moment, then added, "And maybe some others."

The three men sat together and Pasqual put his tiredness aside to act as host. The time passed easily as they waited for one group or the other to return.

The first back were Lotus, Kade, James and Juan. Introductions were made and conversation centered around what was expected of each of them during the gathering. Though each had a general idea about his or her own role, they lacked the hand of experience—they lacked their director.

Jack came along next. Having finished his classes for the day, he went directly to the reservation, still seeking answers about his part in this affair. Juan let him in and introduced him to the newcomers.

When the initial spurts of conversation died off, Lotus called Jack aside. "Do I understand that you've been down into the kiva?"

"No," he answered truthfully. "I looked in after we rolled the stone aside, but the ladder had fallen and Juan approached us only minutes later."

"It is a very ancient place. I am surprised the government hasn't moved in on it yet."

Jack looked down momentarily, feeling caught. "I . . . uh . . . I made a deal with the cops," he said quietly. "I didn't report it to the authorities and the police agreed not to enter without my being present."

The Tohono O'odham woman laughed delicately. "That's good thinking," she said. "Let me tell you about the inside, then. There is something about it that seems important, but I don't yet know what." Lotus explained that the rocks on the site were weathered basalt and that exfoliation had resulted in the breaking apart of the outer shell, creating scales and layers.

"You know," she said, getting into her subject, "the temperature goes from intense heat to freezing cold, there is rain, the rock surface expands and cracks, then refreezes and so on over the centuries."

"I understand exfoliation," Jack replied. "Remember what I do?"

The woman stopped and looked embarrassed. "Of course. Please forgive me." She shrugged. "I've just gotten so used to explaining things like that. I'm sorry."

"It's nothing," said Jack. "Please go on."

"The inside is a volcanic vent. The walls are smooth from the heat, but the floor is lava and may be only a plug. Who knows what might be under there?"

Jack looked immediately interested. "That may be something we need to know more about. In fact, I'm going out there first thing in the morning and take a closer look."

"There were some paintings on the wall in the back." Lotus wanted him to understand that it was a sacred place. "The demon did a lot of damage to them. I don't believe they could be restored."

"I'll look them over carefully. I promised the detective I'd hold off on my report for a week," Jack assured her. "If this isn't settled by Monday morning, I'll contact the university on it right away."

"Thank you, Jack." Her smile flashed with warmth.

They had been speaking in small groups now for hours, but no one had yet made an effort to organize anything more complicated. One by one, they realized they were still waiting.

The sound of a car pulling up outside brought Kade to the window in a rush. He looked out and then turned, relief evident in voice and manner. "The Navajo has arrived." Excitement filled the room. "And there is an Apache with him as well."

"Good," said Lotus. "We can begin as soon as the others return."

Juan looked around the group and shook his head. He did not speak aloud but thought to himself, *Not quite yet.*

Chapter Forty-Three

Salt River Reservation

Gordon and Gerry arrived at the house rested and relieved. Their journey together had offered them a chance to get acquainted and they had taken advantage of it. The drive had been leisurely, the conversation informative and a friendship had begun. The Apache fascinated the Navajo.

Gordie was amazed that Gerry appeared so matter-of-fact about his dual nature. For Gordon, this new experience represented yet another wonder—but only one of many since Archie's death. His companion claimed he had been Geronimo. Was he crazy or not? The whole idea of reincarnation conflicted with basic Navajo beliefs. The dead stayed dead, to be mourned and lamented. Had he not seen the change of personalities, he would have rejected such a claim without debate. Now, he did not feel so sure.

It called more than a few basic beliefs into question. His people were renowned for many things. Their crafts were superb, their sense of humor—especially punning—exceptional, their ability to adapt to the white man's world remarkable. Unfortunately, their stubborn adherence to superstition had become just as well known.

The dead must be buried. Only witches—Navajo wolves—dealt with them after death. The Evil way and the Enemy Way existed to protect the living from troublesome spirits, to cure the ills they brought from the grave.

How could it be that this man had once been the famous Apache medicine man and warrior? Was it simple schizophrenia or could it be true?

Gerry appeared rational, intelligent and confident. Gordon could not help but be impressed with the way he handled their meeting, the acquisition of the car and the journey to Tom Bear's house. He wanted to trust the Apache, but there were many questions roiling in his mind.

Getting at last to the home of the Pima had ended that particular speculation. There were many people to meet, many explanations to be given, many other questions to be asked.

A half hour after their arrival, Tom, Danny and Harold returned from the hospital. The relief on the Pima Witch's face when he saw the Navajo was plain to see.

Again, there were introductions. Gordon watched each face and counted off the tribes in his mind. When they had finished, he looked at the others and spoke. "Where is the Pai?"

Juan nodded to himself.

"We don't have any pie," said Danny, "but there might be a biscuit in the kitchen."

Tom smiled and said quietly, "Not pie, Danny, but Pai. He means the Havasupai named Rattle."

"Oh." Danny felt foolish.

"English is a strange language," said Gerry.

"I thought you were making a pun," said Gordon, dismissing it. "We are lacking only that one as far as I can see." He looked around with concern.

He saw a strange group of faces. The Zuni, Pasqual, showed the strain of his two heart attacks—he looked fragile. The Hopi, his broken leg in a cast still hardening, sat in a drugged stupor on the couch. The woman, Lotus of the Tohono O'odham, distracted him. He had expected a man. He did not know how the presence of a woman would affect the ceremony.

Gordon wished again that Archie could be here. His great-great-grandfather knew these things. Gordon knew only some songs. His youth and inexperience threatened to betray him at every turn, but he had seen upon arrival that these people all expected him to lead. He tried hard to exude confidence.

"There are others who wish to find you," said Tom. "Two men were here early this morning seeking Gordon Smythe. One is a Tempe policeman, the other of your people. They asked that we call them when you arrived." He passed over Johnson's card. "They have questions about Chaco Canyon."

Of course they would, thought Gordon. *I probably am the last one to leave there alive.* Looking at the card he said, "I will call them when we are finished here."

Tom nodded but did not speak.

Gerry looked at Gordon and smiled. "We're all waiting for you to tell us what to do, Fly. Everyone knows part of it, but you are the only one who knows all."

"Each has a part to play," explained the Navajo youth. "No part is more important than the others, yet all must be flawlessly accomplished or it is over for us and our people. Later, when we would have taken our evening meal, I will sing instead the song of the Great Gathering that you may know the past and better understand the future."

"Instead of?" Danny did not understand.

Gerry said, "We all fast tonight."

Gordon explained. "We must purify our bodies and hearts by fasting and prayer. Only in this way will we be able to stand unharmed before the demon when it comes."

Everyone exchanged resigned glances, then turned their attention back to the Navajo.

"Is there anything else we need once the Havasupai arrives?" Lotus was businesslike.

Fly looked around the group curiously. "Who has the Charm?" he asked.

The others looked confused, but Jack stood up suddenly and cursed. "Damn! That's what it was." He turned to Juan. "You kept asking me what I did at the site and I kept patting my pockets, remember?"

The Yaqui nodded.

"I was looking for the charm I found just under the rock."

"Describe it to me," commanded Gordon.

Jack shook his head and remembered. "It was predominantly silver, small but heavy. It was maybe two inches wide by an inch high, but almost an inch thick because of the hunk of turquoise."

"Go on."

"The turquoise part made up the sky, the silver a desert floor. In the middle an inverted funnel of gold had been inlaid."

"That is it," said Gordon enthusiastically. "Where is it?"

Jack looked blank for a moment, then patted his pockets again. "It's got to be here somewhere . . . ." He trailed off. "Did I ever take it out of my pocket after that first time?" He gestured for the others to stay quiet and closed his eyes, willing himself to remember. "Let's see, I had it before I went out and found Don's ring. Where did I put it after that?" Try as he might, he couldn't recall. He shrugged.

Michael said, "You've got to remember, Jack, this is vital."

Jack stood, perplexed, frustration evident in every movement as he wracked his brain. Then they all heard the car pull up outside.

When they peered out the window, they saw a stranger, a young white man.

Chapter Forty-Four

Phoenix

Rattle had been taken to Speed Perkin's house in West Phoenix instead of the Salt River Reservation. Speed had explained that he had an errand to run before he could drop the old man off. When they arrived, however, the Havasupai had been taken inside and locked in a closet. Shocked and exhausted, he had soon stopped struggling with the door and fallen asleep. He had been awake and on edge now since Sunday. During the ride, Bob had pumped the Indian for directions to Tom Bear's house, who would be there and what they were to do. The directions were given, but the other information withheld. The white men had taken turns guarding the door all night, but the old man had not stirred.

Today, after arguing all of the morning, Speed had left for the Reservation. He was to evaluate the situation and see if the old man they held prisoner was worth real money or if they were, as he put it, "jacking off in the closet."

Second thoughts and nervousness plagued him so he delayed going to the Pima's house until well into the afternoon. When he arrived, he went cautiously toward the door. A moving curtain indicated he had been seen and, a moment later, a strange collection of Indians came out and stood along the porch rail.

One of the older men stepped forward and spoke. "I am Tom Bear," he said. "Who are you and what do you want?"

"Nuthin'. My name's Speed."

"If you want nothing, Mr. Speed, why are you here?"

The man looked down at his feet, moved a toe in the dirt. "I might be able to help you find somethin' you want," he said too quietly.

"What did he say?" Pasqual leaned on the rail.

"I think he has something we want," said Juan to the others. He turned and stepped forward as well. "What do you have?"

"Not what," said the Bartender/Kidnapper. "Who."

The faces remained blank.

"Who then?" Juan's voice had gotten suddenly cold. He put something into his mouth and started chewing.

"A Havasupai that calls himself Deer Man," said Speed. He noticed a nervous tic starting under his nose. He chewed his lip before he went on.

No one else spoke.

"He's your Upperworld Warrior, he says. He tells me you can't do what you want to unless you've got him."

Tom exchanged looks with Juan and they both turned to the newly arrived Gordon Smythe.

Fly nodded slightly.

"Where is he?" Gerry asked. He looked menacing.

Speed took a step back before he straightened and returned the look, challenge in his eyes. "He's safe. He's on the west side of town. I could find him and bring him here if it was worthwhile."

No one but Lotus saw Juan step back behind the group and return to the house.

Tom scowled. "What would be worthwhile?"

"Ten thousand bucks," said the bartender clearly. It was the figure he and Bob had decided to start with. Looking at the house and the area, he felt sure they would be lucky to actually get a hundred.

That inscrutable blank look was replaced on all their faces with distress and consternation.

Speed felt immediately better. He held control here. He stepped forward, swaggering as he walked toward the porch.

No discussion ensued among the Indians. They exchanged glances, all nodding.

Tom turned back to the white man and said, "When must we have the money?"

It took a great deal of self-control for Speed to conceal his start of surprise. He had been prepared to drop the demand significantly. In deals like this, haggling had to be a big part of the plan.

"When do you want him?" He could think of no other reply.

"We need him now." Gordon had spoken.

Speed smiled and looked at his wristwatch. "If you can get the money, I'll meet you at eight p.m. in front of the Denny's on Thunderbird and Tatum."

Jack stepped from the back and looked down on the man. "Do you realize this is kidnapping?" he demanded.

"Chill out, dude," said the other. "We aren't talking kidnapping, but the sale of information. You don't want it, you don't have to buy."

Gerry laid a restraining hand on the archaeologist's shoulder.

Tom looked one more time around the group before he answered, "We will be there."

Gerry spoke. "Be sure the Pai is unharmed," he warned. "If anything happens to him, you'll find out how Custer felt at the Little Big Horn."

"He seemed okay when I saw him earlier today," Speed replied. "There's no reason that should change."

"Get out of here, then," said Tom, barely concealing the contempt in his voice. "We will be there at eight with the money."

"Sounds good to me, dude," said the bartender happily. "But remember, no cops. I might just forget where the Deer Man is if I see cops anywhere nearby." With a careless wave, he returned to his car, got in and pulled away.

As he sped down the uneven dirt road, he hooted in delight. "Piece of cake, man! Piece of cake!" He did not see the large crow winging high overhead.

*   *   *   *   *

Juan realized immediately that this task had been meant for him. He feared he might have trouble calming his mind enough to summon the crow, but it came to his window immediately.

He made the transfer and had no difficulty following the car as it departed the house and pulled away at top speed.

The traffic was heavy, but the VW made good time, weaving in and out of the lanes, passing with impunity the larger vehicles of the wealthy.

When it drove on to the old farmhouse, the bird glided down from the sky and landed on a ledge before an open window.

Bob Murphy had bitten off all his nails as he passed the day worrying about his cohort. The Indian had awakened and begun hurling himself against the closet door. It had taken half an hour of yelling before the old man would listen. He explained that Rattle would be safe, unharmed and returned to his friends before the day ended. Only then had silence fallen over the closet.

When the VW pulled up in front, he had rushed out to greet Speed and learn what happened.

As they entered the house, they talked excitedly, words stumbling over each other, smiles of glee lighting their faces.

"I couldn't believe it," said Speed. "They never even made a counter offer. They'll pay off at eight."

Bob jumped up and down, pounding the bartender's shoulder.

"Hot damn!" he exclaimed. "We're rich!"

Speed consulted his watch. "It's four now. We'll leave at seven-forty-five. It'll make us late, but let 'em sweat."

"I wish there were more than two of us," said Bob. "It means I got to watch this guy while you make sure it isn't a trap."

"More people means a smaller cut of the Pai, boy," said Speed, laughing at the pun.

"Hey, that's great!" said Bob, chuckling. "When we take all their money, these injuns won't have-a-sou!"

Both collapsed onto the sofa, slapping their knees and laughing uproariously. Neither saw or heard the crow leap from the window sill and launch itself into flight.

Chapter Forty-Five

Salt River Reservation

Juan came back to the reservation house nearly exhausted after flying frantically across town. Always a drain of life energy, transference to the crow usually compensated him with extended periods of leisurely observation. This time the resting period had been but moments and Juan had been forced to push the crow beyond its abilities. In effect, he normally left the flying to the crow but today he had been forced to flap the wings himself.

Lotus sat on the edge of his bed, watching his face with a look of wonder as the crow landed and then both changed before her eyes.

Intelligence faded from the bird and the slack face of the Yaqui came alive. Juan opened his eyes.

"This is a wondrous gift," she said quietly. "Can it be taught?"

Juan shook off his lethargy and sat up. "Ask me when this is all over, my sister. Now is not the time." He walked out into the other room.

The rest sat together, arguing over what course of action to follow.

"Gordon should call the two policemen now," said Tom. "Perhaps they can help."

"No," admonished Cord. "The white man said no police."

"But we must tell the authorities," insisted the witch. "We can't come up with ten thousand dollars."

"You would risk the life of the Pai," added Michael.

"We should go out and search," suggested Kade.

"All over West Phoenix?" Danny shook his head. "We could take weeks and have no luck."

"He's right," said James. "There's no way we'd find them."

"We can't just sit here," shouted Harold, his painkillers wearing thin. "If we need the Pai, we have to find him today."

"We gotta get the money," urged Pasqual. "We gotta do what they ask."

"We don't have that kind of money, grandfather," said Gordon. "We'll have to find another way."

Gerry, who had been sitting back with his eyes closed, spoke without even looking around. "We will find him," he said simply.

Juan looked at them, a kindly expression, understanding and compassionate. "Quiet, all of you. I know where he is and can lead you there."

"What? How? Where?" They all reacted at once, incredulous but relieved.

Lotus stood in the doorway and watched attentively.

"I have my ways of finding things," said Juan quietly. "I have seen the place. There are only two of them. Our friend is well and unharmed but we have little time. We must go now."

Gerry stood. "We'll take my rental car," he said. "We can accommodate five besides myself."

Danny, Michael, James and Cord accompanied Gerry.

Tom insisted on going in his truck otherwise they wouldn't have room for Rattle on the return trip if they were successful in rescuing him.

Kade decided to ride with Tom.

They loaded up and Tom led off with Juan giving directions.

When the others had gone, Pasqual and Harold stretched out in the living room to try and get some sleep.

Gordon went out back and sat on the edge of the gorge, watching the sun sink lower in the evening sky. It promised to be a beautiful sunset in a few hours. He let his legs dangle over the edge, allowed his thoughts to reach out toward Archie and his family.

All were gone now. For the first time since realizing Chaco Canyon had been destroyed and his great-great-grandfather killed, he allowed the emotion to run through him. In moments his eyes were filled with tears that fell prodigiously down his cheeks and dripped off his chin. He made no sound, however, nor did he move.

Lotus went to him, much as she had to Danny. She knew what she had to offer was healing. At first he seemed reluctant, but—just as with the Pima—she gentled and led the Navajo, coaxed and praised, and soon they were as one while the day faded in magnificence around them.

*   *   *   *   *

The pickup and the Ford pulled off the road just out of sight of the farmhouse. Tom waited with the vehicles while the others moved up and fanned out, covering the possible exits. His watch read seven thirty. They could hear Bob and Speed inside.

"We're taking you to your friends now, Deer Man," said Bob. He had apparently been celebrating already since "friends now" came out as "frengenow."

"If he gives you any trouble, use the sap," called Speed from the front room. "Hurry up. Water him and get him out to the car."

The bartender came out the front door looking back over his shoulder and walked directly into Gerry's arms. The scuffle was brief. The Apache outweighed the white man by a half. Speed soon lay unconscious in the yard.

Cord, James, Michael and Danny went in. Kade covered the back door while Juan stood by the side entrance.

Those outside heard a startled shout that was quickly cut off by the sound of breaking glass.

Bob Murphy came out the window head first under his own power, did a perfectly executed tuck and roll and came up running. No one pursued him.

A moment later, the rest of them came out of the house escorting Rattle who looked disheveled but otherwise no worse for his incarceration. When he got to the truck and saw Tom, the old Havasupai embraced him.

A happy group returned in triumph to the reservation just as the sun disappeared.

After a quick search through the house, Danny ran out back to tell Lotus of their success. The good news and excitement died un-uttered when he saw her wrapped in the arms of the Navajo.

He turned and stumbled blindly around to the front of the house, seating himself at the foot of the steps as he had . . . was it only the night before?

Angry. Betrayed. Hurt. Confused. Danny wanted to put it out of his mind, but it seethed within him like a festering sore.

An hour later, Lotus came looking for him. She appeared as fresh and beautiful as ever and called softly, urging him to hurry as they were about to plan the Great Gathering.

Taking a deep breath, he stood and turned.

She gazed at him innocently, not understanding. When he refused to meet her eyes, she realized what must have happened. She walked up to him, put her arms around him and pulled him close.

He did not return her embrace and remained standing, unresponsive.

Without letting go, she pulled his face down by the chin and tried to give him a deep, passionate kiss.

He stood unmoved.

She looked up at him with pleading eyes. "I am a healer, Danny," she said.

His face remained expressionless. Carefully, he unfolded her arms from around him. Gently, he moved her aside. Still without speaking, he walked into the house not looking back.

Chapter Forty-Six

Salt River Reservation

Detective Greg Johnson and Twohats Redfield arrived at the reservation home of Tom Bear that evening to interview Gordon Smythe about the Chaco Canyon disaster. Both were eager for the meeting. Greg wanted it because he hoped it would end all the talk of a demon or evil entity. Twohats sought a resolution of his mission so he could get back to New Mexico and end the constant nagging of his father, the Lieutenant.

They knocked at the door and were ushered in by Danny Webb, who directed them toward two folding chairs set in the middle of the living room. Greg moved to the seat immediately, but Twohats looked around the room nervously.

"Thank you," he said respectfully, "for allowing us to come here. I know your time is valuable."

There were a few nods from those who sat around the room.

Greg noticed that there were more people present than before— thirteen Indians and Jack Foreman. He nodded to the archaeologist and received a barely perceptible wink in acknowledgement. He could feel significant tension in the air.

Twohats crossed over and stood before a young man seated cross-legged on the floor on the end facing their chairs. "Ya-deh-hay," he said in greeting.

"Ya-deh," came the response.

"Thank you for seeing us." He turned slightly, gesturing toward the chair next to Greg. "May I sit?"

The young man said, "Please do."

After they had sat and fidgeted for a moment, Twohats pulled out his notebook and looked at Gordon.

"As you know," he said in Navajo, "the dineh have suffered a great loss."

"Let us speak in English," said Gordon quietly. "It is the only tongue common to all here."

"Very well," said Twohats and repeated his opening remark in English, then continued. "Though there is much speculation about the cause, no one seems sure what happened there. You are, as far as we can determine it, the last to have left Chaco alive. We hope you can tell us what happened."

All eyes turned on Gordon.

He looked around the circle of his peers and then at the detectives in the middle. "There are two answers," he said. "The first is the one the white man will be most comfortable with. It is, simply, that I know nothing." He sat up straighter and faced Greg directly. "When I left Chaco Canyon two hours before dawn, my great-great grandfather bid me an unhurried goodbye and everything seemed well. I travelled to the home of my uncle and delivered a message and then went on to Shiprock. I saw nothing unusual, heard nothing out of the ordinary, went in my ignorance to safety as was the old man's plan."

Twohats looked disappointed. Greg felt relief wash over him. They exchanged glances.

"If we leave it at that, Twohats," said Greg, "you can get on the plane tonight."

"I know," replied the Navajo, "but that would not answer our questions."

Tom Bear spoke from his seat off to their side. "Are you sure you really want the answers?"

In the awkward silence that followed, each man searched his soul for the truth.

Twohats would be forced to confront his beliefs, the Navajo fear that accompanied the dead or the magical. He was better equipped to accept the existence of a demon than the white man, but less likely to act on it.

Greg knew what the other answer would be, but could not accept the supernatural as an explanation. If he could find a logical way to explain what had happened in Agate and Chaco, he would be free of this challenge to his basic beliefs. On the other hand, once he had identified the cause, he was more likely to act effectively in dealing with it—no matter what it turned out to be.

They both knew they had no choice. With a resigned nod from Greg, Twohats asked the next question. "Tell me, my brother, what is the second answer?"

"The Demon." Gordon looked at Greg, then continued. "We each have our origin myth," he said, gesturing around the circle. "I will generalize in the interests of harmony. Be patient with me, my brothers and sister. It is a long story I must tell."

Gordon knew he was treading on dangerous ground. Who was he to speak for those around him who were both older and wiser? Still, he had no real choice. The question had been asked.

"The gods placed people on the earth to live in harmony with it, to farm and hunt and share the bounty of their work in creating it. For a long time, the people lived according to those precepts. After a time, however, some began to stray away from the wishes of Those Above. They no longer sang their praises to the gods, stopped keeping the traditions, started breaking the laws. The gods grew angry.

"The world ended several times. With each ending came a new beginning, for the gods were reluctant to destroy the people who kept their faith. At one such time, a demon was sent to end all life. The demon took the shape of a desert storm, a great wind. It punished those who had forgotten the right way. It fed on those who had abandoned the gods.

"It grew very big and very strong. No one could stand alone before it and remain unharmed. Many tried but all failed. As time passed, this demon—just as the people—strayed from the wishes of its creator and began to feed on the innocent as well as the guilty. It stopped being an instrument of the gods and became a thing unto itself. The more strength it had, the more destructive it became. It is conscious, you know. It has a mind not unlike our own. At first, it had a just and directed way of thinking. Later, it became bent. It forgot its purpose. It grew fat and arrogant and cruel.

"The gods tried to call it back, but it would not listen. It had become sick—twisted, not weak—and thought of itself as a god. Since nothing could stop it here in the desert where it roamed, it believed itself above everything.

"The people had those among them who were faithful to the gods, those who spoke to the creator through his servants. These were the wise men of the tribes, like those who are gathered here.

"Each of our tribes has a belief we are the chosen of Those Above. Each has carried the legends forward as faithfully as possible from the beginning till today. Each is sure that their story is the real story.

"But time and retelling can change a thing. It may be only a word, but the next retelling may change yet again. As the stories are told, they are adapted to the times. I believe much of our disagreement comes from this. No matter how faithful the singer, the songs change.

"Finally, a little over five hundred years ago, one of the tribes—the Pima—found itself hard pressed by the demon. When they realized they could not stop it, their medicine man envisioned a gathering of the wise in which they would unite to do what none could do alone. It was a very imaginative thing, this thought he had. Few of the tribes cooperated in those days. Runners were sent to all the tribes and they requested that the strongest and most powerful shaman in each one come here and represent his people.

"Thus came into being a wonderful thing, the first Great Gathering of the Wise. Only the Ute could not send a representative as they had been almost destroyed by the demon and all their medicine men had died. For this reason, not for any deficiency in the Utes, they are not represented here today. Twelve tribes answered the call, as we have today. They were the Pima, the Hopi, the Navajo, the Yaqui, the Pai, the Apache, the Zuni, the Tohono O'odham, the Mohave, the Chemehuevi, the Cocopah and the Maricopa.

"The Yaqui lived further south, but they came. The Zuni lived further east but they came. Despite their differences, all came when called. It was a great thing. It took weeks to prepare the ceremony—for each of the tribes wanted to be represented well and to play an important part—thus there was much discussion and maneuvering by the medicine men. They chose a site after much argument. They selected the mouth of the fire god that once had belched flame into the air. The rocky top rose into the air, the sides felt smooth like glass beads, and the floor proved to be soft, easy to shape. At that time, the heat from the underworld could be felt through the floor. It took many days and many workers to make it deeper.

"The artists were set to work in creating a charm, a symbol in which all the wise would invest a part of their magic. They worked with things that pleased the gods—the shiny metals of silver and gold and the blue rock, turquoise. They made it as long as the longest finger on the artist's hand, two fingers wide and one thick. When they had finished, the Zuni brought it to the gathered shamans and each sang over it and prayed and asked the spirits to bless his particular contribution. It is said to be very beautiful.

"When all had been prepared, the wise travelled to the site and formed a great circle. They made a sand painting showing the whole world and all its parts. Every medicine man made part of the painting. It took them a whole day for it was very big. That night, they summoned the demon and it came. At first, it acted unafraid for they were all only men and it thought itself a god. When it got too close to the charm, however, it found itself drawn in, as if the talisman had become a magnet and the beast metal, unable to pull away. One of the magics given to the charm was that it could reduce the size of what it caught. Thus the demon found itself pulled to the center of the circle, kept off the earth by the painting and shrunken by the magic charm into a condensed ball of force. One man of the wise stood and held the charm in the center of the circle, protected by this talisman yet alone under the rage of the demon.

"Then, the demon worked magic of its own. Feeling its control slipping away, it took the shamans and spirited them away to other dimensions. In five different places the wise were forced to battle it. They realized immediately the loss of a single battle would mean victory for the demon. In the underworld, in the middle world, in the upper world, in the spirit world and in the world of the mind, the battle raged through the night. With the rising of the sun, exhausted but triumphant, the wise had defeated the demon. It could not be killed. Only by returning it to the fires of the earth could it be truly destroyed. But it was chained to the charm, helpless unless another took the talisman away. The charm, with the beast still tied to it, was placed inside the fire god's mouth and a rock put over the top so no one would remove that binding magic.

"When it was done, there was much rejoicing and the word was sent by swift runners to all the people, telling them the demon was gone. Each of the shamans returned to his tribe to grow old in honor, a hero to his people. Thus it was five hundred years ago."

As Gordon's voice died away, there was silence.

Greg stayed quiet as long as he could, but eventually could not keep himself from speaking. "And then Jack Foreman and Don Hunnicutt let it out."

Jack nodded unhappily. "We didn't know."

Gordon smiled at the archaeologist. "It had lain under the earth unresolved long enough," he said. "Either we are ready to live in harmony or we are not. This time the Great Gathering must solve the problem, not place it as a burden on the shoulders of those who will come after."

Twohats looked around the circle. He shrugged. "How can we help?"

"Keep interruptions away from us once we begin," said Tom. "It will be impossible to do anything if this turns into a circus."

"Find a way to help us keep track of the demon," said Gerry. "If it gets here before we've finished preparations, all this will have been for nothing."

"When will you begin?" Greg remained unconvinced, but it could do no harm.

"We have begun," said Gordon. "The start of it all is telling the story of the First Great Gathering."

Chapter Forty-Seven

Phoenix

Jack left only a few minutes after the policemen. He drove home and began a systematic search for the charm. After an hour, he felt frustration building.

"Why is it I can never find things when I want them?" On hands and knees, he crawled through the house looking under furniture, checking behind stacks of books.

Useless accompanied him, weaving around his thighs, rubbing past his forearms, butting him with his head, purring.

Jack stopped and picked the cat up, cradling him in his arms. "Hi, buddy. I guess I've been ignoring you, haven't I. I'm sorry. I'm a little preoccupied."

"Brrrrrrrrrrppppppppppp," the cat chirped contentedly.

Jack sat back on his heels, gently stroking the animal, trying to reconstruct in his mind the last few days. When exactly had he held the damned charm last?

His house was not large. It should not be taking this long. To his best recollection, he had found the charm after taking his shower Sunday, when he kicked that pile of laundry. What the hell had he done with it then?

He set the cat down on his feet and rose, heading for the kitchen. "Ready to eat, guy?" He was rewarded with the usual nonchalance.

Useless washed himself, his head ducking down in that wonderful loose-jointed way as he licked his chest.

Jack moved to the kitchen and opened a can of cat food, the electric opener making the usual whirring sound. The cat peered around the corner, his tongue still fully extended but momentarily forgotten.

Jack laughed. Cats were extremely comical in their own way. When you attracted the attention of a feline, it riveted on your action no matter what the animal had been doing. Tongue out or foot and paw fully extended in the air, the concentration of moments before was abandoned while it assessed this new wonder.

"Don't give me the raspberry, furball," he said chuckling. "I'm the guy who buys the vittles, remember?"

Useless licked his chops and stepped delicately into the room, moving to his feeding station as Jack bent and set the dish next to the water bowl.

Leaving the cat in the kitchen, Jack moved back to his bedroom. He sat on the edge of the bed and looked around the room, trying to reconstruct his activities. "I called the dorm from here, then the police," he muttered to himself. He simply could not remember. "What did I do then?"

He checked the bathroom, the bedside table, under the bed, behind and under the dresser. No luck. He did find two buttons, a safety pin and a stale cigar. He went to the closet and hauled out his laundry bag, dumping it on the bed.

Patiently, he sorted through the clothing, checking pockets. It had only been four days, for God's sake! He moved the stack aside and looked carefully on the bed. No charm, but he noted that he had managed to get sand in the sheets. He rose and retrieved the laundry bag, turning it inside out. Not there.

He could have sworn he put it in his right pants pocket. He patted the pair he was wearing absently—only the usual junk, keys and change. He scratched his head.

Carefully, he separated the other pants from the rest of the laundry. He put his hand in the right front pocket of each pair. One had a big hole in it, the other two had lint and he found a quarter.

Leaving the laundry on the bed, he got to his hands and knees again and looked under the bed. Forearms flat to the floor, ass in the air, he must have presented a pretty picture.

Useless came bounding in through the door and jumped up onto Jack's butt, springing from there to the bed.

Not expecting it, the cat's weight—eighteen pounds—caught Jack off balance and his forehead hit the bed rail.

"Ouch! Son of a bitch!" The archaeologist pushed up off the floor and onto his knees, lifting a hand and rubbing his head.

Useless sat on the edge of the bed, his face at eye level and licked his paws in the after-meal ritual.

"Will you be careful, please?" He felt no anger at the cat, but his forehead still stung. He reached out and playfully pushed the animal over on its side. When he did, however, its usual friendliness disappeared.

Useless growled and backed away, swatting once at the stack of clothing before turning, then leaping off the bed and fleeing the room.

"What the hell?" Jack reached over to where the cat had lain and patted the clothing, something heavy and pointed was in the hem of the trousers. A moment later, he held the charm. A glance at his watch told him it was eight-forty-five at night. He still had time to return to the reservation and pass the talisman on to the Navajo, thus ridding himself of the last obligation in this affair.

He stopped. He knew in his heart there was no way to eliminate his feelings of responsibility. He would have to stick it through to the end, but wasn't this all crazy?

Was it possible such a thing as a demon could exist in the modern world? Was he allowing himself to be sucked into a grand hoax?

His mind returned to the faces of the Native Americans gathered in Tom Bear's house. He heard again the tale of the Navajo called Gordon or Fly. His imagination was captured by the image of the demon, the Great Gathering, the ultimate battle.

No, crazy or not, he would see this through. Irrational as it seemed, he believed the Indians knew what was going on better than anyone in the modern world. They would do as they were meant to and the threat would end forever.

He decided to get a good night's sleep and return to the reservation house in the morning. He had a part to play. He would rest and do it right.

Then the phone rang.

Chapter Forty-Eight

Phoenix

Matt Sharp was still trying to track down the ASU archaeologist Jack Foreman. Once he interviewed the professor, he would know about the earliest incident in this incredible series of events. If Foreman could tell him, for instance, from what direction the storm had come, he might be able to track it back to a previous flare-up and eventually even determine its point of origin.

He had been right about the phone calls from both coasts. New York and LA were interested in a bright young man who could scoop the networks. It seemed like the entire industry had been buzzing since his broadcast. He had appointments with two major stations next week, assuming of course that the storm finally blew out and he could break free.

The toll-free number had been a master-stroke. There had been hundreds of calls reporting damage from a wind storm of one size or another. Oh, there were spurious calls and reports of other perfectly natural storms in other areas of the state, but a swarm of reports from northeastern Arizona indicated that Matt's killer storm had returned and might be turning south toward Phoenix.

The producers had agreed when Matt suggested they bring in a technician to see if the radar could be adjusted to greater sensitivity. The man worked even now in the studio trying to set the machine so it would register smaller particles and dust storms without rain.

The destructive force involved in this storm had not been measured. In the back of his mind, Matt envisioned himself reporting from the center of the storm, wind whipping debris around him, uprooted trees flying in the background. It would bring him awards and accolades from his peers and the security of employment by one of the big networks. The possibility of danger never entered his mind.

"Matt," the excited voice of Diedre Carroll came from the living room.

"What is it, honey?"

"I have Professor Jack Foreman on line five."

"Great. Thanks, beautiful. I owe you dinner." Matt picked up the phone and stabbed the button. "Hello, is this Professor Foreman?"

The voice on the other end sounded hurried.

"Yes, this is Jack Foreman. What can I do for you, Mr. Sharp?"

"Oh, call me Matt, please," said the weatherman. "I'm doing a national broadcast on the killer storm and I need to talk with you as soon as possible. I realize you must be very busy, but is there a time when we can meet?"

"I'm afraid that's out of the question, Matt." The voice was unsure. "I have to sleep. I need to deliver something over on the Salt River Reservation at sunrise tomorrow. I'm sorry, but I don't know when I'll be back." There was a momentary hesitation. "Besides, it isn't really a storm . . . at least I don't think so . . . it's, uh, something else."

"I really need to speak with you, Professor." Matt wasn't about to lose the guy now. "Perhaps I could meet you at your destination?"

"I don't know." The archaeologist's voice betrayed his indecision. "Oh, hell. Why not? But I warn you, Matt, this will not be what you expect."

Matt wanted to ask what the professor meant, but sensed he had just achieved a major concession and wanted to take advantage while he could.

"Give me the directions," he said, whipping a pen and pad out in front of him. "Exactly where is it that you're going?"

"To the home of a Pima witch," said the voice with a chuckle. "The man's name is Tom Bear. You take Pima Road north from McDowell and turn right on Shea Boulevard. After three miles, you'll see a Bait and Tackle shop on the right with a sign that says DONNO'S. Make a right onto the dirt road and follow it for exactly three-quarters of a mile. There are a lot of side roads and branchings, so watch the odometer carefully. Take a left at that three-quarter mile mark. The house is isolated and alone two-and-a-third miles further on. Have you got that?"

Matt, who had been scribbling furiously, repeated the directions, then added, "Is there a phone number in case I get lost?"

"No." Jack's reply was short and to the point. "Look, I have to go. I'll see you in the morning. Goodbye."

Then, on Matt's end, only the dialtone remained.

Chapter Forty-Nine

The Desert

The beast continued on its southwesterly course, leaving Diablo Canyon and skirting around Happy Jack, Stoneman Lake and Rimrock. It swept by Montezuma's Castle and crossed the Verde River just south of Camp Verde. When it reached Turret Peak, elevation six thousand feet, it climbed to the top, halted, and lay low.

Ahead, it sensed the increased density of larger settlements, towns and even cities. These were new experiences for it. Before its imprisonment, it had dealt only with the smaller Native American settlements.

The destruction of Agate Junction had been exhilarating, but disturbing. No matter how hard it had tried there, it could not level the huge block constructions. The weaknesses had been found, of course, and the roofs peeled back, the contents sucked out, but the main shells had been stronger than its own fury. If these larger concentrations of humanity meant more of the same, it would have to proceed cautiously.

This terrain could not have been more ideal for the beast. Aside from an isolated house or two, the towns and cities were clusters of humanity. It could pass unnoticed between them and approach any of them undetected. Its awareness of the minds around it remained limited. Surface thoughts were clear and sharp, but it experienced a feeling of unease when it dealt with anything else. There were so many of them. Subtler patterns of thought immersed themselves in the mass of minds it could not unravel, a knot of words and feelings that muddied themselves in combination.

It had grown strong now. Expanded over the ground, it would stretch in a circle three miles in diameter. It could lift objects that weighed thousands of pounds and hurl them into others at speeds in excess of three hundred miles per hour. It had become larger and more powerful than it ever had before. And it knew now that there was no upward limit. In time, it could grow ten times, a hundred times, larger and rage unchecked over the whole world.

It had no eyes. It saw through the eyes of those it fed upon. It lived and understood by virtue of their minds alone. The beast had seen through those eyes. It had seen mountains and canyons and sunlight. And it had seen the lights in the night sky.

Points of light, yet more than that. If it understood correctly, those points of light were suns. Those suns might light worlds like this one, other worlds.

The beast began to understand ambition.

It developed—in that moment—imagination.

It imagined itself grown large enough to envelop the world, huge enough to add the moon. It saw them crash together in a moment of splendor and magnificence. It saw itself in the aftermath, a vortex of force spinning unrestricted in empty space. It looked out and wanted the stars.

Thursday, July 13th

Chapter Fifty

Salt River Reservation

An hour before sunrise, Jack Foreman arrived at the reservation house of Tom Bear carrying a three-inch by one-inch artifact known to be at least five hundred years old. The Second Great Gathering had become possible when Gordon Smythe told the story of the first. It began when the medicine men of all the tribes were finally together. The story had been told, the doubts dispelled. Now there were preparations to be made.

The work of the second Gathering began when Jack Foreman delivered the Charm.

Gordon greeted the professor at the door, a wide smile on his face as he accepted the offered silver, gold and turquoise talisman. The others stood solemnly around in a half circle. No words were spoken. None were needed. The metal and stone spoke more eloquently than language.

"Now we can begin," said the Navajo. "It is time."

The wise stood there, awaiting instruction, a group of individuals willing to surrender individuality, a malleable and powerful force ready to accept direction.

Gordon, the youngest of them all, would point them at the demon and lead the battle. "First," he said, "we must strengthen the charm. Each of us must give what he or she has to offer. The past has done what it was required to do. It is time for the present to act."

"Who is first?" asked Tom.

"As history requires, Tom Bear, the Pima are first. No matter that they may be few in number, your people were responsible for bringing the first Gathering into being."

Tom and Danny looked at each other and the older man nodded. It was Danny Webb who stood up and approached Gordon.

"Then I am first." He was surprised to hear his own voice rise over the others. The Danny Webb who stood there now was a much different man than the one who had walked to Tom Bear's house the Saturday before. He stood tall and moved with confidence.

He held out his hand and Gordon passed the charm to him. It felt heavy. Gold, silver and turquoise had been melded into a talisman of power. He could sense its antiquity and its strength. The charm represented more than the sum of its parts.

Gordon spoke to all of them. "We will each take a turn. When your time comes, you may take this thing and walk with it. Think carefully what you will give to it and, when you are sure, begin your magic. When you are done, give it to the next." To Danny, he said, "Pass it on to Harold Laloma of the Hopi when you have finished."

Danny nodded and looked once all around the room, meeting each pair of eyes with a level gaze. When he reached Lotus, he smiled. When his eyes met Tom's, he saw the old man bursting with pride. He turned once again to Gordon.

"How long?" he asked.

"Waste no time. There are many and the day is just beginning."

So Danny left the room and walked outside carrying the charm as the sky in the east lightened with the promise of the dawn.

In a vato, one of the arrow weed sheds behind the house, Danny sat with his back to the mesquite tree and thought of what he could give the charm. Next to him on the ground were his medicine pouch and the feathered wand. In his mind were the faces of his father and grandfather. In his heart dwelt a peace and contentment he had never known before. This felt right. This was what he had been born for.

He concentrated first on the visage of his father. The face was as he remembered it, scarred but strong despite the years of abuse. "You were wrong, father. The medicine way is still needed even in the modern world. This demon would destroy all the people were it not for these men and the woman and me."

The face glared sternly and began to change. In its place, Danny saw movement, a swirling cloud—and in it he saw his father's eyes, saw his father's mouth. He had no fear. Then he realized that he held the charm.

"Who are you that dare challenge me?" The voice of the demon echoed harshly in his mind.

"I am Danny Webb of the Pima," he responded.

"Do you think you can defeat me, Danny Webb?"

"We will send you back to the father of winds, demon, for only he can judge you. Yes, we will defeat you."

The face changed again and became his father, but this time the features twisted with pain, the flesh torn and bleeding.

"Danny," it cried, "do not do this thing! The beast can reach into the world of the dead and avenge itself on us!"

The vision changed swiftly yet again and the serene countenance of his grandfather floated before his eyes.

"Do not be fooled, grandson," said the well-loved voice in Danny's mind. "The dead have nothing to fear from this creature. If any demons plague and torment your father, they are of his own devising."

A new picture formed. This time he could see a mountain in the north with a whirling storm hovering above it. At the foot of the mountain stood a man, looking up at the storm. Danny's sight swooped in and around until he could see the face.

"Jon!" He gasped as he recognized his friend Jon Steele.

The demon's voice spoke again. "Does this one mean something to you, boy? Would you have me spare this wretch? It would be easy. All you must do is go home and forget. You do not belong in the battle your misguided friends prepare to enter. Stop now and I will spare the weaver."

But his grandfather's voice spoke. "Steele is not yours to mold, grandson. Jon has placed himself at peril and you must let him meet his destiny alone."

In the vision, Jon Steele held a feathered wand upraised in his hand. He shouted up at the storm above, but his voice could not be heard.

"He found his wand," murmured Danny to himself.

"One last chance, Danny Webb," said the demon. "Agree to withdraw from this and I will spare him."

"I will not."

"Then watch retribution at work!"

The storm over the mountain began to move downward, growing in intensity, ripping up trees and boulders, denuding the slope as it raced toward the human below.

Steele apparently saw it begin its descent for he stiffened and looked around, fear suddenly on his face.

Danny watched helplessly as his friend fell before its violence, ripped to pieces.

The vision faded only to be replaced by Jon's face floating as had the others in the young man's mind. Crushed out of shape and battered, the lips moved and accused. "Your fault," it whispered. "Your fault."

"No." The voice of his grandfather spoke again. "Tricks meant to rob you of courage will not succeed, grandson. You are the only medicine man of the Pima now and there is a task for you."

Danny nodded. He knew now what he would give to the charm.

He lifted it and held it at arm's length in front of him with both hands, offering it to the light in the eastern sky. Gently he lowered it to the ground before him and reached for his pouch. Within, he found a small bundle of pollen with which he blessed the talisman. Then he lifted the metal and stone object again and held it to his forehead. Into it he willed the memories of his grandfather, father and of Jon, cushioning them in unconditional love. In doing so, he contributed the strength of simple faith, ever the Pima way.

When he looked around, Danny realized with surprise that only minutes had passed. The sun had still not risen, though the sky was lighter than before.

Returning to the house, he passed the charm to Harold Laloma as the priest sat upon the couch, his leg up, the weight of the cast supported by cushions. As the young man handed the talisman over, he felt compelled to warn the Hopi. "I saw the demon," he said. "It spoke to me."

Harold nodded. "I know. I have spoken with it several times. It is necessary that all of us know what we must face. This demon sees our weaknesses."

Out of deference to the priest's immobility, the others left him in the house alone and went out onto the porch.

Harold made an altar on the coffee table using two baskets, flowers brought to him by Lotus, and taking pahos and cornmeal from his bag, he placed the charm before him. Lighting his pipe, he smoked for a few minutes.

The plaster cast itched distractingly, but Harold put it from his mind and concentrated on the task ahead. He did not know what to give the charm. The object inspired awe in him, a thing which had been held by a nameless predecessor five hundred years before. He could feel the medicine radiating from it, could sense the power it contained.

He closed his eyes and prayed, scattering a little cornmeal in offering, stacking pahos in the limited space before him. The smoke lingered in the air.

"Taknokwunu, spirit who controls the weather, I await your wisdom."

"I am pleased with you," replied the spirit in his mind. "You have done well. The People of Peace are well-represented."

"Oh, Spirit," said Harold aloud, "before me is the charm that once imprisoned the demon. What gift shall the Hopi give to it?"

"Cornmeal to sustain it, pahos to honor it, and reverence to the gods," said the weather spirit.

"I have cornmeal and pahos," said Harold, "but how shall I give reverence?"

"With your heart," said the spirit gently. "Lift the charm and show it to me."

So Harold reached down and took the talisman in his hands and lifted it up that Taknokwunu might see, lowering his own eyes humbly as he did.

"So beautiful," said the spirit in a soft voice. "Now place the charm upon your breast, my Priest."

Harold did as commanded and immediately felt something akin to an electric current, a barely perceptible vibration not at all unpleasant.

"This is the flow of reverence from your heart to the charm and back," said the spirit. "It makes a circle, like the earth itself. Always the People of Peace have given their reverence and their faith to the earth and Taiowa, the Creator."

"I thank you for your wisdom, Taknokwunu," said Harold.

"There is much remaining to be done," cautioned Taknokwunu. "The battle must still be fought and the outcome is not certain."

"I will do my best," said the Priest humbly, and then he felt the spirit withdraw. Gently he took the charm from his breast and placed it on the altar. Reverently he prayed, offering more cornmeal and stacking the last of the pahos he had prepared.

"You are a fool, Peace Man."

The voice, though expected, jarred the Hopi from his reverie.

"I am only a servant of the spirits," said Harold quietly. "I represent my people."

"You remain a fool, Priest," said the beast. "I am coming for you—all of you."

"It must be the will of Taiowa," said the Hopi. "What must be done will be done."

"I could have given you power, Peace Man. I could have raised you above the little men around you. I could have rid your people once and for all of the Navajo plague that surrounds your mesas."

"I am learning that we must live together here in Tuwaqachi," replied Harold. "There is no more room for hate and envy."

"I will see you on the battlefield, Priest. Be prepared to die."

"If the spirits will it, then it will be so."

And Harold was left alone.

When the Hopi called the others, the sun had just risen over the mountains to the east. Gordon next took the charm.

Moving out to the ravine, he returned to the spot where Lotus had shared her healing gift with him. Seated with his legs dangling over the edge, he watched a hawk soar high overhead.

So many changes had come to his life. Everyone he loved most dearly had been taken by the demon—his father, mother, grandfather, brothers and sisters, uncles and aunts, nieces and nephews and, finally, his great-great-grandfather.

Yet I have been healed. Before the Tohono O'odham medicine woman came to him he had been filled with anger and hate, overwhelmed by sorrow and self-pity. After the beauty of her sharing, there was peace.

He had no illusions about a future with Lotus. She meant nothing to him romantically, had been only an instrument of the gods, a sweet and gentle giver of life and hope. It might be she would one day marry, but it would take a very special man to understand and accept her.

Like Danny, Gordon had been transformed. Part of the change had come from Archie, the patient training, the beautiful songs. The dineh had many stories and no one had known more than He-Who-Walked-In-Wisdom. Gordon suddenly realized his mind had changed the name to past tense.

Sitting here on the edge of the ravine, holding the charm that proved the ultimate truth of the demon and the story of that first Great Gathering, filled young Gordon with wonder.

Those questions he had been asking himself about relevance and the worth of his singing had been answered now. He could finally embrace the old world and the new without conflict.

Closing his eyes, he summoned the memories of his great-great-grandfather and reviewed them one by one in his mind. The old man had known that he could not live to see the final battle with the demon, Gordon recognized that now. Archie had given him the knowledge that would enable the young man to lead.

And what a group of shamans he would lead!

The cream of every southwest tribe, the wisest men and woman the people could produce. They were here, summoned by their hearts or their gods or totems. They had come and placed themselves under his direction to do battle with an ancient force.

Gordon knew what he would give to the charm. He held it to his forehead and willed into it the wisdom of his great-great-grandfather, the wisdom of the eldest. He felt the metal warming in the sun.

"You are the young one trained by Archie?" The voice sounded harsh but Gordon experienced neither surprise or fear.

"I am that one."

"You are an aberration, boy. You should not be here. All you have done is prolong the inevitable. You and these fools cannot defeat me."

"Are you so sure, demon?" Gordon spoke with confidence. "You were sure once before, weren't you? Didn't you think you were invincible five hundred years ago when our ancestors locked you beneath the rocks?"

"It was a trick," snarled the voice. "I did not understand what they had done until it was too late. I will not fall into the trap again. Nothing you can do will stop me. I will destroy you and the others, and your people will have lost their magic forever."

"Perhaps," conceded Gordon. "It may be that the world has strayed too far from the wishes of Those Above. If that is so, you will triumph and man will die." He made it a simple statement of fact.

"Why are you not afraid, boy?" The voice had changed, subtly. It no longer rang with arrogance.

"I am only a singer," replied Gordon. "I have this thing to do because I am one who can do it. I am no warrior, no scientist. I am a scholar. I study and remember. That is all. Why should I be afraid? The gods will decide."

"I could be your god. I have seen wonders through the eyes of men. I am the strongest, the most powerful being in the universe and, one day, all of it will be mine. Do you understand that, boy? I am God as far as you puny creatures are concerned. Worship me! Adore me! Perhaps I could learn mercy."

"Only God is God," said Gordon. "Whatever He or She or even It may wish is what will come to pass."

"We shall see when we are on the battlefield, singer," said the beast. "Prepare yourself for death. Your hogan is broken rubble so no one will seal the door and break a hole in the other wall. Your body will not be safe from your ghost for I shall trap both within me. I will torment it, boy, in ways only I can conceive. You will never know rest."

Gordon felt the demon withdraw. It left not in triumph, gloating and victorious, but rather slunk away, unsure and filled with doubt.

Gordon returned to the house and passed the charm to Juan Mapoli. No words were necessary.

Juan took it into the bedroom and closed the door. He placed it on the bed and took mushrooms from his pouch. One by one, he popped them into his mouth and chewed, the musty flavor that had once seemed so unpleasant now an old friend.

He looked at the charm. The gold dust devil spun on a silver plain under a turquoise sky.

He thought of Maria, waiting for him in Barrio Libre. He thought of Carlo, the disappointment of his life when he refused to follow in his father's footsteps and rejected his heritage as a sabio.

What gift would the Yaqui give to the charm? What strength could he offer?

All of his life he had lived simply, learning the ways of the desert, studying the magic that dwelt in life. What could he offer that would enable the charm to last, to protect, to preserve?

And the answer came as he waited. "Patience."

So Juan picked up the charm and held it with both hands, closed his eyes and willed the strength of patience into it. He felt it flow through his arms and chest, felt it pass through the metal which vibrated slightly in response. When he had finished, he sighed. Truly, all things come to those who wait.

The demon came into his mind cautiously. "Who are you, old man?"

"Mapoli of the Yaqui," replied Juan.

"Why do you join these fools? I sense knowledge within this mind. Go back to the Barrio, to your woman. Let the others die if they wish."

The old man smiled. "Perhaps you would be wise to re-evaluate," said the sabio. "This is no longer a thing you can wish away or ignore. This gathering of the wise is as strong and powerful as that which defeated and imprisoned you five hundred years ago. More," he added, "it is composed of modern men from a new world, a world you do not yet understand. Things have changed."

"What kind of changes could matter to something like me? I am invisible, invulnerable, all powerful." The beast could not disguise its curiosity.

"Man has learned new tricks, demon," said Mapoli with a chuckle. "He has learned to split the atom, to descend to the deeps of the ocean, even to climb upward toward the stars."

"I have seen the stars," said the beast.

"Besides," added Juan, "there are too many now for a creature like you to rule them. There are cities of millions, not only here but across the waters. You may have some success until they learn what you are, but in time they will rise against you and their science will find a way to crush you. The world you used to know is gone."

"There is no upward limit on my growth, old fool. I can envelop the world. I can sense it. Once I have filled all the land with the swirling magnificence that is my body, I will fill the rest and twist this world apart. Once free of it, I will spin into the vastness beyond, devouring everything and growing more godlike. The universe is mine, old man. How dare you puny men stand in my way?"

"But we do stand in your way, demon," laughed the Yaqui. "We few pitiful mortals dare to bar your dream of stars. What will you do about it? We may be strong enough to defeat you, even to destroy you."

The Beast offered no answer in response to Juan's last question. It had withdrawn again.

The Yaqui took the Charm to Rattle. The Pai accepted it and went outside into the desert. He knew a happiness here that he had missed since leaving his beloved Canyon. He felt at home with the others, all so different and yet so much alike. These were his peers, old and young, even the woman.

Once away from sight of the house, he sat in the shade of a cactus and began to chant his summons to the deer spirit. Only a little while passed before he saw it approaching from behind a low hill.

Rattle never questioned where the great deer came from. He knew it for a supernatural creature, a manifestation of something beyond the physical world. It was not a thing he required answers about—why, where, what, when, who, how. These were the mundane questions of men and had to do with mortal lives. With the deer spirit, Rattle needed no explanations, no accounting. With his totem, he stood at one with the world.

The great buck approached and posed before the medicine man, head held high, its large frame ripe with the essence of life. He saw the broad chest expanding with breath, nostrils flaring at it tested scents the old man could not even guess at.

Rattle felt love wash over him like a gentle tide. He held the charm out and the velvet muzzle of the deer touched it, sniffing.

"This is a thing of power," it said. "It is also a thing of beauty. What shall we give to it?"

"I was hoping you would tell me," said the old man honestly. "The only magic I got I was given by you. I don't know about these charms and demons and things."

"Let us give it something special," said the deer. "Stand up and come to my side."

Rattle did as asked and stood beside the buck.

"Place the hand holding the charm over my heart," said the spirit.

Again, the old man complied, and as he did he felt a strange vibration in the metal and stone of the charm. At the same time he became aware of the steady beating of the heart of the deer under his hand.

"What is the gift?" The old man wanted to know.

The large buck turned carefully so as not to hurt the human with its horns and gazed into his face with the peaceful, dark, liquid chocolate eyes and spoke one word. "Harmony."

Rattle understood.

Not many minutes later, the Havasupai returned to the house and handed the charm to Gerry. The Apache took it out onto the porch and sat alone in the shade.

Within his mind, George and Geronimo spoke together.

"It is time for you to come forth again," said George.

"Perhaps," agreed his other self, "but this is a thing we can do together. We must give a gift. What would you suggest?"

"I do not know, my warrior brother," said George honestly. "I will go where I must and do what is required, but this is all beyond me."

"Are you afraid, George?"

"Yes."

"Yet you will go into battle despite the fear?"

"Yes."

"Then you have courage." Geronimo was matter-of-fact.

"I don't understand," said George.

"If you were not afraid, you would be a fool. We stand on the brink of a battle with a creature so different from ourselves that we cannot comprehend it. It is a force so strong and careless of what we feel that it is alien, yet we must face it and risk our lives."

"But I am afraid."

"And therefore courageous," agreed Geronimo. "It has always been the hallmark of our people. We fight—not without fear—but despite it."

"Then this should be our gift," said George, understanding at last.

"Yes," agreed Geronimo. "We shall give Courage."

Gerry lifted the charm and placed it over his heart. Immediately, he felt the vibration as the talisman took his gift.

Thus it went all through the morning and into the afternoon. Each of the remaining medicine men and the medicine woman gave a gift.

Pasqual Quatero, whose Zuni craftsmen had originally created the charm, gave Understanding.

Kade Wonto, the Maricopa, gave it Grace.

Lotus Farley, the Tohono O'odham, gave Healing Love.

Michael Coyoma, the Mohave, gave it Imagination.

Cord Hames, the Chemehuevi, gave Honor.

James Bluesky, the Cocopah, gave Dedication.

The demon stopped coming after the Yaqui, silent as it prepared for a struggle it now knew it could not avoid.

Chapter Fifty-One

Salt River Reservation

At two-fifteen in the afternoon, Matt Sharp pulled up in front of Tom Bear's house on the reservation. Despite his intention of arriving early, the logistics of his day prevented him from getting to the rendezvous before then. He had done the morning show, the ten o'clock show and the hourly reports. He took a risk even now, though Diedre had a taped report she could feed to the station if he were delayed past four.

The house surprised him. It spoke of poverty. The ramshackle appearance put him off. What kind of man could live in a shack like this? What did these savages think when then looked out at the real world, saw the way real people lived? He could not help himself. His prejudices had been born in a childhood of squalor—an alcoholic father, his mother a suicide when he was seven, his sister a whore at fourteen.

Matt stopped himself. He shook his head as if that act of negation might clear it. He had not thought of Angeline in ten years.

His sister had gone to LA in search of a career in show-business, a common enough story. After only a few weeks the money had run out and she turned to the streets. Almost exactly a decade ago he had received that midnight phone call from the LAPD asking him if he had a sister, if she might possibly have been in California, if she had a birthmark on her left thigh in the shape of a half moon.

It had been handled quietly. He had flown out the next morning, identified the body and arranged for a quick burial. It had all been so long ago. Why had coming to this godforsaken place on an Indian Reservation triggered memories?

"You'd better get yourself under control, Matt," he said to himself aloud. Then he looked up at the porch and saw the front door open.

Out of it came a middle aged man with a broken leg, escorted to the old couch and seated there by a young man. Behind them came a beautiful woman supporting an old man who looked very frail, his lips almost purple. He, too, took a seat on the couch. After them came others.

Matt counted. There were thirteen Native Americans and last out the door was an older, overweight white man who had to be the archaeologist, Jack Foreman.

He stood there stupidly for a moment, unable to shake the image that had come unbidden to his mind of the little red car in the circus that comes out and drives frantically around, then stops, the doors open and out come dozens of clowns. Where the hell did they keep all these people?

"Are you Jack Foreman?" He finally had the presence of mind to engage his brain and mouth.

"Yes," said Jack. "And you must be Matt Sharp."

"That's right," said Matt. "I apologize for showing up so late, Professor, but it's been a hectic morning. I won't need long. I just want to ask you about the storm last Saturday."

"I'm afraid it isn't that simple, Matt," said Jack. "I told you on the phone that it wasn't really a storm. I think you might like to hear what I . . . that is . . . what we have to say."

One hour later, Matt sat quietly on the steps, a look of shock and consternation on his face.

"You guys expect me to believe that?"

"I don't think they care one way or another," said Jack with a gesture at the others. "There is only one thing you need to decide. That is whether or not you're going to help us. Only you can deal with your suspension of disbelief."

"But it's too wild," said Matt, more to himself than anyone else.

"I'll agree with that," chuckled Jack. "It's the craziest thing I've ever heard of . . . but it's too logical to discount. Look," he said. "This so-called storm has hop-scotched around two states, zig-zagging around big towns but hitting little homesteads and ranches on both sides of them. It isn't following any weather patterns I've ever heard of. It travels a hundred miles in a night and then disappears for lengthy periods of time, only to pop up again hours later at more than its previous strength in an impossible place. The only way it makes any sense at all is if it could be sentient."

Matt looked around at the others.

"Are you all telling me the same thing?"

"We are," said Tom Bear. "We have spoken to it."

"What?" Mat looked incredulous.

Jack felt uncomfortable. "They mean in their minds. They say it communicates telepathically with them."

Matt put his head in his hands. "C'mon, Professor, you don't really expect me to swallow this."

The archaeologist shrugged. "Once you've shot the dog, you don't worry as much about the fleas."

"If I believed all this, how could I help?" The weatherman looked like a prizefighter on the ropes.

"We need to know where it is," said Jack. "The only thing it can do now is try to destroy the Gathering. It has to be coming here."

"I can give you access to the reports on the toll-free number, but we haven't licked the radar problem yet. Without rain, we just can't seem to track this thing."

"Whatever. Anything you can do will be appreciated," said the archaeologist. "A few minutes of warning might make a difference."

"Does anyone else know about this?" asked Matt.

"Cops, DPS, and maybe the friggin' FBI by now. We have a couple detectives of police, Tempe and Navajo Tribal, who promised to back us up."

"Greg Johnson?"

"Yeah, him and a guy called Twohats," agreed Jack.

"I know Johnson. If he backs you up, I'll give you the benefit of the doubt. Greg gave me a ration of shit the other day when I said this thing was a storm. He's the most conservative cop I've ever met."

"He isn't a happy camper," laughed the archaeologist, "but he's decided to play along."

Matt looked at the Professor frankly. "You realize I have to play this straight, keep working on it as a storm of some kind?"

"Yeah," agreed Jack. "I figured you'd have to. That's okay. Just feed us any information you have as soon as you get it. We'll do what we're supposed to do."

"Hey, Professor?"

"Yeah?"

"What if all these people are wrong? What if it's just a freak storm after all?"

"Then you'll report it as it happens and we'll be just west of Phoenix holding a Native American Ceremony." He looked suddenly very serious. "There could be worse things."

"I suppose you're right," agreed the weatherman. "What next?" The preliminaries out of the way, Matt remained simply curious.

Gordon answered. "We have to prepare the site. Our ceremony will begin at noon tomorrow."

Chapter Fifty-Two

Salt River Reservation

Gordon called them together after the weatherman left. "We must go to the place of battle," he said. "Between now and noon tomorrow, we must cleanse and purify it." He turned to Gerry. "You have seen the sand painting. You must recreate it. The Zuni and Hopi will assist."

"I want to look inside the kiva again," said Jack. "I think Lotus may have found something that we can use."

"Go, then," said the Navajo. "In the morning you will not be able to enter."

"I could use some help," suggested the archaeologist.

"I can go," volunteered Danny.

"And I, too," said Lotus.

"Very well," agreed Gordon, "but come back here tonight. I must talk with all of you about the ceremony."

"Thanks." Jack turned to the two young people. "My Rover is just outside, the shiny one."

Jack, Lotus and Danny drove out to the kiva. His watch read five in the afternoon and the sun would be up for hours yet. Jack used a rope to lower himself down into the site, followed inside by the other two.

He first examined the floor. As Lotus had said, it was a lava plug, probably less than five feet thick. Under it might be further levels. He felt heat.

Next he examined the separate chamber containing the painting. It had been scoured almost opaque by five-hundred years of the demon's frenzied activity within. A glance told him it was not critical. A real effort at restoration would result in nothing of importance being saved. He regarded it as non-essential.

This provided the last of the equation for Jack. Simple calculations told him how much dynamite would be required. The rest would depend on the Indians.

They went directly from the site to the university. Jack took a few minutes to look up the number of the supply administrator and used up several old favors in requisitioning the explosives he required. One of the best things about working in archaeology remained access to supplies as needed.

He dropped Lotus and Danny at the house before returning to the site.

The couple paused at the foot of the steps leading to the porch. They had not spoken privately since he walked away after discovering her with Gordon.

The Pima hung a little behind the beautiful young Tohono O'odham woman. The others were obviously all asleep.

Lotus went up the first two steps before turning and facing the young man. "Do you wish to talk?"

Danny did not answer.

"I am willing to talk if you want to," she said quietly.

"What is there to say?" asked Danny.

"Why, whatever you would say. You have not spoken to me since you returned from rescuing the Havasupai, Rattle. I think I know why. I tried to tell you then that I am a healer. You know that this is my work. The Navajo had been crushed. His entire family had been destroyed by the demon. His great-great-grandfather, to whom he paid the highest respect and love, had been killed to prevent him from attending this very Gathering. He needed me. We needed him. I offered what I could. Do you not understand?"

"I do understand, Lotus Farley. Though I felt surprise and pain at your seeming disregard for me, I came to understand what you did and why."

Lotus looked perplexed. "Then it is I who do not understand, Danny. Why have you been so remote to me?"

Danny looked uncomfortable. "We have been busy, Lotus. I did not mean to ignore you."

"Why do you think I slept with you, Danny Webb?"

"Because I had pain and required healing," he said, not meeting her eyes.

"Ah," she said. "No wonder." She took his face in her hands and stepped down so that her face met his. "It was not as a healer that I called you to me. It was as a woman."

It took a moment to sink in.

"You mean . . . are you saying . . . was it different with us than with Gordon?"

"Of course," she said whispering into his ear. "I chose you because I fancied you, not only because you needed me."

"Then you want . . . uh, that is . . . could we . . . ?"

"Oh, Danny," she said huskily, embracing him. "I have wanted nothing else since the other night."

Friday, July 14th

Chapter Fifty-Three

Phoenix

Before dawn, they loaded their gear into their vehicles and drove to the site. Twohats and Greg Johnson had arranged for the area to be cordoned off. Yellow banners proclaiming "Police Line" stretched across all approaches and, though there were few actual police, it looked very official. Detective Johnson had gotten three officers assigned on the strength of his own authority, a back-up request from Jack requiring protection of a possible archaeological site, and a request from Gordon as leader of a Native American Religious Convention.

They arrived just as the sky grew light enough for them to see, and the next few hours were busy ones. Forming a line, the shamans moved across the site, shaking rattles, scattering pollen and cornmeal, chanting in time with the drum which Tom played. Seven times they passed across an area about the size of half a football field and surrounding the rocks which marked the site of the beast's imprisonment.

When that had been done, the Charm was brought forth and Gordon spoke over it, dedicating it to the will of the gods and invoking the aid of Those Above in the battles to come.

Gerry, Pasqual, Harold and Lotus began the sand painting. It became a massive affair, fully twelve feet in diameter. Gerry had laid out the outer border, divided it into lower, upper and middle world, and designated where the symbols had been in his vision. The basic white sand of the background had been obtained from a landscaping company the previous afternoon. The other colors were prepared by Harold and Pasqual in accordance with their regular practices.

The Zuni and Hopi, less mobile and more bound by ceremonial tradition, did the detail work. Lotus helped wherever she felt needed.

Each of the others contributed to a greater or lesser degree. Some did not normally do sand painting, but were still required to handle the symbols and representations of their own tribes. The work continued until noon.

Just after mid-day, as they prepared to start the ceremony itself, Matt Sharp called on the cellular to tell them that the technician had juked the radar and it now tracked something heading toward Phoenix.

"The signature is amazing," he told Jack. "It covers an area over three miles in diameter and has no eye. In fact, there's something strange about the middle of this thing anyway. It's just as dense as the outer ring of wind and dust, but it doesn't behave like it. I can't figure it out."

"Exactly where is it?"

"It's coming in from the Northeast—looks like it's heading for Cave Creek and Carefree. We've already ordered a weather alert. The Highway Patrol has begun evacuation since the path of this thing is like an arrow."

"Where's it heading?"

"Straight at you, Jack."

"Have you got an ETA?"

"Impossible to tell because we don't know what will happen when it hits the Cave Creek area."

"Okay. Thanks, Matt. Keep us posted." Jack handed the phone back to Twohats and turned to the others. "It's heading toward us. Is there anything we need to do?"

"Now that the charm is here, the demon won't be able to approach us physically, at least not close enough to matter." Gordon smiled, grimly. "If it does come, it will be drawn in and trapped."

"Is that what happened before?" asked Jack

The Navajo laughed. "How would I know, Jack? I wasn't around back then. I know the story as it was told to me and nothing more. Remember, this is new to me as it is to all of us. It happens that my great-great-grandfather taught me both the history and the ceremony.

I know what to do. In some cases I even know why I do it. The rest of it is sort of like reciting a poem in Latin without speaking the language. I learned the sounds, the order of calling, the form to follow. What I don't know is what specifically we are trying to accomplish—other than, of course, to stop the demon."

Jack shook his head. "I'm sorry, Gordon. I keep forgetting. You act so confident that it's easy to think you've been around longer than you have."

"That's Archie's influence," said the Navajo. "He knew so much more and I could have learned it . . . if he had lived."

"Are you worried?"

Gordon leaned close and whispered confidentially. "Don't tell anyone, but I'm scared shitless."

Jack looked blank for a moment, then burst out in laughter. "I'm sorry. I'm sorry," he said, trying to catch his breath and stifle his mirth. "I didn't mean to laugh, but it was so unexpected."

Gordon turned to him and grinned. "It seems to me, Jack, that we haven't any choice. Either we can see the humor or we might as well fold up and drop dead right now. We must see the light side of our lives. If we can't laugh at ourselves, we must surely cry."

The archaeologist looked at the young man with even deeper respect. There were levels to Gordon he hadn't suspected. Privately, he hoped the Navajo would come out of this all right. The responsibility laid on the boy's shoulders must be enormous and he had already been through so much. "You're going to be a hell of a yataalii, Fly," he said, using the nickname he had heard Gerry use some time earlier.

"Thank you, digger," the boy replied.

As Jack walked away, Lotus came up and placed a hand on Gordon's arm.

"They are almost ready."

"Are you ready, my Tohono O'odham maiden?" His voice was tender.

"As ready as I will ever be," she replied. "And you, singer?"

Fly nodded. "I hope Archie will be proud of me," he said. "He took a lot of time to teach me what I must do. I remember it all. It remains only to do it."

"You'll be fine," she said, patting his shoulder.

"For all our sakes, and the safety of our people, I hope you are right, Lotus Farley." Then he shrugged. "Regardless, I will do my best."

Chapter Fifty-Four

Phoenix

It was an assemblage from another time. Jack found it difficult to accept that it could be taking place in the modern world. Each of the others had changed to ceremonial dress and stood around the painting in the appointed place. Jack, in plain shirt and slacks, stood at the top of the circle holding the charm. He felt incongruous, a jarring exception to the scene around him. With the rocks before them masking the construction yard, it was a desert scene that might have been captured from any time in the past. Representing twelve tribes, the dozen men and one woman had a strangely similar, determined, expression on their faces.

Gordon Smythe, Navajo yataalii, great-great-grandson of the famous Archibald Smythe, stood up in his place. He felt nervous there before the others, but he heard Archie's voice speaking from deep inside.

"Be brave, grandson. You are the only one left now who remembers what must be done. You will do it for all of us. You will do it perfectly. You are my successor."

"Ya-deh-hay," Gordon said, looking around the circle at each in turn. "Another should be standing now before you, but the demon took him and I am all that remains of what he knew." He looked at the white man. "I am Thoughts-Never-Stop, a singer of my people." He signalled to Twohats, who lit the bonfire they had constructed twenty yards to the rear.

Young Smythe stood dressed in full ceremonial garb. Several strings of beads hung about his neck, surrounded by furs. He wore a breechclout, resplendent with embroidered designs, leggings and moccasins. Over it, he wore a tunic belted at the waist. On his head were eagle feathers held in place by a beaded headband. He stood tall and proud.

He began with a short form of the one-day Hoh-chon'jih Hatal, the devil-chasing chant. In it, Gordon evoked the lightnings, black, blue, yellow and white. He did not simply speak the words. He sang in a clear melodious voice so that all who heard nodded to themselves. Here, indeed, was a singer.

Upon Gordon's signal, Tom began to play upon the drum. It made a lonely sound in the middle of the afternoon and it seemed strange to have a fire in the heat of the day. No one else spoke. There were no whispers. The sparks rose up over the flames and sailed upward into the air, carrying the song and the beat of the drum to Those Above.

Juan Mapoli rose and moved around the circle in a counter-clockwise direction, symbolizing the movement of the demon, contrary to the way things are. He offered tea from a bowl, tea made from *Rivea Corymbosa*, Morning Glory. Everyone but Tom drank deeply. In the background, the drum sang.

Over the ensuing hours, two separate events occurred.

To someone from the outside, it would have seemed strange indeed. The Indians and the archaeologist stood in a circle and listened to the Navajo boy sing. During the course of the ceremony they rose, one after another, and stepped to the center nearest the fire to perform some part of the ritual. It was beautiful and awe-inspiring, poignant and artistic, simple and yet unbelievably complex.

On another level, experienced only by the participants, something far more important occurred. There was a blending of consciousness, a unification of minds and wills. On this level, what science might have called telepathy became the norm. On this level, the magic began.

Jack had never experienced such a thing before, but Juan's help and coaching had prepared him for the moment of disorientation that occurred when their minds linked. As he had been advised, he quieted his thoughts and concentrated on the beat of the drum.

Loud within their minds, clear and pure, the voice of Thoughts-Never-Stop continued to sing. It directed them as their hearts beat in perfect time with the drum.

Tom could feel it. even as he played upon it—the drum began to play upon them.

They rose. Leaving their physical forms around the fire, they rose in unison, shining in their psychic sight like a multi-colored rainbow of spirit. High above the desert, they united and circled and intertwined. Patterns of consciousness they could see, woven tapestries of mind, floated in the air, bright and alive like a cloud of butterflies.

"We must journey into the upper world," said Thoughts-Never-Stop in their minds. "Rise up with me and let us go to the city beyond the clouds."

They entered a tunnel—a cloud tunnel—in the afternoon sky that was nonetheless lit by the sparks from the fire receding now below them. The Yataalii continued to sing. Below them, Tom continued to play the drum and, up ahead, they heard other voices joining in the song, voices that were not all human.

Gradually becoming visible to them, lining the sides of the tunnel like a gallery, were hundreds of faces—faces of all kinds and types—birds and animals, men and women, winged beings and creatures not so easy to describe. All were singing, like a great chorus.

Then the tunnel widened and seemed to fade. Rising out of the smoke ahead, they saw a golden mountain. It glowed and pulsed with the colors of a sunset, rich and deep and fiery. Atop the mountain was a beautiful building, a palace constructed of pale green crystal that radiated golden light.

Thoughts-Never-Stop spoke again within their minds. "It is the palace of the Phoenix that we see before us, the undying one. This is the first stop on our journey. It is from here that we will go to the different levels and confront the force that seeks to end the world."

Jack looked around in wonder. Somewhere his conscious mind knew this was illusion, a pretty picture induced by the drug in the tea—but it looked and felt as real to him as anything he had ever experienced.

Even as these thoughts passed through his mind, he felt the others—in particular Juan.

"Steady, Jack. Remember what I told you. Just flow with it. This is real on a certain level. Breathe deeply. Listen to the drum. Pay attention to Thoughts-Never-Stop. He will guide us."

The archaeologist's acknowledgement came as silent assent.

"We shall be greeted by the great bird itself," explained Gordon. "It is our host. The Phoenix will provide strength when we need it, sustenance, passage to the other dimensions and will safeguard our return. It is a great spirit, ancient as time. Treat it with respect and reverence."

And before them they saw a huge winged creature rise up from behind the glowing crystal palace, rainbow light reflecting from its feathers as if broken and split by a prism.

When Jack saw it, he felt his heart expand in his chest. He experienced an overwhelming sense of belonging, as if he had come home. The eyes of the Phoenix invited him to relax, rest, feel comfortable—to surrender all care. They conveyed a message of love.

At a gesture, a graceful sweep of its wing, a panel opened in the crystal wall of the palace and they felt themselves invited to descend, passing through the portal and into a room almost as magificent and grand as their host.

Delicate crystal chandeliers and sparkling sconces illuminated a room walled with stained glass and rich tapestries and furnishings at once strange and wondrous, for they were not designed for man alone.

The twelve Shamans and Jack floated down and came to rest on the sparkling crystal floor and were greeted by attendants who were winged men.

The voice of their host spoke in welcome. "You are the warriors of light. Here shall you rest and refresh yourselves until it is time to meet the dark. Be at peace here in my house."

Those who waited on them were as lordly as kings and queens and no class or distinction marked them as servants. Each acted, instead, as if he or she—determining their sex seemed next to impossible—was the host. Their movements were grace beyond measure, their voices, when they spoke, like beautiful music.

One by one, the members of the Gathering were seated on soft, luminescent cushions and lay back on a nest of the softest pillows, lulled into peace by exquisite music.

Gordon spoke to them in a gentle voice. "Drop your cares for a while now," he said. "This is the heart of the kingdom of peace. When it is time for the struggle to begin, I will call and awaken you. Rest now."

Jack felt himself drifting into a sleep peopled by delicately haunting dreams, filled with the sensations of gentle hands and musical voices.

In the most private part of his mind, he heard Evelyn's voice singing as she used to when in the next room sewing. It was as if she had never gone, and he slept contented for the first time in years.

Chapter Fifty-Five

Cave Creek, Arizona

Cave Creek and Carefree are small communities just to the Northeast of Phoenix. Combining country and country-club life-styles, each town provides a variety of diversion, from small crafty shops to Arabian Horse Farms. Residents enjoy the wide open spaces of a leisurely desert clime, yet still have the advantages and convenience of metropolitan centers with restaurants, bookstores, shopping malls and movie theatres.

To live in either community year-round requires an economic base both affluent and independent. To say the residents are spoiled might be overstatement, but they are not prepared to leave their homes on the basis of a phone call from the police. As a result, the weather alert had no major impact until the local constabulary started driving up and knocking on doors.

Despite Matt Sharp's enhanced radar system, the storm caught everyone by surprise when it swept down from Turret Peak and raced across country toward the Cave Creek area. Police had only two hours warning and, in retrospect, were extremely lucky to get seventy-five per cent of the residents in the direct path of the killer to evacuate to outlying areas.

Tarleton Crabb was a geezer, a bit of wild west color who traded on his resemblance to the immortal Gabby Hayes. Each year during the Randolph Scott festival, he served as Grand Marshal of the big parade. Some years, this had meant tying him to his horse, Mincemeat. "Tacky" Crabb spent the rest of his time caging drinks at the

Short Branch Saloon or over at Harold's Place . . . when he was not in jail for drunk and disorderly conduct or disturbing the peace.

Arizona allows its citizens the god-given right to carry unconcealed weapons. Tourists are often intimidated by the sight of cowboys with guns on their hips.

On this particular day, Tacky played at being stubborn. He felt he had the right to be orn'ry and pig-headed when he wanted to be. When the deputy suggested politely that he grab his boots and flee, he became so outraged that he literally sputtered. "Dang, Charlie! Are you shittin' me? You expect me to run from a little dust storm?"

Charles Borden felt no amusement. He had an urgent schedule to keep. "Tacky, I ain't got time to argue. The same storm as wiped out Agate Junction is headin' here fast. You'd be wise to take my advice and skedaddle." He looked at the set square jaw and the narrow eyes and sighed, deciding to try just one more time. "Honest, Tacky, it's comin' fast. You want a ride?"

The old man brought his cane-seated oak chair back onto four legs and leaned forward, spitting a wad of tobacco juice that just missed Charlie's feet.

"Not only says I should run, but says I should abandon my horse!" He stood, weaving slightly and put his hand on the pommel of the Colt .45 on his hip. "Get outta here, deputy, or I'll forget you're wearin' that badge."

No fool, the lawman backed up immediately. Not only could Tacky be crotchety, but he was a crack shot. "Okay, hoss," he said. "Have it your own way. I tried."

As Borden drove away toward the next cabin, Tacky chortled to himself. "Asshole. He don't unnerstan nuthin'. You can't run from a little dust storm in Arizona. Hell! Everybody'd be outta breath all day long."

The more he thought about the incident, the more it pissed him off. Charlie was a yahoo anyway, one of them city boys who thought a white wide-brimmed hat made him a cowboy.

For just a moment, Tacky remembered pictures he had seen of Agate. It had sure been a clean sweep—nothing left standing. It must be quite a storm.

The hill behind his house had been cleared the year before so the phone company could set up a tower. It stood above the tree line and afforded a hell of a view.

Tacky wondered if he could see the damned storm coming from there. It wouldn't take but fifteen minutes to ride on up and have a look-see. Besides, then he wouldn't be bothered by these friggin' do-gooders. As soon as Charlie reported his failure to dislodge the old man, the sheriff would be along to force the issue.

Tom Darcy was a good man. He had pulled Tacky off the streets more than once when he would probably have died of exposure or dehydration. Even Crabb was forced to admit there were times he drank too much. It was just that whiskey tasted so smooth after a while, like mother's milk.

Worse, Sheriff Darcy could make the old man do anything he wanted. Not only was he six-foot-four, weighing almost two hundred-forty pounds, but he knew Crabb wouldn't really shoot at anyone. If he said move, even Tacky obeyed.

Despite the ten slugs of Hiram Walker he'd sucked down within the past hour, it took only a few moments for thought to translate itself into action. He went into the house and scribbled a note.

> "Dear Sheriff Tom,
>   Fuck off! I ain't going!
>   Yours affectionately,
>   T. Crabb"

Chuckling at his fine sense of humor, he used his bowie knife to stick the note to the front door. No one would dare take it, but it would surprise the sheriff.

Staggering to the corral, he took a little longer than usual to saddle up his horse. He couldn't decide which of the two Mincemeats was the real one. It only slowed him up a little though. Ever an innovator, Tacky used the process of elimination. When he threw the saddle up on the first horse and it fell to the ground, he nodded sagely, retrieved it and slung it up on the other. The horse ignored him.

Five minutes later, he rode on the trail that led from behind his cabin in a winding course up the hill.

Two miles further north lived Agnes and Melvin Proctor. Mel had been an alderman in Chicago before retiring to Arizona. Their luxurious home atop a stubby mountain had cost over a million to build twenty years before. Each year, Proctor petitioned the council to name the mountain after him. Each year, the council politely refused. Mel did not like that.

It was not as if the damned thing had a name already. The map called it N4E7, which simply meant it was the fourth stubby look-alike mountain north of an arbitrary survey point and the seventh east.

Agnes had grown up thinking of herself as rich, but marriage to Proctor had increased her expectations considerably. Chicago politics being what they were, Mel had accumulated a rather large nest egg over the years. She never asked where it came from and had no trouble spending it.

Childless, the couple spent much of their time traveling after Mel's retirement. Nowhere had pleased them as much as Cave Creek. They didn't live in town, of course. That would have put her on a par with all the other former East-Coast society matrons. No, they had a house on a mountain top and threw lavish parties almost every week.

The staff consisted of two Mexican maids, a cook, a butler and a chauffeur. Agnes did not understand why they needed two maids, but Mel insisted and she knew better than to cross him. He was not such a bad man, after all. Oh, he occasionally struck her when she irritated him, but it was, after all, her fault. After thirty years of marriage she should know better.

But he had such silly rules. For example, she could not enter the part of the house that contained his office. This didn't mean just the office, but the suite of three rooms that comprised it. She had tested Mel's resolve on that issue only once. The lacerations had healed without scars, thank goodness.

Proctor spent several hours a day in his office, making long distance calls to Chicago, manipulating investments, doing "business" as he put it.

This left Agnes with too much free time. It was not as if she could just walk outside and into town. It meant getting permission to have the chauffeur drive her there, something she had to do in advance. There was no spontaneity in her life.

Fortunately, the chauffeur had proved quite spontaneous.

When the weather alert came over the ten o'clock morning news, Agnes buzzed Mel's office to see if they should leave. He did not answer . . . as usual. She toyed with the idea of just leaning on the buzzer until he answered, but wisely chose not to.

Annoyed with her husband, a little frightened at the idea of the storm, she buzzed Reggie's extension.

"You called?" His voice still sent a thrill coursing through her body.

"Yes, Reggie. There is a weather alert and I can't get Mel to answer. I suspect he's incommunicado again. Would you mind terribly coming up to talk with me? I'm a little nervous."

"Of course not, Mrs. Proctor," said the chauffeur. "I'll be just five minutes."

"Oh thank you, Reg. You're such a dear."

She took every moment of that time to brush her teeth, apply perfume and make up. She stood there naked in the vanity, trying to decide what to wear—decided not to don anything and then paused. She gave a critical look at her reflection in the mirror. "Not too bad for fifty-one," she murmured. Pirouetting she lifted her arms and watched the effect on her breasts. It was still, if she did say so herself, spectacular. Her forty-four inch bust remained firm and shapely. Of course it ought to—poor Mel had paid enough money to keep it that way.

Reggie knocked at the door and she called, "Come in."

He entered and carefully closed the door behind him.

In response to his raised eyebrow she said, "Bolt it."

*   *   *   *   *

The beast hurried. It wanted to arrive at the Phoenix site before the Shamans could complete their preparations. It was, however, hungry. Except for the Pima weaver, it had not fed for over twelve hours and its increased size necessitated vastly accelerated feedings.

It hit Carefree with winds of almost four hundred fifty miles per hour, sweeping a clean path four miles wide and causing considerable destruction for an additional mile on each side as it hurled debris in a continuous mass.

Within its center there were no survivors whatsoever. In the mile-wide swath on each side, where flying rock, trees, auto parts and cement block were thick, casualties ran just over fifty percent.

It had not intended to slow, certainly not to stop, but the sweet smell of fear was a tonic that drew it to pause and savor. Once the carnage had begun, the urgency faded in the ecstacy of indulgence.

Agnes and Reggie were busily engaged in the numerical act when the beast destroyed the mountaintop. Coincidentally, Mel and Rosita were in his wing doing the same thing. It happened too quickly for any of them to suffer. The house simply flew apart.

Tacky Crabb and his mount came up over the hilltop just as the beast hit it.

In an instant, both man and horse were mincemeat.

Chapter Fifty-Six

City of the Phoenix

Gordon awakened Danny, the Pima and James, the Cocopah. They sat up, their faces alight with half-remembered dreams.

"Where are we?" asked Danny, looking around.

"Still in the city of the Phoenix," said Gordon, "but it is time for our first meeting with the demon."

"Which world?" James rubbed sleep from his eyes and looked around.

"Ours is the world of the mind," said the Navajo. "The struggle may not take place in a physical scene as we know it. I believe the demon is insane by human standards. It has had days to study the minds of those it destroyed. We cannot know what it will use."

"I think we can be sure it won't be the images spun for it by innocence and love," remarked James with a wry expression.

"What has it done since we began?" Danny stood and stretched, and one of the winged attendants stepped forward offering a goblet of liquid.

"Say no," cautioned Gordon. "We still must fast." He turned to the Pima. "I do not know. We are not connected to the temporal world while we rest here as guests of the Phoenix. When we are finished with our task, we will no doubt discover what the beast chose to do."

Danny shook his head at the offering and smiled his thanks. The attendant nodded and withdrew. "How do we do this?" In the young man's mind were confusing images. A part of him knew that his body sat now with the others in the large circle around the sand painting in the desert outside of Phoenix. A glance at the beauty surrounding him convinced yet another aspect of his mind that he stood in the crystal city above the clouds. He shook his head.

James smiled and laid a hand on the Pima's shoulder. "Do not work so hard at sorting it out," he advised. "Just accept that there are many wonders when mind and spirit are linked."

"Good advice," agreed the Navajo. "Come, a place has been prepared for us."

Gordon led the way down a wide opalescent hall toward two huge ornate doors that gleamed and sparkled and seemed to lighten at their approach. When they arrived, the doors swung open to reveal yet another of the winged attendants. The creature smiled in welcome and beckoned them enter.

Within this separate chamber were three comfortable chaise-style couches and each sat upon one, then lay down.

Gordon explained, "It is here that we will confront the demon."

Danny looked over at the other two men. "We're just going to lie here?"

The Navajo laughed. "This battle will be in the field of imagination as all such are fought between good and evil. Be wary. The mind holds many chambers we would prefer not to open. If the demon is to defeat us, it will be with our own secret thoughts."

"You mean like tapping our fears?" James thought he understood.

"Yes," said Gordon. "Whatever it is that you most fear will probably confront you. Harold told me that the demon seems unable to sense the deeper levels of thought but reads the surface mind clearly. If that is the case, we must be very careful what we let out of the confusion that is the subconscious. I do not know if it will battle one, two or all three of us. The choice is not ours.

The three men looked at each other for a long quiet moment. Each had learned, even in this short time together, a deep and abiding mutual respect.

"When do we begin?" Danny licked his lips which were suddenly dry and cleared his throat.

The Yataalii smiled.

"Now."

All of them closed their eyes and thought of the demon, of the storm that swept the real world they knew surrounded them. From that time on, fate hung in the balance for each of the three. On some level, back in the real world, their minds were linked and they worked toward their common goal. In the world of mind, however, each man is alone.

Danny knew not to become attached to any of the sensory images he was bound to see. Floors, walls, ceilings, landscapes—all would be illusions spun from his own mind by the consciousness of the demon. It did not prepare him.

He was suddenly hurled off a cliff and, though his feet scrambled for purchase, he fell, twisting and screaming forever. The wind of his passage whistled upward fleeing from his body, and he heard, as in a nightmare, his own voice following faintly as it raced along behind.

For the young Pima, lack of control represented the ultimate horror. When Lotus had called him to the porch, the tears on his face had burned like flaming oil. Now, as he fell endlessly, unable to stop the twisting, tumbling motion, he cried out in helpless rage. He felt the overwheming power of the demon as it played upon his fears.

He could see nothing, for the air whistling past his face stung his eyes and filled them with a milky veil of tears. His hair whipped his face and shoulders, got in his mouth, stung like a thousand tiny barbs. He could not get his breath, the force of falling ripping the air out of his lungs.

When the end came, it arrived just as suddenly and unexpectedly. He plunged face first into water—a lake, an ocean, he could not tell—but it burned bitter and bitingly cold, as cold as liquid can be without turning to ice. He felt the sting of impact and imagined the welts raised by his fall from such a height, but his outraged skin erupted in protest to the freezing cold.

Danny sank quickly. He struggled to reverse his progress. His lungs were already bursting from lack of oxygen and every foot of depth meant that much longer before he would be able to reach the surface. Spread-eagled under water, he finally achieved an end to descent and began to claw frantically at the thick viscous liquid that enveloped him.

He almost gave up. Every inch of his body, inside and out, revolted against the strain and abuse endured. Even as he cupped his hands and kicked his feet in a desperate race to propel himself back to the surface, his mind whispered that it would be easier to surrender. The numbing cold closed in and seemed to coax him to stop, to cease his struggle, to end the contest.

Only then did Danny recognize the mind of the demon lurking in the dark recesses of his own thoughts.

He broke free of the water, exploding and gasping for breath. "Not yet!" he yelled, though his voice sounded hoarse and raw. "You won't win that easily!"

"Ah, Danny," whispered the beast. The sound surrounded him, echoed though his mind and reverberated endlessly with a physical vibration akin to that experienced when one bumps his funny bone— painful, nerve-wracking, uncontrollable and promising worse. "Almost, Danny Webb. I almost had you there . . . and we have only begun, boy."

Confidence sang in the mind of the beast. It had been shaken during the blessing of the charm. The shamans had been so controlled, so sure, so invincible. After that confrontation, the prospect of other battles had seemed perilous. Now that the first of these had arrived, its combative nature and hunger for growth drove it into the conflict with insane glee.

Danny concentrated on quieting his ragged breathing, treading water and trying to orient himself. He could see nothing. The only difference between the surface and the deep was the air. Everything looked black. He could literally not see his hand in front of his face when he lifted it to check.

He felt himself tiring, knew that his muscles were beginning to draw on reserves that no longer existed. He had been fasting for two days, had just fallen what seemed thousands of feet and nearly drowned. His body could not take much more.

Then he stopped.

This was not his body—at least not his real body. It was a projection of mind, either his or the demon's. The only exhaustion he could feel was illusion. His own mind drained his strength, his own imagination dragged him ever closer to surrender.

For the first time, Danny took the offensive. He closed his eyes and ceased struggling. With a calm and steady strength he had not realized he possesed, he changed the reality around him. Picturing the images in his mind, he saw himself rising out of the mire that surrounded him and standing on dry land. He envisioned himself, whole, confident, rested—and, as he saw it in his mind, so it was.

The Pima warrior opened his eyes and stood regally upon solid ground. It was the earth of his home as it had been in elder days when the Pimas farmed and played and loved without interference from the outside world. He stood as close to paradise as he could imagine.

Then Danny saw the figure materialize before him. He felt shock. Standing opposite and crouched ready to spring stood his father. The well-remembered features glowered with rage and shimmered, a personification of insanity.

"I taught you that magic was like addiction, destructive, habit-forming and useless. You didn't listen. You disobeyed. The only thing you really understood was the back of my hand. Well now, my son, I'm going to beat sense into you and, when I'm convinced you truly understand—when you beg me to end it—I'm going to kill you."

The younger Pima reeled back before the old. Memories of beatings in his childhood rushed in and the wounded child within cried helplessly.

"No, papa. No!"

But the figure of Jed "Bearclaw" Webb stood unmoved. It leaped instead to a position directly before the boy and swung a ham-sized fist at his head.

The blow drove all coherent thought out of Danny's mind. He fell hard, pain and fear submerging him as had the water of the previous vision. Jed stepped in and kicked viciously at the boy's ribs. The sharp agony and the sound of cracking bone were real enough.

"Little bastard," screamed his father as he kicked again. "Magic your way out of this!" The toe of the steel-tipped boots connected with the side of Danny's head and his vision clouded in a bright flash of cascading stars.

Without let-up, Jed grabbed the boy by the shoulders and hauled him to his feet. Propping him up with one hand, he swung the other up from behind his back in a roundhouse right that shattered teeth and nose cartilage, split the lips and lifted Danny's body backward off its feet in a flying arc that ended with bone-jarring impact on the hard ground.

The boy curled up in a ball, hands over his head, knees up tight to protect his groin. Blows rained furiously from above, battering flesh, sending further flashes of brilliant lightning through what little consciousness remained as the brain bounced about inside the skull.

"Never disobey your father!" Jed's face twisted in an insane grin, his eyes glassy with delight in the satisfaction of venting all the years of pent-up rage. He kicked again and heard the rewarding crack as he broke Danny's left forearm. The sound and pain were loud in the surrounding stillness. It seemed as if nature had been reduced to shocked silence as witness to the raw violence.

Jed reached down and twisted the broken limb, watching the shattered bone break through the tortured flesh, laughing as he heard the boy cry out.

"Want some more, Danny-boy?" The older man could not contain the gibbering and hoots of joy as he waded in for more. The heavy booted feet stomped down on the boy's feet and heels, the snap of breaking bone ringing out like a shot. More kicks to the rib cage, a full arc kick to the testicles that lifted the body up off the ground almost a foot and propelled it a yard and a half along the ground. This engendered maniacal laughter.

"Get up! Get up, Danny-boy!" Jed taunted the figure in the dirt. "Stand up, medicine man and work a spell on me! Come on you little bastard, get up and tell me how you're going to follow in the footsteps of that useless Donald Webb. The son of a bitch wasn't even my real father, just a poor substitute your grandmother dragged back from the refuse pile after your real grandfather dumped her."

The boy's mind hovered on the edge of unconsciousness, the pain and agony of his battered body banishing any other thought. Only then did he hear the voices in his mind.

"Illusions, Danny." He recognized Gordon's voice. "Don't give in. Don't surrender. It can't defeat you. This is all taking place in your head."

"C'mon, Danny," urged the voice of James. "You can do it. Come back against it. Use the things it fears."

"Up!" screamed Jed. "Get up so I can knock you down again, you wimp!"

The mind of the young Pima had become so multi-faceted that it took a long moment for him to begin the process of orientation.

One part of him knew that he sat in the desert at the Great Gathering. Another knew that he lay on the chaise in the crystal city. A third was quietly rejoicing in his escape from near drowning in the blackness. The last part had almost gone, a mere flicker of life in a body so broken and ravaged that it couldn't have stood even if it had the will.

The voices of Gordon and James faded and grew louder again like poor reception on an old radio. The taunts of Bearclaw Webb continued, but they too took on the wavering insubstantiality of dream.

Reorganization suddenly became reintegration and the mind of Danny Webb was whole again. The pain, which had overwhelmed his will moments before, vanished. He stood, peacefully and lovingly, before his father. The figure of Jed seemed to have shrunk somehow, or Danny had gotten taller. The look of insane glee that had shown on his father's face had transformed to a grimace of pain.

"You lose, Demon," said the boy in a calm quiet voice.

The figure of Jed Bearclaw Webb faded from existence never to trouble Danny again. Once it was gone, the world of the mind faded as well.

Chapter Fifty-Seven

The Upper World

Rattle awakened to find himself seated on the edge of a cloud. Next to him sat a large black crow that tilted its finely shaped head and peered at him out of one bright black eye.

The Pai looked down and saw the mosaic of the earth laid out below like a crazy quilt of texture.

The crow spoke. "Don't you think we ought to get on with it?"

Rattle turned slowly, afraid and yet separate from the fear. He looked at the bird for a long moment in wonder. "Juan? Is that you?"

"Of course it's me," said the Yaqui. "Don't you think it's time to summon the deer? We have a battle to fight, you know."

"But I never thought . . . . " The old man's voice trailed off as he gestured helplessly around them.

"We are in the upper world, my friend," said the crow. "All things are possible here."

"What am I supposed to do?" The Pai felt bewildered.

"Summon the Great Deer Spirit," said Juan with a shake of his feathers. "The demon may appear at any moment."

Rattle had difficulty concentrating on the sending. He knew both joy and terror. He had never once in his life flown on an airplane, never even seen a television picture of it. Now he sat on a seemingly substantial cloud in the middle of a clear blue sky with the earth far below.

"Try closing your eyes," suggested the crow.

When he did, Rattle felt an immediate sensation of vertigo, and fear of falling assailed him.

Opening his eyes quickly, he still felt troubled. How could the deer spirit come to him here in the sky? What kind of battlefield was this?

"You really must begin," said Juan. "I suspect we will have little or no warning."

Rattle started to chant. It took longer than usual, but he soon achieved that feeling of harmony with nature and the world.

He heard a familiar voice raised in song. He continued his chant, eyes closed. The voice grew clearer and sang in harmony to his chant. "Oh spirit of my heart," he chanted.

"I am yours," sang the voice.

"Answer me I pray," he sang.

"We are never apart," replied the voice.

"I seek your guidance," Rattle's voice cracked.

"You are mine," responded the voice.

"Come to my side," he continued.

"I am here," said the spirit.

When the Pai opened his eyes, he was amazed to see the great deer floating in the air before him. He looked from the spirit to the crow and back.

"Why are you so surprised?" asked the deer, its magnificent antlers sparkling almost silver in the sunlight. "Did I not tell you I would come?"

"But I never thought it would be here," protested the old man. "How can I fight a battle in the sky?"

"From my back," said the spirit quietly. "Come, climb up. The demon approaches."

Gently, tentatively, Rattle reached out and placed his hand on the flank of the huge buck that stood suspended in mid-air in front of him. He felt frightened and unsure and did not know what to do, but he would not disobey his totem. At the moment of contact, he sensed new strength and confidence flood through him. From the instant his hand touched the soft hide, his mind and that of the deer spirit were linked.

He pulled himself comfortably upon the animal's back and felt a sudden freedom he had never before known. Tears of joy sprang into his eyes and he could not speak.

"You do not need to speak, my love," said the spirit within his mind. "I am here as I have always been."

"Look!" warned the crow as it hopped from the edge of the cloud to Rattle's shoulder. "Look to the west."

Darkness grew where moments before there had been light. In the western sky, clouds billowed and darkened as they watched and lightning played along the edges.

"What form will it take?" Rattle blinked at the brightness of the storm.

"It has no limit," said the crow. "It may choose even as we have chosen."

At first, the clouds began to swirl like the demon itself, a huge circular vortex of force that quickly took on the shape of a hurricane. As it approached, they heard the demon's voice.

"I have come," it said in a deep sonorous rumble. "Who dares to face me?"

The swirling ceased its advance and hovered still some distance away. Red, yellow and green lightnings flashed from the interior, lighting the sky with eerie shadows and seeming to draw new clouds from all sides.

To Rattle's eyes, they floated in the center of a huge arena, cloud tiers of stepped opacity climbing up on all sides. Though they could see no one, they began to hear voices, as if they were surrounded by a vast audience.

"Ten souls on my brother," yelled a harsh and inhuman voice. "I'll wager ten souls!"

"You're on, wind bag," called another in response. "I think the deer is the hunter today."

"I'll back your brother," laughed a third voice. "I want to see him eat crow."

The laughter all around them was deafening.

"Put them from your mind," instructed the deer. "They are not part of this, merely illusion meant to distract you. The demon wants you to forget you are in a sacred place."

"It's doing a damned good job of it," remarked the crow.

As if in answer, the phantom arena dissipated and the cloud smoothed out below them, flattening into what looked like a level plain.

"What now?" Rattle looked over the deer's shoulder, through the shining rack of horns and saw something coming out of the wall of cloud ahead.

"Oh no," croaked Juan.

"Interesting," commented the spirit.

Before them, stepping out onto what seemed a solid floor came a dragon. It was immense, standing fully twenty feet tall from ear tip to rear claw, majestic wings swept back over a massive scaly back.

"Take your weapon," said the spirit.

"His bow?" Juan fluttered his wings in frustration. "A bow and arrow against that?"

The deer turned its head and looked at Rattle. The deep eyes searched his and its voice echoed in his mind. "Do you believe in me?"

Deeply moved, the old Pai bowed his head and pressed his forehead to the neck of the huge buck. "Of course," he said and reached behind his back where he found his bow and a quiver containing two arrows.

The crow squawked and flapped its wings above his shoulder. "Two shots?"

The spirit answered in a sweet quiet voice. "There will not be time for more. We must make them count."

The dragon roared and called to them, belching smoke and flame.

"Come to me," it rumbled. "Let us see if this thing you see is as powerful as men claim."

"Time for me to go," said Juan, launching himself off Rattle's shoulder and spreading his wings. "I'll be nearby." But to his consternation, he fell back and the Pai had to grab quickly or he would have fallen.

"Ah," called the dragon, snorting and laughing. "I forgot to mention about the flying, didn't I. We can't."

"No time," said the deer spirit, tensing suddenly. "We are starting to sink into the cloud."

Indeed, the deer was forced to dance in order to stay unmired in the surface below them—which had begun to take on the consistency of mud.

Rattle thought quickly. He pulled an arrow from his quiver, nocked it and leaned forward. "Go!" he said.

The deer reared once and then charged forward, angling to the left so the old man would have a clear shot over its shoulder.

They closed the distance swiftly and the dragon hissed as it blew a plume of flame directly in their path. The deer swerved and dodged while still closing the gap between them.

Rattle loosed the first shaft. It had been many years since he let fly an arrow while on horseback, let alone on the back of a massive charging buck. It missed with inches to spare to the right.

Juan in the flightless body of the crow had all he could do to hang on as they sped closer to the huge winged saurian ahead.

Rattle drew and nocked his second arrow, conscious of the need for accuracy with this shot. The deer cut once to his right, closing quickly, then shot off to the left, leaving the dragon on the right presenting the best possible target.

Rattle loosed his shot and the arrow sped true, coming to rest in the dragon's right eye.

With a bellow of rage, it stopped and opened its mouth, shooting a tongue of flame that resembled a flame thrower across the intervening ground. It missed by scant yards but singed the three as they continued to close.

"Use me!" Juan spoke from behind Rattle's back and the Pai turned to find that the Yaqui had been transformed from a bird to a serpent, but the serpent was rigid and spoke breathlessly.

"A final arrow, my friends," it said, its split tongue tasting the air. "Fire quickly."

Without thought, Rattle took and nocked his final shot, speaking as he loosed it. "Fly true, my friend."

The dragon now loomed only yards away. It opened its maw and prepared to give them a final withering blast of fire. The serpent that was Juan Mapoli passed directly into its mouth, through the cavity behind and into the brain of the beast, striking with poisoned fangs as it buried itself within.

The upper world dissolved.

Chapter Fifty-Eight

The Spirit World

When Pasqual opened his eyes, it was to behold the presence of the twin gods, Ahaiyuta and Matsailema—the gods of war. "Oh twin children of the sun, immortal youths, have I died?" he asked.

The two laughed and shook their heads. "We will go with you, Priest, to see this evil thing. Perhaps we shall deal with it as we did Atahsaia and there shall be a new red star in the heavens."

The two merrily waved their war clubs and shook their magic shields, just as might any children at play.

Pasqual looked upon them and laughed delightedly, clapping his hands together like a child himself. He knew in his heart now that the demon could never win.

A noise from behind caused the old Zuni to spin in alarm, but the twins only laughed and said, "See, Pasqual. It is the Hopi."

Indeed, Harold stood there on two good legs and a part of Pasqual's mind knew that this, therefore, must be illusion. At Harold's side were two strange figures that shimmered and changed shape too rapidly for the eyes to follow.

"Welcome, my brother," said the Zuni. "Who have you brought with you?"

Harold spoke, his voice tinged with awe. "I have the honor of being accompanied by Taknokwunu, the spirit who controls the weather, and Yaponcha, the god of winds."

Pasqual bowed before them, then indicated the Twins. "These are Our Beloved, the Terrible Two, Ahaiyuta and Matsailema," he said reverently.

If some greeting passed between the four, neither Harold nor Pasqual was aware of it.

"Is it to be just the Hopi and the Zuni?" asked Harold.

"No," replied a voice from off to the side. "I also have been sent to confront the demon in the spirit world." Lotus Farley of the Tohono O'odham stepped forward into the light . . . or rather brought the brightness with her, for she seemed to pulse and glow with a pale green radiance.

"We three then," said Pasqual.

"Seven," said a rumbling voice. Thus spoke Taknokwunu.

The Zuni bowed low. "I'm sorry," he said. "I meant just us three people. I never been this close to gods before."

For the first time, the three mortals looked around them. They were surprised to find themselves surrounded by rock walls.

"I did not expect to find the spirit world enclosed in stone," said Lotus. "What place is this?"

Neither man nor spirit answered. When the reply did come, it was a harsh and threatening sound.

"A place of my choosing, whore of the Tohono O'odham."

Lotus reddened at the insult.

Pasqual had been looking around, searching the shadows but could not locate the source of the voice.

"It is not here," said Matsailema. "It still hides."

"Come out," called Harold. "Face us."

"Peace Man," spat the voice. "I see that you appear whole now. Why not face me as you are?"

"But I am whole, demon," replied Harold. "The injury to my leg is not who or what I am."

"I hope you are in pain, Priest. I will come for you as I did the old Navajo."

"Words will not defeat us, demon," challenged Pasqual.

"Yes," agreed Lotus. "Come out and face us. Are you going to talk us to death?"

"Perhaps when the time is right, whore," replied the voice, "I will find something large and jagged to insert in your healing center."

"Words, again," said Harold. "Come, let us do what must be done."

A moment of silence followed in which Pasqual thought he heard something akin to a sigh.

"Very well. Let us get on with it."

The roof above them suddenly split asunder and a fiery red light shone upon them. The walls tumbled outward as if shaken by an earthquake, but none fell on the little group within.

The twins had put up their hands and deflected the rock. It was ever their purpose to shelter and guide.

All saw a landscape that shifted, tilted, rolled, and erupted, but the spot upon which they stood did not move.

A vast blackness rolled up from the horizon and swept toward them at incredible speed. They saw a wall of water, a tidal wave that crashed across the level plain and bore down on the seven figures like darkness descending on the earth.

When the humans would have run, the twins gestured for them to stand firm and turned toward the wall as it towered above them. Taknokwunu and Yaponcha moved in front and the god of winds blew a tremendous gale into the onrushing water, splitting it as if it had been cut into two streams. As the wave passed, the waters moved in from the side and flooded the plain, but the twins again acted swiftly, almost playfully.

They took the kiaallan, the water shield, and laid it down, lifting the others to safety upon it. Though there was soon no land in sight, the seven figures floated serenely on the surface of the water and waited for the demon's next move.

A huge fin rose out of the water, indicating the approach of a great fish. In a moment, Lotus identified it as a killer whale. The beast sped toward the floating shield like a runaway truck. Ahaiyuta only laughed and lifted them out of the water to hover in the air just out of the killer's reach.

Abruptly, the scene changed again. The seven found themselves standing in a small valley completely surrounded by high rocky hills. The entire enclosure could not have been more than a football field in length or width.

Suddenly, the earth began to shake violently. The rocks and boulders on all sides jarred loose, bouncing and rolling toward the center where the warriors and gods stood.

Pasqual smiled at Lotus and Harold. "It is losing," he observed. "It continues to play with illusion as if we did not know that such cannot harm us."

Again, the wind god blew and the rocks changed course, crashing into others and sending vast chunks of stone flying through the air like shrapnel. The twins used their magic shields to protect the others.

"Fight fairly," cried the demon in frustration. "What kind of battle is it in which I must submit myself to such as you and have only illusion as a weapon?"

"What kind of battles are they when you sneak up on a village of women and children and smother it?" asked Lotus.

"I must feed," shouted the demon. "Growth is destiny. I must feed and grow that I may reach the stars."

"This is my world," said Taknokwunu. "You cannot either feed or grow here. Tell me, demon, are you still growing in the middle world?"

The question was a distraction, a horrible diversion that caught the beast off guard. It found itself dividing its attention, trying to be in two places at once—the real world and the spirit world.

Was it growing? It tried to assess, to measure. It had come so far in only seven days.

For just a moment, the beast forgot about the seven who challenged it in the spirit world. For a split second, it neglected to conceal itself behind the rock.

What the others saw was an ogre, a huge giant from fairytale that hurled rocks and boulders down on the unwary. It wore the hide of some large animal and carried a spiked club. It glared down under bushy brows and let out a bellow of rage.

The demon raced down the side of the hill, club flailing the air, spittle flying from jaws that could not close over the rotten oversized fangs that filled its mouth. It roared as it charged and covered the ground at an alarming pace. The humans huddled behind their gods and their shields.

Taknokwunu spoke to Yaponcha and the wind blew, trying to deflect the monster's course. It failed.

The charging beast laughed at their weakness. It sensed triumph at last.

Pasqual, Lotus and Harold had been crouched behind the twins when the gods suddenly leapt directly into the air, leaving the three humans unprotected.

The beast gave a shout of triumph and sprang at them from only a few yards away.

At the apex of the arc that would have brought it crashing down upon them, crushing them to pulp beneath its massive weight, twin beams of energy slashed through the air and blasted the ogre apart.

The twins had used their rainbow bows and turquoise tipped thunderbolt arrows. They leapt high into the air, celebrating their victory . . .

. . . and the spirit world faded from the human's view.

Chapter Fifty-Nine

City of the Phoenix

Gordon awakened the others. "Come, it is time to return to the middle world," he said, shaking Danny and James.

The Pima was the first to recover from the effects of his slumber. He felt tired but his face split in a wide grin.

"We did it!" he exclaimed. "We beat him."

The three men smiled at each other, but Gordon turned serious quickly. "We have won three of the five battles," he said. "That is very good. But we still have two more to go. The last are the hardest."

James nodded. "The middle and under worlds," he said. "Battles to be fought in real time in the modern world."

Bowing respectfully to the attendant who remained as passive and regal as before, the three exited through the door and returned to the room where the others waited.

Smiling faces greeted them. Lotus, Cord, Kade, Rattle, Michael, Pasqual, Juan, Gerry, Harold and Jack all waited, apparently whole and hearty.

They had brought nothing so there was nothing to gather, no preparations to be made. They stood in a group and turned toward the place in the wall through which they had entered.

The winged beings who had served as their hosts all bowed as one and the shamans returned the courtesy. Silently, the crystal door opened and the thirteen rose once again into the air. The sound of the drum could be immediately heard.

As he left the palace behind, Gordon saw the majestic form of the Phoenix as it perched regally on the highest parapet and heard the melodious song of its goodbye. He waved a regretful farewell.

The clouds before them thickened and the passage between narrowed until all could see the mouth of the cloud tunnel through which they had ascended. The heavens remained golden and inviting.

Not one of the thirteen found it easy to reenter the tunnel. The sweet song of the Phoenix, the warm feeling of well-being, the experience of lavish comfort and gentle peace all made departure from this realm a difficult choice.

Knowing what lay ahead made it even worse.

As they entered the tunnel, sparks from the fire below rose up as if in greeting. The chorus of voices that had welcomed them upon arrival sang now a melancholy song of farewell. The faces of the singers lining the tunnel looked on them with love and grace. The drum grew louder, stirring something within—something visceral and primitive. Each of them left the sight of the crystal city consumed by a passionate appreciation of beauty.

Jack came to himself as he sat cross-legged in the warm desert afternoon before the sand painting prepared by Gerry, Harold, Lotus and Pasqual.

First he noticed how bright the colors seemed in the painting. The upper half glowed with golden highlights and, in his memory, he could still see the ethereal light of the palace of the Phoenix. He imagined he could hear faint traces of the music sung by that strange chorus.

He next saw that all the others sat in similar positions around the circle. Each of the Indians appeared to be just coming back after the experience of the morning glory tea. Tom Bear stood off to the side beating the drum, but, at Gordon's signal, he stopped.

"Be careful when you try to stand," cautioned the Navajo. "From the appearance of the sun, we have been here for about three hours. Some of you may experience re-circulation tingling and a little pain."

The archaeologist thought about that for a moment before experimentally trying to straighten his right leg. He had no feeling in it whatsoever . . . for about ten seconds. Then he realized he was mistaken. Returning circulation first tickled the nerves and then outraged them. The sensation was not pleasant, but he knew it would stop hurting after a while. Meanwhile, he groaned.

It did not help to find that he had company. Pasqual, Juan, Rattle and Kade all made similar sounds of their own. Age has its price.

Gordon rose and stretched. "Thank you," he said, looking around the circle. "You have all done very well. We have been lucky, and the best news is that the last part of this may not be as difficult as we once feared."

Gerry stood slowly and also stretched. He winced but didn't groan. When he did speak, he cautioned Gordon.

"I sense something new about the demon," he said. "We may have succeeded on the other levels, but it has not given up yet. In fact, what I'm getting is a feeling of elation."

"It won't matter if we can draw it here to us and the charm," said the Navajo. "Once it gets within a mile, we'll be able to trap it."

"How?" asked Jack.

"The charm is our weapon," replied Gordon. "If the creature gets too close, it is drawn in and cannot escape. That's how it was caught originally."

Pasqual added, "And it makes it smaller too. That's why we gotta lure it here."

"That's right," agreed Harold. "The closer it gets to the talisman, the more it is compressed. Once it touches the charm, it cannot get free. Only removal by an outside force can break it free."

All of them had, by now, gotten to their feet and were working out the various kinks and cramps that resulted from their long immobility.

"What do we do now, Singer?" asked Lotus.

"We concentrate on calling the demon here. It is furious at us for defeating it on the other levels. It wants to crush us because, if it succeeds, there are no others like us to stop it."

Twohats and Johnson approached the Yataalii with deference. "Forgive me for interrupting, my brother," said Redfield, "but I have just received a most disturbing report."

"What is it?"

"The storm swept through Carefree and Cave Creek during the last hour causing a lot of destruction and loss of life," replied Greg.

"They had a little warning and managed to evacuate some so it could have been a lot worse."

"I am sorry to hear it," said Gordon.

"Yeah, well, the thing is, you see, Matt Sharp's jury-rigged radar is tracking it. It headed west instead of south."

"It isn't coming here?" Lotus didn't sound disappointed.

Gordon turned and met her eye. "It will come," he said levelly.

"You're probably right," agreed Johnson, "but it looks as if it plans a detour on the way."

"That will give us more time," said Michael.

The detectives exchanged glances.

Twohats continued. "First it went west, and now it looks like it has decided to go south."

"Less people out there anyway," commented Cord. "Maybe it's best."

Johnson didn't look relieved. Instead, his face creased with lines of concern. "You don't understand," he said. "Southwest of Phoenix. What is west and a little south?"

"A lot of open spaces," said Gerry.

Jack suddenly caught on. His eyes went wide and he felt a chill start at the base of his spine. "Good Christ!" he exclaimed. "The Nuclear Plant! The sonofabitch is going to roll right over Palo Verde!"

The Phoenix detective looked grim as he added, "Packing winds in excess of four hundred miles per hour."

"Can the plant withstand it?" Jack was still stunned.

"No one knows. It sure as hell wasn't designed to," replied Greg. "They're shittin' peachpits out there right now."

The shamans and police exchanged a long, meaningful look. "Is there anything you can do?" Johnson asked.

Gordon shook his head. "We are bound to this site—the original kiva, the sand painting. It must come to us."

Jack looked at Gordon, then spoke. "Forgive me if I think out loud, but maybe one of you can come up with something less frightening than what I'm thinking now." He looked around hopefully.

No one responded.

"This demon or creature or whatever it is sucks up emotion and body fluids and what-not, is that right?"

"This demon or creature or whatever it is sucks up emotion and body fluids and what-not, is that right?"

"It absorbs the life force, the life energy. The emotional responses of the victims are like the seasoning," said Gordon, struggling a little with the images.

"Okay," said Jack looking urgently around at the group. "What about nuclear energy?"

"Oh fuck!" exclaimed Greg. "I hadn't thought of that. I was only worried about the radiation in case it damages the plant." He turned to Gordon. "It can't grow on nuclear energy, can it?"

The Navajo shrugged. He didn't know.

Jack's voice was grim. "I don't think we can afford to find out."

There was a long silence. No one could think of anything to say.

Gordon finally broke it. He looked directly at Jack as he did. "You'll have to take the charm and beat it to Palo Verde, digger. Once the demon has turned away from there, it will come here. Get back as quickly as you can."

"But that would leave you out here in the open, unprotected," protested Jack. "You people can't stand against the storm without the charm."

Gordon shrugged again. "We don't know that, digger. We are the medicine people from twelve Native American tribes. We have assembled the Second Great Gathering. Perhaps the charm will prove to be unnecessary."

"That's a hell of a gamble," said Twohats.

Gordon looked from face to face around the circle. He received an almost imperceptible nod from each of the shamans. He turned last to Jack. "Go, digger," he said, "and keep it from the plant. We will wait here for the demon's arrival."

Jack looked to the detectives, then back at the others. "If you think I should, I will, but the charm belongs to you, not to my world. We wouldn't all die if the reactors are breached, but we might if the storm destroys you."

"It is a risk we must take, digger," said the Navajo. "You were right to ask about the energy. We don't know how strong it might get, how large it would grow. We can't take the chance."

Greg spoke into his cellular phone. "This is Johnson. I want a chopper here in three minutes."

Five minutes later, a police helicopter rose from the site and set off at top speed for the Palo Verde Nuclear Plant west of Phoenix. On board were Jack and Greg plus the regular crew.

"What do we have to do?" asked the detective.

"Get there before the storm, I guess," said Jack. "Gordon and the others think it will have to turn aside if we're between it and the plant."

The pilot called back over his shoulder. "Take a look to the right."

Both men turned to the window and saw the storm for the first time.

"Sweet Jesus!" said Jack.

Greg nodded in wordless agreement.

The dust and debris rose three miles in the air, swirling furiously. Nothing could be seen under the vortex for it did not taper to a small point like a dust devil or tornado. It looked like a satellite picture of a hurricane only on a smaller scale.

Jack smiled grimly. Who was he kidding? A smaller scale? The storm was over four miles across, almost a perfect circle. From their angle, they could see the wide barren swath of nothingness that stretched behind it.

For the first time, Jack was able to think of it as the demon. The last vestiges of doubt vanished when he saw its unnatural perfection, its awesome power. This was no manefestation of nature. It was the essence of destruction.

"Palo Verde just ahead," reported the pilot. "We already have clearance."

"We made it," breathed Greg.

"Just," agreed Jack.

*   *   *   *   *

The beast had thoroughly enjoyed its sojourn through Carefree and Cave Creek. The thinning of the population through forced evacuations had actually lessened the distraction. It had taken too long, it knew, but the delay had been minimal and the rewards great.

In Cave Creek, it had found and devoured an employee of the Nuclear Plant, an engineer who understood what went on there better than the general public. When it tapped his mind, it had learned about the power of the atom.

Still enraged by its defeat in the other levels, it seized upon this new knowledge as a way to even the odds. The humans who opposed it were powerful. They had already demonstrated their courage, much to the beast's detriment. It had begun to think it would lose the final battles. Three defeats in a row had badly shaken its confidence.

But this was perfect. A place that produced energy—more energy than the beast had imagined could exist—a marvelous source of sustenance and growth.

It knew now that the humans had found some way to track its movements. The thinning of the population through flight had told it they had been warned. They might, therefore, be able to determine its course and realize the destination it had chosen as an alternative.

That would be fine.

They would be forced to watch helplessly while it grew larger and more powerful. It would take this energy and then go to the place the shamans had gathered. They would be helpless before its might and fury.

Chapter Sixty

Phoenix

Matt Sharp decided to leave his studio when the storm, or whatever it was, approached Phoenix. Diedre remained behind and watched the instruments for him as he commandeered the traffic helicopter on the roof of the KTVC Building. He had to see this thing himself.

He had started at the station as a traffic reporter, moving into the weather slot after six months of flying the helicopter over the city during morning and evening rush hours. The steady and rapid whup-whup-whup of the rotor was a familiar companion as he headed west from downtown.

Looking below at the modern city that Phoenix had become, he considered the existence of a six-hundred-year-old demon ravaging the countryside.

Matt was not like the detective, Greg Johnson. The weatherman had an abiding belief in the supernormal, in telepathy, ghosts, magic, witches, astrology and the like.

He saw no conflict between these beliefs and his scientific orientation. The works of Charles Fort had been fodder for his imagination as he grew up. Without a secure and happy home to go to, he had haunted the library both at school and downtown. The discovery of *Lo!*, *Wild Talents*, *New Lands* and *The Book of the Damned* had demonstrated to his teen-aged mind that science did not hold all the answers.

After returning from his interview with Jack Foreman, Matt had checked the backgrounds of the Indians gathered at the house. It was an impressive gathering of powerful men, and the woman was praised by the Tohono O'odham. Quatero of the Zuni was one of the most powerful priests of modern times according to sources within the tribe. Laloma, the Hopi, was—though not the most powerful or famous—highly respected by his people. Mapoli, the Yaqui, was famed in Barrio Libre. All the others, though to a lesser degree, were the best their people had to offer in the traditional ceremonies and sacred rites of Indian magic. It wasn't likely that such men would spend their time on spurious pursuits.

He stood prepared to accept their claim that the storm was a sentient creature. His own study of its movements had certainly indicated it was not a normal weather event.

When Matt looked ahead through the windshield and saw it for the first time, he became convinced.

Dominating the landscape ahead, a vast column of wind, sand, dust and debris towered over the desert. Four miles wide and stretching three miles into the air, it looked solid enough to be a huge building—until one realized that the walls shifted and changed constantly and that it moved remarkably fast.

It was still six miles ahead, but Matt could hear the roar of the four-hundred-mile-per-hour winds. As it raced to the south at forty-five-miles-per-hour, it left a clean and barren trail behind. Where was it going? Matt had no difficulty now with the imaginative leap that turned this swirling column of storm into a thinking creature. The Indians had told him it fed on life energy and fluids, yet it moved away from densely populated Phoenix and headed south across open farmland and desert. If purpose directed it, what would draw it to the west?

He turned the chopper and ran parallel to the storm. Looking in that direction, he saw nothing but more emptiness. The checkerboard of cultivated fields alternated with desert.

"CCV-23 to weather control," he said as he thumbed the radio mike button. "Are you there, Diedre?"

"Weather Control to CCV-23. This is Diedre, Matt. I was starting to worry."

"No sweat. I have it in sight now. It's moving due south along the west edge of Phoenix. Can you plot me a course for it and tell where it's heading?

Reception began to include considerable static, apparently due to some kind of interference from the storm itself.

"Palo Verde," said the voice on the speaker. "Unless it alters course again, it'll hit the Palo Verde Nuclear Power Plant in twenty minutes."

"Patch me through to Greg Johnson," said Matt tersely. He hoped the detective was near the phone.

After a few crackling moments, the speaker squawked once again. "Johnson here."

"Greg. This is Matt Sharp. I'm in the air running alongside this thing and it's heading for Palo Verde."

"We know. I have Professor Foreman and the charm with me. We're at the plant. If these people are right about the nature of the storm, we should be able to turn it away once it senses our presence."

Matt thought about that. Of course! If the storm was sentient, it would want to avoid the charm. The talisman was the trap it had fallen into five hundred years before. Once it realized the charm was close, it would turn and go . . . where?

There were apparently only two things the creature feared—the charm and the Great Gathering.

Matt chewed his lower lip. When it realized the shamans were unprotected, it would turn toward them, wouldn't it? "Greg. Do you understand where it has to go next?"

The reply was grim. "We've already figured that out. This is the way they wanted it."

Matt looked again at the storm as it sped across the desert. "I'll stay with it a while longer."

*   *   *   *   *

The beast had moved quickly across the land, the energy source drawing it like a banquet set before a starving man. It burned up reserves at an accelerated rate, avoiding the city but alert to the needs that continued to grow within. Its senses stretched ahead, eager to reach this place, ready to satisfy its hunger.

Then, suddenly, it felt something—an almost tangible pain in the forward wall of its advance!

The mind of the beast filled with disappointment. It knew and recognized the charm.

For just a moment, it felt despair.

Every time these men acted, they kept it from what it desired. How could this be? How did they learn so much in so little time? The beast did not stop or slow. It could approach the site without danger as long as it did not get too close to the charm. Disappointment was a bitter drink.

It's mind reached out and became aware of the shamans as they stood in their circle to the east. They were filled with confidence, fresh from their triumph on the other levels. They reeked of satisfaction and content.

Ahead, it sensed the thoughts of the one who had set it free. The beast experienced a series of mixed emotions. This man had been the one to remove the hated charm, to loose it from the long imprisonment. It felt almost fond of him. Yet he stood now between the beast and its goal. It also hated him.

The men were puny and insignificant, but they evidenced a spirit of heroic resistance that frightened the beast.

Jack Foreman had left the helicopter on the inner court and walked with Greg Johnson and the Plant Supervisor, Miles Tucker, out to the east perimeter of the complex. Behind him, the three reactors reached into the sky.

"This seems a little crazy to me," said the supervisor. "I have a major crisis on my hands and they send me an archaeologist."

"There isn't time to explain," said Greg. "You just do what you would normally do. Ignore us. We'll stay out of your way."

Tucker laughed, a humorless sound. "Normal? What about any of this is normal? From all reports, this is the most severe mainland storm in history and I'm in charge of a nuclear plant directly in its path."

"I understand your difficulty, Mr. Tucker," said the detective sympathetically. "Go on with your preparations. We'll head over to the north gate."

Tucker left them and returned to the hoard of engineers trying to button up the facility.

The detective and archaeologist watched him moving away.

"I wouldn't want his job," said Greg.

"Me either," agreed Jack.

The two men moved alone across the grounds and approached the high chain link fence that surrounded the plant. Security guards at the gate were the only other people around.

"Is there anything I can do to help?" asked Greg.

"All we have to do is be here," said Jack. "The charm is a trap. If the demon gets too close, it starts to shrink and lose its power. Once it senses the charm, it will turn and head off toward the beltway site."

In the distance, they could see the storm approaching. The column stretched far into the air. To those who watched, everything else in the world stood still.

Chapter Sixty-One

Phoenix

The City of Phoenix would never forget this day. When the storm swept through Cave Creek and Carefree, the reports of damage and loss of life sent government into a frenzy of activity.

Since it is the state capital as well, the machinery set in motion was complex and ponderous. The Governor declared a state of emergency and called out the State Militia and the National Guard. The Red Cross moved into the armories and set up shelters with medical facilities. Hospitals were placed on alert and all medical personnel not usually on duty were called in. Television and radio stations broadcast non-stop reports and evacuation plans were put into effect.

With the first reports from Cave Creek, the Phoenix Mayor ordered an evacuation of Northeastern Phoenix. Then the storm turned west. This left the northern streets clogged with traffic moving without unified purpose. Some people were fleeing—others had heard of the change in course and were returning to their homes.

As the storm turned south, the danger from Palo Verde became known and west-side residents began to flee as well. The result was panic and grid-lock. Looting and vandalism broke out everywhere.

Twohats and the other three officers had their hands full. The beltway site was still under construction, but the road had been laid down from Baseline to Camelback and people fleeing in panic soon discovered that it would serve as an escape route to the south.

In very little more time, the roadway had been choked with traffic and people began turning onto the access in an effort to go around. Soon, cars and trucks were pulling into the desert in a frantic search for a way out.

Gordon and the others stood guard around the painting and the site. Refugees who had abandoned their cars and struck out on foot suddenly encountered fourteen Indians, all but one in full ceremonial regalia, and three policemen who barred their way, directing them back to their vehicles.

The storm continued to advance on the nuclear plant. It showed no signs of slowing or stopping. When the leading edge was only a mile and a half away, it swung to the west and then drew closer, beginning an orbit of the facility.

"It's trying to outflank us," yelled Greg over the din. Telephone poles and huge chunks of debris began to rain down around them. They ran back toward the reactors, seeking shelter.

At Greg's direction, the helicopter rose into the air and moved away from the storm toward relative safety. Getting it back would take precious time and delay their departure if the demon turned toward the east, but they could not afford to risk the machine if they were to outrun the storm later.

"It doesn't have to come close enough to be trapped," shouted Jack. "It can pulverize us with debris and still remain far enough away."

"If we don't want to glow in the dark," yelled Greg, "we'd better get right in the middle of the reactor cluster. It's the only way the charm can protect them from a direct assault."

The storm continued to circle the plant, now turning south but still remaining safely away from the power of the talisman.

"How strong are those towers?" Jack realized he wouldn't want to hear the answer if it was bad news, but he could not help asking.

As if in response, a loud crash was heard as an automobile came flying overhead to slam against the building wall and then slide in a grinding, tortured slow motion fall to the ground below.

"Looks tough enough to me," said Greg.

"But how much can it take?" asked the archaeologist.

"Steel reinforced concrete," said the detective. "It should hold up."

"Look!" Jack pointed up to the northwest sky. "The chopper!"

Both men watched in horror as the wildly bouncing machine was struck by a tree trunk. It came apart in mid-air, rotor and tail separating from the crushed body and spinning out of control. Amidst the twisted wreckage, they could see the torn human forms of the crew just as the entire mess was engulfed in a blinding, orange sheet of flame.

Neither man moved or spoke for a few stunned seconds, then both went into motion once.

"What the fuck do we do now?" yelled Jack.

Greg was already shouting into the phone he still carried. "I need another chopper out at Palo Verde Nuclear Power Plant." He listened for a minute and then looked up, his face pale and serious. When he spoke, his voice was low and steady. "They can't get another bird here for an hour."

The archaeologist sank down, leaning against the wall behind him.

"If it turns now, it can reach Gordon and the others long before then," he said.

"Jesus," said the detective, "I hope Gordon was right about them not needing the charm."

Both men looked to the south. The storm had just made its last turn. It was completing the third side of its orbit of the plant.

They watched for a long moment before Jack spoke. "It's angling east."

"Yeah," agreed Greg. "It knows."

Chapter Sixty-Two

The Desert Outside Phoenix

The beast turned back with a song of triumph in its heart. The foolish men could be outmaneuvered, could be tricked. Now it raced at top speed back toward the shamans as they waited unprotected in the desert.

It had tapped into the mind of its liberator. It had divined the purpose of the machine that flew in the air near the plant. Luckily, it had carried within its bulk the wherewithal to destroy it.

Now it had time. Now it could approach the fools who thought they could stop it—crush them.

It broadcast its thoughts ahead to the Zuni, the Hopi and the Pima. "I am coming for you," it sent. "I want you to know it and realize how futile your struggle has been. This is not a battle in the world of illusion, but a meeting at last with reality. You and your weather god are powerless here. Your twins are indeed helpless children. Your fathers and grandfathers are ghosts of little substance and no influence. Prepare for me if you can."

It roared through untenanted land west of Metropolitan Phoenix, then turned east at Thomas Road, heading toward the city.

Gordon and the others saw the storm as it approached. The people whose presence had threatened to disrupt the ceremony also saw it and fled, abandoning cars, hopelessly buried in the sand, bumper to bumper on the roadway.

Twohats spoke urgently into the phone. "Greg, are you there? The demon is here. We need you and the professor right away." Static was the only reply. "Greg, where are you?"

Silence.

Twohats looked over to Gordon and shook his head.

"All right," said Gordon. "Let us continue, my brothers. The demon has come to us as we wished. Now we must force it to reenter the kiva."

Tom began beating the drum, a heart rhythm that quickly brought the others into sync. Ignoring the huge whirlwind that towered over them just to the west, the shamans took their places and concentrated on the sand painting in their midst.

Gordon spoke over the rising din. "Since the charm is not here, we must recreate it in our hearts and minds. The thing itself is nothing, but the power within it came from us. Remember the gift you gave and give it again now."

Like the individual tones in a musical chord, the twelve shamans each created again the element of the charm that was the gift of his or her tribe. Faith, Courage, Wisdom, Patience, Harmony, Reverence,

Understanding, Grace, Love, Imagination, Honor and Dedication—these, the noblest of human qualities, manifested within the circle.

The voice of the demon spoke to each of them, trying to break their harmony and disrupt the spell.

To Danny, it spoke yet again with the voice of his father, but he stood unswayed. The struggle in the world of the mind had freed him forever of that particular ghost. He sang his simple faith in a clear voice.

To Gerry, it spoke of defeat in battle, of long years of imprisonment and the coming of death, but Geronimo was an extension of George and the modern man was not moved. He sang of courage against overwhelming odds.

To Gordon, it bragged about the death of his family, brought into his mind the screams of his mother and father as it levelled Chaco Canyon, but the Navajo had been healed of that hurt. He was not distracted and sang lovingly of He-Who-Walked-In-Wisdom. The gift of Archie's wisdom was given yet again.

One by one, the shamans confronted their worst fears and found them trifling. Step by step the recreation of the charm progressed until it was complete.

At last, Gordon spoke again. "It is done," he said.

The beast approached the shamans filled with confidence and in no hurry to end the game. It saw them turn back to their circle and begin the ceremony. It reached out and touched their minds.

One after the other, though it confronted them with the darkest thoughts and fears, they rejected it, rose above it and became more.

It felt the power of the charm and the first twinge of panic. What if they succeeded? What if they could call forth the power of the talisman even though it wasn't present?

It moved toward them, then halted again. What if this were a trap? The First Gathering had not looked significantly different than this and the beast had spent the last five hundred years under the earth.

It began to think. They would not be sitting there so calmly if they hadn't found something to replace the charm. What could it be? The intangible power from this ceremony couldn't be a threat. It hadn't been affected. It was still as large and strong as it had been . . . wasn't it?

It moved closer, but not too much closer, then stood without forward motion, spinning in the desert west of the site, a huge tower that dwarfed everything close by. It whirled and swirled as if its outer edge were a wall, a perfect construction of sand, wind and rock. It could see the shamans through the eyes of Twohats and the other police.

The beast divined their plans from Gordon's thoughts—to force it once again into the hole in the earth. It felt amused. The fools thought it could be trapped again.

Suddenly, it became aware of the drum. The steady beating was a thing felt, not heard, but the hollow pounding began to strike its leading edge like hammer blows on thin metal. It felt that perfect outer wall bend and warp. What was this?

It retreated a little, seeking to alleviate the discomfort wrought by that vibration. As it backed away, it became aware of a tangible pressure behind, as if it had brushed against a wall.

What was that? It searched in the space behind it for a mind to tap . . . and found Jack Foreman.

*   *   *   *   *

After the destruction of their helicopter, Jack and Greg had watched helplessly as the storm turned away and raced toward Phoenix. Greg had tried to commandeer a truck and been refused. All the staff at the plant was needed to inspect the damage and insure the integrity of the facility.

Jack, unwilling to wait, was about to steal a car, when the phone rang. It was Matt.

"Do you guys want a ride?"

The two men on the ground exchanged glances as they began searching the sky. Just to the north, they saw a small helicopter with KTVC emblazoned on the side.

"You bet," said Greg in relief. "Get down here quick. We're on minus minutes."

"Your wish is my command," said Matt, and the chopper dropped toward the ground before them.

When they set out in pursuit, the elapsed time had been only five minutes.

They followed the demon to the site, hanging well back where it would not accidentally discover their presence. When it came to rest, they landed, and moved up on foot.

Now they stood behind it, Jack holding the charm high in his right hand. Greg looked at him from a few feet back and remembered the scene in the old movie, *War of the Worlds,* where the priest advanced holding a bible before him. Despite the serious circumstance, Greg smiled grimly at the sight. Even in his imagination, Jack Foreman in the role of a priest was probably criminal miscasting.

Jack began to advance, the charm held before him.

The beast apparently felt it.

On the other side of the storm, the shamans rose as one and began to advance as well.

Twohats—who stood back and to the side—did not know about Jack, Greg and Matt, but he did see something miraculous. The towering wall of wind and sand grew misshapen, slowing and shrinking back from the advancing group. It had been a column of pure destructive force until the Gathering started to move closer. Now it was a bank of dense fog and the sound of crashing objects filled the sudden silence.

Trees, rock, crushed automobiles and building block rained down from where they had been supported within the storm.

As they advanced, the shamans began to spread out, circling to both sides. It took time. The storm had been almost five miles in diameter at its peak.

An eerie scene presented itself to Greg and Matt to the west and Towhats and the policemen on the east. The wind whispered and, after the howling when the storm was at full force, the contrast was profound.

Greg and Matt followed a few yards behind as Jack advanced into the storm that was now like a thick cloud. It retreated.

Twohats and the three policemen stood together near the construction and saw the Great Gathering form into a large half-circle, the cloud thinning and dissipating before them.

The beast was in pain, stunned and reeling. It had been so careful this time, so sure. The charm had been marooned miles away, unable to reach out with its agonizing magic. The men had been left helpless and unprotected, yet they had wrought a new force among them, had struck when they should have retreated.

The relentless advance kept forcing it to retreat, but the retreat was to its own center. Stubbornly, it tried to resist, but the magic of the charm burned. It could not stop shrinking before the pain. Reluctantly, it acknowledged to itself that it had been trapped again. The inevitable result would be imprisonment in the hated chamber. Its mind grappled with the disappointment and anger, but accepted.

Eventually, the archaeologist came in sight of the others. It had been a long weary walk and his right arm ached from holding the charm before him.

The Indians stood in an almost complete circle and Jack finally took his place, closing it. They were spaced well apart and within the circle brooded the beast. They could not see it, but the creature's presence lay heavily on all their minds.

Chapter Sixty-Three

Phoenix

The rock had been moved aside and a tall wooden ladder lowered into the kiva. One by one, the representatives of the tribes had entered and stood now in a circle on the lava floor. Jack was the last to descend, still in possession of the charm. The beast, chained by invisible bonds to the talisman was dragged in with the archaeologist.

Twohats, Greg and Matt, with the other policemen, waited outside.

Gordon spoke. "We must give thanks, my brothers and sister. The struggle for the middle world is done. The demon is once again imprisoned by the charm."

Danny looked around the circle and asked, "What of the underworld? We still have to meet the demon there."

"Here," corrected Tom, standing back against the wall, still holding the drum.

"Yessss." The voice echoed in all their minds. "You forget my little human bugs, that I am not powerless even in the presence of the charm."

"What does that mean?" Jack turned suddenly alert.

Gordon had become glassy eyed, his posture rigid and his face twisted. "Give me the charm." The Navajo reached out and grabbed the talisman from Jack's hand.

"Look out!" yelled Tom.

Suddenly, the air filled with stinging sand as the center of the chamber erupted in a whirlwind.

Lotus cried out, flinging her hands over her eyes.

Harold, who had needed help just to descend the ladder, was struck on the temple by a flying rock and crumpled.

Pasqual turned to help Lotus but suddenly clutched at his chest and buckled, sliding down the glassy wall.

Juan turned and grabbed for the ladder, but the figure that had been Gordon Smythe flung him aside like a toy and hurled the charm up and out the opening above.

Turning, eyes red and blazing, the voice roared in triumph. "Now you are mine," it rumbled. "Nothing you can do will ever stop me again."

Danny and Gerry threw themselves across the room and onto Gordon. They were flung away like matchsticks.

"Everybody get out!" yelled Jack.

Kade, James and Michael joined the struggle with the Navajo.

Tom tucked the drum under his arm and scrambled up the ladder. Whirling dust and sand filled the air.

Jack reached down and grabbed Lotus' arm and pulled her to her feet. "Help me with Pasqual," he said urgently.

Juan had recovered and was once again halfway up the ladder. He turned and helped hand the still form of the Zuni up to where Tom waited.

A few feet away, Gordon's body was writhing and heaving under the combined weight of the others. The voice of the demon issued from his throat, a tortured cry. "You cannot win!"

Next to be passed up the ladder was Harold, moaning in delirium. His cast had broken.

Once the Hopii had been handed up and dragged away from the opening by Tom, Jack called up. "Tom, you've got to find the charm and throw it back down to me!"

Danny had ripped the medicine pouch from around his throat and offered the thong to Kade. They wrapped it around Gordon's wrists. James and Michael both ripped at their clothing, pulling loose other thongs and they continued to try to bind the struggling Navajo.

Tom called from above. "Got it, Jack!"

The archaeologist looked up and deftly caught the charm as it dropped into his hands from above. Immediately, the struggling Navajo quieted.

"Get him out!" Jack commanded. He could feel the demon trying to take control of his mind. It still possessed strength.

Guided by Lotus, Gordon's limp form was lifted and carried up and out of the kiva by Danny and Gerry. One by one, battered and bruised, the shamans climbed the ladder and into the light above.

Finally, only Jack remained below with the charm and the beast. The archaeologist felt himself weakening.

Lotus peered down from the opening above. "Come on, Jack. All you have to do is climb out and leave the charm on the ledge. That will imprison it once again."

The archaeologist looked up at her, a strange expression on his face. He knew that was not true. He was linked now to both the charm and the demon. He could not get out and still do what had to be done. "No," he said in a quiet voice. He walked over to the ladder and kicked at the base. It fell into the chamber. "Roll the rock over the top and then get out of here. You have less than three minutes before this place goes up."

"What?" Lotus turned and called over her shoulder, "Danny!"

The young Pima's face appeared at the opening. "What are you up to, Jack?"

The older man shook his head. "We can't just lock it up this time, Danny." He displayed a wan smile. "You've got to do what I ask. Roll the rock back over the hole and then get clear. I've mined this floor with dynamite and I'm going to blow it in."

The voice of the demon echoed in Jack's mind. "Don't be foolish, old man. You can't destroy me by closing the door. Climb out. Take me with you."

The archaeologist smiled in grim satisfaction. "Yes I can destroy you," he said. "The floor underfoot is only a plug and the shaft from this old vent may drop deeper into the earth than even you can imagine—you and I and the charm are all going down." The sand and dust began to swirl again.

The beast wrestled for control of the archaeologist's mind, but Jack sat with his back against the wall and held the charm in his lap.

"No good," he said. "You're too late." Struggling to keep his facial expression under control, Jack looked up to the opening. "You have only ninety seconds! Do what I ask!"

There was a rumbling sound and the light began to fade. The last thing Jack heard from his friends above was a quiet goodbye from Juan. "Goodbye, my friend," he replied.

In darkness, Jack reached into his vest pocket for the electronic detonator. Thumbing the safety off, he spoke aloud. "See you in hell, demon!"

The chamber erupted in a cataclysm of fire and crushed lava. The floor disappeared and Jack, the charm and the demon began to fall.

Chapter Sixty-Four

Phoenix

As the dust cleared and the earth became quiet, those around the site were hushed, still in shock at the rapid chain of events. Danny held Lotus. Her left eye had been lacerated by the whipping sand, but she would be all right. Gerry stood with Juan behind them.

"Why did he do it?" asked Kade.

"Why did any of us do this?" replied Tom. He shrugged. "Because it needed to be done, of course."

Michael and James ministered to Gordon, who had not yet recovered completely from the physical strain his body endured while possessed.

Cord Hames sat with Harold, who had recovered consciousness but suffered in great pain.

Pasqual's body lay by itself in a place of honor. His heart had finally failed.

Greg Johnson and Twohats Redfield stood atop the rubble that had once been a volcanic vent and then a kiva. Nothing identifiable remained.

"I never thought he had it in him," said Greg.

"Heroes rise up when least expected," observed Twohats. "My people will remember him."

Greg shook his head. "Mine will never know," he said.

"Perhaps that is best," said Tom walking up to them. "The modern world has enough trouble without the past rearing up to remind it of ancient evils."

"It hardly seems fair," said Juan quietly, "but then no one ever promised that life would be fair."

"Does he have anyone we should notify?" Danny and Lotus had come up to join the others.

"The university, I guess," said Greg. "I know his wife passed away years ago. I don't think they ever had children."

Danny stepped forward. "Jack Foreman shall be a Pima."

"And a Hopi," said Harold through his pain.

"And Tohono O'odham," added Lotus.

"He shall be one of all our tribes," said Gordon, leaning on Michael and James as he approached. "He saved us from my arrogance."

"Don't blame yourself," said Tom. "You did what no one else could have done. You too shall be remembered."

"Indeed, my brother," said Twohats, walking up and bowing to the young yataalii. " I will tell of this when we return to Windowrock."

A truck had been brought up by the police and the ambulances arrived for Pasqual and Harold. The Shamans climbed up into the vehicle, weary and sad, but still proud of what they had done. The demon was gone. They had lost two of their number, but the Second Great Gathering would live on in the stories told for generations by the singers of their people.

The white world would never really know what had happened. Matt Sharp would take the job in New York and rise to the pinnacle of his profession, marry Diedre and raise a family. Greg Johnson would file a report claiming that Jack Foreman's death had been an accident during excavation of a suspected archaeological site, then go back to Tempe and start a meteoric rise in his police career.

Lotus and Danny would marry and both tribes would benefit from the union of two such powerful medicine people.

Kade, Michael, James, Cord, Juan and Gerry would return in honor to their homes and families.

Tom Bear looked around at the others. "We must not forget this day," he said. "You are invited to return to my house every year from now on to remember and reunite the Great Gathering."

And so it would be for many years to come.

Epilog

Under the Earth

Deep under the earth, in tunnels immemorial, the beast cried piteously. Unfair! Unfair! It had done what it was bid to do by the master. The hated men had resisted, had brought it pain, had once again imprisoned it beneath the earth—this time behind barriers no careless man could possibly remove, barriers as ancient as the earth itself.

It dashed and spun down endless corridors, hurling itself against the solid rock walls and spinning off again without form. The barren rock was hard as iron, cold and non-porous, unwilling to surrender even a grain of matter that the beast could use.

As it raced through the strange tunnels, the beast tried to stop, to end the dark descent, but every movement drove it deeper.

In time, the temperature in the maze began to increase and a deep red glow lit the miles still ahead. Only then did the beast recognize and understand its fate.

It tried in vain to reverse itself, to halt the inexorable downward fall, but forces greater and older pulled it eagerly toward the glow.

The heat increased and the beast began to sense a deep rumbling vibration that mounted as the ruddy light grew brighter. Soon, the tunnel shook with the force of the sound, an all-penetrating roar that drove the last vestiges of its sanity whimpering into the darkness.

"Oh, Father," it cried, "Father Ithaqua, why have you forsaken me?"

But there was no reply from the Elder God of Winds. The only sounds were the roaring of the fires of the earth and the final wail of the beast as it plunged into the planet's core.

- The End -